The Deception at Lyme

OTHER MR. & MRS. DARCY MYSTERIES
BY CARRIE BEBRIS

Pride and Prescience (Or, A Truth Universally Acknowledged)

Suspense and Sensibility (Or, First Impressions Revisited)

North by Northanger (Or, The Shades of Pemberley)

The Matters at Mansfield (Or, The Crawford Affair)

The Intrigue at Highbury (Or, Emma's Match)

The Deception at Lyme

OR, THE PERIL OF PERSUASION

A Mr. & Mrs. Darcy Mystery

Carrie Bebris

TOR®

A TOM DOHERTY ASSOCIATES BOOK

NEW YORK

This is a work of fiction. All of the characters, organizations, and events portrayed in this novel are either products of the author's imagination or are used fictitiously.

THE DECEPTION AT LYME

Copyright © 2011 by Carrie Bebris

Map and illustrations by Jon Lansberg

A Tor Book
Published by Tom Doherty Associates, LLC
175 Fifth Avenue
New York, NY 10010

www.tor-forge.com

Tor® is a registered trademark of Tom Doherty Associates, LLC.

Library of Congress Cataloging-in-Publication Data

Bebris, Carrie.
   The deception at Lyme : or, the peril of persuasion / Carrie Bebris. — 1st ed.
      p. cm.
   "A Tom Doherty Associates book."
   ISBN 978-0-7653-2797-0
   1. Bennet, Elizabeth (Fictitious character)—Fiction.   2. Darcy,
Fitzwilliam (Fictitious character)—Fiction.   3. Married people—Fiction.
4. Murder—Investigation—Fiction.   5. England—Fiction.
I. Title.   II. Title: Deception at Lyme.   III. Title: Peril of persuasion.
PS3602.E267D43 2011
813'.6—dc22

                                                                2011021551

First Edition: October 2011

Printed in the United States of America

0 9 8 7 6 5 4 3 2 1

To my father
and my godmother

Acknowledgments

I realize, dear reader, that you are anxious to page through all of this front matter and reach the prologue, where the story begins. But it actually begins here. For while it is my name that appears on the cover of this novel, there are a great many individuals who contributed to its creation, and were it not for them, the story you are about to enjoy would not exist in its present form.

I must, as always, first thank my family. In addition to the very patient and understanding husband and children who live with me during the day-to-day writing, I am blessed with an extended family whose support and encouragement also nurture my creative soul. For this novel, I am particularly grateful to my father for accompanying me to England as my research assistant, for taking countless photos and walking countless miles, for helping me see the navy through the eyes of one who served, and for flinching only a little bit on our first day of driving on British roads.

I thank my editor, Kristin Sevick, for her editorial guidance, for her belief in this book, and for all her support that enabled me to write the story as it needed to be told; my agent, Irene Goodman, for

Acknowledgments

her sound advice and humor that keeps everything in perspective; and my publicist, Cassandra Ammerman, for her promotional efforts on behalf of me and the Darcys.

Artist Teresa Fasolino amazes me with her ability to take my novels and capture their essence on canvas. For the painting on the cover of this book, and those of all the Mr. & Mrs. Darcy Mysteries before it, she has my continued admiration and gratitude.

Friends and fellow writers Mary Holmes, Pamela Johnson, Victoria Hinshaw, Anne Klemm, and Sharon Short offered ideas, criticism, and support at critical stages of the book's development. I am also grateful to the Sisters of St. Joseph for providing a quiet retreat where I could regain my creative focus and write.

Of the many individuals who answered numerous research questions, I am especially indebted to two people who not only shared their specialized knowledge but also helped me apply it to the unique circumstances of my story: gynecological surgeon and Regency medical expert Dr. Cheryl Kinney, and historical weaponry and military expert Kristopher Shultz. Thanks also to the guides and staff of Portsmouth Historic Dockyards (particularly the HMS Victory), the Royal Marines Museum, National Maritime Museum, and Lyme Regis Museum. Special thanks to Natalie Manifold of Literary Lyme Walking Tours for her private tour of Jane Austen sites with an extended concentration on the Cobb. Closer to home, the reference librarians at Woodbourne Library hunted down all sorts of obscure old books and managed to obtain them for me.

From the day I joined the Jane Austen Society of North America twenty years ago, its members have generously shared their knowledge, enthusiasm, and friendship, and I deeply appreciate the support I have received since I first started writing the Darcy series. I also thank the Jane Austen Centre in Bath and the staff of Jane Austen's House Museum in Chawton for their warm reception.

Finally, I thank you, my readers. Your comments, criticism, and enthusiasm have helped shape this series, and are a daily inspiration.

The report of the accident had spread among the workmen and boat-men about the Cobb, and many were collected near them, to be use-ful if wanted, at any rate, to enjoy the sight of a dead young lady, nay, two dead young ladies, for it proved twice as fine as the first report.

—Persuasion

"We none of us expect to be in smooth water all our days."

—Mrs. Croft, Persuasion

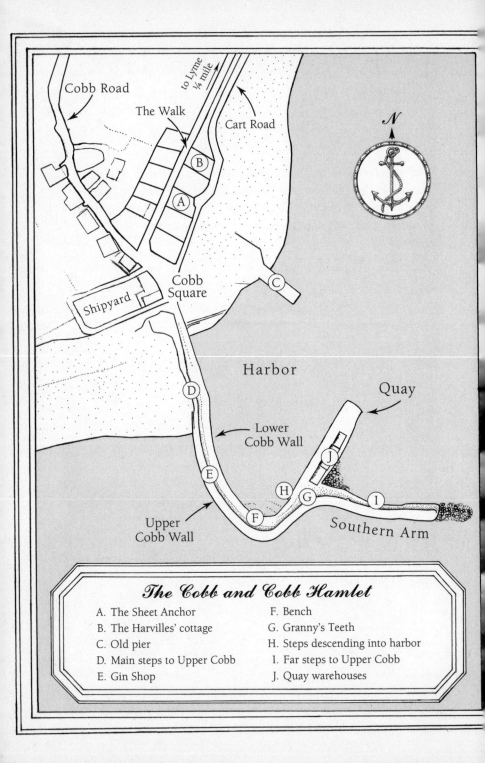

The Cobb and Cobb Hamlet

A. The Sheet Anchor
B. The Harvilles' cottage
C. Old pier
D. Main steps to Upper Cobb
E. Gin Shop
F. Bench
G. Granny's Teeth
H. Steps descending into harbor
I. Far steps to Upper Cobb
J. Quay warehouses

The quay and southern arm of the Cobb, where the Darcys form more than one new acquaintance . . . not all of them pleasant.

The "gin shop," where a lost hat leads to an unexpected find.

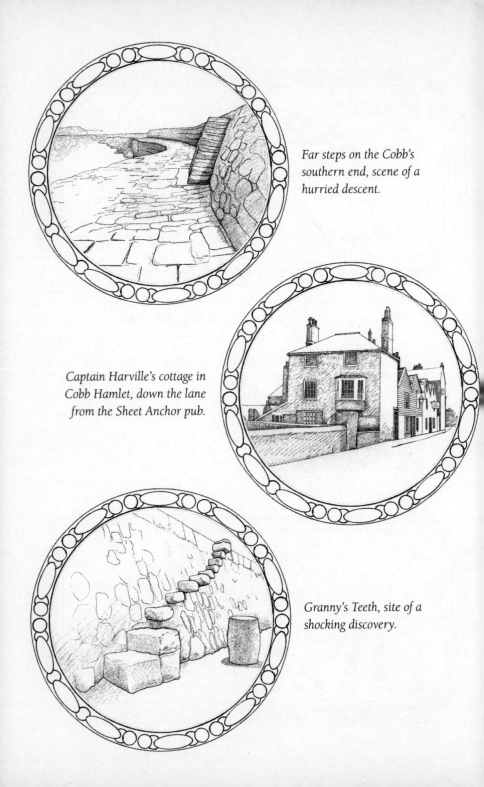

Far steps on the Cobb's southern end, scene of a hurried descent.

Captain Harville's cottage in Cobb Hamlet, down the lane from the Sheet Anchor pub.

Granny's Teeth, site of a shocking discovery.

The
Deception at Lyme

Prologue

The Cobb itself, its old wonders and new improvements . . .
are what the stranger's eye will seek.

—Persuasion

*O*n the southern coast of England, near the town of Lyme Regis, an ancient seawall rises from the water.

Like a great openmouthed serpent, its head reaches into the sea, its jaw acts as a quay, its body curves round to form a harbor, its tail stretches to the shore. Known as "the Cobb" for reasons lost to time, this man-made barrier more than half a millennium old is but a youthful newcomer to a wild, unstable coast where prehistoric creatures once dwelled.

Were it not for the Cobb, there would be no harbor, and were it not for the harbor, there would be no Lyme, for the rugged shoreline the seawall faces offers no natural protected anchorage. The construction of the wall proved the making of the town, their fates and fortunes entwined. From simple medieval beginnings, the Cobb, the harbor, and the village together evolved into a thriving port worthy of royal notice.

In this haven, ships were built and launched, trading vessels unloaded exotic wares, sailors returning from distant lands found welcome, and visitors invested hope and fortunes in the alleged restorative powers of seabathing—all sheltered by a mighty stone guardian from the caprice of the sea and the violence of Mother Nature.

In the summer of 1815, however, even the Cobb could not safe-guard Lyme from the tempests of human nature.

One

After securing accommodations, and ordering a dinner at one of the inns, the next thing to be done was unquestionably to walk directly down to the sea.

—Persuasion

*E*lizabeth Bennet Darcy had yet to glimpse the Cobb as she negotiated one of the steep cobblestone streets that wended through Lyme's cliffside dwellings and shops. The close buildings obscured her view of the renowned seawall and harbor some half-mile distant from the town. Yet even had the breakwater been within sight, her gaze coveted a still more remarkable spectacle: the sea itself. In all her three-and-twenty years, she had never before laid eyes upon the sea, and the narrow glimpses she managed to catch between buildings as her small party walked down to the shoreline only whetted her impatience to behold it unobstructed.

At last they reached the end of Broad Street, where a promontory opened up a commanding prospect, and she stopped to absorb the sight. She could see not only the harbor, but also miles beyond. The sun traced its descent toward the horizon, its rays diffused by clouds into muted green and yellow light that slid across the dark water rolling toward the beach.

"Is it as you imagined?"

Had her husband not stood directly beside her, his question

might have gone unheard. The wind blowing across Lyme Bay tugged insistently at her bonnet, the ribbons beneath her chin straining to prevent its taking flight.

"I could not possibly have imagined this." Though she had seen depictions of the sea, no canvas could capture its magnitude, nor the latent power she could feel even from their elevated vantage point. Tall-masted ships moored in the harbor, their mighty hulls dwarfing the smaller fishing boats bobbing round them with the incoming tide. Still more great vessels anchored beyond the seawall, majestic silhouettes against the horizon.

She turned to Darcy. "Thank you for indulging my eagerness to walk down to the sea tonight. You and your sister have visited the coast on enough previous occasions that it cannot hold for you the novelty it does for me."

"I have never visited this part of the coast before. And I believe my appreciation of the sea is the greater for viewing it this time with you."

"Despite my having drawn you and Georgiana out of our lodgings nearly the moment we arrived in Lyme?"

"The more so, because you did." Darcy smiled. "I believe you are even more keen to experience the sea than is Lily-Anne."

Elizabeth had felt a touch of guilt upon leaving their young daughter with her nurse while the adults walked to the shore. Their family had been speaking with such anticipation about this holiday that although Lily-Anne's vocabulary was limited, "sea" had been among her most-used words for the past fortnight. The journey to Lyme, however, had tested the eighteen-month-old's temper beyond endurance. She would enjoy her first sight of the sea in the morning, after the proper night's rest for which her nurse was now settling her down.

Georgiana clamped a hand upon her hat. "Lily-Anne would have been carried off by one of these gusts of wind. Do you think it will rain?"

Darcy glanced at the sky. "Not tonight. However, more clouds are forming, and sunset is not long off. We should continue to the beach so that we can see it and return to our lodgings before full dark."

As they descended steps down to the square, another gust swept the cliff, catching hold of Elizabeth's wide-brimmed straw bonnet. "If I do not adjust my hat, the wind will carry *me* off," she said.

An inn, the Lion, stood not far up the street, with a narrow passage between it and its neighbor that would provide shelter from the wind. They walked to the building, and Elizabeth entered the alley while Darcy and Georgiana waited at its entrance.

She removed her gloves and tried to untie the bonnet. The wind, unfortunately, had strained the ribbons so taut against her jaw that now, though the ties had slackened in the sheltered space, they formed a knot so tight that she struggled to work it free. She glanced at Darcy and Georgiana, thinking to summon one of them for assistance. They, however, had become engaged in conversation with a couple she did not recognize. The lady appeared of an age similar to Georgiana's; the gentleman, about a decade older. The animated manner with which Darcy's sister spoke with the lady suggested the familiarity of previous acquaintance.

Electing not to interrupt, Elizabeth continued her solitary struggle. As she tried to coax the knot, she became aware that Darcy and Georgiana's conversation was not the only one taking place near her. Voices drifted through an open window of the inn.

"Do not deny it—I saw you leave the Sheet Anchor with one of them, and later walking on the Cobb with the other." The voice was a woman's: sharp, high-pitched. "You told me you had done with them."

"I have not seen either of them in I know not how long." This voice was male. Cultured. Condescending. "I was not aware they were in Lyme until we happened to meet today."

"Do not insult me with your lies; I know you better than anyone. And were that not enough, I have talked to each of them myself. You never stopped. All this time, I thought the business had ended. But you have been carrying on behind my back."

Elizabeth tugged harder at the ribbons. Uncomfortable with the accidental eavesdropping, she wanted to secure her hat and move along as quickly as possible.

"My affairs are none of your concern."

"*Your* affairs? Those affairs never would have begun had I not been so foolish as to introduce you. We came here to meet them, did we not? You allowed me to believe we were on holiday, when all along you were planning these rendezvous."

"Of what have you to complain? You *are* on holiday," responded the man, who Elizabeth presumed was the woman's husband. "You spend my money as if you were."

"Your money! And where is mine? Where is my share of what they have received all these years?"

"Do I not provide for you? You are wearing your share. You dine on your share. You drive about town in your share, patronize half the shops in London with your share. So long as you live under my protection, whom I meet and why is *my* business."

"Your business—and *you*—can go to the devil."

"Madam, at times I believe myself already in his company."

There followed an expletive which Elizabeth had never before heard uttered, let alone by a woman. She edged away from the window to distance herself from the scene of marital discord.

"What of the promise you made me?" the wife continued, her shrill voice rising to a volume Elizabeth could not escape despite the increased distance. "Did you ever intend to keep it?"

"In time."

"You have run out of time."

"Not quite yet. I suggest you keep that fact in mind."

"Depend upon it, I have."

A brief silence followed. Elizabeth hesitated to take another step, lest her retreat be heard and her presence realized.

"I have friends in Lyme, you know." The wife's voice was calm, steadier.

The man issued a low, scornful chuckle. "No doubt you do. Half the navy is ashore. Though in your current state, you hardly present an enticing object."

"Certain individuals might be very interested in learning what I know. I am not the only person *your* affairs have betrayed."

"You are hardly guiltless yourself. Unless you are an utter fool, you will keep your mouth shut."

The next sound was that of a door opening.

"Where are you going?" the man said.

"Out."

Though Elizabeth had failed to free her knotted ribbons, she hastened to rejoin her party. An accidental witness to the domestic drama, she had no desire to meet its actors.

Georgiana and Darcy were alone once more; the couple with whom they had been speaking were now a good twenty yards up the street, slowly negotiating the steep incline.

"You just missed my friend Miss Ashford," Georgiana said. "What a delightful surprise! I had no idea of her being in Lyme. She is here with her brother, who comes regularly. In fact, he likes it so well that he leases a house here throughout the year. They arrived a se'nnight ago. They were just come from a promenade on the Cobb, which they highly recommend. Sir Laurence said the view from the top is very fine. They have gone every afternoon, and invited me to join them tomorrow."

Elizabeth took Georgiana's arm and continued walking, hoping to move their party along. "I am glad you have found friends here. Are they Derbyshire acquaintances?" She could not recall having heard the name before.

"No—their family home is in Somerset. I know Miss Ashford from London; she and I have studied with the same harp master since we were girls. I met her eldest brother once about three years ago, but this is the first time I have seen him since he inherited the baronetcy from his father. He is Sir Laurence now. That makes him sound older than merely 'Mr. Ashford,' do you not think? Yet he is not too old—" She turned to her brother. "I believe about the same age as you, Fitzwilliam. I did not realize until today that you know each other."

"We have met occasionally at White's," Darcy said.

Georgiana, noting the unaltered state of Elizabeth's bonnet, offered her assistance, but Elizabeth declined.

"It can wait. I am impatient to reach the waterfront." She glanced over her shoulder toward the inn's entrance, but saw no one who answered her mind's image of the couple she had overheard.

In but a few steps more they passed the Assembly Rooms and arrived at the beach. From here they could see the Cobb half a mile southwest. Small boats bobbed in the harbor created by the semicircular breakwater, which extended at least a thousand feet from mouth to shore. The seawall met land near a cluster of buildings their landlady had referred to as Cobb Hamlet. Separated from Lyme proper by an undeveloped cliff prone to landslips, the harbor and hamlet were linked to Lyme by an elevated promenade known as the Walk, which ran parallel to a cart road that skirted the beach.

Elizabeth, Darcy, and Georgiana ambled along the Walk, taking in the sights, sounds, and smells of the sea. Dusk approached, and waterfront activity both on- and offshore was winding down. Vendors packed up their wares; sailors finished unloading goods from recently docked ships; horses pulled the last of the carts toward the Customs House for clearance. Four bathing machines, having long since completed their service for the day, were parked on the beach out of reach of the lapping tide.

A set of steps led from the Walk down to the cart road and the beach itself. The rising tide brought the water quite close, and Darcy asked whether Elizabeth would like to go down and dip her hand in the seawater breaking onto shore. She responded enthusiastically.

At the base of the stair, a young gentleman who had been about to ascend moved aside to grant them clear passage. Even in the fading light, his features evinced considerable time spent at sea. The sun had tanned his skin to a rich hue and bleached to pale gold the long hair tied back beneath his hat. The result was not unfavorable; in fact, he possessed a mien of health and vigor superior to most of the other sailors they had passed as they walked through Lyme. He nodded politely at Elizabeth and Darcy as they reached the bottom step—a civility they returned—but when his gaze shifted behind them to acknowledge Georgiana, a spark entered his blue eyes, and an expression of patent admiration overtook his countenance.

Elizabeth turned to regard her sister-in-law. A well-favored, graceful girl even in ordinary moments, Georgiana at present appeared altogether fetching. The wind that had played such havoc with Elizabeth's bonnet had brightened Georgiana's eyes and loosened tendrils of honey-blond hair that fluttered becomingly around cheeks pinkened by the persistent sea breeze—or perhaps by consciousness of being the object of so admiring a look. No one could be insensible of such attention from a handsome gentleman, certainly not a young lady of nineteen.

And certainly not her brother.

Darcy glanced from the sailor to Georgiana, and saw his sister through the stranger's eyes—the eyes of a man. A man who was not her brother, not her protector, but a warm-blooded buck who could not help but respond to the sight of a beautiful woman. Worse—a man turned onshore after months at sea entirely deprived of women's company. Decent women's company, anyway.

Though there had been nothing improper in the sailor's expression or manner, his interest put Darcy on guard. It reminded him all too vividly of the last time he and Georgiana had been at the seaside, and the evil she had so narrowly escaped. Darcy had thwarted the designs of one fortune hunter, but scavengers of Mr. Wickham's breed flocked in watering-places like gulls.

Before Darcy could offer his hand to assist Georgiana's descent, the stranger offered his own. She accepted his aid, placing her hand in his. She negotiated the stairs without incident, but as she stepped onto the beach—her attention entirely upon him, to the neglect of her own feet—a small mound of shingle shifted beneath her, throwing her out of balance.

The gentleman quickly caught her, preventing a fall. Darcy stepped forward to help steady Georgiana, relieving the sailor of any need—or excuse—for further contact with his sister. Georgiana took Darcy's arm, but required it for only a moment. She had regained her equilibrium. Her composure, however, was not so easily recovered. She cast her gaze about, fleetingly meeting the stranger's, then shifting it to look at anything but the man's countenance.

His face reflected amusement. Hers was in high color. She stammered a few halting words of gratitude, by all appearances directed at the wall behind him. The edges of his mouth upturned to a half-smile.

He tipped his hat—"Your servant, miss"—and continued on his way.

Though she had refused to meet his eyes, Georgiana watched his back as he nimbly cleared the stairs and hastened along the Walk.

"He thinks me a careless featherbrain."

Darcy, too, observed the retreat of the man who had found his sister's discomposure charming. "The opinion of a common sailor you will never again set eyes upon should cause you no distress."

"He is not a common sailor. From his manner and dress, he is a gentleman. I wager he is a naval officer, as Gerard was."

Indeed, there were enough ships in the harbor that the stranger could well be an officer on one of the small naval vessels, if not the master of a merchantman. Darcy doubted, however, that the man could ever wear a uniform as proudly as their late cousin had worn his the last time Darcy and Georgiana saw him. A newly commissioned lieutenant of the Royal Navy, Gerard Fitzwilliam had died three years ago in action aboard the *Magna Carta*.

"Even if that fellow is an officer, neither dress nor stripes make a man a gentleman," Darcy said. "Put him from your mind."

They strolled along the beach a little way, but the sun soon dropped so low that the filtered light faded quickly. The wind picked up, and the temperature, which had dropped decidedly since they began their walk, caused both Georgiana and Elizabeth to shudder. Electing to postpone the pleasure of their first promenade on the Cobb itself until the morrow, they headed back toward their lodgings.

Darcy looked at the sky once more. Clouds obscured the young moon. Perhaps a storm was gathering after all.

Two

There was too much wind to make the high part of the new Cobb pleasant for the ladies, and they agreed to get down the steps to the lower.

—Persuasion

*L*ily-Anne, stay with mamma and papa!" Elizabeth called after her daughter. Her admonition, however, was spoken in vain; her voice drowned in the crash of waves against the Cobb.

Darcy pursued their racing toddler. His strides overtook the child's short steps well before Lily reached the edge of the seawall upon which they walked. Built to hold back an ocean, the breakwater was wide enough for their whole party—and then some—to comfortably walk abreast. Nevertheless, Lily-Anne had given her mother a scare. They were on the upper Cobb, which rimmed the lower Cobb on one side and fronted the open sea on the other; beyond either of the upper wall's edges was a sheer drop—onto merciless pavement or into the ocean itself.

As Darcy's arms closed around Lily and lifted her, the child squealed in delight, oblivious to the hazard toward which she had raced. He brought her close and bent his head to her ear. Elizabeth could not hear his words as she left Georgiana's side to catch up to them, but Lily-Anne nodded, and when Darcy set her down, she remained at his feet.

"So, you have decided to be obedient, have you?" Despite her stern tone, Elizabeth was not cross with her daughter. Lily-Anne was normally a well-behaved child; her sprint had been inspired by the novelty of new surroundings, and in truth, Elizabeth remained as eager as her daughter to see them. In fact, it had been Elizabeth who suggested walking to the Cobb shortly after breakfast. Despite sharing Lily-Anne's exuberance, however, Elizabeth longed for the day when her little girl would possess sufficient understanding of the world to have a care for her own safety.

The great seawall had two levels. The lower Cobb—the harbor side of the wall—was level with the shore, and as the Cobb stretched into the sea, maintained a height equal to the harbor's water level at high tide. It served as a broad walk upon which pedestrians and horse-drawn carts could access the harbor and reach the quay at its mouth. The lower wall was edged by the upper Cobb—the ocean side of the wall—which rose some nine feet higher than the lower Cobb to shelter the harbor from the sea's great waves and winds.

Because of its height, the upper wall blocked much of the sea from the view of anyone on the lower. A broad stone staircase where the Cobb met the shore provided access from the lower wall to the upper, and upon their arrival, Elizabeth, Darcy, Lily-Anne, and Georgiana had climbed it to look upon the sea. Lily-Anne, however, had immediately gone charging to the wall's edge.

Lily-Anne now wrapped one arm around Darcy's leg and pointed with her other toward the ocean. "Sea."

"Yes, Lily, that is the sea," Darcy said. "And we would rather you not topple into it."

The clouds that were building during last evening's walk had settled in thick masses overnight. Mist hung heavy in the air, obscuring the horizon and coating the Cobb with a thin film of moisture. "She could slip on these stones," Elizabeth said. "Perhaps we should turn back and resume this walk another time, when the sun will have dried the pavement."

"We are on a seawall, Elizabeth. There is a good chance these stones never entirely dry. Lily-Anne will be safe; we shall keep a close hold on her."

"Sir Laurence *did* particularly recommend the view from the upper wall," Georgiana said as she reached them. "Surely he would not have advised us to walk on it were it not safe."

The top of the Cobb indeed offered an impressive view, even if at present the mist obscured it. They could no longer see the Portland lighthouse to the southeast that had been visible last night, and even nearer objects proved difficult to distinguish. Two ships approached port. The closer one, about to enter the harbor, appeared to move as if in a dream; the more distant vessel was barely discernible.

Elizabeth assessed the sky. Despite the rising sun, it was not growing lighter. However, the rain threatened by the clouds seemed to be holding off. She allowed herself to be persuaded.

They strolled on the upper wall at a leisurely pace. People from all strata of society left their footprints on the damp stones. Looking down to their left, they saw sailors on the lower Cobb hustling about their duties. A woman sat on a bench, resting her hands on the handle of a walking cane, watching the harbor—observing the dockmen at work, the carts headed toward the Customs House, the bobbing of fishing vessels and larger boats as the incoming tide freed them from their sandy groundings. The upper Cobb was less populated than the lower, doubtless due to its height and more weathered surface that pitched toward the open sea at a daunting angle along some stretches. Nevertheless, they were not the only pedestrians venturing upon it.

The thick mist seemed to suspend time and movement, yet the wind that buffeted them was anything but gentle. Completely exposed to the sea, those atop the high wall had no shield from the elements, and last night's determined breeze had become this morn's full gale. The damp air held a chill, enhanced by the sea spray that cascaded onto the wall when particularly forceful waves crashed against its base. Elizabeth was grateful that she had dressed Lily-Anne warmly, and wished she had thought to wear a spencer over her own muslin dress. She envied the foresight of a solitary woman standing near the harborside edge of the upper wall, away from the worst threat of the sea spray. The lady wore a long grey cape that ballooned about her in the wind.

The woman's back was to their party, but as they passed, she turned her head. Her gaze met Elizabeth's. There was a hardness in her countenance at odds with the fluid billowing of her attire, almost an embodiment of the unforgiving stone on which she balanced. Immediately discerning that Elizabeth and her companions were nobody of interest to her, the lady returned her attention to the shoreline.

At this point the lower Cobb forked. The branch along the harbor was a quay which hosted several buildings that seemed to primarily serve those loading and unloading docked boats. The southern arm, running behind the quay, extended the outer seawall at both upper and lower levels by an additional few hundred feet.

Another large wave crashed against the wall, sending up the highest spray of seawater they had yet seen. Cascading droplets christened them and fell in their path, forming rivulets that ran across the Cobb's surface to puddle in the stone's many depressions. Lily-Anne giggled, delighted by the unanticipated fountain.

Though not soaked, Elizabeth shivered. "Perhaps we should turn back."

"We are almost to the end," Georgiana said. "And Sir Laurence said—why, look! I believe there is the gentleman himself."

A small stone staircase offered access to the lower wall at this end of the Cobb. Considerably narrower than the stairs Elizabeth and her family had used to mount the upper wall, these were hidden from view along most of the Cobb by the serpentine curve of the seawall and the buildings on the quay. Elizabeth might have entirely overlooked them had Sir Laurence's ascent not drawn her attention.

When he reached the top and glanced in their direction, the baronet appeared as surprised as they to be meeting thus. "Miss Darcy!" He came immediately to them. "I did not expect the pleasure of escorting you on the Cobb until later today."

"Nor I."

Now that she had a closer view of the baronet, Elizabeth's earlier impression of his good looks was confirmed. He had dark hair and eyes, strong, well-formed features, and an agreeable demeanor that was aristocratic but not pompous. Though he stood a little shorter than Darcy, he was his equal in handsomeness. From her sister-in-law's demure smile and manner, Elizabeth suspected the bloom on Georgiana's cheeks had little to do with the wind.

Sir Laurence greeted Darcy, who introduced Elizabeth and Lily-Anne. The baronet was all courtesy, expressing his happiness in meeting Elizabeth, and acknowledging the child with kind attention.

"Sea." Lily pointed, in case the baronet had not noticed the vast expanse of water.

"I do see the sea," he assured her with all seriousness—save a good-humored brightness in his eyes. He then turned to Georgiana. "And while this is not ideal weather, I think the sea exhibits a different sort of beauty—a wild magnificence—on days such as this. Did you walk down to the very end of the Cobb?"

"Not yet."

"Then I beg you to allow me to accompany you." He spoke to Georgiana, but his gaze extended the invitation to them all.

"I should like that very much," Georgiana said.

They walked another twenty yards or so, past the steps up which Sir Laurence had come. Elizabeth looked again at the sky and the churning water. Though she agreed with the baronet's opinion of the sea's untamed splendor, at present she would rather appreciate that splendor from the shore—or better still, from the interior side of a window in a room with a fire warm enough to banish the damp chill that had crept into her bones. Yet she did not want to deny Georgiana the pleasure of Sir Laurence's company.

"I pray you will understand a mother's anxiety and let us postpone taking Lily-Anne farther out to the point until fairer weather," Elizabeth said. "However, do escort Miss Darcy. We will wait here."

Sir Laurence bowed. "We shall not be long."

As the pair walked away, Elizabeth noticed how closely Darcy observed them. "This is not Ramsgate," she said, "and your sister is four years older than the last time she visited the sea. I believe it is safe to take your eyes off her for a moment."

"It was not the sea that posed danger in Ramsgate."

"No, it was one of her oldest acquaintances, someone she should have been able to trust. Would you deny her a new acquaintance now because of Mr. Wickham's deceit? Surely the baronet is not a fortune hunter."

"No, Sir Laurence inherited considerable wealth along with his title, and the sense to protect it. That fellow last night who ogled her on the stairs, however, is another matter."

Elizabeth had thought the gentleman's conduct unobjectionable. "He did not ogle. And what makes you suspect him of being a fortune hunter? He appeared perfectly respectable."

"One cannot be too wary."

"Sea." Lily-Anne squirmed in Darcy's hold. Tired of being carried, she was growing restless, but Elizabeth wanted to provide Georgiana a few more minutes' uninterrupted conversation. Sir Laurence was pointing toward the ship still approaching port. Though it was a good-sized vessel, with cannons lining its sides, its progress appeared hampered by the strong eastern wind.

She took Lily-Anne into her own arms. Lily rested her chin on Elizabeth's shoulder and stilled, content—at least for the moment—to gaze at the view behind her mother, but the tranquility would not last. In truth, the sea had temporarily lost its allure for Elizabeth, as well.

"Given the weather, we need to cancel our plans to go seabathing this morning and find some other diversion," Elizabeth said. "Have we any other engagements today?"

"Only my appointment with Lieutenant St. Clair, but that is not until evening."

"Where are you meeting?"

"He will call at our lodgings at half past seven."

Sir Laurence and Georgiana returned, retreating from the Cobb's point more hurriedly than they had walked out to it. Georgiana held fast to the baronet's arm.

"The wind has shifted," Sir Laurence said. "Storms can arise very quickly in Lyme, and those from the east are the worst. You can see how that ship struggles to make port. I advise walking back to town without delay."

Scarcely had he uttered the words than an enormous *crack* rent the sky. A lightning bolt struck the mainmast of the struggling ship. Aflame, the mast fell toward deck but got caught in the rigging of the foremast, igniting that, as well. Suddenly, the ship was a fiery spectacle of burning sails, ropes, and wood. Smoke billowed up from the lower decks and out the gun ports. The blazing mast, having incinerated the ropes that trapped it, crashed to the quarterdeck.

But the worst was yet to come.

In seconds that seemed to stretch to eternity, the flames reached gunpowder.

The explosion was so forceful that Elizabeth felt its thunder ripple past her. Instinctively, she tightened her hold on her daughter, who cried out and clung to her. Had the ship been closer, all on the upper Cobb would have been in serious danger from flying debris.

The Cobb erupted in motion. Those who knew the sea hurriedly prepared to search for survivors—futile though their efforts might prove—or to scavenge the ship's cargo. Everyone else rushed to get out of the rescuers' way and find safety for themselves.

Another thunderbolt lit the sky. Elizabeth's heart raced so hard that surely Lily-Anne could feel its palpitations. "Sea, Mama! Sea!" She practically climbed up her mother's chest and over her shoulder toward the harbor. Even the child realized that her former source of delight now posed peril.

Elizabeth felt she could not get off the exposed seawall fast enough.

Before she even turned to Darcy, he was taking their daughter into his own arms. "Come." His voice was calm, but she heard the underlying urgency. He motioned toward the steps Sir Laurence had ascended but a few minutes ago. "We must move to lower ground." Georgiana and Sir Laurence were right behind them.

The steps were narrower than Elizabeth had realized, and water puddled in their crevices and depressions. Under other circumstances she would have eschewed them in favor of the broad stairs at the other end of the Cobb, but they had not that luxury—the sky threatened greater hazard than the stone.

Father and daughter descended first, followed by the ladies and Sir Laurence, and their party hurried along the lower Cobb toward shore. Though they were now alee of the upper wall, the breakwater offered only partial shelter, for the harbor opened to the east whence the wind blew from Charmouth along the cliff face. The wall's bend at this section restricted their view of a considerable portion of the Cobb ahead. Elizabeth was anxious to reach the point where this particular curve ended; from there she would be able to see the remaining distance to safety. Drops of water landed on her: two on her arm, another on her neck. Were they sea spray, or had rain begun to fall?

She moved faster with each step to keep pace with Darcy's ever-lengthening strides. They approached the curve, rounded it—

And stopped.

The solitary woman they had seen standing on the upper Cobb now blocked their path on the lower. Her back to them, she did not turn this time. Indeed, she took no notice of them at all. And her cape no longer billowed about her.

It covered her body, lying motionless on the cold, hard stone.

Three

The horror of that moment to all who stood around!

—Persuasion

*T*here is never a particularly good time to stumble upon a body, but Darcy could not help thinking that this was one of the worst. The sky had darkened to the state of dusk, and the droplets that struck the pavement could no longer be dismissed as sea spray by even the most optimistic observer. Thunder sounded again.

Sir Laurence came up beside him. "Is she dead?"

"I see no blood," Darcy said, "but she does not appear to be breathing." He transferred Lily-Anne to Elizabeth, who tried to shield the child's view while he approached the prostrate form.

Lily-Anne, however, seemed intent on watching him. She wrestled against Elizabeth's embrace. "See!"

"Not now, Lily." Elizabeth drew their daughter closer to her.

Darcy knelt beside the inanimate form tossed on the ground like one of Lily-Anne's rag dolls. The lady's right arm was trapped beneath her, the other hidden with her bent knees somewhere beneath her long cape.

"She must have tried to descend Granny's Teeth to escape the storm," Sir Laurence said.

Carrie Bebris

"Granny's Teeth?"

The baronet nodded toward the wall. Beside them rose a set of steps so narrow that they had escaped Darcy's notice entirely when they passed them above. "Steps," in fact, was too generous a word to describe the weathered rectangular stones protruding at uneven intervals from the sheer face of the wall. The flight was so steep and treacherous that only the most intrepid—or foolhardy—individual would hazard it in trousers and fair weather, let alone skirts in a storm.

Darcy put his hand on the woman's back and detected a slight rise and fall. "She breathes. I feel broken ribs, however." The lady likely suffered other broken bones as well, but Darcy could not with propriety examine her. He turned to Elizabeth, who was already consigning their daughter to Georgiana.

As his wife moved to the other side of the injured lady, Darcy looked about. Had nobody else noticed the inert figure lying on the wet pavement? The quay's warehouses blocked this stretch of the Cobb from the view of most of the dockworkers, and the attention of those within sight was consumed by the frantic activity of launching rescue efforts and battening down hatches before the storm unleashed its full fury.

"Good heavens."

Elizabeth's words wrenched his attention back to her. She had lifted the woman's cape, and now raised her gaze to his. "She is with child."

"Is the baby—"

She reached toward the woman's abdomen and was silent for several very long minutes. "Yet alive," she said at last. "I feel movement. She needs a surgeon."

"Sir Laurence," Darcy said, "if you would escort my family to our lodgings and send a surgeon hither, I would be most obliged."

"Nay, I should be the one who remains."

Much as Darcy would prefer to conduct his family safely home himself, the baronet was the logical choice to go. "You are more familiar with Lyme. You know better than I the fastest way back through the town and where a surgeon might be found."

"You will be escorting only Miss Darcy and Lily-Anne," Elizabeth added.

Both gentlemen objected to her not seeking shelter, but she refused to yield. "This woman is unconscious, with child, and has just suffered a traumatic accident. If something occurs with that baby before the surgeon arrives, have either of you any notion what to do for her?"

Darcy and Sir Laurence exchanged glances.

"Very well," said Sir Laurence. "I will send a surgeon with all possible haste and return myself after seeing Miss Darcy and your daughter to safety."

Lily-Anne offered the only additional objection. "See, Mamma!" The toddler lunged so violently toward her mother that the unexpected weight shift nearly caused Georgiana to lose her hold on the child.

The baronet reached for Lily. "We can walk faster if I carry her."

But Lily-Anne would have none of that, and clung to her aunt with tenacity. Sir Laurence attempted to disengage her, but Georgiana shook her head. "I can carry her. Let us not lose another moment."

Darcy watched them depart. Sir Laurence walked between Georgiana and the harbor, so that Georgiana and Lily received as much shelter as possible from the wall. His left arm circled Georgiana's back to hold her far elbow, supporting her balance on the slick stones and the arm which bore most of Lily's weight. It was a posture Darcy would have adopted with his wife under similar conditions, and he never would have countenanced such familiarity between the baronet and Georgiana were the safety of his sister and daughter not in question. As it was, the sight of the trio—man, woman, and child—so intimately grouped gave rise to a fleeting image of Georgiana established in a family of her own. Though he had given matters such as her marriage settlement due contemplation, the marriage itself had always been a vague, distant event. He was not ready to admit a specific face into his indistinct visions of Georgiana's future, but he wondered whether his sister was.

More lightning flashed, and he forced these thoughts aside. He had a crisis demanding his full concentration. He turned to Elizabeth, who ministered to their patient as best she could. "I wish you had gone with Georgiana and Lily-Anne," he said.

She met his gaze. "I could not in good conscience leave."

"I would have managed."

"I know." The look she gave him left no doubt of her confidence, nor her devotion. "But just because you are capable of handling difficulties by yourself does not mean you should have to. I would not abandon you to deal with this alone."

It seemed, however, that they were no longer entirely alone. Despite the storm and rescue efforts, some of the men working on the dock had at last noticed the injured woman and paused in their activities long enough to cast occasional curious glances their way. Discovering a surgeon among them would be a stroke of fortune too propitious to come Darcy's way this dark morning, but he approached them nevertheless. They might prove helpful in another way.

"Do any of you know that lady?"

"I don't know her, but I've seen her before," piped a gaunt, pockmarked fisherman. "Comes to Lyme every so often. Usually see her around the Cobb with a gentleman. I've not seen him this morning, though."

"I did," said a burly fellow. "Well—I think it was him. Didn't pay 'em much mind, but she was talkin' to someone up there on the wall before she fell."

"Did you witness her fall?"

"No, sir. But there was another young lady fell off the wall not too long ago, and I saw that. Thought she was dead for sure, but she recovered. She stayed with the family in that house until she was mended." He pointed toward a small group of modest cottages in Cobb Hamlet.

"Does anybody have additional information regarding *this* lady?"

No one did, and all were anxious to resume their own business. Darcy returned to their patient. The unfortunate lady had not moved in the slightest since they came upon her. "I hope the surgeon does not arrive too late."

"I wish she would open her eyes." Elizabeth had removed the lady's bonnet, revealing dark blond hair—and swelling at her temple.

"Ma'am? Can you hear us?" The woman's facial muscles tensed, and it appeared that Elizabeth might be granted her wish. It was the hope of a moment, however, dashed as the stranger's face became expressionless once again.

More drops fell from the sky. Darcy removed his coat and placed it over Elizabeth's shoulders. The patient received some protection from her own cape, but the weather was worsening, and her likelihood of recovery diminished the longer they waited for a surgeon. He peered toward the beach, barely able to discern Sir Laurence and Georgiana in the misty darkness. They had reached the Walk but yet had a considerable distance before reaching the town. Once there, Sir Laurence still had to locate an available surgeon, who then would have to travel back through the elements to reach his patient.

"We need to move her to shelter," Darcy said.

"I had the same thought. But where?"

The nearest buildings were the quay warehouses—full of frantic activity and rough workmen. They might provide protection from the rain, but were hardly an appropriate venue for the surgeon to treat a lady, particularly one in a family condition.

Yet transporting her all the way to town was impractical, if not impossible. Darcy looked toward Cobb Hamlet. As he tried to recall whether he had seen any promising sanctuary there when they had passed through on their way to the Cobb, he became aware of someone approaching.

"Darcy, is that . . . ?"

It was. Of all people, the sailor they had encountered on the beach last night—the one who had prevented Georgiana's fall—now strode in their direction. Darcy presumed he was headed to the quay to assist the other seamen, but he instead came straight to them.

"Is the lady all right? Oh! I see she is not."

"We have sent for a surgeon but need to get her out of the rain," Elizabeth replied.

"Of course. How might I be of use?"

Despite Darcy's unfavorable previous impression of the man, he appreciated the offer of assistance. "We do not know where to take her."

The stranger assessed their options, as Darcy had done a minute ago. He scarcely glanced at the quay buildings, focusing instead on the hamlet. "A naval captain lives in one of those cottages. I do not know him well—have met his wife only once—but they are good people. Let us take her there."

He approached the injured woman and grimaced at the head contusion. "Has she been conscious?"

"Not since we discovered her," Darcy said.

"She also has broken ribs," Elizabeth added, "and is with child."

He nodded. "We shall take extra care." He lifted the edge of the woman's cape off her and spread it behind her on the ground, then asked Darcy to help him roll her onto her back. "Slowly," he cautioned.

When she lay more or less centered on the cape, the sailor slid his hands beneath her shoulders and under her arms. He looked at Darcy. "When I lift her on this end, you lift her by the knees. If you can pull the cape taut to support her back, so much the better. And you, ma'am"—he turned to Elizabeth—"help me hold her head still as we carry her."

Given his air of authority, Darcy believed he might indeed be a ship's officer, as Georgiana had speculated. Under other circumstances, Darcy would have chafed at being commanded as if he and Elizabeth were subordinates, but as the officer seemed to have experience in moving injured persons, he accepted his direction.

They carried their patient off the Cobb as quickly as the rain allowed. When they reached the naval captain's home, Elizabeth knocked on the door of the modest cottage. A boy of about seven answered.

"Is your father at home?" the officer asked.

"No, sir." The boy stared at the injured woman, who Darcy believed grew heavier each minute.

"Caleb, who is at the door?" called a feminine voice from within. Before the boy had a chance to answer, a woman who, given her unmistakable resemblance to the child, could be none but the boy's mother, appeared beside her son.

"Good day—" Her gaze shifted to the injured lady. "Good heavens! What has happened?"

"This lady fell on the Cobb in the storm," the officer said. "I beg your pardon for the imposition, Mrs. Harville, but your home is the nearest shelter I could think of."

Mrs. Harville ushered them in without hesitation. "Poor creature! Here, bring her this way." She led them through the small main room to an even smaller side chamber that held a bed onto which Darcy and the officer lowered the patient. The injured woman stirred slightly as her cape was removed and handed to a maid with orders to set it out to dry beside the kitchen fire. "Caleb," Mrs. Harville added, "go with her and bring wood to light the hearth in this chamber."

Two small boys—Caleb's younger brothers, Darcy presumed—moved aside to allow them passage, then hovered in the doorway, observing the scene with wide eyes.

Mrs. Harville turned back to the patient. "Her head! Lieutenant, do you know where to find Mr. Sawyer?"

"If Mr. Sawyer is a surgeon, I believe one has already been summoned."

"But was it Mr. Sawyer you sent for? So many frauds flock to Lyme this time of year. Mr. Sawyer will know what to do. A friend of ours had an accident on the Cobb last autumn and injured her head. Mr. Sawyer treated her, and she is mended now."

"If you give me his direction, I shall go at once."

Within a minute, he had departed. Mrs. Harville turned to Darcy and Elizabeth. "Forgive me—in the urgency of the moment I have forgotten my manners. I am Mrs. Harville. My husband, Captain Harville, is out just now. He heard a ship went down before it reached harbor, and he left to see whether he could be of use."

Darcy introduced himself and Elizabeth. "We are visitors to Lyme and appreciate your assistance," he added.

Mrs. Harville adjusted a pillow behind the patient's head in an attempt to make the woman more comfortable. "How could anyone with a heart turn away your poor friend? What is her name?"

"We do not know the lady," Elizabeth said. "We came upon her as we were leaving the Cobb in the rain. She had already fallen."

"Does the lieutenant know her, then?"

Elizabeth glanced at Darcy uncertainly, then back at Mrs. Harville.

"I do not believe so. He was not present when we discovered her; he arrived afterward."

"Her husband must be frantic with worry."

Darcy reproached himself for that thought not having occurred to him. But without knowing the wife's name, how might anyone begin to locate the husband?

"Did those workers you spoke with recognize the lady?" Elizabeth asked him.

"They had seen her earlier with a gentleman."

He wondered whether that gentleman might yet be on the Cobb, searching for his wife. How they had become separated was a matter of speculation for another time, but were Elizabeth missing in this storm, nothing could have forced Darcy to leave the seawall until he had found her, particularly if she were in a delicate condition. If the dockmen to whom he had spoken could provide a description of the lady's husband, perhaps Darcy could find the gentleman.

Rain splattered against the glass of the chamber's tiny, sole window. The last place Darcy wanted to go was back out on the Cobb. The errand, however, could not be delayed.

"I should talk to those workers again while there remains a chance of finding them still on the quay," he said to Elizabeth. "But I will not leave if you or Mrs. Harville have need of me here while awaiting the surgeon."

Both women assured him of his superfluity. Elizabeth, who yet wore his coat, removed it to return to him.

"Oh! Let me fetch you Captain Harville's spare oilskin," Mrs. Harville insisted. "It is not much to look at, but it will provide some protection from the rain. Mrs. Darcy, I will find you some dry things, as well."

The raincoat was well worn—it had obviously weathered many storms at sea—but Darcy was grateful for it as he returned to the scene of the accident. His wet errand was not undertaken in vain; he found the two dockmen just as they were entering one of the warehouses. After soliciting their cooperation, he stepped inside with them.

"You said you had seen the woman with her husband earlier—pray, describe him to me."

The scrawny fellow cleared his throat. "I don't think he's her husband, sir, if you catch my meaning."

The insinuation startled Darcy. From the quality of the woman's attire, he had assumed she was a lady. "Did she appear to be his mistress, or a . . . more casual acquaintance?"

"Oh, I'd say they know each other very well. Saw them the day before yesterday, arguing like me and the missus do." The man laughed. "You know, sir—same argument, different day. Her doin' most of the talking."

"What did they argue about?"

"Couldn't say. Something about the air. Maybe the seashore don't agree with her."

Darcy was eager to find and inform the woman's patron—or whatever the gentleman was to her—and have done with the whole matter. "Can either of you tell me what the gentleman looks like?"

"He's a fair-looking chap, I s'pose. No worse than most other gen'lemen."

"Can you provide more particulars? His height, his age?"

"No need," said the dockman, looking past Darcy's shoulder. "That's him right there."

Darcy followed the man's gaze outside, where a gentleman had come into view. He was short, of an age approximating Darcy's own one-and-thirty years, with agreeable but not handsome looks due in part to an overpronounced lower jaw. Well prepared for the weather, he possessed both an overcoat and an umbrella. He scanned the dock, then ducked into the warehouse to search the faces of those inside.

Darcy thanked the workers who had identified the gentleman, then approached him.

"I beg your pardon, sir, but I have urgent news for the family or friends of a woman whom, I have been given to understand, you might be able to identify." Darcy spoke in a tone that barely rose above the noise of the warehouse activity. Depending upon the nature of this gentleman's association with the woman, he might not be inclined to admit an acquaintance with her. "She is perhaps thirty years old, with dark blond hair and freckles. This morning she wears a white dress and long grey cape. Does that description sound familiar?"

The gentleman regarded Darcy warily. "What sort of news?"

"She has suffered an accident."

"An accident? Here on the Cobb? Did she fall?"

"Indeed, she did."

"Whatever was she thinking, walking upon the upper wall on a morning such as this? Rain and wind that could knock a man down." He paused, his expression sobering as the situation settled more firmly upon his understanding. "Is she injured? She must be injured—you said the news was urgent. Where is she?"

"She has been taken to a nearby house. Come, I shall bring you to her."

They reentered the elements, which had worsened while Darcy was inside the warehouse. The gentleman opened his umbrella and carried it between them, but the wind drove rain at them at such an angle that it provided little protection. Darcy put up the hood of Captain Harville's oilskin, allowing the gentleman full use of the umbrella as they walked with all possible haste.

"Did you witness the accident?"

"No," Darcy replied. "My wife and I came upon her afterward."

"How badly is she injured?"

"A surgeon has been summoned." Darcy searched for the proper words to convey the gravity of the situation to someone who must hear the news from a stranger. His hesitation must have said enough.

"I am sure you must have noticed her delicate condition," the gentleman said. "Do you know whether the child survived the fall?"

"It was yet alive when we found her."

"Did she tell you how the accident occurred?"

"She has not regained her senses since the fall."

Thunder boomed. A powerful gust of wind caught the umbrella, forcing it inside out. The gentleman swore under his breath and paused to fix it, but the umbrella was beyond repair.

"Damn this deuced thing!" He flung the umbrella into the harbor, then apologized almost immediately. "Forgive me—I am not myself at the moment."

They resumed walking. They had covered about half the distance to the Harvilles' cottage, and now advanced with still more rapid strides.

"So she has not spoken?" the gentleman asked. "She cannot tell what happened?"

"I am afraid not. Though perhaps she has awakened in my absence."

"Let us hope so. I appreciate your trouble on her behalf. Might I ask to whom I am obliged?"

Startled, Darcy realized that in the urgency of delivering his news and the fury of the weather, he had failed to introduce himself properly. "Fitzwilliam Darcy. My wife is with your friend now, along with Mrs. Harville, to whose house she was taken."

"I am indebted to you all."

They had reached the cottage, and Darcy stopped before its door. "Might I, in turn, ask your name?"

The gentleman offered his hand. "It is Elliot. William Elliot."

Four

Her eyes were closed, she breathed not, her face was like death.
—Persuasion

*E*lizabeth helped Mrs. Harville and the maid exchange the patient's wet dress for a dry bed gown, then followed the servant upstairs to another small bedchamber where she changed into dry clothing herself. Afterward, Mrs. Harville deployed the maid to fetch smelling salts while she herself prepared a plaister for their patient's head. Elizabeth was assigned to watch over the patient while Caleb was enlisted to light the fire in the hearth. From the efficiency with which the naval captain's wife took charge, one might have thought it was she who regularly commanded a warship and its crew.

Left alone with the unconscious woman once the fire was lit, Elizabeth covered her with a blanket. "You are in good hands," she said, hoping that the sound of her voice might penetrate the unnatural slumber. "Mrs. Harville seems to know what she is about." Elizabeth could barely bring herself to look at the head contusion, which was turning a hideous shade of purple. The swelling at her temple had doubled since she and Darcy first came upon her.

In the relative privacy of the moment, she felt the woman's abdomen again to check on the dependent being within. It was alarmingly still. But then . . . a faint kick. Weak, but perceptible. As if to confirm that it had not been merely an illusion of her hopeful imagination, she felt a second movement.

"The surgeon is coming," she said, unsure whether she spoke the words aloud to reassure the baby, its mother, or herself.

The maid returned with the salts, then went to check on the children. Elizabeth passed the vial of hartshorn beneath the woman's nose, holding her own breath as she did so. The powerful odor always brought tears to her eyes, and reminded her of her mother's nervous fits.

The woman's countenance tightened. With what appeared great effort, her eyelids fluttered, but her gaze appeared unfocused.

Encouraged by this sign of consciousness, Elizabeth leaned closer. "Can you hear me, ma'am? You have suffered a fall."

"No . . ." The woman winced.

"I am afraid so—a bad fall, ma'am."

"Ell—" Her eyes drifted closed, as if she had not sufficient strength to at once hold them open and speak. "Elliot . . ."

"Is that your name? Elliot?"

She did not respond. Mrs. Elliot—if that were indeed her name—had drifted back out of consciousness. Elizabeth attempted the hartshorn again, but without success.

Mr. Sawyer at last arrived, so familiar with the route to the Harvilles' home that there had been no need for the officer who had summoned the surgeon to accompany him. Elizabeth somewhat guiltily recalled that Sir Laurence was also to have sent a surgeon, and hoped the second medical man was not wandering the Cobb in the storm wondering where his would-be patient had disappeared to. She supposed that if there were any survivors of the ship explosion, his services would be needed there more than here anyway, now that Mr. Sawyer had come.

He immediately set about examining the patient, assisted by Mrs. Harville. Their communication betokened familiarity, and references to "last time" and "Miss Musgrove" implied that Mrs. Harville's nursing experience had proved indispensable to him in the past.

Elizabeth described the state in which she and Darcy had found the woman, and the baby kick she had just felt. "She regained consciousness briefly," Elizabeth finished. "That is a good sign, is it not?"

The surgeon nodded absently as he felt the woman's ribs and took her pulse. "Unfortunately, she shows other signs that are not as encouraging. Was she able to speak?"

"She was very disoriented, and said only the name 'Elliot.'"

"Elliot?" Mrs. Harville glanced up from her ministrations. "Are you quite certain?"

"Yes. I assumed that to be her name, though she lost consciousness again before I could confirm it."

Mrs. Harville returned her attention to the patient. "I wonder whether she is connected to the Elliots of Kellynch Hall. The two younger daughters of that family are well known to us. Mr. Sawyer, you will recall them from Miss Musgrove's accident." She smoothed the woman's hair away from the plaister she had applied. "Mary is wife to Miss Musgrove's eldest brother, and Anne recently wed Captain Wentworth." She looked at the patient's rounded abdomen. "This cannot be the eldest sister, however, for Miss Elliot is a spinster."

Mr. Sawyer determined that leeches must be used to reduce the head swelling. As he prepared for the bloodletting, the maid entered to inform them that Darcy had returned. Elizabeth left the patient with the surgeon and Mrs. Harville, and entered the main room to find a rather wet Darcy with an even more soaked gentleman. He introduced his companion as Mr. Elliot.

"Mr. Elliot! Thank goodness my husband found you. The surgeon is with your wife now."

An odd expression passed over his countenance. "My wife passed away little more than a year ago." Despite his rumpled appearance, he stood stiffly.

Elizabeth flushed with embarrassment. "I beg your pardon. I assumed—"

"I believe, however, that I am acquainted with the woman Mr. Darcy described to me. Might I see her?"

"Of course."

She led him into the bedroom, where Mr. Sawyer was applying

leeches to the woman's temple. Mr. Elliot looked at her face, then averted his gaze from the business under way.

"I do know her. This woman is Mrs. Clay."

Elizabeth was relieved to at last have a name with which to address their patient. "Where might we locate Mr. Clay?"

"Penelope is widowed."

"Oh." Elizabeth was not certain who engaged her pity more—the mother left to raise her child alone, or the child who would never know its father. "She is fortunate to have friends at such a time. She asked for you."

Mr. Elliot started. "She is awake?"

"Not at present, but she woke briefly."

"What did she say?"

"Only your name: Elliot."

His features relaxed. "Yes, well . . . she has been under my protection for the past several months."

A moan from Mrs. Clay drew the attention of all in the room.

"Does she waken again?" Mr. Elliot asked.

Mrs. Harville called Mrs. Clay by name several times, but received no response. "Poor dear. I wonder whether she feels the leeches." She adjusted the blanket, which had become rumpled during Mr. Sawyer's examination. As she smoothed it over Mrs. Clay's abdomen, the patient released another soft moan.

Mrs. Harville stopped mid-motion and frowned. Pushing aside the blanket, she placed her hand firmly on Mrs. Clay's belly. Her expression of concentration alarmed Elizabeth, who crossed and placed her own hand beside Mrs. Harville's.

Time seemed to creep as she waited for the baby to signal her again, but in fact little more than a minute passed. This time, however, she did not feel a kick, but a hard tightening. She met Mrs. Harville's gaze, and saw that she had recognized it, also.

"Is she—"

Mrs. Harville nodded. "Mr. Sawyer, I believe Mrs. Clay has begun to labor."

Five

*Mrs. Hall of Sherbourn was brought to bed yesterday of a dead
child, some weeks before she expected, oweing [sic] to a fright.*
—Jane Austen, letter to her sister, Cassandra, 1799

*A*s birthing chambers are no place for gentlemen, Darcy and
Mr. Elliot quit the bedroom directly. Their adjournment to
the main sitting room, however, afforded Mrs. Clay and her atten-
dants little privacy, and the gentlemen little relief from noises and
other signals of the trial so near. Moreover, as Mrs. Harville had
pressed all able female hands—namely, her maid and Elizabeth—
into service to assist Mr. Sawyer with the lying-in, the gentlemen
found themselves left with Caleb and two smaller sprites whom
Darcy guessed to be five and two.

"Who are you?" the five-year-old asked.

"Two gentlemen come to call," Mr. Elliot replied. "Pray, do not
stare so." He shifted under their continued scrutiny. "I cannot believe their mother countenances such impertinence," he muttered.

Though the children's curiosity was poorly concealed, Darcy considered it natural. He and Mr. Elliot—not to mention the laboring
woman in the next room—were, after all, strangers in the boys' home,
and their arrival had been dramatic. He supposed, however, that
anxiety for Mrs. Clay and the physical discomfort of damp clothes

left Mr. Elliot little patience for conversation with young children. Darcy himself could have done without their surveillance at present.

"As we can be of no use," Mr. Elliot said, "I shall retreat to my lodgings."

Darcy regarded him with surprise. "You are going?"

"The rain has diminished, and I want to change into dry clothing. I will return later to enquire after Mrs. Clay."

Mr. Elliot seemed curiously detached from Mrs. Clay's plight. From his demeanor, his connexion to her would seem a slight acquaintance, yet the dockworker had suggested a much more intimate relationship between the pair. Darcy could not help but wonder whose baby Mrs. Clay was about to deliver. Mr. Elliot had implied to Elizabeth that the child belonged to the late Mr. Clay. Had the dockworker presumed too much, on too little intelligence? Darcy was not inclined to invest a great deal of credibility in the speculations of a man with more tattoos than teeth, and so withheld judgment. "If you are wanted before then, where might I find you?"

"In Broad Street, at the inn."

With that, Mr. Elliot was gone.

Elizabeth pushed hair away from her damp forehead with the back of her hand. It was warm in the room, almost intolerably so, and the maid had just banked the fire with more wood. The heat mixed with the scents of perspiration and blood and other effusions to create a heavy musk that gave rise to memories of her own lying-in and other births she had attended, including that of Darcy's cousin Anne Fitzwilliam little over a month ago. Anne's lying-in, however, seemed a world away from this one. Though not of especially robust constitution, Anne had at least been a conscious, active participant in the proceedings, awake to not only the travail but also the joy of presenting a healthy son to her husband once the ordeal ended. She had rapidly recovered her strength, and the Darcys had left the new family a happy threesome.

Mrs. Clay, however, hovered on the edge of awareness. Due to her accident, the baby was coming quickly. Her distressed countenance and the soft moans that heralded each contraction revealed that she felt pain, but she remained insensible to every attempt to speak to her.

Once, Mrs. Clay had roused enough that, at Mr. Sawyer's direction, Elizabeth and Mrs. Harville had raised her to a sitting position, supporting her through a contraction and urging her to push. Mrs. Clay had opened eyes that appeared filled with confusion. As the pain receded, Mrs. Clay met Elizabeth's gaze. "Pushed."

"You did a fine job, dear," Mrs. Harville replied. "Stay awake with us now, and help with the next one."

"No—I . . . before . . ." She closed her eyes and brought a hand to her head. "Pushed . . ." She lost consciousness again.

Mr. Sawyer, his expression grim, withdrew a set of forceps and other medical instruments from his bag. "Her pains are coming so rapidly now, it will not be long."

"Another pain is starting already," said Mrs. Harville, whose hand was on Mrs. Clay's abdomen. "The child is coming now."

Caleb, Adam, and Ben. Those were the names of the Harvilles' children, though Darcy was begun to think the elder two would have been better named Cain and Abel. Though of good dispositions, they competed fiercely: whose turn it was to sit on the tallest stool; who had played with the bilbocatch longer; and most especially, who could command the greater portion of Darcy's attention. The youngest, meanwhile, had stationed himself immediately outside the bedroom door, where he called alternately for his mother or the maid.

When the bedroom door opened, Darcy hoped to see Elizabeth emerge. Instead, it was the maid, so full of purpose that she did not pause to share any news, only retrieved additional linens and hurried back into the bedroom. Anxiety evident in her every movement, she did not even notice that the youngest child, Ben, trailed after her, and she unknowingly shut the door in the little boy's face.

The toddler erupted in tears.

Darcy picked up the child, who burrowed his sniffling nose into

Darcy's shoulder. Between the rain and the toddler, his new serge coat would never recover.

Thankfully, their father soon appeared. Captain Harville stood a few inches taller than Darcy, with dark hair and a face weathered by the sea. Despite his rough features, he had a kind face and genial manner. He walked with a slow limp.

The boys greeted their father with the exciting news that they once more had a lady with a head injury receiving treatment in their home. When they paused for breath, Darcy introduced himself. Captain Harville listened soberly as Darcy summarized Mrs. Clay's accident on the Cobb, how he and Elizabeth had come to bring her to Harville's cottage, and what he knew of Mrs. Clay's present condition. He omitted the questionable nature of the woman's connexion to Mr. Elliot.

"Mrs. Clay could ask for no better care than what she is receiving from Mrs. Harville and Mr. Sawyer," the captain said.

A tiny cry from the next room announced that Mrs. Clay's travail had ended. Darcy was heartened by the sound; the infant had survived its mother's fall and its own birth. Captain Harville grinned. "What did I tell you? All is well."

Several minutes later, Elizabeth emerged from the bedroom. Darcy expected her countenance to reflect relief and cheer, but her face was drawn, her manner grave. Her gaze swept the room—not a lengthy process in the confined space. Her resulting frown indicated she had not found what she sought. She crossed to Darcy, acknowledged Captain Harville, and enquired after Mr. Elliot.

"He is gone back to his lodgings and will return later," Darcy said. "He did, however, leave his direction. Does Mrs. Clay ask for him?"

Elizabeth shook her head. In the bedroom, the newborn renewed its cry. The sound seemed to settle on Elizabeth's shoulders like a heavy weight.

"Mrs. Clay is dead."

Six

A Mr. (save, perhaps, some half-dozen in the nation) always needs a note of explanation.

—Persuasion

*I*t was with heavy steps and a heavier heart that Elizabeth climbed the sharp incline of Lyme's main thoroughfare. The strain of the morning's events made it hard for her to believe that it was now only early afternoon. After powerlessly witnessing Mrs. Clay's death in childbirth, she wanted nothing more than to return to her own lodgings and hold her own child. However, Mrs. Clay's next of kin must be notified without delay, and provisions made for the care of the new son she left behind.

Broad Street, she and Darcy learned from the Harvilles, held multiple inns. As Mr. Elliot had not specified which one enjoyed his patronage, Mrs. Harville suggested the Darcys seek him at the Lion or the Three Cups, two of Lyme's finer establishments. They went first to the Three Cups, where the innkeeper confirmed that he had a guest by the name of Elliot.

They were directed to a room on the second floor. The manservant who answered the door did his professional best to conceal his appraisal of their appearance. Though Elizabeth had changed back into her own gown and Darcy's coat had dried, they both had a rather sodden, weary look about them. When Darcy gave their names and asked for Mr. Elliot, the servant stiffly replied that he would see whether the baronet was at home, and left them standing in the hall while he disappeared into the apartment.

Of course, the servant knew whether his master was within; "at home" was a tacit code in better society for "receiving visitors"—or, depending upon the particular visitors, "receiving *you*." What puzzled Elizabeth was not the possibility that Mr. Elliot had somehow become lost in a small inn chamber, but the manner in which the servant had referred to his employer.

"You did not tell me that Elliot is a baronet," she said to Darcy.

"He did not tell *me*," Darcy replied. "I wonder that he did not introduce himself properly."

From within, they heard a lofty male voice. "Mr. Darcy? Who is this *Mister* Darcy? Is he a gentleman?"

The voice was unfamiliar. Darcy glanced at Elizabeth. "I fear we have disturbed the wrong Elliot."

Though it seemed their luck could not turn any worse this day, Elizabeth harbored hope. "Perhaps he is a relation of our Mr. Elliot?"

A moment later the servant returned. "Sir Walter is not at home."

As the servant began to close the door, Elizabeth said quickly, "Pray, advise Sir Walter that we have news regarding Mrs. Clay."

"Mrs. Clay?" said the voice within.

Mention of the unfortunate woman won them entrée. Elizabeth and Darcy found themselves in a small but superiorly appointed sitting room, being assessed by a gentleman who indeed bore resemblance to the Mr. Elliot they had met earlier. This man, however, was older, of their parents' generation, but more fashionably dressed than many gentlemen half his age. He was a fine-looking man, well preserved, with a complexion any woman would envy and not a hair astray on his powdered head. Soft white hands with neatly trimmed fingernails rested on crossed forearms as he studied Elizabeth and Darcy.

A younger woman was also present. Elizabeth guessed her to be at most thirty, but yet quite handsome—and she held herself with the air of a lady who knows she is handsome. She did not rise, but remained seated stiffly. Her impassive gaze took Elizabeth's measure.

After a minute, a slight nod of greeting indicated that she had tentatively judged Mrs. Darcy acceptable.

"You seem a decent fellow, by the look of you," Sir Walter pronounced. "Mr. Darcy, is it? One meets all manner of individuals in a watering-place, Mr. Darcy. Where is your home?"

"Pemberley, in Derbyshire."

"Derbyshire! How unfortunate. I hear it is ghastly cold in the Peaks during winter. Frigid air is brutal on one's complexion—though yours seems to be holding up. You must spend your winters in town."

"Occasionally," Darcy said. "In truth, however, I prefer to spend them at home."

The gentleman regarded Darcy as if he were addled. "Well," he said finally, "I suppose there must be some appeal in Derbyshire, if only that the Duke of Devonshire resides there. I do not suppose you are acquainted with him?"

"Devonshire is one of my closest neighbors. We dine at Chatsworth regularly when he is at home."

"Do you?" This connexion to one of England's most influential peers—a personal friend of the Prince Regent—appeared to considerably raise Darcy in Sir Walter's estimation. The fact that it did, lowered Sir Walter in Elizabeth's.

"Yes, and His Grace dines with us at Pemberley," Elizabeth said. She turned to Darcy. "When was the last time we had him to dinner? Was it when your cousin, the Earl of Southwell, came to visit?"

Neither Elizabeth nor Darcy were given to boasting of their titled acquaintances; indeed, they loathed the practice in others. She wanted to determine just how important their connexions were to the Elliots.

"I believe it was," Darcy said. She could read in the expression of his eyes that he understood what she was about.

At this admission, the lady in the armchair took far more interest in both Darcys. "The Earl of Southwell!" A meaningful look passed between her and Sir Walter.

"Forgive me," Sir Walter said. "I have just realized that I neglected to introduce you to my daughter, Miss Elliot."

Miss Elliot was now all graciousness. "If the earl is your cousin, then I believe another relation of yours is our neighbor in Bath. Our house in Camden Place adjoins the one Lady Catherine de Bourgh takes each autumn."

"Lady Catherine is my aunt."

Elizabeth attempted to imagine how Sir Walter and Lady Catherine got on as neighbors. Were the pair attracted to each other's pride, or did similarity breed contempt? Even the finest Bath town houses could contain only so much vanity.

The confirmation of Darcy's possessing yet a third titled connexion sent the Elliots into raptures. "Do sit down," Miss Elliot exhorted. "May we offer you tea?"

Elizabeth wondered whether a quiz regarding her relations would follow. As much as she would take perverse pleasure in revealing her own grand connexions to a country attorney, a London merchant, and a ne'er-do-well militia officer, the day's events had left her with neither inclination nor patience for idle conversation with strangers. She and Darcy had come on serious business, and they must return to it. "Perhaps another time."

Sir Walter mistook their decline of hospitality for disdain. "With connexions such as yours, you are no doubt used to finer surroundings than these," he said quickly. "I assure you, our occupancy of this inn is but temporary, until we secure more suitable lodgings. When my physician recommended seabathing, we traveled here directly to follow his advice. By this day week, we hope to be established in a style commensurate with that to which we are accustomed—not only at our house in Camden Place, but our family home, Kellynch Hall in Somersetshire."

"Think nothing of it," Darcy said. "We decline only because it seems we have intruded upon you accidentally. We seek a different Mr. Elliot whom we met earlier today, to deliver pressing news. We understood him to be staying at this inn. Is there another gentleman among your party?"

"No," he said coldly. "If you mean Mr. William Elliot, my cousin is not part of our company. You will find him at the Lion. However, you told my servant that your news regarded Mrs. Clay. We are acquainted with that lady. What do you know of her?"

"We are sorry to bear unhappy news, but Mrs. Clay suffered an accident this morning."

Sir Walter appeared confused by Darcy's announcement. "An accident? Where?"

"On the Cobb," Elizabeth said.

He looked at his daughter. "I thought she was in her room. Have you not checked on her today?"

"Have not you?"

Sir Walter scowled. "If this is how she intends to conduct herself—" He broke off, aware once more of his audience. "Well, I hope this incident has made her realize that she cannot gad about as she used to."

"Sir Walter," Elizabeth said calmly, trying to ease him into the news she was about to deliver, "Mrs. Clay fell and injured her head. The surgeon offered what treatment he could, but . . ." She paused, allowing Sir Walter and Miss Elliot a moment to fortify themselves. "Mrs. Clay did not survive."

Sir Walter appeared stricken. He stared at Elizabeth, then looked to Darcy for confirmation. At Darcy's nod, he turned away and uttered a soft oath.

Miss Elliot was emotionless. "I presume the child died, as well?"

"No, that is the good news—if anything good can be considered to have come out of this sad event. She lived long enough to deliver the child."

Sir Walter recovered himself. "Is it a boy?"

"Yes. And healthy, as best one can determine."

"A boy," Sir Walter repeated.

"We must find your cousin," Elizabeth said. "I expect he will want to know this news."

Sir Walter stood. "The boy, and his mother's death, are none of Mr. Elliot's concern."

"But we understood Mr. Elliot to be . . . well acquainted with Mrs. Clay."

"Her name was no longer Mrs. Clay." Sir Walter stepped to a small pier table, opened a silver snuffbox that had been lying atop it, and took a pinch. "She was Lady Elliot. My wife."

Seven

*Miss Blachford is married, but I have never seen it in the Papers.
And one may as well be single if the Wedding is not to be in print.*
—Jane Austen, letter to her niece Anna Lefroy, 1815

*E*lizabeth struggled to overcome her astonishment. If Mrs. Clay was in fact Lady Elliot, why had the other Mr. Elliot—Mr. William Elliot—not referred to her by her proper name, nor directed them to Sir Walter the moment he learned of the accident? And why had Mr. Elliot said she was under his protection, when she had a husband?

"Allow us to extend our condolences, sir," Elizabeth stammered, "and pray forgive our ignorance. We understood Mrs. Clay—pardon me, Lady Elliot—to be a widow."

"We are but recently wed—last night, in fact." Sir Walter set the snuffbox back on the pier table and assessed his appearance in the glass that hung above it. "By special license from the Archbishop of Canterbury, of course."

"Of course," Elizabeth echoed. Because special licenses required a fee and were issued only to persons of a certain station, they were sometimes obtained even if the couple did not need the dispensations they granted to perform the marriage ceremony wherever and whenever convenient, without the necessity of crying banns or marrying in either party's home parish. It was not unheard of to secure a special license merely to show that one had the money and connexions to do so.

Sir Walter smoothed his velvet lapels. "I must order mourning clothes posthaste," he said more to himself than to anyone in particular. "A pity—my tailor just finished this coat." He summoned his servant, directed him to find a reliable local tailor, then turned back to the Darcys. "Now, where can the new Elliot heir be found?"

"He is at the home of Captain and Mrs. Harville, who took in Lady Elliot after her accident while the surgeon attended her."

"Naval people." Sir Walter sighed. "One cannot go anywhere in Lyme without encountering them. At least this Harville fellow is a captain. Where is the house? Uptown, I hope?"

"No, on the waterfront, in Cobb Hamlet." At Sir Walter's horrified expression, Elizabeth hastily added, "They appear a perfectly respectable family. I believe Mrs. Harville mentioned an acquaintance with two of your daughters."

"Naturally, they would boast of the connexion. My daughter Anne married a naval captain, Frederick Wentworth. He did well for himself during the war, and has friends among the Admiralty. His brother-in-law is an admiral—Admiral Croft." The baronet sighed again. "If a naval person must enter the family, one connected to an admiral is tolerable. Fortunately, Captain Wentworth is a decent-looking man, as far as sailors go. The elements have not completely destroyed his complexion, though he does look more roughened than he once did." He turned to his daughter. "Are Anne and her husband still guests of the Crofts?"

"No, they have taken a house here in Lyme. That widow friend of hers, Mrs. Smith, is staying with them, so I have not yet advised Anne of our being in town—we would not want to give the mistaken impression of bestowing notice on Mrs. Smith."

Elizabeth wondered that Sir Walter wanted to discuss his son-in-law's complexion and living arrangements immediately after receiving news of his wife's death, but she supposed the shock of bereavement scattered his attention. She tried to redirect him to the duties now at hand. "We would be happy to accompany you to the Harvilles' home."

"I would never visit such a house. My servant can collect the child."

After he collected the tailor? Were she Sir Walter, or even Miss Elliot, Elizabeth would not lose a moment retrieving that baby herself, no matter where he was. And what about poor Lady Elliot? "I thought you might wish to see your late wife or meet the people who cared for her in her final hours."

"Also," Darcy added, "arrangements must be made."

"Financial arrangements? The surgeon can direct his bill to my attorney, Mr. Shepherd. He is presently in Lyme, having come to handle matters related to the marriage."

"I meant funeral arrangements."

"Of course—an undertaker. There must be someone local who can handle the necessities."

"Perhaps the surgeon or the Harvilles can offer a recommendation."

"Life at sea so ages one that I expect these Harville people have acquaintances expiring all the time. I defy you to show me any sea officer who does not look at least twice his age, and I would wager this Captain Harville is no exception. I suppose they also expect some consideration for their trouble?"

"I do not believe so," Elizabeth said. "They acted out of kindness." She thought of the modest house, barely large enough to contain the Harvilles' three young boys, and of the captain's limp. The new peace had put many naval officers out of work; she doubted an injured one was still drawing full pay. "Though an expression of gratitude might not be unwelcome, were you so moved."

"I shall consult Mr. Shepherd on the matter. Claiming my son is the first order of business."

"When we left them, Mrs. Harville was making enquiries toward procuring a wet nurse."

"My daughter will see to that."

Miss Elliot started in surprise. "What do I know of wet nurses?" Her expression could not have been more appalled had her father suggested she nurse the infant herself. Elizabeth doubted the hard-edged spinster possessed a single maternal instinct.

"Engaging a nurse cannot far differ from hiring any other type of servant," Sir Walter said, "and I know you will ensure we retain a woman of proper character."

"Given the urgent nature of your search, you will be fortunate to find any wet nurse available with no notice," Elizabeth said. "You might reconsider availing yourself of Mrs. Harville's experience and local connexions."

"Nursing the Elliot heir is a privilege. We shall have no shortage of applicants."

Privilege or no, hiring a wet nurse was a challenging business even under the best of circumstances; the most reliable ones were engaged well in advance, timing the weaning of one charge with the birth of the next. Given the urgency of Sir Walter's situation, he would be fortunate to locate one at all. Elizabeth, however, did not think it her place to explain the nuances of the process to Sir Walter, nor did she harbor great expectations of any such attempt penetrating his vain mind.

She made one last, valiant effort to guide him, not for his own benefit, but that of the helpless infant now entirely dependent upon his judgment. "Boarding the child out would likely increase the pool of candidates."

"We most certainly will," declared Miss Elliot.

"We most certainly will *not*," said Sir Walter.

Though Miss Elliot's vexation with her father was apparent, her tone was restrained. "We do not have space for an infant and nurse here, nor at our lodgings in Bath when we return."

"The Elliot heir will not spend the first year of his life living with a family of such ignoble origins that they make ends meet by the wife's nursing a passel of other people's children like a common dairy cow. He will have his own nurse, in his own home, as did you and your sisters."

Miss Elliot gestured about her. "Where is the nursery to be? This is not Kellynch Hall."

Sir Walter sighed heavily. "I must speak to Mr. Shepherd about this alteration in circumstances. It was all very well for us to reside in Bath this past year, but now that I have a son, we should return to the ancestral Elliot home."

Elizabeth hoped for everyone's sake—most particularly the child's—that Mrs. Harville's efforts had proved successful, and that by the time Sir Walter's servant collected the celebrated "Elliot heir," the matter of hiring a wet nurse would be a fait accompli.

She had experienced enough of Sir Walter and his daughter; she wanted nothing more than to complete their melancholy errands and end this wretched day. Sensing that Darcy was of similar mind, she tactfully brought the meeting to an end. Sir Walter and Miss Elliot escorted them to the door, full of expressions of pleasure in having made their acquaintance.

And not at all overcome by grief.

Once on the street, Darcy offered his arm, which Elizabeth accepted as they continued up the hill. "That was certainly not the meeting I anticipated," he said.

"That was not even the person we anticipated meeting."

"I cannot say I feel improved by the acquaintance."

"Nor I," she replied. "I had pitied Lady Elliot for having drawn her last breath among strangers, but now I believe she found more sympathy in Mrs. Harville's home than she would have known in her own husband's. When I die, I hope you take more interest in the event itself than in the modifications it will impose upon your attire."

"It does appear that the Elliots' marriage was not a match of affection."

"How could it be, with Sir Walter already deeply in love with himself?" Elizabeth knew that many people married for reasons other than romantic attachment—her friend Charlotte Collins offered a prime example. But even Mr. Collins would pause to mourn his wife's passing before hastening to Rosings with the news.

"Did you notice that Sir Walter did not enquire into any particulars of his wife's death?" she asked. "Whether her last moments were peaceful? Whether she died knowing that she had given him the son he so obviously wanted? His thoughts and words focused entirely on *his* connexions, *his* social status, *his* heir—as if the child had been created in a fine London shop and delivered by coach, not by a woman who died in the process." She released a sound of disgust. "Sir Walter and his daughter seemed no more affected by Lady Elliot's death than they would have been by a housemaid who quit her post after completing the day's dusting."

"Mr. Elliot might take the news more gravely."

"Though Sir Walter does not wish for us to communicate any news to his cousin, I do feel that Mr. Elliot ought to be informed. Yet even Mr. Elliot—whatever his relationship was to the former Mrs. Clay, and for all his professions of concern—could not trouble himself to remain at the Harvilles' during her travail, and gave us vague directions by which to find him. Do you truly think he will be any more moved by Lady Elliot's death than Sir Walter was?"

Darcy stopped in front of the Lion. "Let us find out."

Although a bored attendant at the Lion confirmed that Mr. William Elliot numbered among the inn's guests, the gentleman was not at home—truly not at home—when Elizabeth and Darcy called. By this point nearly to their own cottage, they went home to check on Lily-Anne and Georgiana before making any additional attempt to locate the elusive Mr. Elliot.

Thankfully, they found all well with Georgiana and their daughter. Georgiana described how they and Sir Laurence had reached Broad Street and sent a surgeon back to the Cobb before the rain increased to an intensity that prevented them from continuing up the steep hill home. Their small party had taken refuge in a pastry shop, where they warmed themselves over tea and cake until the rain ceased and they could resume the walk to the cottage.

"As distressing as the circumstances were," Georgiana said, "Sir Laurence was a reassuring presence. He knew just where to go and what to do, and took very good care of us. He was exceedingly attentive to both me and Lily-Anne, and our conversation in the pastry shop was so diverting that I felt guilty whenever I recalled that the two of you were dealing with such a dreadful situation while I enjoyed his company."

"Pray, do not feel guilty any longer," Elizabeth said. "I am glad one of us had a day that was not miserable."

"Two of us," Georgiana corrected. "Lily-Anne found Sir Laurence delightful, once she warmed up to him. He was so good with her, Elizabeth—it was charming to watch them together at the pastry shop. I think my niece is quite smitten."

The animation in Georgiana's eyes as she spoke of Sir Laurence made Elizabeth long to ask whether Lily-Anne's aunt was smitten, as well, but she forbore. Georgiana's regard for the baronet was evident; it was too early to quiz or tease her about its developing into something more.

Besides, Elizabeth was not in playful humor. Though happy that Georgiana and Lily-Anne had escaped the worst of the day's events, she yet felt the weight of Lady Elliot's untimely demise. Women died in childbed with tragic regularity, but Elizabeth could not help wondering whether she might have survived had she not also suffered a serious accident.

The company of her own child, however, helped lift Elizabeth's mood. So, too, did a bath and fresh clothing. As her maid completed a simple arrangement of her hair, Elizabeth watched Lily-Anne play on the floor with her two favorite dolls. When the servant left the bedchamber, Elizabeth called Lily-Anne to her. Lily approached the dressing table, set her dolls upon it, and climbed into her mother's lap. Elizabeth embraced her, saying not a word.

Lily asked to go for a walk. Elizabeth wished she could indulge her daughter immediately, but she and Darcy had agreed to make one more attempt to call upon Mr. Elliot. They also felt they ought to return to the Harvilles' home. Upon reaching their lodgings, Darcy had sent a note advising them to expect Sir Walter or his emissary to call for the infant, but both he and Elizabeth wanted to take more formal leave of the generous couple as they ended their involvement in this whole unfortunate event.

"I am afraid a walk with me will have to wait, Lily. Do you want to play with Betsy and Maggie a while longer?"

Lily-Anne scooted off Elizabeth's lap and reached for the pair of dolls on the dressing table. They were cloth dolls, gifts from

Elizabeth's sister Jane, and their appearance was proof that they were well loved. Privately, Elizabeth and Lily-Anne's nurse referred to the dolls as Bald Betsy and Mangled Maggie. Once upon a time, Betsy had possessed red hair fashioned from yarn, but as Lily liked to carry her by it, most of the strands had disappeared. Maggie owed the preservation of her own hair to a sewn-on cap that matched her dress. However, Lily had decided that gumming Maggie's stuffed legs was her preferred remedy for teething pain. After six teeth, the doll looked like the victim of a horrible carriage accident.

As Elizabeth tied the laces of her half-boots, Betsy and Maggie stood on the edge of the dressing table and engaged in a lively dialogue intelligible only to Lily-Anne, who performed it with great spirit. Unfortunately, the conversation took a hostile turn when the dolls shouted "no-no-no" at each other and Maggie knocked Betsy to the floor.

"Lily-Anne Darcy! That is not a nice way to play with your dolls. Pick up Betsy and treat her gently. Maggie should apologize."

After Maggie delivered the apology, Lily-Anne turned to her mother. "Walk now?"

"Not yet, sweetheart—"

Elizabeth reconsidered. The rain had ceased some time ago; Lily-Anne could come with them to call upon the Harvilles. Surely they would not mind. They had children of their own, after all, and Lily might enjoy meeting the youngest boy. As for their stop at Mr. Elliot's, Lily-Anne's presence would provide the perfect excuse to keep the call brief—if they even found him at all.

"Yes, Lily. Let us take that walk now."

Eight

*"I venture to hint, that Sir Walter Elliot cannot be half so jealous
for his own, as John Shepherd will be for him."*
　　　　　—Mr. John Shepherd to Sir Walter, Persuasion

*E*lizabeth and Darcy's second visit to the Lion proved equally
fruitless; Mr. Elliot still had not returned. They therefore proceeded to the Harvilles' cottage. By the time they reached the shore,
however, Elizabeth regretted her decision to bring Lily-Anne along.
While the streets higher up the hill, near their own cottage, had begun to dry following the storm, those closer to the beach were still
wet and dirty. As a result, Darcy wound up carrying Lily-Anne most
of the way, a circumstance that pleased neither the child who wanted
to use her own legs nor the father who had already endured a long
day. Darcy bore it with fortitude; Lily-Anne, with better humor than
Elizabeth anticipated. All three were grateful to finally reach Cobb
Hamlet and the Harvilles' home.

Mrs. Harville was happy to see the Darcys. She, too, had changed
her attire and tidied her appearance since the morning's exertions.
"My husband is on his way to your cottage," she said. "You must have
missed each other en route. We thought you would want to know
that Mr. Elliot has returned."

"Mr. William Elliot?" Darcy asked.

"Yes, the gentleman you brought here earlier. He has been preparing his own lodgings to receive the injured mother and child. Poor man! He took the news of Mrs. Clay's death very hard."

"Has Sir Walter Elliot been in communication with you?" Elizabeth asked.

"Sir Walter? Not at all."

While Elizabeth cast a puzzled glance at Darcy—which he returned in kind—Mrs. Harville bent to meet Lily-Anne's eyes. "And who is this young lady?"

"Our daughter, Lily-Anne," Elizabeth replied.

"I am honored to make your acquaintance, Miss Darcy," she said with exaggerated formality. "I have a little boy not much older than you. Would you like to meet him?"

Lily-Anne looked to Elizabeth. After receiving a nod of permission, she accepted Mrs. Harville's hand and went inside.

Elizabeth turned to Darcy. "Mr. Elliot means to take the baby?"

"Apparently he is ignorant of Sir Walter's interest in the matter."

They entered the house to find Mr. Elliot holding the newborn. The child was well swaddled and sleeping.

"Mr. and Mrs. Darcy," Mr. Elliot greeted them. "I did not expect to see you again."

"We tried to call upon you at the Lion," Darcy said. "That is where you are staying, is it not?"

"For the time being. As soon as Mr. Sawyer assures me the child is strong enough to travel, we will remove to my house in Sidmouth."

Mrs. Harville was in a corner of the room, where she had led the newly acquainted Lily-Anne and Ben to a basket of wooden blocks. Ben took up a cube and handed it to Lily, who set it on the floor and reached for another while Ben began amassing his own stockpile. The toddlers content, Mrs. Harville returned to the Darcys.

"The undertaker has collected Mrs. Clay." She sighed. "Poor dear! But I have heartening news, as well. I may have found a wet nurse—Mrs. Logan, a young widow whose husband served as a midshipman under Captain Harville. They were married scarcely a twelvemonth when Mr. Logan died, leaving her in the family way and with little on which to live. Her lying-in was a few weeks ago—a tiny little girl, smaller than Mrs. Clay's child—and sadly, her baby died the day before yesterday. I went to see her this afternoon and broached the subject of nursing Mrs. Clay's son. She is amenable, but we did not discuss particulars. I thought the business arrangements would be more properly handled by the child's rightful guardian, but was not certain who that might be. When I returned home, Mr. Elliot was here and said he would take the child."

"Indeed, someone must look out for the little fellow," Mr. Elliot said. "It is the least I can do for his mother."

The infant released a cry. For all the challenges the baby had faced simply entering the world, he apparently possessed a healthy set of lungs.

"There, there," Mr. Elliot said matter-of-factly. "Go back to sleep."

The baby, however, only increased the volume and urgency of his mewing, and strained his limbs against the blanket that swaddled him. Mr. Elliot, discomposed by the suddenly restless creature, tried to shift the child to his other arm, neglecting to support the infant's small neck. The blanket loosened still more in the process, releasing its captive, who was now a noisy mass of flailing limbs.

Darcy, who stood closest, took the baby from Mr. Elliot before the gentleman dropped him. In Darcy's firmer hold the infant ceased his wails and thrashing. The baby's response triggered a memory of holding Lily-Anne this way on her first day of life, the awkwardness he had felt despite his outward show of confidence. He had forgotten how lightweight a newborn is; how tiny its fingers, how fragile its frame. Lily-Anne suddenly seemed impossibly big in comparison.

The baby began to fuss once more, and Darcy did what came naturally to him in such situations. He handed the child to Elizabeth.

"We shall sort this out, little one," she said as she took the infant.

"There is nothing to sort," Mr. Elliot said. "The child is obviously hungry and must be fed soon. If Mrs. Harville approves of Mrs. Logan, I am satisfied. Where can I find her? I shall take the child to her now, and settle whether he will board with her or she will return with me to the Lion." He shook his head. "What a dreadful shock. I had thought I would be bringing both Mrs. Clay and my child home with me."

"*Your* child?" Elizabeth said.

"Surely you assumed as much. I confess that I am not proud that he was born out of wedlock—I had intended to rectify that situation before her lying-in. Obviously, the events of this morning caught me unprepared."

Obviously, Mr. Elliot was unaware that Sir Walter had already "rectified" Mrs. Clay's marital status. "In searching for you, we met Sir Walter Elliot. He claims the child as his."

Darcy's announcement seemed to amuse Mr. Elliot. His lips curved into a half-smile. "Does he? I am all astonishment. Sir Walter is not the type of man to dally with a woman of Mrs. Clay's station, nor to acknowledge a natural child if one resulted from such a liaison. Regardless, Mrs. Clay has been living under my protection long enough that no one can question my claim."

"According to Sir Walter, she was under his protection when she died," Darcy said. "They wed yesterday evening."

The smile faded. "Indeed? Yesterday, you say? What fortuitous timing that would be, were it true. But Mrs. Clay was here in Lyme yesterday. Neither she nor Sir Walter are residents of this parish, and she was not absent long enough to have traveled to Kellynch and back without my knowledge."

"He states they wed by special license."

The muscles of Mr. Elliot's pronounced jaw tightened. Calm control, however, quickly asserted itself. "And who witnessed this felicitous event?"

"I did not ask, as I had no reason to doubt his word on the matter," Darcy said.

Mr. Elliot turned an earnest gaze upon Elizabeth. "As a parent yourself, Mrs. Darcy, you will understand why I cannot relinquish custody of the infant until presented with evidence that this alleged marriage in fact occurred. Indeed, if Sir Walter has such an interest in the child, why is he not here arranging for proper care of him?"

Darcy had been wondering the same thing. Sir Walter had been only too willing to delegate the retrieval of his son to a servant, but where *was* that servant? Their own stop to refresh themselves had delayed them sufficiently that Darcy had expected to find the child gone by the time they reached the Harvilles' home. "When we left him, Sir Walter indicated that he would send an emissary presently." He addressed Mrs. Harville. "Yet you said you have received no communication from his household?"

"None. This is the first I have heard of Sir Walter's involvement."

"By whose authority did the undertaker collect the remains?"

"Captain Harville's," she said. "As no one else was here to assume responsibility, Captain Harville took charge. Mr. Elliot approved when he returned."

"See?" Mr. Elliot turned a smile upon Elizabeth. "Sir Walter clearly takes no interest in the matter. You and your husband must have mistaken his meaning in regard to his connexion to Mrs. Clay and his intentions for the child. Pray, hand me back the boy, that I may convey him to his nurse."

Rather than relinquish the baby, Elizabeth held him still more protectively. "I think it premature for you to take him anywhere until the issue can be discussed with Sir Walter." She looked to Darcy. "If you call upon the baronet again and advise him of the present state of affairs, he might come attend to this matter in person."

The baby started to cry again. Mr. Elliot flinched. "Madam, how long must we endure these wails before you take pity on the poor child—on us all—and allow him to nurse? I insist upon delivering him to Mrs. Logan posthaste."

Darcy could see that pity did occupy Elizabeth's heart, and that she was acutely conscious of the infant's distress. He also could read the distrust in her eyes as she regarded Mr. Elliot. It matched Darcy's own.

"While this confusion with Sir Walter continues, resolving it must be your foremost concern," Elizabeth replied. "I shall take the child to Mrs. Logan myself, or we can summon her here."

Mr. Elliot frowned and stepped toward Elizabeth. "Indeed, I would rather—"

"Accompany me than transport a crying child?" Darcy finished. Mr. Elliot turned toward Darcy with an expression that indicated he had intended to end his sentence with an altogether different sentiment, but Darcy continued quickly. "What gentleman would not?

You make an excellent suggestion, Mr. Elliot. Let us leave the infant in the very capable care of the ladies while we call upon Sir Walter to settle this question without further delay."

Mr. Elliot stared at Darcy. Elizabeth caressed the infant's back in slow circles and murmured indistinguishable words. The baby quieted again, though clearly his state of calm was but temporary. The only voices yet sounding were those of Lily-Anne and Ben, engaged in steady jabber as they divided the few remaining blocks, oblivious to the dissent among the adults in the room.

"Of course, time is of the essence," Mr. Elliot said at last, "which is why I—"

A sudden wail sounded from the corner. Ben lay half sprawled on the floor, his lower lip quivering. Lily-Anne stood over him. In her hand was the last block.

"Lily-Anne Darcy!" Elizabeth strode to their daughter. "One does *not* push people. What has come over you today?" Her face was scarlet with mortification as she turned to Mrs. Harville, who was soothing the bewildered Ben. "Did she hurt him?"

Mrs. Harville shook her head and laughed softly. "He is only surprised. You forget that he has two boisterous brothers who are bigger and far less gentle. I think he spends more time on the floor than on his feet."

"Nevertheless, her behavior is inexcusable." At Elizabeth's prompt, Lily-Anne apologized to Ben and offered him the block. The two-year-old accepted the offering and added it to his trove. "I assure you," she said, "this simply is not like Lily-Anne."

The toddlers' tempest had awakened the infant once more. He now fussed in sympathy, though the principals had made peace. As his volume increased, Mr. Elliot shifted uncomfortably until he appeared on the verge of himself breaking down.

"I cannot tolerate his cries any longer." He turned to Darcy. "If you insist upon consulting Sir Walter before allowing me custody of my own son, then let us proceed."

The gentlemen headed for the door, and opened it to find another man just approaching the house. He was a medium fellow—medium height, medium build, middle-aged, his grey hair neither long nor short, his countenance not striking yet not altogether plain. He was modestly but neatly dressed in a dark brown suit, its sole embellishment a black band round one arm.

Were he not immediately in their path, he might have blended into the busy street and gone entirely unnoticed by Darcy. Mr. Elliot, however, stiffened and pulled the door shut behind them as the stranger reached the house.

"Mr. Elliot." He spoke in a clipped tone. "I did not expect to meet you here."

"Mr. Shepherd." Mr. Elliot acknowledged him with equal rigidity.

"I had to hear this news from Sir Walter? You had not the decency to inform me?"

"I myself only just learned of Penelope's death. When last I saw her, she was quite alive."

The man swallowed and looked away, toward the Cobb that had taken Mrs. Clay's life. After a moment, with greater composure, he turned back to Mr. Elliot and nodded toward the house. "Is she yet inside?"

"The undertaker has collected her."

"Where has he taken her?"

"You shall have to ask the family within. I did not make the arrangements."

"No, I doubt you would trouble yourself, given your passing acquaintance with the expectations of propriety. But that is just as well; I will handle the matter from here. The child—where is he?"

"Do you enquire for yourself or Sir Walter?"

"Both."

"You may tell Sir Walter that I have made provisions for my son's care."

The man released a low, mirthless chuckle. "*Your* son? Not two days ago, you refused to make any such acknowledgment."

Mr. Elliot shrugged. "I make it now."

"It is irrelevant now. Yesterday, Sir Walter married Penelope and legally claimed paternity of the child as part of their marriage agreement."

"Doubtless, you drew up the document yourself. Did Sir Walter even read it before he signed it? When was the last time he decided anything independent of your influence?"

"Where is the child?"

"I suppose you were also one of the witnesses to the marriage. Who was the other?"

"Miss Elliot."

"Oh, that is just capital! The bride's father and the groom's daughter—two people who have even more interest in cutting me out of the entail than Sir Walter himself. Well done, Mr. Shepherd! Your years of managing and scheming have won extraordinary recompense. Your grandson may inherit Kellynch Hall before he is out of short pants."

"I ask you again—where is he?"

"Find him yourself." Without another word, Mr. Elliot walked away.

Darcy watched him go. He was certainly an unpredictable gentleman—solicitous one moment, cold the next, his interest in the child shifting with the sea breeze. Apparently, that interest was more financial than sentimental.

"Sir, might you be Mr. Darcy?" Mr. Shepherd asked. "You answer the description Sir Walter gave me of the gentleman who delivered the news of my daughter's death."

"I am he." Darcy added his condolences, which Mr. Shepherd accepted with a nod.

"Sir Walter told me that you and your wife found Penelope. I thank you for the assistance you rendered her, and regret that Mr. Elliot has forced me to beg still more of you. Do you know where can I find the child? I enquire as both his grandfather and Sir Walter's attorney."

"He is within. Mrs. Darcy is preparing to take him to a wet nurse."

Mr. Shepherd frowned. "Was the nurse engaged by Mr. Elliot?"

"No, by Mrs. Harville."

That fact appeared to relieve Mr. Shepherd. "My commission this afternoon was dual: to collect the child and retain a nurse. I should like to accompany Mrs. Darcy and meet the woman. If she and her references prove satisfactory, the position is hers."

"Mrs. Harville seems a woman of sense and discrimination. I trust you will find Mrs. Logan suitable."

"I am also eager to speak with your wife. I understand she was with Penelope during her last hours."

"She was." Darcy paused. "I assure you, whatever comfort could be provided, Mrs. Darcy and Mrs. Harville offered."

"I am grateful. As you surely surmised from my conversation with Mr. Elliot just now, Penelope's . . . situation . . . these several months past was not what a father hopes. She bore mistreatment from individuals who should have demonstrated higher principles, and censure by those who did hold to high standards—or were better able to maintain the appearance of them. She did not have many friends at the end."

Mrs. Logan met Mr. Shepherd's requirements. Just as important, she met Elizabeth's. Having seen the motherless infant through the turmoil of his first hours of life, Elizabeth could not have easily relinquished him to the care of just anybody. Fortunately, the young widow seemed a kind, well-mannered girl. Still grieving the loss of her husband, and now her child, she was struggling to maintain herself. The offer of respectable work was a godsend, and she was as grateful to enter Sir Walter's employ and household as his vanity could desire.

Elizabeth—and Darcy, who had accompanied them—left the Elliot baby with his new nurse and Mr. Shepherd as the two settled the particulars of Mrs. Logan's removal to Sir Walter's lodgings. While Elizabeth and Darcy walked back to the Harvilles' home to collect Lily-Anne and report the successful meeting to Mrs. Harville, Darcy related the quarrel he had witnessed between Mr. Elliot and Mr. Shepherd.

"The timing of Sir Walter's marriage certainly proved fortuitous," Elizabeth remarked when Darcy had done. "Otherwise, it might have required the wisdom of Solomon to determine which gentleman possessed a superior claim to the infant."

"This all would have been much simpler if Lady Elliot had been capable of telling us to whom he belongs, or at least more about herself."

"Even were she able, she might have been reluctant to disclose much. Both Sir Walter and Mr. Elliot seem far more interested in the child than in her."

Darcy agreed. "Only Mr. Shepherd seems to be mourning her death, and his grief is tempered by consciousness of the impropriety surrounding his daughter's marriage."

"Minds more drawn to scandal than ours might wonder how she came to get married so close to her lying-in that the child was nearly a witness to the wedding, and to have two men claiming paternity." Elizabeth recalled the image of Lady Elliot standing on the upper Cobb, the hard expression that had overcome her countenance. "When we saw her before the accident, she did not appear a happy woman, let alone a joyful new bride."

"Did she speak at all once in Mrs. Harville's home?"

"A few words. The only significant one was 'Elliot'—though whether she referred to Sir Walter, Mr. Elliot, or herself is anybody's guess. Later, once her laboring began, she recovered her senses briefly and said 'pushed' after having strained toward birthing."

Lady Elliot had said that word twice; it was the last word she ever uttered. She had never regained consciousness again to see the result of those pushes: the fragile little creature who, having been delivered from the womb with his mother's final breath, was now being delivered to his proud father in a hack carriage.

Elizabeth and Darcy reached the Harvilles' home and entered to the noise of childish squeals. This time, however, they were sounds of delight. Lily-Anne and Ben were playing, the shoving incident utterly forgotten.

Forgotten by the toddlers, that is. Despite Mrs. Harville's assurances, Elizabeth still could not quite comprehend it. Nor the earlier flight of Bald Betsy off the dressing table at Mangled Maggie's stuffed hands. Lily-Anne was not by nature an aggressive child, nor given to violent outbursts. What an aberrant day her daughter was having! But then, there had been nothing normal about this day for any of them.

Lily-Anne, in fact, was probably the least affected by recent events. She had not even witnessed the lightning bolt that destroyed the ship and which, in Elizabeth's mind, had signaled the start of the chaos that claimed them all day. Lily had been looking in the other direction entirely, toward the harbor side of the Cobb. *Sea, Mamma, sea!*

Toward the section of the Cobb where they had seen Mrs. Clay— Lady Elliot—before her fall. An unsettling sensation passed through Elizabeth. Had she misunderstood Lily?

See, Mamma! See!

A lump rising in her throat, Elizabeth tried to recall how far along the seawall they had walked after passing Lady Elliot.

Not far enough.

Not far enough for Lady Elliot to have been out of Lily's view. Not far enough to silence the question now overtaking Elizabeth. Had Lily-Anne witnessed Lady Elliot's fall? Worse, had the accident been somehow preventable, if only Elizabeth had realized what her daughter had been trying to communicate? If only they had been standing closer when Lady Elliot lost her balance?

See, Mamma! See!

Lily-Anne's small voice echoed in Elizabeth's mind. Then, unbidden, so did another.

Elliot. Pushed.

Nine

They set forward, treading back, with feelings unutterable, the ground which so lately, so very lately, and so light of heart, they had passed along.

—Persuasion

*E*lizabeth could not later have repeated the words she stammered while quitting the Harvilles' home, for the disturbing notion forming in her mind occupied it so entirely that it forced out nearly all else. She only hoped that she uttered something intelligible, and relied upon Darcy to convey the proper sentiments one expresses when taking leave of brand-new acquaintances with whom one has nursed a fatally injured woman, delivered a baby, and navigated a custody melee between a baronet and the late mother's former paramour.

At last she and Darcy were alone and headed back to their lodgings. The seafront Walk had dried enough to permit Lily-Anne to toddle between them as they each held one of her hands. Elizabeth's thoughts were jumbled: Lady Elliot's voice mixed with images of Lily-Anne pushing Ben, and Betsy tumbling off the dressing table.

"I have been contemplating Lady Elliot's fall," Elizabeth said.

"Her accident and all that resulted from it is an event neither of us will soon forget."

They were nearly to the end of the Walk. Ahead stood the Assembly Rooms, where well-dressed ladies and gentlemen were begun to arrive for some gay event. Their merriment was jarringly discordant with her own sober thoughts.

She stopped. Lily-Anne strained to continue, tugging on their hands and leaning forward with all her weight. This conversation was probably best postponed until it could be carried on undistracted, but Elizabeth needed Darcy to help her throw off the disquiet that had taken hold of her. "I fear it might have been no accident."

"What has led you to such a notion?"

She related the incident with the dolls, and how it, when taken in context of other events of the day and Lady Elliot's own few words, had caused her to reconsider their meaning.

His expression settled into a pensive frown. "Have you asked Lily-Anne what she saw?"

"Not yet." Even could their daughter recall what she had seen, could she articulate it well enough for them to understand? Moreover, did they *want* her to recall so disturbing an event?

Darcy lifted their daughter. She twisted in his arms, trying to return to the ground. "Lily, your mother has an important question for you." The child stilled.

Elizabeth struggled to formulate her query. "Lily—" How did one ask a young child such a thing? "Lily, do you remember when we took a walk this morning with Aunt Georgiana, before the rain?"

Lily-Anne pointed toward the Cobb. "Walk."

"Do you remember how we found a lady who was hurt, and then Aunt Georgiana and her friend took you back to our cottage?"

She smiled and spoke a string of syllables that Elizabeth interpreted as "Sir Laurence"—indeed a mouthful for someone just learning to speak.

"When we were walking, did you see the lady standing on the big wall? Before she got hurt?"

"Walk!" She threw her weight against Darcy's arm, nearly landing on the ground faster than intended. Darcy, practiced with their daughter's unexpected lunges, reacted quickly enough to prevent her tumbling out of his grasp.

"Lily—"

"Walk!"

Lily's attention could admit no other focus, and the evening witching hour known to all mothers and nurserymaids drew nigh. "This has been a long day for Lily, as well," she said. "Let us simply go home and try again another time, if at all."

They continued homeward. "Are you hoping she saw what happened," Darcy asked, "or hoping she did not?"

"I honestly do not know," she admitted. "And you?"

"However Lady Elliot's fall came about, I hope our daughter did not witness it. If she did, I hope it is forgotten. There are other ways—more reliable ways than the word of a child—to confirm or dispel your doubts about Lady Elliot's demise."

"Do you believe my suspicion reasonable?"

"Your instincts have proved valid in the past, but I also believe an intellect fatigued by events such as we have experienced today is more susceptible to anxiety and misinterpretation than usual. Let us revisit this subject on the morrow, when our minds are rested."

"If you are promising that all will look better in the morning, I may retire as soon as we reach the cottage."

"Have you forgotten our engagement with Lieutenant St. Clair? Or do you wish me to convey your regrets?"

Indeed, she had entirely forgotten their expected visitor. "Oh! No—no regrets. Our appointment this evening did escape my memory, but I would not forgo the pleasure of meeting Lieutenant St. Clair. It is half our reason for coming to Lyme."

"Not half, but much anticipated."

Lieutenant Andrew St. Clair had served in the Royal Navy with Darcy's late cousin Gerard, younger brother of Colonel Fitzwilliam. St. Clair, in fact, had been first lieutenant aboard the *Magna Carta* at the time of Gerard's death. Now recently returned to England after numerous foreign deployments, St. Clair had written to Gerard's family stating that he had in his possession Gerard's sea chest, which he had promised to deliver in person. As Darcy and Elizabeth had already planned a journey to Lyme upon quitting Colonel Fitzwilliam's house, they had arranged to meet St. Clair here.

Though Elizabeth had never met Gerard, he had been a beloved cousin, and remained a subject of conversation among Darcy, Georgiana, and Colonel Fitzwilliam. Elizabeth hoped that tonight's meeting would provide an opportunity to learn more about the promising young man they remembered. Darcy, she knew, had been looking forward to the appointment far more than the seabathing and other diversions that had first inspired their interest in a seaside holiday.

When they reached their cottage, it was not an early Lieutenant St. Clair, but another visitor whom they found just emerging from the house. Sir Laurence greeted them warmly.

"I called to enquire after Miss Darcy . . . and, of course, you, as well. All was at such sixes and sevens when we parted earlier, that I could not rest easy tonight without assuring myself of everybody's well-being. I was saddened to learn from Miss Darcy just now that Mrs. Clay succumbed to her injuries."

"We, too, regret that turn of events," Darcy said. "I thank you, however, for your assistance in ensuring my sister's and daughter's safety."

"I was pleased to be of use. Both the misses Darcy are charming ladies." He tipped his hat to Lily-Anne, who, at last weary of walking, was once more in Darcy's arms.

Lily burrowed her face into the crook of Darcy's neck, then peeked at Sir Laurence with a smile. Elizabeth could hardly believe it—eighteen months old, and her daughter was flirting with a baronet.

As he turned to Elizabeth, Sir Laurence's expression became serious once more. "Miss Darcy told me you were out just now attempting to notify Mrs. Clay's next of kin. Were you able to locate them? If not, allow me to offer whatever help I can."

"That is most kind of you," Darcy replied, "but we have spoken with both her husband and father."

"Her husband? I understood her to be a widow."

Darcy paused. "Were you acquainted with the lady?"

"I? No—Miss Darcy had said as much. The fact that Mrs. Clay left behind a child compounded the tragedy, but if she was married, at least the baby is not orphaned. Her death is still pitiable, nonetheless. After we left you on the Cobb, did anyone come forward who had witnessed the accident?"

"Unfortunately, no. Two dockworkers recognized Mrs. Clay and provided information that helped us find her family, but no one saw the event itself."

No one, Elizabeth thought, except possibly their impressionable young daughter. As her anxiety began to return, however, a new thought struck her. "What about the gentleman who helped you carry her to the Harvilles' cottage?" she asked Darcy. "Perhaps he witnessed her fall?"

"If he did, he said nothing of it, and I should think he would have."

"We were all so concerned by the immediate need to remove her to a safe place and treat her injuries that perhaps he simply never thought to tell us."

"Surely he would have mentioned it," Sir Laurence said. "I am glad, however, that someone happened along to assist you. I did not feel quite right about leaving you to deal with the crisis alone, despite the commission entrusted to me and which I was honored to fulfill. What was the gentleman's name?"

Ten

*There was a very general ignorance of all naval matters through-
out the party; and he was very much questioned.*

—Persuasion

At precisely half-past seven, a confident rap sounded on the
Darcys' cottage door. Lieutenant St. Clair had arrived.

A servant admitted the long-anticipated visitor and announced
him to Darcy, Elizabeth, and Georgiana. Their guest entered, carrying a leather-bound wooden sea chest.

Georgiana released a faint gasp; Darcy better concealed his own
surprise. The man just arrived in their sitting room was the officer
they had passed on the steps at the beach the evening before, and
who had assisted with Mrs. Clay. On official business tonight, he
wore his full dress uniform. The dark blue coat with its stand-up
collar formed a striking contrast to the white waistcoat and breeches.
Gilt-brass buttons accented the white lapels and cuffs, and a single
gold epaulette rested on his right shoulder. A sword hung at his side.
From tall cockade hat to highly polished buckled shoes, it was a
uniform meant to impress, and it did.

Lieutenant St. Clair appeared as surprised as they to discover that
he had already met Gerard Fitzwilliam's family. His gaze took them
in, lingering on Georgiana before finally reaching Darcy.

"Well," he said, "this is a happy coincidence."

"Indeed." Darcy had not decided yet whether "happy" was the term he would use, though St. Clair's quick-thinking aid with Mrs. Clay had raised him higher in Darcy's regard. Darcy gestured toward the sea chest. "Please, let me relieve you of your burden."

He moved forward to assist St. Clair, but the sailor set the chest onto the floor in an easy motion. "It is no burden, I assure you. I only regret that I have been unable to deliver it before now."

"We appreciate your having kept it in your custody all this while."

"That commission has been my privilege." The officer's manner was all that any bereaved family member could wish from an emissary of the service for which his cousin had given his life.

Darcy made the proper introductions between St. Clair and the ladies, whom the lieutenant acknowledged with a bow.

"It is a pleasure to meet you on more stable ground, Miss Darcy." The allusion to Georgiana's slip on the steps brought color to her cheeks. "I trust you suffered no ill effects from our first meeting?"

"I am quite well, thank you." Despite her evident self-consciousness, Georgiana answered with composure, even offering him a faint smile.

"I am relieved to hear it." The lieutenant's gaze rested on her a moment more before turning to Darcy. "Had I known during our previous encounters that you were the party I was engaged to meet tonight, I would have taken the liberty of introducing myself before now."

"All of our thoughts were occupied by more pressing concerns this morning," Darcy replied.

"They were, indeed. I regret that our rescue efforts proved insufficient to save Mrs. Clay. When I called upon the Harvilles this afternoon to enquire after her, they told me her fate. At least, however, the child survives. Is he yet with the Harvilles?"

"No, with his father," Elizabeth said. "Sir Walter Elliot."

"Sir Walter? I understood Mrs. Clay to be under the protection of a Mr. William Elliot."

"It seems to have been a rather complicated state of affairs," Darcy said.

"We are grateful that you came along on the Cobb when you did," Elizabeth added, "else I do not know how we would have found a safe place where Mrs. Clay—Lady Elliot—could deliver her child, let alone have transported her there. Did you simply happen upon us, or did you witness the accident?"

"As I approached the quay, I saw her on the ground, with you attending her."

Disappointment crossed Elizabeth's countenance. Darcy, too, wished that Lieutenant St. Clair had been able to put to rest her doubts regarding the cause of the accident.

"I assumed at the time that she was of your party," St. Clair continued, "though I later realized that you were merely passers-by, like myself. How *did* she come to injury? I expect she fell from the upper wall, or descending the steps?"

"We do not ourselves know with certainty," Darcy replied. "We had seen her on the upper wall not long before, but paid her little mind. After lightning struck the merchant ship, we took the far steps to lower ground and found her as she was when you arrived."

"When you saw her before the accident, was anyone with her?"

"No." It now struck Darcy as odd that Lady Elliot had been on the Cobb unescorted. Propriety dictated that women of her status did not roam public streets unaccompanied, let alone in such a delicate condition.

"I suppose, then, that we shall never know the particulars," St. Clair said.

"Nor will her child," Georgiana said softly. Until now, she had followed the conversation in silence. Like the rest of them, she wore a sober expression—they spoke of a tragic matter, after all—yet hers held something more, and Darcy suspected what might occupy his sister's thoughts. Their own mother had died within hours of giving birth to Georgiana. The circumstances had been far different—she had died peacefully, in her own bed, their father at her side—but Georgiana possessed a heart that could not help but empathize with the baby Lady Elliot left behind.

A change of subject was in order. "Will you take a glass of wine with us, Lieutenant?" Darcy asked. "We would very much like to hear about your voyages with my cousin, if you would be so generous as to indulge us."

Elizabeth, too, recognized the need to shift the mood. "Yes— please sit down." She gestured toward an armchair. "We have been looking forward to this meeting."

As Darcy signaled a footman to bring wine, Elizabeth and Georgiana settled on the sofa. Lieutenant St. Clair did not take the chair that Elizabeth had indicated, but one opposite it—a chair with no arms that could interfere with the sword hanging at his side. The seat also put the officer closer to Georgiana.

Georgiana cast off the melancholy that had temporarily claimed her and addressed Lieutenant St. Clair with the attentiveness due a guest. "You mentioned in your letter that you are recently returned from the West Indies," she said. "Have you spent much time in that part of the world?"

"Most of my career." St. Clair accepted a wineglass from the servant. "I first sailed there as a midshipman under Captain Croft— Admiral Croft, now—and returned many times. As you know, that was the destination of the *Magna Carta,* the ship on which I served with Lieutenant Fitzwilliam."

"That was his first voyage across the Atlantic." Darcy's gaze strayed to the sea chest as he took the chair nearest it. The small trunk elicited in him feelings of both curiosity and sorrow. Gerard had died much too young, his naval career barely begun. The contents of the chest were all that remained of his service to the Royal Navy, and Lieutenant St. Clair, one of few people—the only one Darcy had personally met—who had known that side of him. "Were you well acquainted with my cousin?"

"Fairly well. As you might imagine, living for months in the confines of a ship rather restricts one's society, and the higher an officer's rank, the fewer his equals. The *Magna Carta* had a complement of nearly three hundred fifty, but of that number only a handful were commissioned officers. Lieutenant Fitzwilliam had just been made, and so was the most junior lieutenant. As first lieutenant, I took him under my wing, though he needed my guidance in few matters. By the time we left Jamaica on our return voyage, I relied upon him as confidently as I did the other lieutenants. More so, in some instances."

"Why is that?" Elizabeth asked.

"He was quick-minded, brave but not foolhardy, loyal to the navy and proud to be serving His Majesty. He reminded me of myself not too many years earlier. Indeed, we had much in common—both younger sons making our own way in the world, and determined to make our fortunes in the process."

Lieutenant St. Clair shared several stories of Gerard, tales that rekindled Darcy's memories of his cousin's integrity, intelligence, and good humor, while also casting him in new light. Darcy found it revealing to hear someone so close to him described by a stranger.

Darcy's gaze drifted to Georgiana. But fifteen when she had last seen Gerard, she had been so proud of her older cousin—proud of his dedication to the service, his sense of honor and duty, the fine appearance he presented in navy blue. It was little wonder that shortly afterward she had fallen prey to the reprehensible George Wickham, another lifelong acquaintance who looked dashing in uniform. She had learned, nearly too late, that impeccable regimentals cannot dress up a scheming, selfish soul.

The conversation ebbed temporarily, one of those quiet pauses when new acquaintances are unsure where the discussion should next lead. It was Georgiana who broke the silence.

"We were told that Gerard died in action," she said. "I have always wondered about the particulars."

"He died bravely," Lieutenant St. Clair said. "We were escorting two merchant ships back to England when we encountered a French frigate—the *Dangereuse*—traveling with a sloop of war. Her cannons crippled our rigging, but when her boarding party breached our deck, they found us rather disinclined to surrender. We forced them to retreat, but Lieutenant Fitzwilliam took a pistol ball during the melee."

Darcy knew St. Clair was leaving much unsaid. War was a brutal business; Andrew St. Clair and Gerard Fitzwilliam had lived the violence merely summarized in the battle accounts published for public consumption in the *Naval Chronicle*. While Darcy appreciated the officer's discretion—the horrors of battle were no subject for ladies' ears—he himself longed to hear more. He had no taste for gore; rather, he wanted to fully understand his cousin's final moments. For all of Darcy's responsibilities, many of them settled upon him at an early age, his own life seemed sheltered and safe compared to Gerard's and that of Colonel Fitzwilliam. Darcy had faced danger, but only when it came looking for him—he had not deliberately committed himself to a profession that actively sought it, as his two cousins had.

"Did Gerard suffer a great deal of pain?" Georgiana asked.

"I did not see him take the shot; I came upon him afterward. By that time he had lost consciousness. A seaman and I carried him down to the surgeon, but we had scarcely laid him on the table when he died." He paused. "This may seem small consolation, Miss Darcy, but the final expression of his countenance was peaceful, so I believe he was insensible to pain at the end."

"I was under the impression that my cousin's request to you regarding his sea chest had been a deathbed wish," Darcy said.

"No, he had asked me some time earlier, after we lost two of our midshipmen in another engagement, and a number of seamen to fever, all within a se'nnight. Ours is a hazardous profession, and we try not to dwell upon its risks, but the spectre of death does hover, and after a week of seeing dead crewmen's belongings sold before the mast, the possibility of an untimely demise was much on everyone's minds. An officer's belongings, of course, are not subject to such an auction, but Lieutenant Fitzwilliam asked me, should he perish at sea, to personally convey his sea chest to his family were it within my power to do so, rather than leave it to be transported by unknown personnel with the rest of his effects. It was a promise I readily gave, and regret that duty prevented me from carrying through until now. I appreciate your meeting me here in Lyme, though I gladly would have traveled to Buckinghamshire to deliver the chest to the earl."

It was just as well that Darcy's travel plans had coincided with Lieutenant St. Clair's arrival in Lyme, for the Earl of Southwell—Darcy's eldest Fitzwilliam cousin—was not the most tactful individual, nor did he hold the navy in particularly high regard following his youngest brother's death. His reaction upon receiving Gerard's sword and other effects forwarded by the navy had been acrimonious; Darcy winced to think of what Southwell might have said to Lieutenant St. Clair upon receiving the chest in person.

"It is amazing to me that you have been so long from England," Georgiana said. "Is it usual for a ship to be away for such an extended period, even during war?"

"I have served on numerous ships," St. Clair said, "and been appointed to them at the will and convenience of the Admiralty. Some of the transfers occurred in foreign ports; on other occasions my new ship was leaving so soon upon the arrival of my former that there was no time for shore leave."

"You must be grateful, then, to finally stand on English soil once more," Elizabeth said.

"I am, indeed." He set his wineglass on a side table. "Mr. and Mrs. Darcy, Miss Darcy—I appreciate your kind interest in my history, but no doubt you would much rather examine the accoutrements of Lieutenant Fitzwilliam's career than politely endure an account of mine."

"I assure you, our interest is not feigned," Elizabeth said. "But if you have another engagement . . . ?"

"I am entirely at your disposal, madam."

"Then I beg leave to quiz you awhile longer, for we have no other acquaintance in the navy, and are intrigued by that life."

"I shall do my best to offer intelligible replies. However, my society has been limited to shipmates for so long that I cannot guarantee conversation worthy of such fair company."

"You have acquitted yourself perfectly well thus far," Elizabeth assured him. "Now, do present duties bring you to Lyme, or are you here by choice?" Though Lyme boasted a shipyard, it was not a naval base. The navy, however, maintained a presence along the entire south coast. Lyme appeared to have a higher naval population than Darcy had anticipated; he had also seen a number of marines.

"I expect to remain here until joining another ship." St. Clair glanced at Gerard's sea chest. "And when I do, I imagine I shall feel strange not bringing that chest aboard with my own possessions.

After traversing the world together, at least one of us is finally where it belongs."

"I can scarcely comprehend the distances you have traveled," Georgiana said. "Lyme is as far as I have ever journeyed from home."

Darcy regretted the truth of that fact. His sister's life had been more circumscribed than he would have wished for her, and as her guardian he felt keenly this gap in her education. Georgiana longed to see more of the world; for that matter, so did he. However, circumstances beyond any individual's control had prevented fulfillment of that desire. Though the rest of Europe stood but a brief sail across the Channel, politics had created a vast gulf that made travel difficult and dangerous. England had been at war with France for most of Darcy's life and all of Georgiana's, and the hostilities had encompassed other countries, as well. Gone were the years when a young gentleman's Grand Tour marked his coming of age, or when a lady might visit Paris to acquire the latest fashions. While a few intrepid individuals yet traveled for pleasure, most foreign journeys were undertaken by necessity, as Darcy's rare trips had been.

Napoleon's recent defeat, however, had made the seas safer and travel possible once more. He hoped, after the political climate stabilized further, to take his family to the Continent. Elizabeth and Georgiana both possessed natural curiosity and strong intellects that would be stimulated by exposure to the art, music, and culture of other countries, and even Lily-Anne, young as she was, would benefit.

"Now that England is at peace, perhaps we shall travel abroad," Darcy said.

"Truly?" Georgiana's eyes lit at the prospect. Elizabeth, too, appeared very pleased by the suggestion.

His sister was still smiling when she turned back to Lieutenant St. Clair. "My brother knows how much I would enjoy that. I have long wanted to visit other places, to see people and landscapes and buildings I have only read about. Has your naval service taken you to the Continent?"

"Which one?" he asked in good humor. "I have seen more of the American continents than 'the' continent of Europe. Most of my time in the New World, however, has been spent among the islands."

"I have not read as much about the New World as the Old," Georgiana confessed. "What do they look like—the West Indies?"

"Like no other place you have seen. The sea is different there—not the cold grey of the Channel, but warm and bright—vibrant blues and greens." His own eyes lit with his subject. "All colors seem more brilliant, in fact—perhaps it comes from being so close to the equator."

"I had always envisioned that part of the world as quite wild," Georgiana said, "but you make it sound enchanting."

"It is both. Parts of the islands do remain untamed, and even the civilized areas have their less pleasant sides. Though the commerce of slavery has been abolished, many of the plantations still use slaves to work in the fields and great houses, a condition that it troubles me to behold. Yet the islands possess a beauty of their own, one very unlike England's and which I have grown to admire as much as that of my native land. If you ever have the chance, Miss Darcy, you should see them with your own eyes. My poor description cannot begin to do them justice."

"Your description is not poor at all, for it has certainly engaged my imagination and made me wish I could view them myself. However, I doubt very much that such an opportunity will ever come along."

"If it does," he said lightly, "and we ever have the fortune to meet again, you must tell me how you liked them."

Their visitor rose. "It has been an honor to conduct Lieutenant Fitzwilliam's chest to you, and to formally make your acquaintance. But I shall depart now, so that you can open the chest in private." He glanced at the chest once more, removed a handkerchief from his pocket, and wiped a smudge off the escutcheon. "You *will* be able to open it, will you not? That is a very clever lock. Lieutenant Fitzwilliam never revealed its code to me."

A letter lock secured the hasp; it had been the suggestion of Gerard's father to avoid the risk of losing a key in the course of many long voyages—and so that, should the unthinkable occur, his family could open the chest under these very circumstances. The late earl had predeceased his youngest son, and so never knew how prescient his advice had been.

"I know the lock combination," Darcy said. Colonel Fitzwilliam had shared it with him. It was the late earl's name: HUGH.

Lieutenant St. Clair nodded. "I assume the chest contains the typical items of a sea officer. Should you discover anything unfamiliar that sparks your curiosity—navigational equipment, perhaps, or some souvenir of the West Indies—I would consider it an honor to call upon you again to explain it."

They thanked him, and the officer took his leave. When he had gone, Elizabeth turned to Darcy. "I found him perfectly agreeable," she declared. "A gentleman in all respects."

"It was kind of him to stay and talk with us about Gerard for so long," Georgiana added.

Darcy conceded that it had been a pleasant evening, even if Lieutenant St. Clair had paid a bit more attention to Georgiana than Darcy liked. However, he was now anxious to conclude it by having a look inside the sea chest. Elizabeth and Georgiana were equally curious, and the three of them gathered round it.

This weathered box of wood and iron had accompanied Gerard from the time he was first made a midshipman; it had traveled across oceans with him, and in the earliest days of his naval career had contained every personal possession he had aboard. The silver escutcheon on its leather-covered lid declared its owner's name— G. Fitzwilliam—in engraved script. The plate shone so brightly against the darkened leather that Lieutenant St. Clair must have polished it before bringing the trunk to them.

Darcy took the lock in his hand, rotated the rings to the proper letters, and tugged the shackle. After years of disuse and exposure to salt air, the lock resisted release, but at Darcy's persistence it opened.

The chest indeed contained the usual items of a sea officer: Gerard's dress uniform—he had died in his working rig for the battle— spare shirts, neckcloths, stockings, smallclothes; shaving apparatus and other grooming items; foul weather clothes; nautical instruments; a writing box and several books; silverware and a knife for the mess. Toward the trunk's bottom lay more personal objects: a backgammon set and a deck of cards, a packet of received letters tied with string, a miniature of a young lady.

"Is that Miss Wright?" Georgiana asked.

Darcy nodded. At Elizabeth's enquiring expression, he clarified. "The eldest daughter of one of Riveton Hall's neighbors." He passed the tiny portrait to her. "She and Gerard formed an attachment while quite young—before he first went to sea—and when he was made lieutenant they became formally betrothed."

"How sad, that they never had a chance to marry."

"She did not go out in society for a considerable time after Gerard's death," Georgiana said. "I heard, however, that she wed this past season. They say it was a marriage of affection, so I hope she has found happiness."

On the floor of the chest lay a money purse. It was small and worn, the fabric thin, and it contained only a modest sum—not at all what Darcy expected a commissioned sea officer, let alone the son of an earl, to have. Darcy supposed paydays might be few and far between on voyages to the West Indies.

One more item remained: a leather-bound journal.

"His lieutenant's log?" Elizabeth asked.

"No," Darcy said. "Gerard's official log was naval property, and would have been turned over to the Admiralty with those of the other officers at the end of the voyage." He opened the volume and scanned the first pages. "This is his private diary."

Eleven

"I felt my luck . . . I was as well satisfied with my appointment as you can desire. It was a great object with me, at that time, to be at sea."

—Captain Wentworth, Persuasion

I passed the exam—I am made! "Lieutenant Fitzwilliam"—does it not sound well?

I have been appointed to the Magna Carta, a sixty-gun fourth-rate commanded by Captain Tourner. I cannot wait to tell my father—to be assigned as a brand-new lieutenant to a rated warship is a choice commission. She is berthed in Portsmouth, where I am to join her after a brief leave to visit my family.

My first stop in Buckinghamshire, however, shall be at Hollycross, to surprise Miss Wright with the news. I shall not tell her directly of the promotion, but simply appear with the epaulette on my shoulder and at last voice the unspoken question between us. I have not wanted to offer myself to her—more to the point, to her father—as anything less than a commissioned officer, though thankfully the inheritance my own sire left me frees us from dependence upon my lieutenant's pay for our maintenance. I could never ask her to live on £8. 8. 0 a month! Though she, of course, will bring a settlement to our marriage, a gentleman hopes to at least equal his wife's fortune; the Magna Carta would have to capture a great many enemy ships *for me to make up the difference with prize money, and Captain Tourner is not known as the boldest captain in the fleet.*

When I have secured Miss Wright's hand, I must then meet my ship in Portsmouth and assist in preparing her to set sail. We are under orders to Jamaica, a frequent deployment for the Magna Carta. *(There—I write the name again!)* Magna Carta. Magna Carta. *Gerard Fitzwilliam, Fourth Lieutenant of the* Magna Carta.

I met Captain Tourner today—a stern man, though no more so than other captains under whom I have served. Many of his crew are staying on, but we are in need of more men—particularly able seamen. I hope we find volunteers—even landmen—and need not resort to the press to fill out our complement.

I also met my fellow lieutenants. I am the most junior of four. Our first lieutenant is one Andrew St. Clair—businesslike, very disciplined, and expects the same of the men. He does not lord his position over us, nor does he resent my birth. Since joining the navy, I have learned that being the son of an earl has its advantages in influence with the Admiralty, but can be a liability in daily life aboard ship—as a midshipman I had to prove my worth to my colleagues on more than one occasion, and I hope I will not face similar prejudice among commissioned officers.

The other two lieutenants, Wilton and Fletcher, are amiable enough, though this is Wilton's second crossing aboard the Magna Carta, *and he has an air of the know-all about him. St. Clair has also sailed to the West Indies before. This is his first voyage with the* Magna Carta, *however, and I sense some umbrage on Wilton's part at the newcomer's outranking him. I overheard the master's mate tell the boatswain that the decision was an Admiralty dictate, not Captain Tourner's preference. . . .*

We are now three weeks at sea, and settled into daily routines. Watch duty has been uneventful, to the disappointment of many, but gun drills keep us occupied and disciplined. The men hope for action, and the prize money it can yield, but ours has been a quiet voyage thus far—a blessing, as a squall our first week out employed ten hands at the pumps for two days straight and brought down our foremast. The ship's carpenter built a jury mast that should—barring further trouble—carry us until we reach a port for repairs.

Life aboard ship for a lieutenant differs from what I have previously known, beyond the increase in responsibility. I have my own tiny cabin off the wardroom, made smaller by the fact that I share it with one of the ship's cannons. Its walls and "door" are but canvas stretched across frames that are removed when we prepare for battle, but these accommodations nevertheless afford me more privacy than I knew in any midshipmen's berth. We have shared wardroom servants, including our own cook.

As officers, we eat fairly well. The lieutenants mess in the wardroom with the master, chaplain, and captain of marines. We pool our messes, and our cook supplements the standard rations with provisions purchased with our own funds. St. Clair acts as our caterer; he contracted for the provisions, and we each subscribe for a share. I have fewer dining companions than I did as a midshipman, especially since one lieutenant is always on watch and St. Clair is invited to the captain's table more often than are the rest of us. Sometimes we invite the surgeon to join us, for variety of company and discourse. We also have entertained the captain himself on occasion; Tourner is a gracious guest, though the wardroom definitely lacks the ambiance of his lavishly appointed cabin, and the meal, despite our cook's sincere efforts, cannot help but be inferior to what he enjoys in his own quarters. Captain Tourner likes his luxuries and keeps an abundant table.

The confines of a ship can feel all the smaller for the individuals who occupy it, and tolerance of varying temperaments is essential to harmony among the officers. The captain of any ship establishes its tone, but that set by Tourner changes, it seems, with the tide. He is moody as the sea; we bask in his calm days, and do our best to ride out his turbulent ones. I am told he was never a particularly strong leader in his youth, and that age has made him even less so. Some years ago, as captain of the Stalwart, *he lost his ship to capture and spent many months in a Spanish prison. It is said that he has not been the same since. He seldom initiates engagements with the enemy; I have overheard the men complain of his reluctance to pursue even merchant ships that might be seized as easy prizes. Any ship under his command is not a vessel set on a course to quick wealth. The crew is careful, however, not to voice their complaints too loudly, lest Tourner hear them and order out the cat-o'-nine-tails.*

As for my fellow lieutenants—St. Clair is not the man I took him for at first. He is serious about his responsibilities and efficient in their execution; he holds himself in reserve and keeps his own counsel. Yet there is in him an amiability that emerges upon better acquaintance. Wilton, however, does not see this, and continues to nurse resentment over his own second-lieutenant status, a bitterness that at times spills over to encompass Fletcher and me—if Wilton cannot be first lieutenant, he will employ the full measure of his authority over the third and fourth. Fletcher is of an easy enough disposition to mollify Wilton's waspishness; I endeavor to ignore it. . . .

The West Indies are beautiful, but hot. We have been here now for three months, performing various assignments to protect Britain's Caribbean interests. It is important work, and we have seen a few battles, but none have yielded much in the way of prize money, and the men grow restless as a result. They long to be closer to the main action of the war. Their wish will soon be granted, for we leave Kingston on the morrow.

We are under orders to escort two merchant ships back to England. They carry cargoes comprising mainly Jamaican rum and sugar (muscovado— brown sugar that will be further refined in Bristol or London; I have learned more about the sugar trade in three months here than I ever expected—or wanted—to know). The owner of one of the ships—the Montego—*has won over our crew with a gift of numerous casks of rum for the men's consumption during the voyage home. He is a wise man—doubtless, they will now defend the* Montego *with extra zeal. He has also given each officer enough rum to last the voyage and then some, as well as casks of finished white sugar—illegal to import for sale in England, but allowed on board as part of our personal possessions. Rumors circulate that the captain's private stores hold more Jamaican rum and sugar than wine and beef. . . .*

We are halfway home, and I look forward to our return to England's fairer climate with each passing day. The sea has been calm—too calm—and we bake in the heat as our sails hang slack. The men are bored and frustrated.

I believe the captain is, as well. He has formed the habit of inviting three passengers of the Montego *to dine with him regularly. One gentleman, a Mr. Smith, is the owner of a sugar plantation between Kingston and Spanish Town; it is his sugar and rum the* Montego *carries, and which the crew and officers of the* Magna Carta *received in gift. Our crew does not grumble about having civilians aboard, or the trouble of transporting them from one ship to another for the sake of dinner, as the quality of Mr. Smith's rum—which they enjoy on Sundays in lieu of their standard issue—is superior to Pussar's. The best that can be said of the other two fellows is that they are unobjectionable, though one of them seems at pains to impress upon us that he is a future baronet. . . .*

A most extraordinary mystery presented itself today. Upon my return to the wardroom after watch duty, our cook begged a private word with me. We moved to my cabin and drew closed the canvas. He then recounted in a low voice how, while he was retrieving sugar from a partially used cask, the scoop struck something hard. He dug out the object—an incredible discovery—a small gold figurine fashioned in the form of some sort of fantastic creature. Additional excavation produced a second figurine of similar design.

The poor fellow was in some terror of this find, though it is difficult to name the greater source of his fright—superstitious dread of the wrath of whatever heathen god the idols represent, or fear of being accused of theft aboard ship and sentenced to flogging. He had been threatened with such punishment some days previous by a midshipman whom he had surprised in the stores taking inventory for St. Clair. I assured him of my faith in his innocence, took the idols into my possession, and told him I would handle the matter.

Where did the gold figures come from, and how did they find their way into our sugar cask? Did one of Smith's slaves plant them for some superstitious purpose before the cask left the estate? Did a member of our own crew secrete them in there? Perhaps they are stolen, and the thief needed to hide them hastily. How else would such valuable objects come to be in such an odd, unsecure location?

Someone comes—

————

The "someone" was St. Clair, and I confided to him the discovery. He appeared surprised—yet there seemed something disingenuous in his manner. He obliquely deflected my speculation as to the idols' provenance, and discouraged me from bringing the matter to the captain's attention. "He is entertaining Mr. Smith and the others at present," said he.

I asked whether the cask in question appeared on the inventory, and he replied that all items on the ship had been entered in the manifest before we set sail. I clarified that I meant the inventory he had ordered Mr. Musgrove to complete last week. "Hart told me of it."

"Did he?" There was a transient wariness in his expression, almost immediately eclipsed by something harder. "Do not concern yourself about the inventory."

He was all brusque authority; there was none of the warmth I had come to know in months of service with him. He held out his hand. "Give that to me; I will attend to this myself. Meanwhile, say nothing to anybody else about it, and instruct Hart likewise." He was in that moment entirely the First Lieutenant, and I, the Fourth. There was no question but that I must follow orders without argument.

I surrendered the idol I had shewn him, but they remain fixed in my thoughts. My conversation with St. Clair, far from relieving my suspicions, has only heightened them.

At present, however, we have more pressing concerns. I hear the drum—we are beat to quarters—my cabin must be cleared for the gun crew. Two warships have been spotted, bearing French colors.

Darcy closed the diary. There were no further entries; the last had been dated the day of Gerard's death.

After scanning the first pages the night they had discovered the volume, Darcy had deliberated for some time before reopening it. He wanted to know more about his cousin's life, to hear the tales he might have told in person had he ever had the opportunity. With Gerard's voice silenced by a lead ball, his writings offered the only means by which he could yet speak. To read his personal diary, however, seemed to violate the privacy of a man who had already lost all else.

It had been Elizabeth, observing Darcy repeatedly taking up the journal only to set it down again unopened, who had ultimately persuaded him. "By reading the record that Lieutenant Fitzwilliam left behind, you do not disrespect your cousin. If anything, reading his words honors his memory, for doing so enables you to appreciate more fully the value of his life."

"Would you ever want someone else reading *your* diary?"

"Nobody would want to read my diary."

"Why do you say so?"

"It would be an extraordinarily brief diversion—I never remember to write in it."

Gerard, apparently, had not suffered Elizabeth's lack of discipline. He had filled nearly all the pages of the bound volume with close-written lines, so many that reading through them had occupied a considerable portion of the following two days, when intermittent rain had restricted their enjoyment of Lyme's outdoor pleasures. Darcy had read slowly, savoring Gerard's words and descriptions, hearing his cousin's voice once more and seeing the confident young sea officer Lieutenant Fitzwilliam had become as he related his experiences aboard the *Magna Carta* and its tour of the West Indies.

The abrupt end and its references to the impending battle foreshadowed Gerard's death more dramatically than could a novel. While Darcy knew the hero's fate, he wished it could be rewritten. Yet it was a secondary character who most occupied Darcy's thoughts when he finally closed the diary.

On the sofa, Elizabeth added stitches to an infant blanket she was embroidering for Lady Elliot's son. Though Sir Walter had likely commissioned a fleet of seamstresses to outfit the Elliot heir with the most au courant infant fashions and all the linens one small creature could require, she had wanted the motherless child to own something sewn with more than mere thread. Georgiana was helping her create the gift, though at present she had already retired to her chamber for the night.

He watched his wife pass the needle through the fabric several times before she became aware of an audience and looked up.

"What is your impression of Lieutenant St. Clair?" he asked.

"And here I thought it was I who inspired your reverie." She smiled and went back to her work. "He seems a conscientious gentleman. Another individual might have passed off to someone else the trouble of conveying that sea chest to your family, rather than have the burden of it himself for so long a time—your cousin, after all, would never have known the difference. But he took that responsibility seriously. And we were certainly fortunate that he happened upon us on the Cobb when we needed assistance with Lady Elliot. Between the foundering ship and the rising storm, everybody else was too busy, but Lieutenant St. Clair suspended his own business to render aid to strangers. I think that reflects well upon him."

Darcy silently contemplated her words, frowning in thought.

"Have you a different impression?" Elizabeth asked.

He did, but it was not fully formed. "I wonder what business brought him to the Cobb on such a morning. He was not in uniform, and therefore not performing any official duty."

"What business brought us? Or Sir Laurence? Or any of the other people we saw promenading before the weather turned so suddenly?"

"*We* thought it turned suddenly. Lieutenant St. Clair is an experienced sea officer. While aboard ship, it is his job to monitor the weather, because his life and that of the entire crew depend upon it. If he is worth his epaulette, he knew that storm was coming before we did."

"Will you next accuse him of conjuring the storm himself?"

"He was not on the Cobb for leisure."

"Does it matter? As you say, he is a mariner. Any number of reasons could have brought him to the Cobb. Mrs. Harville told me that the new peace has forced many in the navy to seek other work."

That much, Darcy knew to be true. They had seen solicitation notices posted throughout Lyme by masters of private vessels offering prime wages for able seamen. Officers were also in demand, promised recompense more attractive than the half-pay they received if not actively employed by the navy.

Elizabeth set aside her work. "You have just finished reading Lieutenant Fitzwilliam's diary, yet it is Lieutenant St. Clair who occupies your thoughts. Why? Did your cousin write ill of him?"

"Not directly." Darcy was troubled by Gerard's account of the gold figurines he had discovered—and Lieutenant St. Clair's response. Perhaps the last two entries would not have bothered him so much had they appeared earlier in the diary. But falling as they did, as the final scenes in a narrative—a life—cut short, invested them with significance, real or imagined. "They had a difference of opinion over a protocol matter shortly before Gerard's death."

"Well, that is hardly something to hold against him." She fixed Darcy with a penetrating stare. "I think you dislike him because of the way he looks at your sister."

His first instinct was to refute her accusation—but it held a grain of truth, and he could not deny her perceptiveness.

"Georgiana can do better than a naval lieutenant," he said.

"Her own cousin was a naval lieutenant."

"Between Gerard's determination and his family's connexions, he would have been promoted to captain in due course. Once he made post, advancing to admiral is merely a matter of seniority. However, even had he remained a lieutenant, he would have come into the same inheritance—modest though it may be—that Colonel Fitzwilliam received when their father died, which enabled him to betroth himself to Miss Wright knowing they could live respectably. St. Clair, by contrast, has had many years in which to rise to captain, yet he has not so much as achieved the rank of commander. He is still a lieutenant, and with England now at peace, is likely to remain so indefinitely, with an income of a mere one hundred pounds a year—less, if not on active duty."

"You assume that Lieutenant St. Clair's income is limited to his naval earnings, when in fact we know little about the man beyond the fact that he served with your cousin. However, I expect any discussion of his fortune, or lack thereof, is irrelevant in regard to Georgiana, as her thoughts seem to be occupied by Sir Laurence Ashford since our arrival in Lyme. Did you observe how much more interested she became in attending last night's public ball after Sir Laurence enquired whether she was going? I believe she would have danced every dance with him, had decorum allowed. And I am begun to think he might have asked her to, could he have done so. As it was, they spent a considerable portion of the evening in conversation with each other, not dancing with anybody."

"Georgiana does appear to have become the object of Sir Laurence's particular attention—and to be receptive to it," Darcy said.

"Are you?"

"An object of the baronet's distinguished notice? No. He did not ask me to dance even once. Which is just as well. I would not want to compete with my sister for his regard."

Elizabeth laughed at his unexpected jest. "Did I just hear my husband approve of a gentleman—*any* gentleman—courting his sister?"

He would not give her the satisfaction of a firm reply. "Perhaps."

"Perhaps? The Darcy I know is more decisive than that."

He met his wife's gaze, held it a moment . . . and conceded. "It *is* time Georgiana considered marriage. Probably past time." He returned Gerard's diary to the sea chest and went to sit beside her. "Sir Laurence possesses tangible assets—a title, fortune, property, family, connexions—along with his intelligence and pleasing manners. If he is her choice, she has made a sensible one."

"Sensible—now *there* is a romantic word, from a man whose own choice defied the expectations of his entire acquaintance, not to mention his own judgment. I hope your preference for a sensible match for Georgiana does not mean you regret our experiment."

"Indeed not." He spoke softly, and she moved closer to hear him. "In fact—" He brought his hand to her cheek and bent his head toward hers. "I would say it has worked out rather well."

Twelve

"I am quite convinced that, with very few exceptions, the sea-air always does good. There can be no doubt of its having been of the greatest service to Dr. Shirley, after his illness. . . . He declares himself, that coming to Lyme for a month did him more good than all the medicine he took; and that being by the sea always makes him feel young again."
—Miss Henrietta Musgrove, Persuasion

Although the weather had cleared and the morning dawned sunny, evidence of the storm three days past yet cluttered the shore as Elizabeth and Georgiana walked down to the beach. Splintered wood and other pieces of the foundered ship lay strewn amidst the shingle, left by the tide like an offering. Occasionally a barrel washed up, exciting great interest—the merchantman had been returning from the West Indies—but most of the cargo had been lost or destroyed by the lightning bolt that claimed the ship.

The two ladies had reserved a bathing machine, one of the curious vehicles lined up on the sand like hackney cabs in Covent Garden following a theatre performance. Essentially small wooden huts on four wheels, they were designed to go where no ordinary carriage ought—straight into the water. This was to be Elizabeth's first experience seabathing, and she looked forward to it with a mixture of excitement and trepidation. She wondered what it would feel like to completely immerse herself in the water, but also doubted the wisdom of doing so. After all, neither she nor Georgiana knew how to swim. She did not want to drown, of course, but she was almost equally fearful of making a public spectacle of herself.

Georgiana, who had bathed at other seaside resorts, assured her she had nothing to dread. "The whole process is quite safe and civilized. We will climb steps to enter the machine, and once inside, change into our bathing costumes. Then a horse will pull the machine into the water to the proper depth. The dipper—our attendant—will assist us into the water."

"Will the water be very cold?"

"Compared to the indoor baths, yes, though it is August, so the sea will not be as cold as at other times of year. I have also gone in November and February, as physicians advise winter seabathing as most efficacious, but I could not bear to stay in the water above ten minutes. I much prefer the hot baths in winter."

"What does one do once in the sea?"

"I mostly move around trying to keep warm."

"Even in summer?"

"Even in summer. Depend upon it, by the time the machine takes us back to the sands, you will be grateful for this morning's sun."

Their machine was not yet ready for them, it being still in use by another patron who, the attendant informed them, was changing out of her bathing costume. At last she emerged, dressed in a modest but neat gown, a heavy shawl draped round her shoulders. She was a thin woman, with an angular face that looked to have been pretty once, before illness etched premature lines upon it. Her untied bonnet strings fluttered in the light breeze. Small hands gripped a cane, which she used to cautiously negotiate the steps.

She was accompanied by a plump woman of middle years, who attended her with warm solicitude. The two were in high spirits as the large woman helped the frail one down to the sand. They had apparently enjoyed their morning's bathing, for they laughed and chattered almost girlishly, and thanked the dipper for a fine outing. "I was happy to immerse myself in the water again after the recent days of rain," the slender woman said. "Provided the weather remains fair, we will return at our usual time tomorrow."

They walked a few steps away from the machine, so that the next patrons could enter it, but the woman with the cane moved so slowly that Elizabeth and Georgiana held back so as not to make her feel rushed.

"The sedan chair is late," the plump woman said to her companion. "If you wait here, I shall engage another." She departed, walking as quickly as one can over shifting sand. In a few minutes, she had left the beach and disappeared from sight, headed toward Broad Street.

The breeze strengthened. The gust lasted only a moment, but in that moment it caught the thin woman's bonnet. As the wind carried it off, she tried to recapture it, but the effort upset her already precarious balance on the unstable sand, and she fell.

Elizabeth and Georgiana rushed to her.

"Are you all right?" Elizabeth asked.

"Yes, yes." The woman laughed self-consciously. "Merely clumsy."

The bathing attendant retrieved a stool from inside the machine, and Elizabeth and Georgiana helped the woman onto it. She thanked them profusely, rubbing one of her calves through the fabric of her gown.

"Are you certain you are not injured?" Elizabeth asked.

"I will be fine. I suffer from rheumatic fever in my legs," she explained. "Earlier this year I could not even walk, but having benefited from the hot waters in Bath, I have come to Lyme in hopes that the sea will advance my recovery still more. I try to bathe every morning, but with the recent rain, I have missed several days, and I suppose I overexerted myself." She sighed. "I think when my nurse returns, I shall tell her I wish to go directly home. Usually after bathing we sit a while looking upon the harbor, simply inhaling the saline air. Both my doctor and Nurse Rooke claim it is quite medicinal."

"Apparently, it can also be quite strong," Elizabeth said.

The woman laughed. "That, it can. I do love to feel it on my face, though. It reminds me that despite ill health and other difficulties, I am yet fairly young, and among the living, and that is something to be grateful for."

Her bonnet lay on the sand several yards away, and Georgiana went to retrieve it. When she returned, the woman thanked them again for their assistance. "Do not allow me to trouble you further—I am keeping you from your own seabathing."

"You are no trouble," Elizabeth said. "We will wait with you until your nurse comes back."

"You have both been so kind. May I ask your names?"

"Mrs. and Miss Darcy."

"It is a pleasure to make your acquaintance. I am Mrs. Smith."

Tendrils of fine brown hair had come loose when her hat took flight, and they now blew round Mrs. Smith's face as she put the bonnet back on her head. She tried to tuck them beneath, but they defied her.

"Would you like some assistance?" Elizabeth asked.

"If you do not mind. My hands are sometimes stiff after bathing, and the water was cold this morning."

"We do not mind in the least," Elizabeth said. Georgiana removed Mrs. Smith's bonnet and held it while Elizabeth used Mrs. Smith's hairpins to secure the wayward locks. When she had done, she put Mrs. Smith's bonnet back on her head and tied the ribbons for her.

"I am much obliged to you, Mrs. Darcy. Nurse Rooke should return soon with the chair to take me home."

"Is your house very far?"

"It is not my house, actually, but that of my friends the Wentworths— the most thoughtful, generous friends one could wish for! Mrs. Wentworth is a former schoolmate of mine. We fell out of communication for many years, but last winter we discovered ourselves both in Bath at the same time and renewed our friendship. She has been very good to me. When my physician advised me to try seabathing, she and Captain Wentworth invited me to come to Lyme and stay with them, despite their being recently married and just establishing their home." She laughed. "I told them that newlyweds did not need a poor widow intruding on their privacy, but they so kindly insisted that I could not decline."

"They sound like very good friends, indeed," Elizabeth said.

"Oh! There is the chair now."

Nurse Rooke approached, leading two bearers carrying a sedan chair. The conveyance—a windowed box with a seat inside, borne on two long poles—was as common a sight in Lyme as it was in Bath, for it offered advantages over horse-drawn carriages. Often, the chair men could negotiate the town's narrow lanes and steep hills more easily than drivers of wheeled vehicles, and they could collect and deliver their passengers in places such as sandy beaches or inside buildings. Elizabeth found the chairs confining and generally used them only in the rain, but for a debilitated person such as Mrs. Smith, they were an ideal form of transport.

"Here we are at last!" the nurse called out cheerfully. "I am sorry to have taken so long—a chair was not immediately to be had. Are you ready to go to the Cobb?"

"No, let us simply return home today."

"Very well." The nurse picked up Mrs. Smith's cane, which lay forgotten behind the stool she had been sitting on. "Here—I will help you into the chair."

As the nurse handed Mrs. Smith her cane, Elizabeth realized that she herself might have seen Mrs. Smith once before. There had been a woman on a bench on the lower Cobb the morning of Lady Elliot's accident. Elizabeth's party had been on the upper wall, looking down from an angle, so the woman's bonnet had prevented a clear view of her face, and even had it not, Elizabeth had no reason at the time to closely observe her. But the woman had possessed a cane.

Mrs. Smith rose. Leaning on her cane with one hand, she extended her other toward Elizabeth, which Elizabeth took. The widow's hand was bony, her knuckles swollen.

"I feel so fortunate to have met you, Mrs. Darcy—and you, too, Miss Darcy. Thank you once more for your assistance. I hope our paths cross again while you are in Lyme."

Elizabeth hoped so, too.

Thirteen

"No one can be really esteemed accomplished who does not greatly surpass what is usually met with. A woman must have a thorough knowledge of music, singing, drawing, dancing, and the modern languages . . . a certain something in her air and manner of walking, the tone of her voice, her address and expressions. . . ."
—*Caroline Bingley*, Pride and Prejudice

*E*lizabeth found that she enjoyed seabathing. Though shockingly brisk upon entry, the water temperature was not unpleasant after one became accustomed to it, and the dipper's advice to immerse one's whole self immediately rather than ease in proved sound. The water reached their shoulders, alleviating any modesty concerns Elizabeth had harbored, and the two sisters—though Georgiana was her sister by marriage, Elizabeth loved her like a sister of blood—conversed freely and cheerfully on all manner of subjects, their discourse drifting as unconsciously as the tide.

Boats dotted the waves farther out to sea. Most of them were small fishing vessels, but a larger passenger ship caught Georgiana's attention.

"Do you think my brother is seriously contemplating a tour abroad for us all?"

"You know your brother—he would not have voiced the possibility aloud unless he were sincerely entertaining it."

She smiled. "I am simply so delighted by the prospect that I can hardly believe he said it."

"You are that eager to travel?" Elizabeth was pleased by the prospect herself, but Georgiana's enthusiasm was palpable.

"I would like to see something of the world beyond Pemberley and London. I have wondered what it might be like to hear Mozart performed in Vienna, or see the ceiling of the Sistine Chapel. Sir Laurence has traveled a great deal. He has mentioned a few of his trips, and Miss Ashford has shown me some of the gifts he has brought home for her. Did you notice the diamond ear-bobs she wore to the ball?"

"I did. They were lovely." Elizabeth also noticed how animated Georgiana had become. Journeying abroad seemed a subject that had been in her thoughts for some time.

"Even if I do not travel, however, I am eager for some sort of alteration in my life. I enjoy my musical studies, our visits to London, the society of my friends. I adore my niece. I am blessed with an excellent brother, and you, Elizabeth—you have brought me the happiness of at last having a sister." She looked at Elizabeth with such genuine affection that Elizabeth would have hugged her were she not expending so much energy simply keeping her head above water as the tide moved toward shore. "But I cannot exist forever in the manner I have been. I need more to occupy my mind and hours." She looked out toward the sea again. "Whether that is the novelty of travel, or a home of my own of which to be mistress, or something else I have not yet discovered."

Elizabeth understood. For all that polite society praised an "accomplished" woman, it offered few outlets for one to employ those accomplishments in a meaningful manner. Georgiana was fluent in four languages, but when did she ever have opportunity to use them? As it was, she was fortunate that her father, and in turn, her brother, had valued women's education enough to encourage her to cultivate her mind as well as her manners. There were many ladies of richer birth with poorer intellects.

On the horizon, a ship of the line sailed east toward Portsmouth, and both could not help but admire the majestic image of a first-rate flagship under full sail.

"Do you think Lieutenant St. Clair will ever captain such a ship?" Georgiana asked.

"He might, in time," Elizabeth answered. "Though now that the war is ended, I expect that opportunities to distinguish oneself for promotion will be fewer, and captaincies will not become vacant as frequently."

"I suppose that is both good and bad for naval families. Advancement will be much slower, but there is a greater chance that one's husband—or father, or cousin—will live to an old age."

"I have sometimes wondered how the wives of sailors and soldiers bear the long absences and uncertainty," Elizabeth admitted. "My younger sisters, before they were married, would have said that the uniforms make up for it." Kitty, now wed to a clergyman, had developed more maturity, but the ever-flighty Lydia likely still held that opinion. Elizabeth hoped for her youngest sister's sake that something made marriage to her untrustworthy militia officer tolerable.

"I think it takes more than a uniform," Georgiana said. "Though . . . Lieutenant St. Clair did look terribly handsome the other night, did he not?"

"He did indeed—second only to your brother, of course. If Darcy had first appeared to me with a gold epaulette, I might have been utterly lost."

The climb up Broad Street toward their lodgings seemed steeper following their exertions in the sea. Elizabeth and Georgiana paused to catch their breaths before continuing, and found themselves in front of a fossil shop that they had passed numerous times since their arrival in Lyme but had never entered.

"Sir Laurence says that Lyme is becoming as famous for its fossils as for its seabathing," Georgiana said.

"Indeed?" In the reflection of the shop window, Elizabeth regarded her with an arch look. "What else does Sir Laurence say?"

"That the region's landslips uncover extraordinary specimens that attract collectors. He owns several himself."

"Sir Laurence is a fossil collector?"

"Not specifically—he collects all manner of things. He has a great interest in history, and art, and antiquities. He admires Lord Elgin tremendously for having rescued the Parthenon marbles."

Elizabeth read the esteem in Georgiana's eyes and doubted they glowed for Lord Elgin. "Does Sir Laurence admire anybody else?" she asked softly.

Georgiana turned away from the shop window to look directly at Elizabeth. "He says he would like to show me his collection one day."

"And would you like to see it?"

She smiled.

Elizabeth was tempted to ask whether a title enhanced a gentleman's appearance to the same extent as did an officer's uniform, but forbore, not wanting to chance Georgiana's misconstruing her gentle teasing. Whatever feelings about a certain baronet might be developing in Georgiana's heart, Elizabeth left it to her sister-in-law to confide them to her when and if she chose.

Their tête-à-tête was interrupted by the emergence of one of the shop's customers, a spectacled man in his middle thirties whose clothing boasted an extraordinary number of pockets. A man whose countenance lit with delight upon recognizing Elizabeth.

"Why, Mrs. Darcy!"

"Professor Randolph!" Elizabeth's pleasure matched that of her friend; she and Darcy had not seen Julian Randolph in two years. They spent more time at Pemberley than in London, and even when they were in the city, the professor's work as resident archaeologist of the British Museum often took him away from it.

"And Miss Darcy," he continued. "Imagine, meeting you here in Lyme. This is the very best of surprises."

"Indeed, it is," Elizabeth said, "though I cannot say I would be altogether surprised to meet you anywhere."

A specialty in New World artifacts—Professor Randolph was American by birth—had earned him the attention of the museum, but a scientific passion that comprehended artifacts of all cultures and eras had taken him around the world. His eclectic knowledge had proved critical in assisting Elizabeth and Darcy in two adventures early in their marriage.

"I am here at the invitation of the Philpot sisters—have you met them?"

"I have not had the pleasure."

"Lovely ladies, all three—prodigious fossil-hunters. Their collection is considered one of the best, and includes several discoveries that are the first of their kind. Lord Chatfield introduced me to Miss Elizabeth Philpot at one of his dinner parties. We had a most enjoyable conversation about paleontology and archaeology—how they are really quite similar, both sciences in which their practitioners sift through earth searching for evidence of those—be they creatures or men—who lived before us." He paused. "But *you*—how are you and Mr. Darcy? And your little one? I regret that I have not yet had an opportunity to meet her."

"We are all well, thank you. Lily-Anne is here in Lyme with us. Perhaps you would like to come to dinner one evening?"

"I should enjoy that above all things. I am engaged this evening— the Philpots have invited some promising local young people for a scientific salon—but I am otherwise at your disposal."

"Tomorrow evening, then, at six?" Lyme, she had found, did not keep London hours.

"I look forward to it already."

Fourteen

"*You have difficulties, and privations, and dangers enough to struggle with. You are always laboring and toiling, exposed to every risk and hardship. Your home, country, friends, all quitted. Neither time, nor health, nor life, to be called your own.*"

—*Anne Elliot to Captain Harville,* Persuasion

*D*arcy's pace slowed as he reached the end of the Walk and neared the harborside pub. He was yet uncertain of what he hoped to learn from this meeting with Lieutenant St. Clair, a meeting arranged at Darcy's initiative. He was therefore even more uncertain how to direct their conversation. It is difficult, after all, to set a course without knowing one's destination. And Lieutenant St. Clair struck Darcy as a shrewd enough sea officer to detect any sign of foundering.

What Darcy did know, was that since reading Gerard's diary, he remained troubled by the unfinished business his cousin had left behind. What had happened to the idols Gerard found? Had St. Clair ever determined their ownership? Had he even attempted to?

And now, years later, did it matter?

The tavern sat in a narrow street in Cobb Hamlet. Darcy passed the Harvilles' cottage and continued a few more doors to the Sheet Anchor. Though the meeting had been Darcy's suggestion, the venue had been St. Clair's.

Sailors and dockmen crowded its tables, some eating dinner; fish dominated the menu, from the look of their plates. Others merely enjoyed the local brew; a few of them appeared to have been enjoying it all day. Peace was not an altogether good thing for men susceptible to idleness.

Darcy spied St. Clair in the back of the tavern, where the lieutenant sat with another gentleman at a table abutting one wall. The two were engaged in close conversation, necessitated by the volume of the ballad being sung two tables away by half a dozen seamen deep in their cups. Fortunately (for Darcy, if not the song's hero), the betrayed cabin boy was cast overboard and the *Golden Vanity* sailed off upon the lowland sea just as Darcy reached St. Clair.

"Mr. Darcy! I did not hear you approach." He gestured toward his companion, a weathered, gouty man who could have been any age from forty to sixty. He had a round face, a rounder gut, and a nose that pointed toward intemperance, but his well-made clothes indicated that he had not abandoned all consciousness of his appearance. "Allow me to introduce Captain Tourner, under whom your cousin and I served aboard the *Magna Carta.*" St. Clair turned to the captain. "Mr. Darcy's cousin was Lieutenant Fitzwilliam."

"Fitzwilliam?"

"Gerard Fitzwilliam."

"Of course—the *Dangereuse*," he said. "Do you think I could forget that day?" Darcy could not tell whether his disdain was directed toward St. Clair for his implied suggestion that Tourner had forgotten his fallen lieutenant, or toward the French ship that had been the cause of his death. The captain glanced up at Darcy. "Lieutenant Fitzwilliam was a promising young man. His death was a loss for the navy as well as his family."

"We appreciated the letter you wrote at the time," Darcy replied. In truth, the earl had criticized Captain Tourner's letter as being too brief, the minimum that duty required, with very few particulars. "We are also grateful to Lieutenant St. Clair for having recently returned my cousin's sea chest to us."

Captain Tourner regarded St. Clair critically. "You returned Lieutenant Fitzwilliam's sea chest only recently? Where has it been all this while? I ordered you to arrange for his effects to be transported home with all reasonable expedience, as with any other fallen officer."

St. Clair shifted in his chair and signaled the serving maid. "The rest of his belongings were delivered in a timely fashion; the chest remained in my custody at the request of Lieutenant Fitzwilliam himself. Would you care for another tot of rum, Captain?"

Tourner's heavy face flushed. "Why would Fitzwilliam have wanted his chest floating around the world with you rather than sent home? And when did he make this alleged request? You were not with him when he was shot."

"Some weeks before. I hoped I would never have to make good on the promise."

The serving maid brought rum for three. St. Clair moved his chair closer to the wall and surveyed the room for an unoccupied chair that could be commandeered for Darcy, but Captain Tourner stood.

"You are welcome to my seat, Mr. Darcy. I have business to attend." Apparently, however, the captain had no intention of also relinquishing his rum. Tourner drained his glass and set it beside three empty ones on his side of the table, then picked up his hat and departed.

Darcy sat down, leaning back as the girl cleared away the empty glasses. He noticed that St. Clair had only one glass on his side, and wondered how long he and the captain had been in conference. "Forgive me if my arrival curtailed your meeting with Captain Tourner."

"Not at all," he said. "We were merely reminiscing about past days. Idle talk."

"I am glad for the opportunity to have made his acquaintance. Had you mentioned when we spoke the other evening that he was in Lyme, I would have sought an introduction. Is the *Magna Carta* in port here with him? I should like to lay eyes upon the ship, even if only from shore."

"When last I heard, she was in Bristol. Lyme's harbor is too small to comfortably accommodate many ships of that size. Regardless, the *Magna Carta* is no longer Tourner's ship. He now captains the *Swansea,* an old sixth-rate docked in Plymouth at present. However, there is talk of the Admiralty breaking up the ship now that the war has ended."

"What will Captain Tourner do then?"

"Go on half-pay, I suppose, while he waits for the Admiralty to offer him another ship. It will be a long wait, though, as there are many captains with more seniority and more distinguished service records in similar straits. Alternatively, he could take up an appointment on a private vessel or in another branch of the service—transport, packet ships, or the like. Such duty, however, is hardly glamorous, and would be felt as a demotion."

"Perhaps the Preventives?" Since arriving in Lyme, Darcy had seen numerous ships patrolling the coast to deter smugglers.

"Captain Tourner, command a revenue cutter?" St. Clair chuckled, lifted his rum, and drank.

"He would not find such duty attractive?"

"Actually," St. Clair mused, "he might." He set the glass back on the table. "But unless I am mistaken, we are not here to discuss Captain Tourner."

"No, we are not." Darcy took a drink from his own glass. "Since examining the contents of my cousin's sea chest, I have additional questions about his time aboard the *Magna Carta*."

"You were indeed able to open the chest, then? Before bringing it to you, I had noted some rust on the lock, so I am glad it gave you no trouble. I hope you found his belongings none the worse for their delay in reaching you."

"All appeared in order." He would not mention the diary—not yet. "I wonder, however, now that we are not in the presence of ladies, whether you might relate more particulars about the day my cousin died."

"What do you wish to know?"

"Everything. Whether the day dawned bright or cloudy. Whether the cook burned the porridge. What my cousin's mood and thoughts were—conversations you had." *What happened to the idols Gerard told you of just before he died.* "Anything you recall about that day, before the ship became engaged with the *Dangereuse*."

115

St. Clair released a short laugh. "You do not ask much, do you? That day was years ago."

"I realize that considerable time has passed, but I hope that perhaps its having been a day of battle might have fixed details in your memory more firmly than is ordinary."

"Indeed," the lieutenant said soberly, "battles tend to do that."

St. Clair drained the remaining rum from his glass. Darcy signaled the barmaid to bring another round, wondering how much rum it would require to loosen the tongue of any veteran seafarer, let alone one who had spent half his career in islands known for producing the best rum in the world. Captain Tourner had certainly seemed a man in the habit of consuming generous quantities.

"The day was foggy," St. Clair said. "Mist as thick as the porridge—which, by the way, our cook never burned. Hart was the best ship's cook I ever knew."

"My cousin wrote that the wardroom messes were superior to those he had as a midshipman."

"Did he? Doubtless they were, though I do not know that the fare was worth writing home about. A ship's cook can do only so much. Hart was skilled, however, at making the most of whatever he had to work with. We missed him, after."

"After what?"

"After he died. He lost his life in the same battle as Lieutenant Fitzwilliam."

"How came a cook to be fighting in a battle?"

"When a boarding party breaches your ship, *everyone* fights—cooks, carpenters, coopers. Every hand is needed—if not to wield a weapon, to assist someone who does. Even passengers become involved. It is mayhem."

"I suppose a cook might prove very handy with knives."

"Hart was. Unfortunately, firearms have a longer range."

"He was shot?"

"Yes." He uttered an oath against the French. "The cowards shot him in the back, but I like to think he filleted a number of Frogs before he went."

"You did not witness his death, I take it?"

"I had other distractions."

Darcy could well imagine. "I am sure everyone did, particularly the ship's officers."

"You want to hear more of your cousin, of course." The serving girl returned with their drinks. St. Clair waited until she left before continuing. "Lieutenant Fitzwilliam acquitted himself well that day. I saw his sword take down several of the enemy early in the melee, as he helped three passengers defend themselves. I lost sight of him after that, but the passengers survived, and no doubt have him to thank for their lives."

"You said you discovered him after he had been shot. Did the passengers simply abandon him when he fell?"

"They became separated before then, and had all they could do to save their own skins. Though many gentlemen train in swordplay, controlled single combat at Angelo's fencing school is a far different experience than the pandemonium of hundreds of men on a ship's deck splintered by cannonballs and slick with gore, dodging pistol shots and sniper bullets and falling rigging and the swings of nearby combatants."

Darcy trained at Angelo's.

Although St. Clair's tone had not implied intentional insult, Darcy's pride was ruffled nonetheless. The lieutenant's words essentially questioned the collective honor of all gentlemen not in possession of a military uniform, suggesting that their pursuits were mere playacting.

The suggestion chafed. It was possible to be a man of action without brawling in the middle of an ocean. Was it not? Darcy was vexed at St. Clair, and even more vexed with himself for his own defensiveness. He had nothing to prove to this man. In points of honor, he could match any gentleman, uniformed or not.

He could certainly match St. Clair, who in this conversation still had not alluded to, let alone explained the fate of, the figurines Gerard had brought to the senior lieutenant's attention earlier that fateful day—and who had dissuaded Gerard from sharing the discovery with the captain. Had the first lieutenant ever seen fit to inform his commander? Perhaps Tourner was not the fleet's best captain. Perhaps he was a drunk. But at the end of the day, he was responsible for every thing and every person on that ship. Darcy wondered whether the idols' existence had ever become known to anyone beyond St. Clair, Gerard, and the cook.

The cook who had been killed in battle shortly after Gerard had spoken of the idols to St. Clair.

The cook who, like Gerard, had been told to keep the knowledge to himself.

The cook who had been shot in the back.

Startled by the wild course onto which his thoughts had veered, Darcy took up his rum. As the liquor dissolved the sudden thickness that had formed in his throat, he studied St. Clair, seeking in the lieutenant's countenance some sign that the notion coalescing in Darcy's mind was utterly outrageous—or horrifically plausible. St. Clair, however, declined to make such discernment easy for Darcy. He did not cackle maniacally or radiate a virtuous glow. He merely surveyed the room with his gaze—a sea officer ever on watch, or a guilty man always on guard?

"When you found my cousin, what was his condition?" Darcy asked. "Where did the bullet strike?"

St. Clair hesitated. "It struck his stomach."

"How did he appear?"

His expression tightened. "The effects of lead balls and black powder on human flesh are never pretty, and stomach wounds are among the worst. Are you certain that you want to hear more?"

"I have seen fatal gunshot wounds and gruesome corpses before." Though his statement occasioned mild surprise on St. Clair's part, Darcy did not elaborate.

"Then I will not whitewash the details. Lieutenant Fitzwilliam was lying prone in a crumpled heap on the quarterdeck, sword still in hand. His knees were beneath him—it looked as if he might have tried to raise himself to standing after he went down, but had not the strength. The ball had passed through him, leaving holes in his abdomen and back that bled profusely. I spoke his name repeatedly and received no response, though he moaned and his face contorted as I rolled him onto his back."

"You told my sister that his expression was peaceful."

"I wanted to spare Miss Darcy the images I now relate to you. His countenance did relax at the end, though to describe it as peaceful was . . . generous."

"When you moved him, did he utter any words?"

"No, he only moaned. I was at first buoyed by the sign of life, but quickly realized he was insensible to everything around him. A seaman helped me carry him below deck."

"What did the surgeon do for him?"

"There was little he could do. Your cousin received immediate attention, but Mr. Phelps had scarcely cut away his uniform to examine the wounds when Lieutenant Fitzwilliam expired." He paused. "I am sorry—I wish he had spoken final words that I could pass on to you, or left some other message that could now offer comfort."

Gerard had indeed left a message; Darcy merely needed to determine what it meant. This he knew: it was not bringing him comfort. Suspicion. Apprehension. Distrust. But not comfort.

"I hope the items in his sea chest, at least, provide consolation," St. Clair continued. "Did you find much of interest?"

If you only knew.

Or did he? Both today and the night he had delivered it, St. Clair had repeatedly brought the conversation round to the sea chest. Although having said himself that it likely contained the typical possessions of a sea officer, the lieutenant seemed preoccupied by its contents. Did he know about the diary? In their months of service together, St. Clair could very well have observed Gerard writing in it. Was he concerned about what the junior lieutenant might have privately recorded? Or did a different item altogether spur his fixation with Gerard's effects?

"We indeed found much to occupy our attention." Darcy regarded St. Clair closely as he spoke, hoping to provoke a telltale response.

"Any objects about which I might provide elucidation?"

"No," Darcy replied. "I believe their significance is self-evident."

Though St. Clair maintained his affable expression, its brightness diminished. "Well, my offer stands. If I can ever be of service to you or another member of Lieutenant Fitzwilliam's family, you need only ask. You have my direction here in Lyme." He consulted his pocket watch, a modest but handsome silver timepiece with an anchor engraved on its lid. "I am afraid another appointment commands my appearance now. Pray, give my compliments to your wife and Miss Darcy."

Darcy would certainly remember the sea officer to Elizabeth at first opportunity. He was anxious to show her the diary and relate the conversation just passed, for he wanted her opinion on the speculations forming in his mind.

But tender Lieutenant St. Clair's compliments to his sister?

Never.

Fifteen

*At the bottom of Kingsdown Hill we met a Gentleman in a Buggy,
who on minute examination, turned out to be Dr. Hall—& Dr.
Hall in such very deep mourning that either his Mother, his Wife,
or himself must be dead.*

> —Jane Austen, letter to Cassandra, 1799

*E*lizabeth was not the only person issuing invitations that day.
She and Georgiana returned from seabathing to a note from
Miss Ashford soliciting Miss Darcy's company for an afternoon walk
with herself and Sir Laurence—an invitation Georgiana accepted with
alacrity. As Darcy, too, had gone out, Elizabeth had no one with
whom to share the joy of conversing with two of the most shallow
people in all Lyme when Sir Walter and Miss Elliot paid an unexpected visit.

Sir Walter paraded into the sitting room in his mourning finery,
confident in the belief that black showed his figure and complexion
to best advantage. Miss Elliot seemed blissfully unaware that the
somber shade drained her already pale skin of color, sharpening her
unforgiving features even more than nature had. Although Elizabeth
still could not cast off her misgivings about the cause of Lady Elliot's
death, the widower and his daughter had turned the tragedy into
opportunity.

"There were ten carriages—eleven, counting my own," Sir Walter
said of Lady Elliot's funeral, from which he had just returned to

Lyme. The former Mrs. Clay had been buried at the ancestral Elliot estate in Kellynch, some twenty miles from Lyme, in a manner commensurate with her newly elevated station. "Not so many carriages as the first Lady Elliot's cortege," he continued, "but a respectable showing. Our cousin Lady Dalrymple sent her carriage from Bath, though the dowager viscountess could not herself attend. So did Lady Russell, one of our Kellynch neighbors. Eleven is an entirely respectable number, considering most of my acquaintance received word of the marriage and death in a single announcement. Did you see the notice in the *Times*?"

Elizabeth had indeed seen the notice, which had briefly mentioned Lady Elliot's marriage and death before proclaiming at length the birth of Walter Alfred Henry Arthur Elliot. "I read it with great interest," she said, "including the announcement of your new son's name."

Sir Walter appeared pleased. "He is named for myself, of course, and three of England's greatest kings."

"You named him for monarchs you admire?"

"I—no . . . well, yes. Monarchs of importance, of great reputation. The Elliot heir needs an impressive name, one worthy of inclusion in our *Baronetage* pages."

The poor child might very well inherit his baronetcy before he learned to spell a name that long and pretentious. "Will you call him 'Walter' at home?"

"Alfred, since his namesake was known as—"

"Alfred the Great," Elizabeth finished.

"Precisely."

For little Alfred's sake, she hoped that, free of being called by his father's name on a daily basis, the child might also escape his father's obsessive self-consequence. "And how does Alfred do in his new home after such a dramatic entrance into the world?"

Miss Elliot rolled her eyes ceilingward. "We have not known a single peaceful night since he was born. I do not comprehend how a creature that size can produce so much noise, or what grievance could possibly justify it. I believe Mrs. Logan incompetent."

Her criticism of the helpless child and his nurse moved Elizabeth to defend them. "Newborn babies cry—they have no other way to speak."

"What reason has any child to 'speak' every two hours?"

"I am certain Mrs. Logan has matters well in hand." She paused. "Nevertheless, perhaps I might call upon you and see the child? I have been thinking about him these several days."

"Indeed, Mrs. Darcy," Sir Walter replied with delight, "you are welcome any time. Except mornings, for that is when I endure my daily sea immersion—ghastly ordeal, seabathing, but my physician insists upon its health benefits. Indeed, that is the entire reason we came to Lyme. Mornings, however, are an uncivilized hour for calling, regardless. Evenings used to find us at the Assembly Rooms—now, only private card parties since entering mourning—and we generally promenade along the Walk or the Cobb in the afternoon. But otherwise—yes, do call upon us anytime."

"Does your schedule never vary?"

"Only with the weather. We go nowhere near the sea if it rains, or if the sun shines brightly. The damp is bad for one's lungs, and the sun harsh on one's complexion."

"Did Lady Elliot accompany you on walks along the Cobb?"

"I never visited Lyme whilst Lady Elliot was alive. Fifteen years ago it was not the resort that it is now."

"I meant the second Lady Elliot—the former Mrs. Clay."

"Oh! Of course you did. No, she did not."

Miss Elliot cast a sharp glance at Sir Walter. "Mrs. Darcy, I believe my father finds your conversation so charming that he has entirely forgotten the purpose of our visit."

"Alas, I have indeed." He produced a sealed note addressed to Mr. and Mrs. Fitzwilliam Darcy, Esq., and Miss Darcy. "We are come to personally deliver this invitation to Alfred's christening."

"We do hope you can attend," Miss Elliot said.

"It will be the social affair of the season," Sir Walter declared. "The Lyme season, at any rate. We have hired out the Assembly Rooms for a grand celebration following the ceremony at St. Michael's."

"The christening will be celebrated in Lyme, then—not at Kellynch, where Lady Elliot was buried?"

"Though I would prefer that my son be baptized in the same church as myself and generations of Elliots before him, my physician advises against risking his health by subjecting so small an infant to the ardors of travel. Alfred therefore will be christened in the parish of his birth. Do not fear, however, that this is an inferior alternative. The vicar assures me the rite will reflect all the ceremony due the heir of an ancient and dignified family. The church is named for an archangel, not some obscure saint nobody has ever heard of, and the baptistry dates to Norman times."

Were it not for the Elliots' attire, one would never know they were in mourning as they described plans for the event and boasted of names on the guest list. "Everybody of significance" in Lyme had been invited, as well as notable personages from Bath and London whose names and importance Elizabeth was apparently supposed to recognize but did not.

"Our cousins, Lady Dalrymple and her daughter, the Honorable Miss Carteret, are traveling all the way from Bath," Miss Elliot said.

Sir Walter's chest puffed with pride. "Her ladyship has graciously consented to stand as godmother to Alfred."

"Who is to be his godfather?" Elizabeth half expected to hear they had solicited the Prince Regent himself.

"Sir Basil Morley. Lady Russell, who is godmother to my daughters, will also stand for Alfred, so he shall have three titled godparents. I have also asked my daughter Anne and her husband, so Alfred will have five godparents in total—more than even the Prince Regent."

Elizabeth silently congratulated Sir Walter on having managed to enter the prince's name into the conversation after all.

Sixteen

"Nobody else could have saved poor James. You may think, Miss Elliot, whether he is dear to us!"
—*Captain Harville, speaking of Captain Wentworth,*
Persuasion

*T*he Sheet Anchor had two doors; one fronted the street, the other, the shore. As St. Clair exited through the street door, Darcy quit the tavern harborside, intending to circle round and note the direction in which St. Clair headed to his engagement. For a man at liberty until his next ship posting, the lieutenant certainly had a full schedule.

The door deposited Darcy very near the start of the Cobb. The tide was in, raising the water in the harbor several feet higher than when it was out, and liberating the fishing boats and other vessels that spent low tide grounded in their moorings. With those craft out to sea, the result was a relatively empty harbor that granted Darcy a clear view across to the far curve of the Cobb. He could see nearly the full length of the seawall, excepting the most extreme segment. That section remained obscured by the quay warehouses, beside which two gentlemen engaged in conversation and a few workers went about their business in comparative quiet.

It was not the men, however, who caught Darcy's notice. It was a boy, a very young boy, who toddled along the rough stones of the lower seawall by himself, too close to the harbor's edge for any witness's comfort. A boy who, even from this distance, Darcy recognized.

Ben Harville.

The two-year-old was about halfway along the seawall. There was no one anywhere near him, no one paying heed to that side of the Cobb, no one to act on a shouted warning. Something in the harbor caught Ben's interest, and he moved even closer to the water.

Darcy hurried toward the child, accelerating into a run. If his sudden sprint attracted the notice of anyone near the tavern entrance, he did not know, for his vision focused on the small figure he wished would retreat from the wall's edge. Ben, however, leaned toward the water for a better view of whatever will-o'-the-wisp distracted him.

The sound of Darcy's footfalls striking the hard pavement did command the attention of the gentlemen near the warehouses on the quay. One of them, identifying the danger and realizing Darcy's purpose, himself broke into a run. From opposite ends of the Cobb they neared the toddler, their swift advances at last penetrating Ben's awareness. The sudden sight of two men descending upon him startled the child. As the gap between them closed, the boy jerked involuntarily, upsetting his equilibrium.

Ben teetered over the water at an angle impossible for the child to correct on his own. Darcy reached for him, but his grasp was two strides shy. The other gentleman, however, was just close enough to extend his arm and push the boy toward Darcy, sacrificing his own balance—and tumbling into the water himself.

The resulting splash sprayed Darcy and Ben as Darcy scooped up the child. Ben's rescuer quickly surfaced. Though the water would have been well over Ben's head, the gentleman could stand.

"Is the boy all right?"

"Yes," Darcy said. "Give me a moment to set him down safely, and I will help you out of the water."

"No need." The gentleman retrieved his floating hat, an act that put Darcy in mind of his own hat, which had flown from his head somewhere during his sprint. He would find it later. The stranger then began sloshing toward a set of stone steps that emerged from the water to the quay, doubtless employed more commonly at low tide to load and unload boats.

The splash had drawn the attention of several dockworkers who, seeing that nobody was injured, offered a few comments Darcy could not distinguish, and a few chortles he could, before they headed back to the duty of unloading cargo from a small cutter, the only ship presently anchored in the harbor. Meanwhile, the man to whom the wet gentleman had been speaking before the accident was making his way toward Darcy with as much haste as a person with a bad leg could manage. It was Captain Harville; distance had prevented Darcy from identifying him earlier.

Darcy carried Ben round the walkway and met Captain Harville near Granny's Teeth, at the landing of the steps to which his companion was swimming. His face bore the expression Darcy expected his own would had he just witnessed a similar incident involving Lily-Anne.

"Mr. Darcy, how can I ever express my gratitude? I had no idea— Ben must have followed me out here when I left the house with Wentworth—" The bewildered child lunged toward his father's arms. The captain took him from Darcy. "Ben, do you not know better?" Though his words expressed admonishment, they were gently delivered. He glanced back to Darcy. "I saw you running toward him but I—damn this leg! Damn the French, I should say, and their grapeshot. Were it not for you and Wentworth—"

"Think nothing of it," Darcy assured him.

"I cannot help but think upon it, and offer you my thanks."

The swimmer—Wentworth, he presumed—having reached the steps, Darcy extended his hand to help him up the slippery stones. Wentworth accepted, and soon stood dripping on the quay. Rivulets of water ran into his eyes from his hair, his soaked, tight-fitting coat looked a straitjacket, and he would be very fortunate if his boots were not ruined.

Darcy was a little embarrassed that he himself had emerged from the incident dry save for the effects of Wentworth's splash. "If you must thank somebody," he said to Captain Harville, "thank your friend. It is he who met with greater inconvenience."

Wentworth laughed and pushed his hair back from his forehead. "This old sailor is quite used to getting wet, I assure you." He now extended his hand to Darcy. "Captain Frederick Wentworth."

Darcy would hardly describe Captain Wentworth as old. The man before him could not possess many more years than thirty, and, despite Sir Walter's oration on the detrimental effects of life at sea, looked the model of health and vigor. Even dripping water from his coat sleeves, he bore himself with dignity Sir Walter could not touch. Darcy could easily imagine this man leading a full ship's complement to victory.

He heartily shook the captain's hand. "Fitzwilliam Darcy."

"Darcy?" Captain Wentworth turned to Captain Harville. "Is this the gentleman of whom you were telling me?"

"The same."

"Mr. Darcy, my friend Harville is not the only person here in your debt. My family is much obliged to you and Mrs. Darcy for the aid you rendered my wife's stepmother when she fell on this very pavement. I understand that were it not for you, her child would not have survived."

"I hope Captain Harville retained some of the credit for himself and his wife."

"Not nearly enough, I am sure."

They stepped back against the wall to let a cart pass. The horses plodded slowly, in no hurry to take their cargo from the cutter to the Customs House. The creatures traversed the same road so often that they probably did not at all mind when smugglers managed to by-pass this required review process and spare them their labor. Darcy wondered what these barrels held. French brandy? Spanish wine? Jamaican sugar?

"Lady Elliot was also assisted by another naval officer, Lieutenant Andrew St. Clair." Darcy hoped Captain Wentworth would be able to tell him more about the dubious lieutenant. "Are you acquainted with him?"

"Regrettably, I am not," Wentworth replied. "I shall have to find him out and extend my thanks to him, as well."

Captain Harville shifted a now recovered and impatient Ben to his other arm. "We could stand here for another hour at least, discussing accidents on the Cobb and who among us deserves gratitude. We have not even touched upon last autumn's incident—eh, Wentworth?" Harville chuckled. "But you must be uncomfortable in those wet clothes, and Mrs. Harville must be frantic, looking for Ben. Come—let us find you some dry things. I cannot send you home to Mrs. Wentworth looking like this."

Darcy fell into step with them. The two captains bantered easily, as old friends do, but in a manner that invited Darcy's participation rather than left him feeling an outsider. They had not gone far when Harville spied an object farther down the walk.

"Is that your hat on the pavement ahead, Mr. Darcy? There—near the gin shop."

"The gin shop?"

"Those wooden doors. There's an old ammunition storeroom behind them, built into the wall, from the days when there were cannon on the Cobb. It came to be known as the gin shop for the hoist they used to move the cannonballs and gunpowder." He chuckled. "The name lasted longer than the cannons. At any rate, you had better retrieve your hat before the cart horses trample it. Those animals will not diverge from their path no matter what lies in their way. Wentworth, may we stop a moment to rest my leg? Yes, do take Ben, if you will. No, no—I do not need to sit, only lean against the wall."

Darcy strode ahead to rescue his hat, which indeed lay about ten yards from the gin shop doors. He reached it just before the horses did, picked it up, and moved flush against the Cobb wall to get out of their way. When the cart had passed, he turned to rejoin the captains, but the sound of voices gave him pause.

". . . does not want to be held in soaking-wet arms, and I cannot blame him."

"Ben, if Captain Wentworth sets you down, you must stay at my side. Do you promise?"

The voices were clear as if the speakers stood right beside Darcy. But Captain Harville yet leaned against the stone wall, his friend and son close beside him, at least threescore feet back along the curve from where Darcy stood.

"All right, then. If you misbehave, I will not take you to the ship-yard with your brothers." Harville looked from his son back to Went-worth. "They are preparing to launch a new Indiaman any day now—a thirty-two-gun, the *Black Cormorant*. Have you seen her? I thought I would take the boys over there later today to have a look. . . ."

Darcy was astonished. Somehow, the curved wall carried Har-ville's voice directly to him despite the considerable distance. He had heard of such acoustical phenomena in domed buildings such as St. Paul's in London, but he had never personally experienced an instance of it.

He moved away from the wall gradually, determining the prox-imity required for the effect to work. When he lost the sound, he quickly walked back to the captains. The act of eavesdropping, how-ever accidental, on any conversation, however innocuous, violated Darcy's sense of propriety. Not wanting to embarrass them, he said nothing to his companions about the discovery.

Seventeen

Upon looking over his letters and things, she found it was so.

—Persuasion

*I*f only we could purchase sugar for Pemberley direct from the West Indies," Elizabeth declared as she reached the final leaves of Gerard's diary. "I had no idea that casks of it came with prizes inside. It is little wonder that sugar barons are so wealthy."

"I doubt all sugar casks are thus equipped," Darcy replied.

"Even so, the mere chance of finding such a treasure would sweeten my tea all the more."

She returned her attention to the journal, while Darcy rose from his chair and crossed their small sitting room to gaze out one of the windows. Though impatient for her to finish, he did not want to distract her reading of the critical last entry by staring at her. As he looked upon the street, however, he barely saw the tourists entering the fossil shop on the corner, the gull poking at some morsel on the ground, the gig trying to maneuver round an opposing coach in a side lane too narrow to accommodate both vehicles. His person might stand in a Lyme cottage in the present, but his mind was in the past, on the quarterdeck of a ship in the middle of the Atlantic Ocean.

He turned sideways, as if gazing farther up the street, but in truth surreptitiously watching Elizabeth's expressions as she read. She frowned, eyes narrowed. At last, she finished and looked up at him.

"The approaching vessel, I take it, was the *Dangereuse*?"

"Yes, as evidenced by the date."

She squinted at the lines. "I can barely make out the date. The handwriting on these last pages is inferior to the rest. Though still clearly your cousin's hand, the strokes are not as controlled, and the ink is smeared."

Darcy, too, had been forced to slow his reading when he reached the final entry. Impressions from facing pages, where the ink had not entirely dried when Gerard closed the volume, had resulted in ghostly characters that further hindered legibility. "Indeed, one can see that he wrote the entry in great haste."

"I do not expect, however, that it is Lieutenant Fitzwilliam's penmanship on which you are soliciting my appraisal?"

"No—Lieutenant St. Clair's character."

"Well." She glanced at the page once more before closing the diary. "One must read between the lines for that, and you have had more opportunity than I today. You have been unusually pensive since your appointment. What transpired?"

Darcy came away from the window and sat down across from her. He related the full conversation, from the meeting with Captain Tourner to St. Clair's repeated references to the contents of Gerard's sea chest. Though he censored some of St. Clair's descriptions of the horrors of combat, he included more particulars of the battle and Gerard's injuries than he would have imparted to any other lady in England. As he had hinted to St. Clair, he and Elizabeth had encountered such unpleasantness before, and he was blessed with a wife who could discuss such matters with sense and penetration. He needed both at present.

"So, your cousin and the cook—Mr. Hart—were two casualties of how many?"

"I did not think to enquire." His mind had been so occupied by coalescing suspicion that he had not asked all he might have during his conversation with St. Clair, and the battle itself, though of tantamount significance to Gerard's family, had been of such minor consequence in the overall war that it had received little attention in the *Naval Chronicle* at the time. "St. Clair made it sound a large number, though obviously this was no Trafalgar."

"Perhaps the number of other wounded does not signify," Elizabeth said. "The salient point is that both Lieutenant Fitzwilliam and the cook died shortly after becoming aware of the figurines—objects that somebody else wanted hidden. The question is whether the timing of their deaths resulted from coincidence or malice. As Lady Elliot's demise has already put me in a murderous frame of mind, it is tempting to read homicide into this history. However, ship-to-ship cannon blasts followed by boarding and melee seems a rather inefficient method of murder."

"But a very convenient cover for one—or two."

"You suspect your cousin and Mr. Hart were killed by a member of their own ship's crew?"

"The melee provided a perfect opportunity to silence any questions about the idols."

"Surely you do not think Lieutenant St. Clair himself—"

"It is possible. Or someone acting with his knowledge and perhaps on his instructions."

"But why should he want them dead? He had their trust—he is the person who hired Mr. Hart, and he acted as a mentor to your cousin. He also had the idol in his possession by the time the battle occurred."

"*Idols.*" Darcy emphasized the *s* as he pronounced the word. "Recall that there were two—hence, twice the value and twice the motive for keeping their existence secret."

She perused the final entries again. "Your cousin writes that Hart came to him with two figurines, but the later account of his conversation with Lieutenant St. Clair says he gave up only one: 'I surrendered the idol I had shewn him, but they remain fixed in my thoughts.' Lieutenant Fitzwilliam must have held back the other idol."

"Or in the haste of writing, he accidentally left off the *s* in that single instance—a reasonable possibility, given the general state of those lines' urgency and execution."

"The word is plural everywhere else it appears," she conceded. "Yet if he *did* relinquish only one idol, did he retain the other with or without Lieutenant St. Clair's knowledge? Was St. Clair aware of the second? Perhaps your cousin told St. Clair about only the first. Alternatively, Lieutenant Fitzwilliam might have informed him of both but brought only one with him when he sought out St. Clair."

"St. Clair could have known about both before Gerard even said a word."

"Because he himself put them in the sugar cask?"

"Or ordered someone else to."

"Why would he hide anything of value in a cask to be opened and shared by others, instead of keeping the figurines among his private possessions?"

"Perhaps he did not intend for that cask to be shared, but for it to quietly travel to England with his other personal property." Darcy gestured toward the diary still in Elizabeth's hands. "Gerard writes that many of the officers had purchased small quantities of rum, sugar, spices, and other West Indian goods for themselves or gifts for friends at home. When those goods were loaded onto the ship, a cask intended for St. Clair's stores could have become confused with those designated for his mess."

"Might that not be true of all the officers' goods? The cask in question could have belonged to any one of them."

"Yes, but recall that St. Clair acted as caterer for his mess—he contracted for the group's sugar and other provisions. If a cask from anyone's private reserve was likely to be misidentified as communal, it would be his."

"Again, why would he—or anybody—hide such objects in a cask at all? Why not simply lock them in his sea chest?"

"Perhaps he feared they would be stolen. Perhaps he did not want to be connected with them if they were found."

"He bought two gold figurines as souvenirs of his time in the West Indies. What is the harm in that? Why go to such lengths and risk to disassociate himself from them?"

"Perhaps the idols were something he was not supposed to possess. Given to him by acquaintances he was not supposed to have." Darcy rose from his chair. It was difficult to sit still with his mind so restless. He went back to the window, but saw no more of the view than he had before. "I wish Gerard had described the figurines in more detail."

"Had he known he was leaving behind a mystery for you to solve, no doubt he would have. Unfortunately, he did not expect to die."

"He had the foresight to leave directions for the disposition of his sea chest in the event of his death."

"Yes—ironically, into the care of the very person whom you now suspect of precipitating his demise." She set aside the diary and came to him. "Have you considered that we have only Lieutenant St. Clair's word that your cousin asked him to separate the sea chest from the rest of his belongings and deliver it in person?"

A coldness settled upon Darcy. "I had not. Now that you raise the point, Captain Tourner knew nothing about the request. In fact, he found it extremely unsettling when he heard of it today."

"By taking the sea chest into his custody, Lieutenant St. Clair secured himself unrestricted access to it. Perhaps you are correct—perhaps your cousin did surrender only one of the figurines to St. Clair, and St. Clair wanted time to break into the chest for the other one."

"The chest, however, was never broken into. It is undamaged—other than normal wear—and yet secured by the original lock. Would he not have sawed it off or taken the chest to a locksmith? He has had years in which to do so."

"Maybe he did not need to. Maybe Lieutenant Fitzwilliam told him the combination, or maybe St. Clair figured it out. The code is not difficult to guess by someone who knows even the most superficial information about your family—your uncle's name appears in *Debrett's,* for heaven's sake—and St. Clair is an intelligent man."

"Yet we found all in order."

"Did we? If something were missing, how would we know?"

He pondered this, first imagining Elizabeth's hypothetical scenario, then recalling their actual encounters with St. Clair. "Whatever his intent, I do not think St. Clair ever managed to open the chest. Both here and at the tavern, he seemed very interested in its present contents—almost as if he were hoping we would invite him to examine them along with us." Darcy wondered how he had become St. Clair's defender; he had initiated the conversation expecting Elizabeth to assume the role of devil's advocate.

"I think we have taken this speculation as far as we can without additional information," she said. "We need to either ask him directly about the idols and see how he responds, or find someone with sufficient naval connections to help us investigate. Might Captain Tourner be approached?"

"I doubt any captain would speak against one of his own officers to a stranger, particularly someone outside the navy."

"Might Captain Harville know Captain Tourner?"

"Perhaps. Or—I met Captain Wentworth today, the husband of Sir Walter Elliot's middle daughter and a good friend of the Harvilles. Upon better acquaintance, he might be persuaded to help us."

"Today while seabathing, Georgiana and I met another friend of the Wentworths who spoke very highly of both the captain and his wife. We will have an opportunity to become better acquainted with them quite soon—Sir Walter and Miss Elliot called this afternoon to invite us to Alfred's christening."

"I take it that 'Alfred' is the baronet's new son?"

"Walter Alfred Henry Arthur Elliot." Her brow furrowed. "Or is it Walter Alfred Arthur Henry?" She shrugged. "Yes, Lady Elliot's baby—the new crown prince of the Elliot family."

"Are we to come bearing gold, frankincense, and myrrh?"

"I think gold alone will satisfy Sir Walter, so long as it is delivered with proper homage by magi. Though perhaps he might use the frankincense to preserve himself in all his aristocratic stateliness. Miss Elliot, too." She paused. "From the Wentworths' friend Mrs. Smith, I received the impression that Sir Walter's second daughter does not at all share the eldest's demeanor. What was your sense of her husband?"

"Captain Wentworth has a manner far superior to that of the baronet. I can see why he has risen in his profession. What I cannot see is how he tolerates his new father-in-law, who must sorely try his patience."

"Likely the same way you tolerate my mother—distance and small doses."

In the time they had been speaking, twilight had turned to dark. Though a candle burned beside the seat where Elizabeth had read Gerard's diary, she now moved about the room, lighting more. "Between your recommendation of her husband, and Mrs. Smith's praise of her kindness, I anticipate pleasure in meeting Mrs. Wentworth at the christening. I hope Mrs. Smith might also be there, as I would like to speak with her more—as we parted, I realized I had seen her on the Cobb the morning of Lady Elliot's fall. She was on the bench near Granny's Teeth when we first arrived—I saw her from above."

"There was nobody seated on it by the time we discovered Lady Elliot."

"Even so, I have been wondering whether she might have observed anything that morning which could prove illuminating to our questions about the accident. It is worth at least enquiring, should the opportunity arise at the christening. Meanwhile, however, we have a less extravagant engagement to which we can look forward. I have invited a guest to dinner tomorrow night."

"Sir Laurence?"

"No." She reflected a moment. "Although that is an excellent idea. Perhaps we should invite the baronet and Miss Ashford to join us, unless you would then accuse me of matchmaking—your sister, however, hardly needs my help in that matter. But you will never guess who received the original invitation, so I shall have to tell you. It is Professor Randolph."

"Professor Randolph is in Lyme?"

"Georgiana and I met him in Broad Street this morning. He is here meeting with some fossil collectors. Georgiana mentioned to me previously that Sir Laurence has an interest in fossils—in all sorts of collections, actually—so he and Miss Ashford might make a good addition to our party independent of any thoughts regarding his candidacy as a suitor for your sister."

"Very well. Let us issue the invitation at once. Tomorrow night is little notice."

"Somehow, I do not think the baronet will mind."

Elizabeth retrieved her portable writing desk from the corner and set it on the table. While she wrote the note, Darcy found himself drawn to Gerard's sea chest once more. He opened the lock.

"Are all the contents still in order?' Elizabeth asked.

"That is what I am determining, now that I know what I am looking for."

"I doubt we mistook a gold figurine for a grooming item."

So did Darcy, but reading the diary had made him want to examine all the chest's contents more closely. He withdrew the uniforms, linens, and oilskin, carefully checking folds and pockets. He looked inside the writing box, examined each nautical instrument, set aside the miniature and the letters.

Elizabeth sealed her note and sent it with a servant to the Ashfords' house. She then joined Darcy beside the chest. "Have you found anything new?"

"I am afraid not."

All that remained was the money purse resting on the bottom. Though he had looked inside it before, he lifted it out again now. A sixpence escaped through a small hole in the fabric. The thin coin landed on the bottom of the trunk and rolled to one side, where it became wedged in a narrow gap between the chest wall and base. Darcy grasped the coin. He had difficulty getting his fingers around it, and he wound up extracting it at a slight angle. The action caused the chest floor to shift and rise slightly with the leverage.

"Is that—?" Elizabeth asked.

Darcy already felt as if he had struck gold. "I believe so."

The chest had a false bottom.

He withdrew another coin from the purse and with the pair of them managed to pry up the thin wooden panel that rested about two inches above the true floor of the trunk. The hidden compartment was lined with velvet, a precaution, Darcy supposed, to deter concealed items from shifting around on a rocking ship, and to muffle the sound of any that did. Within lay a larger purse—this one heavier and in superior condition. It contained the pocket money Darcy would have expected the son of an earl to have.

It also contained a gold idol.

Eighteen

"My idea of good company, Mr. Elliot, is the company of clever, well-informed people, who have a great deal of conversation; that is what I call good company."

—Anne Elliot, *Persuasion*

$\mathscr{P}$rofessor Randolph turned the figurine in his hands, studying it from every angle as Elizabeth and Darcy waited in suspense.

About four inches long and nearly as wide, the idol looked to Elizabeth like some sort of sinister angel—a golden Lucifer with an avian head. Fierce and intimidating, its beauty resided in its craftsmanship and history. It was not at all the sort of art object to which she was drawn.

The archaeologist found it fascinating.

She glanced at the clock and wished he would accelerate his examination. Having, at her request, arrived earlier than originally agreed upon, the professor had already spent ten minutes with the idol, and only twenty remained until the Ashfords were due to appear.

"I doubt this is of Jamaican origin," he said at last. "Though your cousin might have acquired it on that island, more likely it was created elsewhere."

They had told the professor that they discovered it among Lieutenant Fitzwilliam's effects. They omitted the part about its having traveled halfway across the Atlantic hidden in a cask of sugar. And the part about suspecting Darcy's cousin might have been murdered because of it. Oh—and the part about the cook getting killed, too.

However, if full disclosure became necessary, Elizabeth knew they could trust Professor Randolph to keep the information to himself. They had taken him into their confidence in the past, and he had proved reliable.

"Created elsewhere in the West Indies?" Darcy asked.

"Elsewhere in New Spain, or perhaps Colombia. It is difficult for me to place it precisely without the opportunity to directly compare it with similar objects of known origin, but my guess is that it comes from the Central American isthmus. Though one does find gold artifacts in the Caribbean islands, they are more plentiful on the continents—or were, until the conquistadors plundered their way through the New World. The Spanish never did find El Dorado, the legendary City of Gold, but they seized plenty of other wealth for the crown. And for themselves."

He turned the idol again so that it lay faceup in his palm.

"What does it represent?" Elizabeth asked. "Is it some sort of ritual object?"

"This artifact is actually a pendant—a bird pendant, a type of ornament Columbus mentioned in his letters as being commonly worn round the neck by indigenous peoples. He called them *águilas*— eagles—but bird pendants can represent other species, generally birds of prey. They were symbols of prestige, worn to demonstrate power. Do you see how the wings are spread, and talons extended? And—oh!"

From a pocket of his coat he withdrew a monocle. Unlike affected London dandies, Professor Randolph carried his for a useful purpose. He removed his spectacles, raised the monocle to his eye, and looked at the figure closely. "I believe that is—yes! That is a fish in its beak." He replaced his spectacles. His face positively glowed. "What a beautiful piece! Your cousin was fortunate to come across it, Mr. Darcy. Though I suspect it cost him dearly."

Darcy started. It certainly had, but in ways the professor could not possibly know. "Why do you say so?"

"Unfortunately, countless relics from the Spanish Empire were lost to greed. The conquistadors wanted gold, not art, and melted ancient treasures without care for their cultural or scientific significance. So much history was destroyed—reduced to merely its metallic value—that surviving items are all the more precious. Collectors pay considerable sums for ante-Columbian artifacts, not all of them legally obtained."

The door knocker sounded. Elizabeth rose and took the pendant from the archaeologist, who relinquished it with the reluctance of a suitor. "Thank you, professor. We appreciate your knowledge—and your discretion."

Dinner proved a success. As Elizabeth had hoped, Sir Laurence and his sister perfectly complemented their party. Professor Randolph found the baronet a worthy conversationalist on subjects both artistic and scientific, and the pair were in mutual rapture over the paleontological promise shown by a young local girl whom the archaeologist had met at the Philpot sisters' home the previous evening.

"Only imagine, Miss Ashford—" A gentleman scholar, Professor Randolph always did his best to draw others into his discourse, no matter how obscure the topic. "Miss Anning was but thirteen when she and her brother discovered a full ichthyosaur skeleton—the first complete one ever found!"

Elizabeth had not the faintest notion what an ichthyosaur was, but Professor Randolph spoke of it with such enthusiasm that she was impressed nonetheless.

Miss Ashford smiled knowingly. "Miss Anning also oversaw the excavation."

Professor Randolph was delightfully surprised by her familiarity with the story. "Do you, too, study fossils?"

"No more seriously than do most visitors to Lyme. My brother, however, maintains such eclectic pursuits that I cannot help but develop a dilettante's knowledge in some of them. His interest in classical antiquities inspired me to read Homer."

"In Greek?"

She laughed. "No, Chapman's translation. As I confessed, I am a dilettante."

Elizabeth turned to Sir Laurence. "Miss Darcy tells me that your interest in Greek antiquities extends to the Parthenon sculptures that Lord Elgin has brought to Britain."

"Lord Elgin is a visionary man who does not deserve the controversy his noble operation and personal sacrifice have generated," the baronet said. "When he saw the damage the building and its frieze had already suffered under the occupation of the Turks, and the continued deterioration to which it was subjected, he took action—at his own expense—to rescue the marbles and preserve them for posterity. And now," he said with disgust, "his detractors accuse him of not having followed proper Turkish legal procedure, or of trying to profit by selling the sculptures."

"Is he not currently in negotiations with the British government regarding a price?" asked Darcy.

"It was always his intention to present the marbles to the nation as a gift for the ages," Sir Laurence said, "but dire financial straits have compelled him to request reimbursement for his expenses—paying his crew and transporting the marbles to England."

"He asks nothing for the value of the sculptures themselves," Professor Randolph added. "A mercy, as I do not know how anybody could fix a price on such treasures."

"All objects have a price." Sir Laurence swirled the wine in his glass. "Even if he did want compensation for his trouble, I would still consider him to have acted unselfishly in saving those artifacts from destruction. Would the world benefit any less from their preservation if he received a reward for having effected it? If he chose at this point to keep them for himself, I would not fault him."

"Do you think an ancient culture's treasures can rightfully belong to an individual?" Georgiana asked.

"Yes, I do." He smiled at her, though his expression soon grew serious once again. "Particularly if that individual values them more than do conquerors into whose hands they have fallen. The Turks did not merely neglect the Parthenon, they used it as a powder magazine, caring not a whit when its roof was blown off during the

Venetian siege. I would support Elgin's rights to the sculptures even if he had not acted under the full knowledge and permission of the Ottoman authorities in removing them. Better such treasures survive in the private ownership of a man who appreciates them than be destroyed by an empire that does not." He turned to Randolph. "As a professor of antiquities, surely you agree?"

"Having seen the sculptures, I cannot imagine where a private individual—even an earl such as Lord Elgin—would display them for his own enjoyment. They require an enormous amount of space. As it is, the museum plans to build a new gallery for them, if Parliament ever finishes its negotiations and enquiries."

"What of smaller artifacts?" Sir Laurence asked. "Are they not better off intact as the personal property of a connoisseur than seized and squandered by unenlightened vandals?"

"Certainly. Not every relic in the world need belong to a museum. Many artifacts were created as personal possessions. Why should they not remain so?" Randolph paused, then added, "If obtained legally, of course. I cannot countenance theft, either direct or through the circumvention of authority."

"Nor could I, of course," Sir Laurence said. "But given circumstances similar to Lord Elgin's, I would have done the same. Would not you, Miss Darcy?"

Georgiana appeared surprised to have her opinion solicited. "I cannot imagine ever finding myself in such a position. But if I were, I should like to think I would act to preserve artifacts from either destruction or theft."

The conversation wandered from there to other subjects, as any conversation with Professor Randolph is wont to do. When the evening ended, Sir Laurence and his sister invited Georgiana, Darcy, and Elizabeth to dine with them later in the week.

Yes, Elizabeth thought as she prepared to retire, from Georgiana's standpoint, the evening was a resounding success.

Nineteen

"Having long had as much money as he could spend, nothing to wish for on the side of avarice or indulgence, he has been gradually learning to pin his happiness upon the consequence he is heir to. . . . He cannot bear the idea of not being Sir William."
— Mrs. Smith, speaking of Mr. William Elliot, Persuasion

I do not understand why Anne was asked to stand as Alfred's godmother, and I was not," Elizabeth overheard one of the Elliots say as she, Darcy, and Georgiana joined the queue of guests waiting to be acknowledged by Sir Walter and his family at Alfred's christening celebration. The religious rite complete, the witnesses—and, judging from the number of guests arriving, a good many others who had not been at the church—now converged upon the Assembly Rooms for a fete so extravagant that all other venues in Lyme (to say nothing of the bounds of good taste) were insufficient to accommodate it.

Sir Walter had enlisted all five godparents to join him and Miss Elliot in greeting the company, that his guests might be sufficiently impressed; he also insisted that little Walter Alfred Henry Arthur Elliot be present for all to admire. The slighted would-be godmother, whom, based on her resemblance to Sir Walter, Elizabeth took to be the baronet's youngest daughter, stood at the end of the receiving line with a gentleman Elizabeth assumed was her husband.

"I have been married much longer and have two children, while my sister has been married but months," the affronted speaker continued. For all her professed domestic experience, she appeared fairly young, perhaps a year or two older than Elizabeth. "What does Anne bring to the godmother's office, of a mother's feelings and sense of duty, that I could not?"

"Mary," her husband said in a low voice, "when we learned Mrs. Clay was in the family way, you declared that you would have nothing to do with the child."

"What does that signify? I still should have been asked, and you should have, too. You have been part of the family far longer than Captain Wentworth."

Further discussion between the couple was drowned out by a cry—the latest of many from the guest of honor. Alfred had cried during his baptismal rite. He had cried upon leaving the church. He had cried upon arrival at the Assembly Rooms. Indeed, the celebrated Elliot heir cried so often and so vehemently that he was at considerable risk of being ejected from his own party.

Sir Walter was not pleased. Clearly, he had expected better behavior from the week-old future baronet. While he might tolerate his son's wails in the privacy of their own lodgings, the public display was an embarrassment, particularly as the infantile protests took place under the judgmental gaze of Lady Dalrymple, to whom Sir Walter offered repeated apologies.

Miss Elliot was even more displeased. When Lady Dalrymple had attempted to hand off Alfred to his eldest sister, he had baptized Miss Elliot with a bit of his breakfast. Miss Elliot now had a damp stain on the front of her gown which a hastily borrowed fichu could not effectively cover as she strove to greet her guests in a dignified manner.

And so Alfred had been passed down the phalanx of godmothers and sisters with each new outburst. Having exhausted the patience of his more exalted patrons, he was now handed off to the last of his godmothers just as Elizabeth was being formally introduced to her: Anne Wentworth, second daughter of Sir Walter Elliot, and wife of the rather handsome Captain Frederick Wentworth, who stood beside her.

Unlike her predecessors—who had awkwardly held Alfred at the maximum distance possible from their own fine attire while they forced the future baronet to face the press of well-wishing strangers— Anne settled the overwhelmed infant against her chest, his head on her shoulder, his countenance turned away from the crowd. As her hand stroked his back, Alfred quieted.

Captain Wentworth greeted Darcy congenially, the unusual nature of their initial meeting having done more to advance accord between them than would have weeks of stilted drawing room conversation. Mrs. Wentworth acknowledged him with equal warmth. Darcy, in turn, introduced the couple to Elizabeth and Georgiana.

"It is a pleasure to meet you," Mrs. Wentworth said. "The Harvilles speak of you with great regard, not only for your recent rescue of their son, but also the kindness you showed to Mrs. Clay. I understand we have you to thank for Alfred's safe delivery."

Elizabeth gazed across the room, to where the Harvilles drank lemonade with a cluster of individuals whom she guessed to be fellow officers. Lieutenant St. Clair was among them. She was glad to see that Sir Walter had, despite their being "naval people," demonstrated the grace to invite to Alfred's christening the couple in whose home his child had entered the world, and the man who had helped carry the injured mother there. "If that is what the Harvilles told you, they were too modest about their own role." Elizabeth turned back to the Wentworths. "Lady Elliot could not have known a better nurse than Mrs. Harville, nor a more compassionate household in which to spend her final hours."

A shadow passed across Mrs. Wentworth's expression, and Elizabeth regretted her statement. "Forgive me," she added quickly. "I did not intend to mention her death at an event intended to celebrate life."

"No—it is only that I am unused to hearing 'Lady Elliot' in reference to anyone but my own mother."

Elizabeth now wanted to bite her careless tongue. She hoped she had not offended Anne Wentworth.

Lady Russell, who stood on Anne's other side, heard her statement and turned to her. "Though the second Lady Elliot may have produced the heir, your dear mother shall always hold superior claim to the title 'lady.'"

Mrs. Wentworth thanked the older woman and turned back to Elizabeth's party with a friendly look that assured Elizabeth that she had not given offense.

"I believe I also have you to thank for the assistance rendered to my friend Mrs. Smith the day before yesterday," Mrs. Wentworth said to Elizabeth and Georgiana. "She told me that two ladies named Darcy helped her after she fell on the beach."

"We were glad to have been of use," Georgiana said.

"Is Mrs. Smith all right following the incident?" Elizabeth asked. "She appeared fine when she left us."

"She is. In fact, she felt well enough this morning that she plans to join me and Captain Wentworth here; we expect her to arrive any time now. I know she would enjoy talking with you again."

"I will watch for her arrival," Elizabeth said, "for I would enjoy speaking with her again, too."

The press of other guests moved the Darcys through the remainder of the receiving line at a pace which allowed for no more than perfunctory acknowledgments of introductions. They formally met Lady Dalrymple, Sir Basil, the slighted Mary Musgrove (indeed Sir Walter's youngest daughter) and her husband, Mr. Charles Musgrove. They then found themselves at liberty to circulate.

It was hot in the Rooms. The number of occupants only increased the August heat that had stolen inside along with them, and sunshine poured through a large window that overlooked the sea. Lemonade had been set out, and Darcy went to retrieve some for the ladies.

Elizabeth had not anticipated knowing many of their fellow guests, but discovered that in addition to the Harvilles and Lieutenant St. Clair, she recognized quite a few others. Mr. Shepherd, apparently not illustrious enough a personage to merit a place in the receiving line—he was only the guest of honor's grandfather, after all—was present with Alfred's brothers, Mrs. Clay's older two boys. Elizabeth judged the boys to be perhaps eight and ten, dressed in mourning as deep as that of Mrs. Clay's father. The family tree had not been kind in planting the seeds of their appearance. The elder boy bore his mother's freckles and crooked tooth, while the younger had shockingly red hair which, for Alfred's sake, Elizabeth hoped he had inherited from his father's side. The boys had stationed themselves beside the refreshment table, a proximity ideal for sneaking rout-cakes each time Mr. Shepherd turned his head.

In the opposite corner, Mr. William Elliot observed the room and its occupants. He wore merely a black armband in acknowledgment of Lady Elliot's passing. The minimal display of mourning for so recent a death declared to the world that he considered his connexion to the deceased only a distant one—a far cry from his efforts just days ago to take custody of her newborn son.

Darcy returned with three glasses of lemonade. Elizabeth gratefully accepted the one he handed her.

"Mr. Elliot is here." She nodded in the gentleman's direction. "Given the scandalous nature of his relationship with Alfred's mother, I am surprised Sir Walter invited him."

"I am more surprised that he accepted," Darcy replied. "The invitation was actually a shrewd move on Sir Walter's part. His marriage to Mrs. Clay thwarted any legal claim Mr. Elliot could make to Alfred or the estate—Alfred was born into a legitimate marriage, however tardily that union was formed—yet socially, the question of the child's paternity remains fuel for gossip. By boldly including Mr. Elliot in Alfred's christening celebration, Sir Walter publicly rejects any speculation regarding the true paternity of his heir, and at the same time reminds his rival that he will now never inherit the baronetcy."

"Meanwhile, the death of the child's mother apparently means little to either Sir Walter or Mr. Elliot." Elizabeth sipped her lemonade. It was tepid, which only dropped Sir Walter further in her esteem.

"I think I am glad not to have met this Mr. Elliot," Georgiana said. "It sounds as if he would never have borne the title of 'sir' as honorably as another baronet in this room."

"Sir Laurence is here?" Elizabeth had not spied him among the guests, but doubted Georgiana meant Sir Walter or Sir Basil.

"Yes, with his sister. They are over there, just behind that gentleman wearing the mourning band." She squinted. "Why, I believe that is the man who brushed past me on the Cobb the morning of Lady Elliot's accident."

Elizabeth and Darcy followed Georgiana's gaze. The only person near Sir Laurence who wore an armband was Mr. Elliot.

Darcy's countenance reflected puzzlement. "When did Mr. Elliot pass us that morning? I did not meet him until after you had returned to our lodgings with Lily-Anne."

"Is *that* man Mr. Elliot? I saw him before the accident."

Upon this announcement, all of Elizabeth's doubts about the nature of Lady Elliot's fall resurfaced. "Georgiana, precisely where did you see Mr. Elliot on the Cobb, and what was he doing?"

"He was on the upper wall. We had just arrived and ascended the steps—you and my brother were distracted by Lily-Anne. He walked right past us, so absorbed by his own thoughts that he would have bumped into me had I not stepped aside. Even then, I do not think he noticed me."

Sir Laurence and Miss Ashford, having spotted Georgiana, now approached. "Do you mind if I leave you for a while?" Georgiana asked Elizabeth and Darcy.

"Not at all," Elizabeth said. "Doubtless you would rather discuss any number of subjects with a handsome baronet than Mr. Elliot's presence on the Cobb with me."

Georgiana's smile held a hint of coyness. "Perhaps." She happily went to meet her friends, leaving Darcy and Elizabeth to themselves.

"So," Elizabeth said in a voice meant for only Darcy to hear, "Mr. Elliot was on the Cobb near the time of Lady Elliot's accident—an accident that could well have taken Alfred's life in addition to his mother's." She met Darcy's gaze and knew she did not need to state the rest aloud. *And that, if it had, would have secured Mr. Elliot the inheritance he has now lost.* "When you met him, did he say anything to suggest he had been on the Cobb earlier that day?"

"On the contrary, he gave every indication that he had not, although one of the dockworkers thought he had seen him talking to Lady Elliot that morning. Georgiana's account, however, suggests that he was leaving the seawall when he passed my sister—which was before we saw Lady Elliot still very much alive."

"Then why should Mr. Elliot prevaricate about his presence on the Cobb before the accident? His conduct that day leaves much to be explained."

Elizabeth studied Mr. Elliot. He had been very eager to take possession of Mrs. Clay's baby after his birth—but what had been his feelings toward the child before it? He had not been attached enough to mother or child to marry Mrs. Clay and legitimize their relationship, as Sir Walter had done.

"The dockworker said Mr. Elliot and Mrs. Clay argued," Elizabeth continued. "I wonder whether she told him she had married Sir Walter."

"He appeared surprised by the news when we told him at the Harvilles' house."

"Yes—*appeared*. What if he already knew? What if the subject occupying his thoughts when he brushed past Georgiana was the revelation that Mrs. Clay was now Lady Elliot, and the child she carried was now Sir Walter's heir? Mrs. Clay's final words were 'Elliot' and 'pushed.' It is possible—perhaps not probable, but possible—that after Georgiana saw him, he circled back on the lower Cobb, ascended Granny's Teeth, and finished the argument in a manner meant to ensure the child did not live to usurp Mr. Elliot's claim to the baronetcy."

It was almost incomprehensible to Elizabeth that anybody could be so cold-blooded as to deliberately take the life of a child who stood in the way of succession. Yet history had proven otherwise; one had only to recall the two princes in the Tower to understand that childhood and innocence offer no protection from adult greed and ambition. And to realize that, though Alfred survived his mother's fall, he might not yet survive the circumstances of his birth. So long as he lived, he was the sole obstacle—presently an utterly helpless obstacle—to an inheritance somebody else had been anticipating for three decades.

"We cannot level accusations against a respectable member of society based solely upon conjecture we have drawn from the utterances of a barely coherent woman on her deathbed and a barely articulate child at play—however pitiable the former, and however intelligent we might believe our daughter to be," Darcy said. "I am more disturbed by his potential motives for trying to seize custody of Alfred after the accident than I am convinced that Mr. Elliot caused it. If he did circle back on the lower Cobb, as you suggest, would not someone have seen him?"

Elizabeth glanced toward the main doors of the room. A sedan chair had just arrived; Sir Walter was directing its bearers to deposit its occupant in an out-of-the-way corner.

"Perhaps someone did."

Twenty

*M*uch to her father's obvious displeasure, Mrs. Wentworth abandoned her receiving line duties, transferring Alfred to her younger sister and following the sedan chair to the unpopulated corner to which Sir Walter had sent it. As Mrs. Wentworth assisted its emerging passenger, Elizabeth turned to Darcy.

"I am going to retrieve more lemonade."

"We have not yet finished these," Darcy said, "and the quality hardly inspires a yearning for more."

"It is not for us. It is for Mrs. Smith."

"I see." He, too, looked toward the corner. The sedan chair and its bearers had departed; Mrs. Wentworth was now helping Mrs. Smith toward a seat beside a large, round table. "Would you like me to come with you?"

Elizabeth considered a moment. Women talk very differently amongst themselves than when gentlemen are present, and she had already established a rapport with the widow. It might be easier to guide the conversation toward the accident without Darcy's company.

"I will introduce you, then perhaps you could go seek the Har-villes' conversation."

She fetched two glasses of lemonade and led Darcy to the la-dies. Mrs. Smith greeted Elizabeth's arrival with the delight of encountering an old friend. "Mrs. Darcy! What a pleasure to see you here! I told Anne about the kindness you and Miss Darcy ren-dered me."

"It is a pleasure to see you again, too." Elizabeth introduced Darcy, whose acquaintance Mrs. Smith entered with equal happiness.

Elizabeth set the lemonade on the table and helped Mrs. Went-worth settle Mrs. Smith into her seat. Darcy, after determining his assistance was not needed, and exchanging a few pleasantries with Mrs. Smith on the subject of the fineness of the day and the beauty of Lyme, excused himself on the pretext of checking on his sister.

Elizabeth chose a chair beside Mrs. Smith. Mrs. Wentworth took another, but perched on its edge in the manner of someone not en-tirely committed to remaining seated. Her attention was divided between their party and the receiving line, where Sir Walter was casting glances at her that proclaimed his desire for her to return to her greeting duties. That he was neglecting his own obligations as a host by ignoring Mrs. Smith did not seem to trouble him.

"Did you have a comfortable ride here?" Mrs. Wentworth asked Mrs. Smith.

"I did—quite smooth. Sometimes the chair men do not take as much care, and one gets jostled or slides forward going down the steep hills."

"You have shown such steady improvement in the two months you have been with us in Lyme, that eventually I hope to see you walk anywhere you wish entirely under your own power, with no need of a chair to transport you."

A smile spread across Mrs. Smith's face. "I look forward to that day, as well."

The receiving line once more drew Mrs. Wentworth's attention. Alfred had recommenced crying, and though Mary appeared to have no patience for him, she rejected an apparent offer of assistance from Captain Wentworth. Mrs. Wentworth's gaze shuttled between the baby and Mrs. Smith, and Elizabeth could read in her expression how divided was her sense of obligation. Even were Alfred in more sympathetic arms, Mrs. Wentworth nonetheless ought to return to her receiving line duties, and even were Mrs. Smith in perfect health, Anne's already slighted friend ought not be abandoned.

"Mrs. Smith, would you care for some lemonade?" Elizabeth handed one glass to the widow and offered the other to Mrs. Wentworth.

"Oh," Mrs. Smith said, "how very thoughtful! It is quite warm in here."

Mrs. Wentworth looked at the glass as if she very much wanted to accept it, then glanced back at the receiving line. Alfred's cries increased.

"Anne," Mrs. Smith said, "if you need to return to your duties, I will be quite all right here."

"Are you certain?"

"I have a comfortable chair and lemonade. Go attend your new godson."

"She also has my company," Elizabeth said. "I would enjoy the opportunity for us to become better acquainted."

Elizabeth's assurance decided Mrs. Wentworth. She returned to her place in the receiving line, where her sister Mary lost no time in delivering the fussing Alfred back to her. Captain Wentworth helped her adjust the child's long christening robe, which had become twisted round his legs during the transfer. Before long, Mrs. Wentworth had soothed the baby back into silence.

Elizabeth turned to Mrs. Smith. "After we parted the other day, I realized that I might have seen you before—taking the air, as you said—on the Cobb."

"It is one of my favorite spots," Mrs. Smith replied. "Soon after arriving in Lyme, I expressed a desire to go out upon it—an idle desire, not one I imagined would be realized anytime soon. Due to my difficulties walking, I expected to enjoy the seawall for some while only as a sight from shore. Captain Wentworth, however, immediately ordered a chair to take me out on the lower wall. Once there, he borrowed a barrel from one of the quay warehouses so that I could leave the confining cabinet of the chair and sit in the open air. I cannot tell you how invigorating it was to feel the sea breeze upon me—it blows onshore, of course, but not like it does on the Cobb. When he saw the pleasure that first outing occasioned, and the strength it restored to my spirits, he engaged the chair to collect me daily, and secured the harbormaster's permission for a bench to be left along the wall for me and Nurse Rooke to sit upon."

"Indeed, then, I believe it was you I saw seated on the bench last week, the morning of the storm that caused the ship explosion."

"What a dreadful morning that was, for so many people! The ship and its crew lost, not to mention poor Mrs. Clay's accident."

Elizabeth was pleased that Mrs. Smith had introduced the very subject she most wanted to discuss. "Did you witness her fall?" Perhaps the widow would be able to put her doubts to rest—or provide information to confirm them.

"We did not stay as long as usual that day," Mrs. Smith replied. "We left when the atmosphere turned unpleasant. I understand from Anne, however, that you and your husband are the couple who found Mrs. Clay. You poor dear—what a start that must have given you, seeing her lying on the pavement like that! Did *you* witness her fall?"

"No, we came upon her afterward. We did not even know who she was until Mr. Elliot identified her later."

"Ah, yes—Mr. Elliot." Mrs. Smith cast a disdainful gaze across the room, to where Mr. Elliot engaged in conversation with Lieutenant St. Clair. "I should be amazed that he has the effrontery to show himself here today, having carried on such a public affair with Mrs. Clay. But I have known him so long that his behavior has lost the power to astonish me. So did hers."

"You knew them both?" Although Elizabeth was disappointed by Mrs. Smith's lack of information about the accident itself, the mention of Mr. Elliot gave Elizabeth hope that the widow might prove a source of intelligence after all.

"These twelve years. Mr. Elliot was a particular friend of my husband when we married, and he introduced us to Mr. and Mrs. Clay. When Mr. Elliot wed not long after, we three couples became intimate companions, as comfortable in each other's houses as our own. Together we enjoyed all London had to offer the young, carefree, and affluent." She sighed. "I have been none of those things since becoming widowed, and as a result have had little recent intercourse with Mr. Elliot and Mrs. Clay."

"I am sorry to hear it," Elizabeth said. "It must have been painful to lose such close friends due to circumstances you could not control."

"In ways you cannot guess. It is in fact Mr. Elliot who is responsible for a great many of my present difficulties. When my husband died, his affairs were out of order—a terribly complex business, property in the West Indies enmeshed in legal tangles—and Mr. Elliot, his designated executor, would not trouble himself to straighten out the matter. Fortunately, Captain Wentworth is now acting on my behalf. He has only just initiated his enquiries, but I trust that in time he will resolve everything. He is a veritable knight gallant."

"How long ago did you lose your husband?"

"It is approaching three years. I have a miniature of him in this locket—would you like to see it?"

Elizabeth indulged her. Mr. Smith had been a pleasant-looking man, with a kind face, though his hair was rather red for Elizabeth's taste. "He was very handsome."

"His Jamaican plantation proved the death of him—he traveled there on business that he thought best handled in person, and returned so ill and weak that he died within a se'nnight of coming home. It is a source of deep regret to me that his last months were spent in the company of his erstwhile friend Mr. Elliot, and not the wife who doted on him till the end."

"Your husband traveled to the West Indies?" Elizabeth repeated. "And Mr. Elliot accompanied him?" Elizabeth would not allow herself to become too hopeful about what she was hearing. Smith was a common name—as common as they came. Surely it was mere coincidence that this woman's late husband shared that name with the plantation owner who had been a passenger on one of the merchant ships under escort by the *Magna Carta*.

The plantation owner who had been traveling with a future baronet.

She now wished she had not sent Darcy off, so that he could hear this intelligence himself. She looked for him in the room, and saw that the receiving line had finally dispersed. He was now in conversation with Captain Wentworth, while Mrs. Wentworth, Alfred still in arms, was headed back toward Elizabeth and Mrs. Smith. Apparently, neither Sir Walter nor any of the other dignitaries had demonstrated any interest in relieving Anne Wentworth of her tiny charge.

Sir Walter, in fact, along with Miss Elliot, was presently engaged in conversation with Georgiana and the Ashfords. Elizabeth could not imagine what had drawn such an unlikely party together, until she observed that Miss Elliot paid particular notice to Sir Laurence, attending the baronet's discourse with keen interest, and smiling more than Elizabeth had witnessed in all the time spent in Miss Elliot's company heretofore.

Aha.

She recognized what Miss Elliot was about, but could do nothing for Georgiana at the moment. She needed to give Mrs. Smith her full concentration.

"Yes, my husband and Mr. Elliot traveled to Jamaica together," Mrs. Smith replied. "Mr. Smith was not in heart or mind a man of business, and lived too long under the notion that money came as easily as it was spent. Though he never said as much to me, I suspect the financial difficulties that now sequester the plantation had already begun, and Mr. Elliot accompanied him as an advisor. Mr. Elliot studied law at Oxford, and my husband was often guided by him—to our misfortune, as Mr. Elliot encouraged us to live as extravagantly as he. Mr. Clay, too, followed Mr. Elliot's lead. I believe he possessed even less business acumen than my husband did."

"Is the West Indian property a sugar plantation?"

"It is, indeed, and it produces the finest sugar you can imagine. Oh, how spoiled I was! We had a French pastry cook who made the most exquisite cakes and confections—our dinner parties were worth attending for the dessert alone. Now I consider it a luxury to have sugar in my tea."

Elizabeth gave up trying to subdue her excitement. She instead gave it full rein. Lieutenant Fitzwilliam's diary had said that Captain Tourner had frequently entertained three gentlemen passengers from the *Montego.* "Did Mr. Clay, by chance, also accompany your husband to Jamaica?"

"No—he had no reason to go, and every reason to stay. Someone needed to keep an eye on his wife." Mrs. Smith cast a glance at Mrs. Wentworth, who was almost upon them, and lowered her voice. "Perhaps it is in poor taste to speak ill of the dead so soon after they have departed this world, but Mrs. Clay was not a faithful spouse. The only thing modest about her life was the size of Mr. Clay's fortune, which she considered too small. She coveted finer things, and solicited the attention of men who would give them to her. She had a particular fondness for naval officers flush with newly won prize money. They would spend it on her, then sail off to their next port, leaving her to enjoy their gifts with no obligation or troublesome entanglements."

"Poor Mr. Clay," Elizabeth said. "Did he know?"

"You have a kind heart, Mrs. Darcy. Do not, however, waste too much of your pity on Mr. Clay. He himself died in flagrante delicto. And not with his wife—with Mr. Elliot's."

Twenty-one

"There is always something offensive in the details of cunning."
—Anne Elliot, *Persuasion*

$\mathcal{D}$arcy had not been long in conversation with Captain Wentworth when Mr. Elliot interrupted them.

"Mr. Darcy—a word, if you will?"

"Certainly." Darcy's conversations and conjectures with Elizabeth regarding Mrs. Clay had left him wanting to speak with Mr. Elliot again, and he was glad for the opportunity to do so at the other gentleman's initiative.

"Shall I withdraw?" Wentworth asked.

"No, my good captain," Mr. Elliot said. "Do stay. I am merely wondering how little Master Elliot gets on, and you might be as well able as Mr. Darcy to satisfy my curiosity."

Probably better, if either Darcy or Captain Wentworth were inclined to divulge any information about the infant to Mr. Elliot—which Darcy was not. Nor was Wentworth, judging from the coolness that overtook his demeanor at Elliot's address.

"He appears to thrive." Darcy offered nothing more.

"I am glad to hear it. I have been concerned for his welfare—poor, motherless child—and Sir Walter has not been forthcoming in response to my notes of enquiry. I was relieved to receive an invitation to this celebration, where I could observe him directly."

"Does your concern derive from a particular cause?" Captain Wentworth asked.

"Not beyond Sir Walter's general state of affairs, with which I am sure you are well acquainted, now that you have joined the family."

Captain Wentworth did not respond, only regarded Mr. Elliot with an expression that Darcy imagined could wordlessly bring an entire ship's crew into line.

Mr. Elliot, however, proceeded undaunted. "I am afraid Sir Walter's heir will inherit nothing but a title, as the present baronet has spent the estate nearly into bankruptcy. That Kellynch Hall is being leased out while Sir Walter retrenches in Bath is an embarrassment to the Elliot name, even if his tenant does happen to be Admiral Croft. At one time I had hoped to exert the influence of a son-in-law to bring what remained of his fortune under better regulation and preserve something of it for future generations, but now that you have taken on that role—not to mention that of godfather to the heir—I wish you luck. You will need it."

"How very magnanimous of you. Perhaps now that Sir Walter's fortune no longer need absorb your attention, you could turn it toward Mrs. Smith's." He gestured in the widow's direction.

"Is that she?" Mr. Elliot peered toward the corner for a long minute, studying the woman in tête-à-tête with Elizabeth. "I must say, she has not aged well. She appears much older than thirty—in fact, she hardly looks herself."

"Is that *she*?" Captain Wentworth repeated incredulously. "Do you mean to tell me that in three years, you have not once called upon her in person to discuss her husband's estate?"

"I see no purpose in such a discussion."

"Fortunately for her, she now has a friend who does," Wentworth said, "and since you have not been forthcoming in response to *my* notes of enquiry regarding Mr. Smith's West Indian property, I have dispatched letters to both London and Spanish Town. Your cooperation, however, could save us all considerable time and trouble, and expedite the settlement of his estate—a matter too long unresolved. That poor good lady—"

"That 'good lady' is a harpy who cannot accept the fact that her husband mismanaged their affairs," he said sharply. "She must blame someone, and so she blames me. I was Smith's friend, not his solicitor nor his steward. I offered him counsel when he asked for it, but he was a grown man responsible for his own choices. He spent beyond their income and jeopardized his estate as a result—a sad truth, but London's clubs are filled with gentlemen who have done so. Your wife has certainly borne witness to the tragedy of a prosperous estate gradually squandered to ruin."

"I take this to mean that I should not expect any information from you regarding the present legal status of the property?"

"There is nothing to be said about it. There is nothing to be *done* about it—by me, by you, by anybody. If you truly wish to act as a friend to Mrs. Smith, leave the matter rest. Your time and effort are better spent encouraging her to look ahead, not back, and in devising some other provision for her maintenance rather than allowing her to continue to pin her hopes on recovering foreign income that will never materialize."

"Thank you for your counsel, Mr. Elliot." Despite the closeness of the room, the air immediately surrounding Captain Wentworth held a chill. "Depend upon it, I shall act in Mrs. Smith's best interest."

Distress shadowed Georgiana's face as she and the Ashfords talked with Sir Walter and Miss Elliot.

Rather, Sir Walter and his daughter talked, commandeering the conversation away from Georgiana and directing it almost exclusively toward Sir Laurence. Miss Ashford was granted the indulgence of an occasional interjection.

". . . three godparents of name—the same number as the Prince Regent—and five in all," Sir Walter said.

The older baronet's painfully evident attempt to impress received polite acknowledgment from the bemused Sir Laurence. "Doubtless, Alfred will benefit from such ample sponsorship."

"How many godparents have you, Sir Laurence?" Miss Elliot asked.

"Only three," he replied. "The Duke of Manchester, and the Earl and Countess of Sommerfeld."

"The godson of a duke!" Though the exclamation was Miss Elliot's, both she and her father were euphoric at the news. Oblivious to the fact that their lofty connexions had been utterly trumped, they exalted in Sir Laurence's as if they were their own. "Are you on intimate terms with His Grace?"

"Not particularly, since he lives so far away."

"My brother did, however, visit him several years ago," Miss Ashford added.

"He is a valuable connexion," Sir Walter said reverently. "You should strive to maintain it."

Sir Laurence accepted Sir Walter's social advice with great civility, though it was neither needed nor wanted.

"And you enjoy the patronage of Lord Sommerfeld, as well." Miss Elliot regarded Sir Laurence as if he were the heir to the throne.

"My godfather was an earl," Georgiana ventured.

Considering the interest Sir Walter and Miss Elliot took in anybody's connexions, Georgiana's announcement ought to have generated the same excitement as Sir Laurence's had. Miss Elliot, however, looked at Georgiana as if she very much wished Miss Darcy would find some other christening to attend, preferably in Derbyshire, and returned her attention to Sir Laurence. "Have you met our future baronet?"

"I have not yet had the pleasure. He was rather beside himself when we arrived."

"Oh, do not let his earlier behavior color your impression of him. He is calm now." She smiled. "Come, I shall introduce you and Miss Ashford."

"That is not necessary. We can wait for another occasion—"

"Why wait? He is such a sweet child—I simply adore him. You must allow me to present my new brother to you—a future baronet to a current one." She turned to her father. "Sir, you should come, too—three baronets."

"An excellent idea," said Sir Walter.

Without waiting for a reply from Sir Laurence, Miss Elliot and her father began walking. After a few steps, she turned to see whether Sir Laurence and his sister followed.

Sir Laurence had no choice. To refuse would embarrass both his hosts and himself. He looked at Georgiana apologetically. "Will you come with us, Miss Darcy?"

Though stunned by Miss Elliot's maneuver, Georgiana had enough presence of mind to decline Sir Laurence's attempt to include her. She harbored no desire to provoke a rival that she had not, until this hour, realized she had. "Thank you, but I think I will get more lemonade instead."

"I will look for you later, then."

She nodded. Sir Laurence took his sister's arm, and Georgiana watched them walk off. Miss Elliot smiled victoriously as they joined her.

"It is not worth your trouble," said a male voice behind Georgiana.

She turned round to discover Lieutenant St. Clair. He was in civilian clothes today, as he had been when she had first seen him. He stood near a wooden column, one of six that dotted the room at regular intervals to uphold the ceiling.

"I beg your pardon?"

"The lemonade." He had a glass in his hand, but stepped forward to set it on a nearby table. "It is too warm to provide refreshment."

"I know." Despite having no interest in her own half-empty glass, Georgiana sipped from it and glanced back at Sir Laurence. Miss Elliot had not gone directly to Mrs. Wentworth, who held Alfred; she had instead paused halfway across the room, and the party was now in conversation again. Georgiana watched them, her expression apprehensive.

"For the record," St. Clair said, "I do not have a single titled godparent."

His statement drew her attention back to him. "It is a wonder, then, that you were admitted to this grandiose affair."

"I keep the fact a closely guarded secret." His mouth quirked, and his eyes held irreverent liveliness. "Pray, do not expose me to Miss Elliot, or I might be shown the door."

His entreaty elicited the beginning of a smile. "I assure you, Lieutenant, your confidence is safely entrusted."

He offered to fetch her more lemonade if she truly wanted it. She declined, setting her unwanted glass beside his. "I would much rather hear how you managed to survive all these years with such shockingly ordinary connexions."

"I am terribly ill equipped, am I not? But my godparents are a most beloved aunt and uncle—two of many. In assorted relations, I am plentifully endowed."

"Have you numerous siblings, as well?" she asked.

"What would you consider 'numerous'?"

"Having grown up with only a single brother, I would deem three abundant."

"I have seven."

Her eyes widened. "Seven! All brothers?"

"Three sisters. The eldest is married and lives in London; the other two are still at home."

"I have often wished I had more siblings. But seven! Have you also a generous number of nieces and nephews?"

"Not quite a full dozen—at least, at last count," he said with a fond look in his eyes. "Incidentally, I am godfather to two of them. We shall have to hope they grow up none the worse for the connexion."

As they spoke, the sun's angle shifted just enough that now its rays lanced the window and raised the temperature in the room still more. Georgiana withdrew a fan from her reticule and waved it slowly. "Whatever is it like, being part of such a large family?"

"When we are all together, rather noisy." He paused, his expression becoming wistful. "But in the best of ways."

"You missed them, while you were so long overseas." It was not a question; she could read the truth in his countenance.

"Very much. I have missed my parents, as well. They all write often, as do I, but it is not the same as being in their houses, enjoying spontaneous conversation and mirth and even the occasional disagreement."

"Have you visited any of your family since returning to England?"

"No, I—there are other matters to which I must attend first."

"You are fortunate to have your parents still alive. You should visit them while you are able."

"Yours, I take it, are not?"

"My father died eight years ago, and my mother . . ." The fan stopped, and her voice grew softer. "Giving birth to me."

"Oh, Miss Darcy!" His expression was one of genuine sympathy. "Forgive me. Had I known the circumstances of your mother's death, I never would have brought up so painful a subject."

"You could not have realized. And I have had nineteen years to make my peace with it. Still, I often wonder how it would have been to grow up under her influence, to have her with me even now."

"Have you spoken with your brother of these feelings?"

"We speak of our mother, but I do not speak of her loss. As much as I regret that I never knew her, he did, and I feel responsible for having taken her from him."

His brows drew together. "Surely he does not blame you?"

"Oh, heavens no. I keep silent because he is such a conscientious brother that it would grieve him to know I have such thoughts."

"It grieves me to know them, and I have only just met you."

A flush crept into her cheeks as self-consciousness overtook her. "Forgive me for having burdened you with such a confidence. I—I do not know what possessed me to reveal it to so new an acquaintance."

"I am not burdened," he said in all sincerity. "And I assure you, Miss Darcy, it is safely entrusted."

"Nevertheless—"

Lieutenant St. Clair's gaze suddenly shifted to a spot behind her shoulder. Georgiana turned to see her brother approaching. He reached them in a few strides and looked from one to the other.

"Good afternoon, Lieutenant."

St. Clair greeted Darcy amiably while Georgiana composed herself.

"I am glad to have spotted you over here," Darcy said to his sister. "I lost sight of you for a while." Again, he glanced between them, wondering what he had interrupted. Georgiana's flustered demeanor suggested that the lieutenant had been speaking in an inappropriate manner. "Is all well?"

"Oh! Yes—quite," Georgiana said. "The rest of my party abandoned me, but Lieutenant St. Clair has been so good as to ensure I was not left entirely alone."

"We were just discussing the subject of godparents," St. Clair said.

"I see." Darcy, in fact, did not see at all how such an innocuous topic could unsettle his sister, and again presumed the lieutenant's manner must be at fault. "Well, thank you, Lieutenant. I can attend my sister now."

The sea officer knew a dismissal when he heard one. Lieutenant St. Clair looked at Georgiana once more. "I enjoyed our conversation, Miss Darcy."

When the officer was out of hearing, Darcy turned to her. "Was he troubling you?"

She opened her fan. "Not at all. He was a perfect gentleman."

"You appear upset."

She watched St. Clair blend into the crowd and shook her head. "Only warm. It is too close in this room." Her fan moved rapidly. "Come, let us find more lemonade."

Twenty-two

"The manœuvres of selfishness and duplicity must ever be revolting, but I have heard nothing which really surprises me."
—Anne Elliot, Persuasion

*M*rs. Smith's history of her acquaintance with Mrs. Clay was interrupted by the arrival of Anne Wentworth and Alfred. The exhausted heir had fallen asleep in Mrs. Wentworth's arms, and now dozed peacefully. Elizabeth helped Anne settle into the chair she had been compelled to abandon earlier.

As the new godmother smoothed the infant's robe, Mrs. Smith observed her with approval. "Look how content he is at last, Anne. You are a natural with him."

"Do you truly think so?"

"He could be in no better arms. You are doing very well by him."

For whatever her opinion was worth, Elizabeth agreed. Of all Alfred's blood relations and godparents, the Wentworths seemed the most genuinely interested in his welfare, and Anne the most attuned to his needs.

Mrs. Wentworth had but little time to enjoy the hard-won tranquility of a sleeping baby before Mary Musgrove appeared and sank into a chair beside her sister.

"Well, here you are, Anne—I had wondered where you were

hiding yourself. I declare, I am exhausted—making conversation with all of these people, having to explain that I am *only* Alfred's aunt, not one of his godmothers, since of course they assume I would have been asked. I would much prefer to sit here at leisure, like you, than perform the social duties incumbent upon us as Elliots."

"I am happy to circulate among the guests if you would care to hold Alfred."

"No, thank you. He might wake and start wailing again, and I have been suffering the headache all day. My headaches, you know, are always worse than anybody's. It is all I can do just to sit here talking to you."

"Perhaps you should try seabathing while you are in Lyme," Mrs. Smith suggested. "I have found it beneficial."

"I said that very thing to my husband, but he thinks seabathing ridiculous, with the machines and dippers and all. I went only the once, all the while we were here last November. I did not care for it, but I bathed in Charmouth, not Lyme. I quite imagine that the bathing in Lyme is superior to Charmouth. It must be pleasurable, for so many people go regularly. Even our father seabathes. Have you been, Mrs. Darcy?"

"I have."

"See! Everybody here bathes—everybody except me! Why should I be deprived simply because my husband does not like it? This is always my lot! Whenever there is something desirable going on, I am sure to be excluded."

"Our father goes only because Mr. Edwards urges him," Anne said.

"I do not think I like this new physician of his. He has our father suddenly fearing that he is halfway to his grave. That is the only reason he married Mrs. Clay, you know."

"Mary," Anne said emphatically, casting a pointed look in Elizabeth's direction. Elizabeth took a sip of lemonade and developed a sudden, intense interest in the pattern of the glass.

"Well, it was," Mary continued. "The marriage was beneath him, but he was not going to leave this earth with Mr. Elliot as his heir."

Wanting to relieve Mrs. Wentworth's self-consciousness over Mary's speaking so candidly about family matters in front of a slight acquaintance, Elizabeth rose and went to the window. It offered a lovely view of the beach and the sea, which was calm today, though the sun's brightness through the glass was uncomfortable.

Anne shifted Alfred to her other shoulder. "Our father could not have known the child that Mrs. Clay carried was a boy."

"Oh, he was certain—Mrs. Clay already had two sons, and kept bringing that fact to his attention the whole while she stayed with our father and sister in Bath. Do you not recall? I said once that I wished I had a daughter instead of only sons, because a daughter would surely be better behaved, and Mrs. Clay declared that she was delighted to be the mother of boys, and believed herself incapable of producing anything but sons. Delighted—ha! There she was, living a life of leisure and amusement in Bath, while her boys were back in Kellynch with Mr. Shepherd. So of course when Mrs. Clay came to our father in Lyme, he believed she carried a boy. And of course she convinced him that the child was his, despite her having run off with Mr. Elliot, because nobody was better at flattering our father than she was—how else could a freckled thing like her have seduced him, right under our noses last winter? And of course Mr. Shepherd was able to persuade him to marry her, because our father is used to following Mr. Shepherd's advice." She released a dramatic sigh. "And of course, while Mrs. Clay got everything she wanted, I still have all the care of my own two boisterous sons, with a mother-in-law who spoils them with too many sweets and then leaves me to contend with their misbehavior."

"I would hardly say Mrs. Clay got everything she wanted," Mrs. Wentworth said. "She is dead."

Mary sighed again. "I suppose." Having failed to gain her sister's sympathy, she turned her attention to Elizabeth. "Mrs. Darcy, do you have sons?"

Elizabeth was happy to come away from the heat of the window and sit down again. "No, only a daughter, Lily-Anne."

"A daughter! How fortunate you are. I would do so much better with daughters. They are quiet and mindful, and one can dress them in such pretty clothes. Boys cannot wear clothes five minutes before something is dirty or torn. But husbands always want boys. Mrs. Smith, do you have daughters or sons?"

"I have no children."

"None at all? How very sad. I do not know what I would do without the cheerful sounds of my darlings at play. I suppose your husband was disappointed to have no son."

Mrs. Smith responded with a polite smile, but Elizabeth saw in her eyes that this was a painful subject to her.

Apparently, Mrs. Wentworth, too, sensed Mrs. Smith's discomfort, for she quickly said, "Mary, I wonder if you might do me a favor and suggest to our father that Alfred's nurse be summoned. He begins to stir—I suspect he will wake soon, and when he does, he will be hungry."

Mary, looking rather put-upon, roused herself enough to cast her gaze about for the Elliot patriarch. With a relieved half-smile, she settled back against her chair. "You may offer the suggestion yourself. He comes this way."

Sir Walter approached, trailing in the wake of Miss Elliot, who parted the crowded floor like a ship's figurehead, with Sir Laurence and Miss Ashford in tow.

"Here you are, Anne. Are you monopolizing the guest of honor? Sir Laurence has expressed a desire to meet our little future baronet. Alfred was out of sorts when the Ashfords arrived, but I see he is in better temper now. You have been holding him some time—here, let me take him from you."

"But he is sleeping."

"I can see that." Miss Elliot reached for him.

"Indeed, Miss Elliot, you need not disturb him," Sir Laurence said.

"A sleeping baby is such a heart-moving image that I cannot resist." Miss Elliot snatched Alfred from Anne, lifting him right out of the blanket that had been loosely gathered around him. Strategically positioning him over the stain the infant had previously made on her gown, she attempted to rest him against her shoulder as Anne had done. Hers, however, was an awkward, insecure hold, not at all convincing her audience of her potential as a mother to a different future baronet—which, given that this sudden display of interest in the baby took place before Sir Laurence, Elizabeth recognized as Miss Elliot's true purpose.

"There—see how he snuggles against me? He is such a sweet little thing."

Until that moment, Elizabeth would have wagered a year's worth of pin money that the word "snuggle" was entirely absent from Miss Elliot's vocabulary. As it was, Miss Elliot appeared oblivious to the fact that Alfred was instinctively seeking the soft shoulder from which he had been so abruptly torn, not snuggling into the bony one upon which he had just been thrust. He squirmed, fully wakening, and released a mew that quickly turned into a full, incessant cry.

"There, now . . . little . . . darling." Miss Elliot's steely voice jarred Elizabeth more than the baby's cries. "Do not cry for your sister—"

Miss Elliot's eyes suddenly widened, and her countenance went rigid. She pulled the mewling infant away from herself and thrust him toward Mary. A damp, uneven circle now darkened another portion of her gown; the lower half of Alfred's sported a matching one. "Would you kindly take this child from me?" Her strained voice came through clenched teeth.

Elizabeth, happening to meet Sir Laurence's gaze, saw that she was not alone in working to conceal amusement.

Sir Laurence coughed. "I should . . . go seek Mr. Darcy. My sister and I have not yet spoken with him today. Unless, Miss Elliot, I can be of use to you?"

"No," she said tightly, a scarlet flush creeping across her cheeks faster than the stain on her dress. Alfred, still in her hands, increased both his agitation and his volume. Sir Laurence bowed and withdrew with Miss Ashford.

Miss Elliot looked at her sister sharply. "Mary—"

"Why must I take him? He has already ruined your gown. I should sacrifice mine?"

As the sisters quarreled, Alfred's high-pitched protests continued. Elizabeth itched to take him from Miss Elliot and offer the neglected baby what comfort she could, but she would not insert herself in a family dispute. Thankfully, Mrs. Wentworth stepped forward and reclaimed Alfred. She wrapped the blanket around him and held him close, murmuring soothing words, mindless of whatever indignity her own gown might suffer in consequence.

Miss Elliot looked down at the damp spot on her dress. The black fabric helped diminish its conspicuousness, but it was obvious nonetheless. "Where is Mrs. Logan? What sort of a nurse is she, who cannot even properly apply a napkin?"

"She is in our rooms at the Three Cups," Sir Walter said. "Where else would she be—here, sipping lemonade with her betters? The inn is mere steps away; I told her I would send Alfred to her if she were needed."

Anne's face was incredulous. "Alfred has not fed nor had a fresh napkin since before church?"

"That was but a few hours ago," Sir Walter said.

"It is little wonder he is so irritable." Mary shook her head with an air of superiority. "Honestly," she said to her eldest sister, "one would think you knew nothing about children."

"That is because I do not have any. Yet somehow I have been saddled with responsibility for a small creature that does nothing but cry and ruin my clothes. Perhaps, Mary, since you possess so much more experience with children, you should take Alfred home to live with you."

"At Uppercross Cottage? I am sure our father wants to keep his new heir closer to him than that."

"As a matter of fact," Sir Walter said, "that idea holds merit. We are quite cramped in our rooms here, and even when we return to Bath, a town house offers nothing compared to a country home in space for a growing boy."

Mary suddenly had the look of a chased fox. "The cottage is already too small for our comfort—it is not as if we live in the Great House yet. Our own two boys—"

"Will be perfect companions for Alfred," Miss Elliot said.

". . . consume all my time as it is," Mary finished. "You have *no* idea. I am a slave to their needs from sunrise till bedtime."

"I thought you employ a nursery maid."

"Of course we do."

"Well, then, with Mrs. Logan's assistance, the addition of Alfred will hardly be noticeable," Miss Elliot declared.

Now Mary had the look of a cornered fox. She glanced at her

other sister, hopeful of sympathy from that quarter, but Anne spoke only sibilant whispers as she swayed in a gentle rhythm that abated but could not eradicate the hungry infant's distress. Mary turned an imploring look upon her father. "Anne has stayed with us at Upper-cross. She can tell you how—"

Mary stopped. She glanced once more at Anne, longer this time, her gaze shrewdly contemplative.

"She can tell you how much better it would be for Alfred to live with her."

Anne's rocking and murmurs ceased as she regarded Mary in astonishment.

"Alfred, live with Anne?" Sir Walter sounded even more surprised than Anne appeared.

Miss Elliot seized upon the suggestion. "Yes, of course—Anne! Who better? She is married now, which makes her far more suitable than I to oversee his care."

"Yet she has no children of her own to demand her attention," Mary hastened to add. "She can devote herself fully to Alfred."

"That is true . . ." mused Sir Walter.

"She is his *godmother*, after all," Mary reminded them. "And Captain Wentworth, his godfather. Why, I should think that office alone obliges them to superintend his upbringing and education."

"Indeed, I believe you have something there," Sir Walter said. "Very well, Anne. I grant you permission to take Alfred home with you. I shall send his things to you, including Mrs. Logan, directly after this celebration concludes."

At last, Anne found her voice. "Captain Wentworth and I are to raise Alfred? Are you quite certain, sir?"

"Yes, quite. Think you that I do not know my own mind? I shall have him for visits in Bath when he is old enough, to ensure he is prepared to take his proper place in society. But until then— Oh! Lady Dalrymple is departing. I must go see her off."

"And I must return to the inn to change my gown," Miss Elliot said.

Elizabeth noticed that she did not offer to take Alfred with her, so that his clothes could be changed, too. Sir Walter and Miss Elliot hurried away, the latter smiling smugly (as smugly as possible for a lady so unceremoniously perfumed) at this turn of events. Mary, realizing how narrowly she had escaped the addition of a third noisy boy to her household, found reason to scuttle off, as well.

Elizabeth was stunned. There was no doubt in her mind that the outcome of the discussion she had just witnessed was the best possible result for Alfred; of all the Elliot family, Captain and Mrs. Wentworth appeared the most capable, most conscientious, and most caring guardians Alfred could have. Yet Anne had acquiesced to a life-altering commitment without so much as a single word of dissent. At a minimum, one would expect her to consult her husband before agreeing to raise someone else's child in their home. Whatever would Captain Wentworth say when she told him?

"Well, that went better than you ever could have anticipated," Mrs. Smith said to Anne. "Your entire family thinks it was their idea."

"I dared not speak much for fear they would change their minds." Anne's rocking of Alfred grew more pronounced. The baby was doing a remarkable job of containing himself, given the overstimulation, lack of nourishment, and wet clothes, but it could not be long before his fussing escalated to full-scale wailing.

"Oh, I believe there is little danger of that. They are all congratulating themselves at having dodged unwanted responsibility by foisting it onto you. Captain Wentworth will be impressed."

"I must find him and tell him I am taking Alfred to Mrs. Logan to be fed."

"Allow me to find him for you," Elizabeth offered. "You have your hands full."

Anne smiled. "I do indeed. And, I suppose, shall for some time." She paused. "May I ask you something, Mrs. Darcy?"

"Certainly."

"I understand you accompanied Mr. Shepherd to interview Mrs. Logan. What was your impression of her? I have heard only complaints from my father and sister."

Elizabeth chose her words carefully, not wanting to insult Mrs. Wentworth's family, but wishing to be fair to the wet nurse. "I believe she has a good heart and wants very much to do well by Alfred.

At the same time, she is young and inexperienced. I suspect, therefore, that she lacks the confidence to question orders given by equally inexperienced persons of higher social rank, whereas a veteran nurse might manage matters with more authority."

"I thought as much. My own experience with infants is limited to assisting Mary during her lyings-in."

"You also appear to have sound instincts and a good deal of common sense, which is all I had when my daughter was born. Between you and Mrs. Logan, I believe you will get along fine."

"With Mrs. Smith as our houseguest, we also have her nurse in residence."

"Then Alfred is in excellent hands, not that I ever doubted. He is extremely fortunate to have you and Captain Wentworth as his godparents. So many occupy the role in name only."

"I have been blessed with a good example," Anne said. "Lady Russell has been an attentive godmother to me, taking her duty seriously and fulfilling it to the best of her capabilities. I lost my own mother at age fourteen, and I do not know what I would have done without her constancy and friendship." Elizabeth followed Mrs. Wentworth's gaze to the lady herself, who was disengaging from a conversation and looked to be headed their way.

"When my father asked her to stand for Alfred, she recognized that my new brother would be even more in need of steady direction as he grew up and prepared to assume the responsibilities of a baronet," Mrs. Wentworth said. "However, she also recognized that she is considerably older now than when she stood for me and my sisters. So she wrote to me and Captain Wentworth, and asked permission to suggest to my father that we be named godparents, as well, in hopes that by virtue of the office we might exert more influence over decisions regarding Alfred than we otherwise would as mere sister and brother-in-law. We readily agreed, and afterward discussed between us offering to raise Alfred ourselves, so that our guidance might be constant and not occasional, and that we would have more power to execute decisions. Captain Wentworth and I had reached an understanding, but had not yet determined how best to approach my father, nor the precise terms of our proposal. And now—" A laugh escaped her, one that sounded disbelief and delight. "We are parents sooner than either of us ever anticipated."

"So Captain Wentworth will not be surprised by this arrangement?"

"Only that our own wishes were effected so easily. In truth, I myself am amazed."

"Then I shall go tell him he is wanted, but leave to you to share why."

"Thank you. Let me take my leave of you now, and say that I have enjoyed talking with you. I doubt Captain Wentworth and I will return here after attending to Alfred—I think he has had as much celebration as he can tolerate for one day."

"Alfred, or Captain Wentworth?"

She laughed again. "Both, I expect."

Elizabeth longed to hear more of the history Mrs. Smith had been imparting to her before Mary Musgrove's interruption—not out of a gossipy interest in scandal, but to better understand the events that had led to Lady Elliot's death. Unfortunately, Mrs. Smith departed with the Wentworths, taking her trove of knowledge with her. Elizabeth and Darcy quit the Assembly Rooms soon after.

Later, she shared what she had learned with Darcy as they walked along the Cobb. It was a lovely, tranquil evening. The heat of the day had eased; both sea and sky were calm. Though a light breeze drifted across the bay, no wind caught her bonnet as it had on their first night in Lyme, when she had been forced to retreat into the alley beside the Lion to unknot its ribbons. Sunlight stretched long upon the waves, a golden contrast to the dark matter of their conversation.

"The relationships between the Clays and the Elliots are more tangled than we ever imagined," she said. "I heard today that Mr. Elliot's late wife had an affair with Mrs. Clay's late husband."

Darcy's brows rose. "I thought I had interesting news to communicate, but you have trumped me. When did this occur?"

"I do not know. Mrs. Smith told me of the affair, but she cut her narrative short when Mary Musgrove joined us. Mary, however, revealed additional information about Sir Walter's relationship with Mrs. Clay. Apparently, she openly pursued him last winter, hoping to seduce him into marrying her."

"Ultimately, she succeeded, though one wonders why she ran off with Mr. Elliot in the interim. She could not have thought it would advance her suit."

"Perhaps Mr. Elliot saw what she was about, and to end her scheme—and obscure the paternity of any child she might have conceived with Sir Walter—made her promises of marriage that he never intended to keep. He would certainly not be the first man in the history of elopements to do so. And Mrs. Clay, believing him, preferred the young heir to the aging title holder."

"An aging title holder whose estate is hazardously close to bankruptcy."

Now it was Elizabeth's turn to express surprise. "How did you learn this?"

"From Mr. Elliot. He spoke of it while I was with Captain Wentworth."

"Well, marrying either of them would procure her the title of Lady Elliot sooner or later—an improvement over her past affairs. Apparently, Mrs. Clay had a proclivity for naval officers before setting her sights on the Elliots."

"Indeed? Then I am surprised Mr. Elliot would bring her to a seaside resort, with half the navy ashore."

Darcy's statement prompted a memory of the conversation she had overheard in the passageway of the Lion the night before Mrs. Clay's accident. *You are hardly guiltless yourself. . . . Half the navy is ashore. Though in your present state, you hardly present an enticing object.*

Elizabeth stopped. Mr. Elliot was a guest of the Lion. And until that night, so was Mrs. Clay.

What of the promise you made me? Did you ever intend to keep it?

In time.

You have run out of time.

Where are you going?

Out.

Her own eyes wide with astonishment, she met Darcy's gaze. He regarded her questioningly.

"I believe I might have overheard a conversation between Mr. Elliot and Mrs. Clay the night before she died."

"How?"

"In the alley beside the Lion, when I stopped to adjust my bonnet. I heard a couple quarreling—I assumed it was a husband and wife, but now, knowing what we do about them both, I believe it was they."

"What was the subject of their argument?"

"Infidelity—on the part of both parties. She was accusing him of continuing affairs he had told her were ended, and of having come to Lyme to rendezvous with his lovers. He responded that she was also guilty of unfaithfulness, but that she was hardly enticing in her present condition."

"That sounds like it could be they."

"Then she brought up a promise he had made to her, told him he had run out of time, and departed—I expect, for Sir Walter's."

"Where she got married, thwarting Mr. Elliot's expectations of inheriting Sir Walter's title," Darcy finished. They resumed walking. "This other affair you mentioned, between Mrs. Clay's and Mr. Elliot's spouses—the couples knew each other for some time, then?"

"Yes, intimately."

"I should say so."

"Darcy!" She glanced round, but there was nobody nearby to hear them. "What I meant was that they, along with the Smiths, were particular friends. Though what happened after the affair was exposed, I did not learn."

"How was it exposed?"

"Let us simply say that Mr. Clay was carried away by his passion for Mrs. Elliot."

He stopped again, searching her face to make sure he had correctly interpreted her meaning. "Mr. Clay died in the act of cuckolding Mr. Elliot?"

She nodded.

Darcy's gaze drifted past her, beyond the edge of the upper Cobb, to the pavement below. Without her realizing it, they had reached the section of the seawall where Mrs. Clay had fallen. "And Mrs. Clay died within hours of leaving Mr. Elliot for Sir Walter."

The chill that passed over Elizabeth had nothing to do with the breeze coming off the sea.

"How did Mrs. Elliot die?" Darcy asked.

"Mrs. Smith did not say—our conversation was interrupted."

"I think we need to find out."

Twenty-three

"As to his marriage, I knew all about it at the time. I was privy to all the fors and againsts; I was the friend to whom he confided his hopes and plans; and though I did not know his wife previously . . . I knew her all her life afterwards, or at least till within the last two years of her life. . . . He was very unkind to his first wife. They were wretched together."
—Mrs. Smith, speaking of Mr. Elliot, Persuasion

The Wentworths lived in a charming two-story house high up the cliff on Pound Street, a dwelling they had taken for six months while they decided where they wanted to settle permanently now that the end of the war had cast the captain ashore. From the exterior, it looked everything a newlywed couple could want in their first home: a neat façade with bay windows and fresh paint, a garden blooming with more flowers than many twice its size, and a door that was always open to friends.

The Wentworths' housekeeper showed the Darcys into a well-proportioned sitting room when they called to deliver the small blanket Elizabeth had embroidered. A day of rain following the christening had enabled Elizabeth to complete the needlework while Darcy wrote a detailed reply to a letter he had received from Pemberley's steward and caught up on other correspondence. Georgiana had spent most of the afternoon at the Ashfords' house; Sir Laurence had left Lyme for a few days on business, and Miss Ashford preferred the company of a friend her own age to that of her middle-aged paid companion.

Mrs. Wentworth welcomed them warmly and received the gift with appreciation, confessing that she had begun a similar project but had not advanced at all since bringing Alfred to live with them. She appeared tired, but in a happy sort of way. The captain, too, looked more fatigued around his eyes than when they had last seen him, though Elizabeth imagined that his profession had probably accustomed him to disrupted sleep. The young culprit was at present upstairs with Mrs. Logan in the hastily established nursery.

"I am finding that I would rather hold Alfred than a needle," Mrs. Wentworth said.

Elizabeth thought of Lily-Anne, back at their cottage with her nurse. She would still rather spend time with her daughter than in sewing. "One cannot fault you for that," she said to Mrs. Wentworth.

"Mrs. Smith, however, has been employing her own to Alfred's benefit—as you can see."

The good woman indeed had needles in hand as she sat beside a table where her work box was laid out. Hers, however, were knitting needles. Her fingers rapidly performed their movements, giving form to what appeared to be the start of a small cap. "I have never made anything for an infant before," she said. "Most of my work has been little thread cases and pincushions, which I sell to support myself. I have not long known how to knit—Nurse Rooke taught me, to help strengthen my hands as I recover—but I am happy for the opportunity to apply my skills, such as they are, to something for Alfred."

If Elizabeth had previously harbored any doubt about the amount of affection Alfred would receive in the Wentworths' home, she now believed beyond question that the little boy would enjoy at least as much attention as he would have known if his own mother had lived—probably a great deal more, judging from the unflattering accounts of Mrs. Clay that Elizabeth had heard at the christening.

Elizabeth enquired after Alfred—his habits, his preferences, his temperament, all the small particulars in which mothers take interest, especially new mothers, who are always quite certain that no baby in the history of babies has ever gurgled, mewed, yawned, blinked, stretched, sneezed, or hiccupped in quite the manner theirs does. Mrs. Wentworth was able to retain some impartiality when it came to Alfred, but one could hear in her voice that her affections were most decidedly engaged. She delighted in the opportunity to discuss such minutiae with Elizabeth, whose conversation was grounded in more experience than Mrs. Smith or even Mrs. Logan were able to provide. The two were soon talking like friends of much longer acquaintance, the timeless experience of motherhood reinforcing their newer connexion.

Darcy was bored nearly to the limit of endurance.

He was a devoted father, and more engaged in Lily-Anne's day-to-day existence than were most gentlemen with nursery-aged offspring. But with rare exceptions, his interest in discussing children began and ended in conversations with his wife, with his own daughter as the subject. Though the manner in which he attended the dialogue between Elizabeth and Mrs. Wentworth was all that courtesy demanded, Elizabeth knew him well enough to recognize each slight shift in his seat as evidence of much greater restlessness.

Captain Wentworth exhibited similar behavior. Indeed, he seemed even more restless than Darcy. After a polite interval had passed, one gentleman's gaze happened to drift toward the other's, and she saw in the slight curl of Wentworth's mouth and the responding spark in Darcy's eyes their identification of a kindred soul yearning to talk about hunting, or politics, or guns, or swords, or brandy, or horses, or dogs—or anything, really, other than the present topic of discourse. The weather would suffice.

The entrance of a servant who needed to consult Captain Wentworth's preference regarding a repair to some item of furniture in his study led to the rapid determination that the captain had better view the article himself before deciding. It was additionally determined that Darcy's opinion might also prove useful, and that he should accompany Captain Wentworth. They made good their escape, eliciting a laugh from Mrs. Smith once they had quit the room.

"My husband would have fled along with them, though I doubt he ever repaired a thing in his life." She laughed again. "But then, people can have all sorts of opinions about things they have never done themselves. Especially men. They must believe that however little they know, their judgment should matter. Mr. Elliot is a prime example of that."

"Mr. Elliot?" Elizabeth glanced to Mrs. Wentworth. "I hope he has not harassed you about Alfred since the child came to live with you?"

"He has not called. I believe he spoke his piece to Captain Wentworth at Alfred's christening."

"Well, you can wager Alfred is still in his thoughts," Mrs. Smith said. "He will not forget a child who cost him his baronetcy. Self-interest is too great a portion of his character. So, too, is a propensity for plotting and scheming."

This declaration, issued with vehemence, unsettled Mrs. Wentworth enough that she excused herself to go upstairs and ascertain Alfred's present well-being. Left alone with Mrs. Smith, Elizabeth was happy for the opportunity to speak privately with the widow. Though this visit to the Wentworths had been motivated by the Darcys' genuine interest in improving their acquaintance with the captain and his wife, and in seeing how Alfred fared, Elizabeth also hoped to learn more about the circumstances of Mrs. Elliot's death.

"Was Mr. Elliot always this way?" Elizabeth asked. "Surely, in the days when he was your friend—"

"I do not believe he was ever my friend, nor my husband's. Not in the true sense of friendship. I do not believe him capable of unselfish feeling for any creature."

"Not even for his wife—before her affair with Mr. Clay?"

"Especially not his wife. It was his heartlessness and neglect that caused the tryst in the first place. I think the months that Mr. Elliot was in the West Indies with my husband were the one period of her marriage when Mrs. Elliot was truly happy. Or at least, not miserable."

"The Elliots' marriage was not a match of affection?"

"It began as one on her side, but for Mr. Elliot it was never anything but a financial transaction. She was of common birth—the granddaughter of a butcher and the daughter of a grazier—but her father was successful enough to provide a decent education and dower her with a considerable fortune. Mr. Elliot wanted money, and she had it, so he wed her despite her lack of bloodline or connexions. At first he was content with the choice he had made—as I said when we spoke previously, we were all living in the moment, and at the moment her money and what it could buy made him happy—but as he became more conscious of his future as a baronet, he grew to despise his wife. Not only did he resent her pedigree and lack of connexions, but also the fact that their marriage had produced no children, and therefore no heir to succeed to the baronetcy after him. He blamed her entirely for their childlessness—men always do—and treated her cruelly.

"I suspected his unkindness toward her, but it was not until both our husbands were overseas that I became her confidante and learned the extent of her mistreatment. She was desperate to have a baby, hopeful that the birth of an heir would appease Mr. Elliot. Mr. Clay having already proved himself able to father a child, Mrs. Elliot deliberately set about seducing him."

"Did she not consider that a betrayal of her friendship with Mrs. Clay?" The former Penelope Shepherd had fallen so far in Elizabeth's esteem that, like Anne Wentworth and Mrs. Smith, she found she could no longer—whether in the privacy of her own thoughts or in conversation with anyone but Sir Walter—refer to the baronet's second wife as "Lady Elliot." It seemed the only thing ladylike about her had been her title, and that, she had enjoyed less than four-and-twenty hours.

"Mrs. Clay had cuckolded Mr. Clay enough times that it was easy for an abused, despairing woman to justify borrowing a husband whose wife was herself so unfaithful," Mrs. Smith said. "Indeed, when Mrs. Elliot told me of additional lovers Mrs. Clay had taken, paramours that I had not known about previously, I, too, lost all sympathy for her. Mrs. Elliot employed the period of Mr. Elliot's absence to engage Mr. Clay's interest, but delayed consummating the liaison until her husband returned to England, so that the child she hoped to conceive would not be born too soon to pass off as Mr. Elliot's. Unfortunately, Mr. Clay died in the act, and their affair was exposed."

"How did Mrs. Clay respond?"

"She was incensed with Mrs. Elliot, but soon saw Mr. Clay's death as opportunity. Free of her husband, she became the quintessential merry widow and set her sights on Mr. Elliot. Tit for tat, as they say, but as a future baronet he also appealed to her social-climbing ambitions. She pursued him, and he casually took what was offered."

"Did Mrs. Elliot know?"

"Certainly. After Mr. Clay's death exposed her infidelity, Mr. Elliot subjected her to even greater cruelty than before. He took no pains to conceal his liaison with Mrs. Clay; in fact, he flaunted it." Mrs. Smith shook her head sadly. "Poor woman. Mrs. Elliot died a very unhappy creature."

"How did she die?"

"She fell down a flight of stairs. It happened only last year, and by then I was no longer on intimate terms with the Elliots, so I do not know the particulars. But given Mr. Elliot's mistreatment of her, I have often wondered whether the event was an accident."

Despite the summer heat, Elizabeth shivered. "You suspect she was pushed?"

"Either physically or emotionally, for I can easily imagine her reaching a state of despair great enough to have thrown herself down rather than endure her bleak existence any longer. Regardless, her death freed Mr. Elliot to marry someone capable of producing an heir, and he certainly lost no time in pursuing his bride of choice."

Elizabeth was confused. "Mrs. Clay?"

"No, Mrs. Wentworth—when she was yet Anne Elliot." Mrs. Smith glanced toward the door through which Mrs. Wentworth had exited, and lowered her voice. "However, shortly before he began courting Anne, Mrs. Clay returned to her father's home in Kellynch village and became the eldest Miss Elliot's bosom friend, visiting constantly at the Great House, so ingratiating herself that when the Elliots removed to Bath they invited her to take up residence with them. All the while, Mr. Elliot and Mrs. Clay affected indifference toward each other whenever he called upon the Elliots, never letting on that they knew each other intimately. In retrospect—I have told Anne this, and she agrees—I believe he installed Mrs. Clay in Sir Walter's household so that she could gather information useful to his suit, or to his financial plans for the estate."

"How did he do that?"

"By convincing her they would both benefit from his protecting his inheritance. If his courtship of Anne proved successful, neither he nor Mrs. Clay would see any reason why he should give up his mistress simply because he had taken a wife. And if it did not, Mrs. Clay would enjoy a more lavish style of living while possibly catching Mr. Elliot for herself at last. However, I think he underestimated Mrs. Clay's cunning. If you recall what Anne's sister Mary said at the christening fete, I believe that once Mrs. Clay infiltrated Sir Walter's household, she developed ambitions of her own, and set her cap for Sir Walter."

"Then why did she run off with Mr. Elliot?"

"Not being privy to their thoughts, I can only speculate based on my knowledge of their characters. I think he realized her scheme, and eliminated the threat she posed by persuading her of his own intentions to marry her. Mrs. Clay was vain enough to believe him. The two of them deserved each other—they were a pair of despicable human beings."

Mrs. Wentworth returned with Alfred in her arms. "He was waking up," she said, "and given the subject of our conversation, I—well, please do not think me silly, but I felt that I wanted him with us in here."

"I do not think you silly at all," Elizabeth said.

Mrs. Wentworth sat down on the sofa beside Mrs. Smith. The widow temporarily ceased her knitting and leaned toward Anne to stroke one of Alfred's palms. The baby grasped her finger in his tiny fist.

"He likes you," Anne told her friend.

Mrs. Smith smiled. "The feeling is mutual."

Mrs. Wentworth offered to let Elizabeth hold Alfred, a suggestion that Elizabeth was happy to accept. "Unless Mrs. Smith would like to hold him first?"

"Not yet," Mrs. Smith said. "I do not want to risk these rheumatic hands dropping him."

From the deftness with which the widow employed her needles, Elizabeth doubted this fear was valid. Her hands seemed as dexterous as Elizabeth's own—and far more skilled at knitting. But Mrs. Smith resumed her work, leaving Elizabeth to indulge in the pleasure of holding a newborn. As she received the tiny boy in her arms, she wondered anew how anyone might wish harm on such a defenseless creature. "Mrs. Smith, you said earlier that Alfred is still in Mr. Elliot's thoughts, and that the gentleman has a propensity for scheming . . . indeed, you have painted such a black picture of his character, that I am unsettled by it. You do not believe Mr. Elliot would go so far as to harm Alfred, do you?"

The needles stopped. "I believe him capable of anything."

Mrs. Wentworth looked warily from Elizabeth to Mrs. Smith.

"I have been relating some of Mr. Elliot's history to Mrs. Darcy—a few of the particulars regarding his connexion to Mrs. Clay," Mrs. Smith explained. "There is bound to be gossip. As the person who discovered her, Mrs. Darcy should know the truth."

"It is not a truth flattering to either Mrs. Clay or Mr. Elliot," Mrs. Wentworth said.

"No, it is not," Elizabeth admitted, "and I hope you will not resent my coming into knowledge of it. I am not interested in scandal, but in Alfred's welfare, as I have been since discovering Mrs. Clay on the Cobb."

She stroked the baby's cheek, then handed him back to Mrs. Wentworth, who seemed anxious to have him returned to her now that the conversation had taken a darker turn. "When heard in context with details of Mrs. Clay's death," Elizabeth continued, "Mrs. Smith's information supports misgivings I had already held regarding the accident. In fact, I believe it is possible that her fall was not an accident at all."

Mrs. Smith gasped. Mrs. Wentworth instinctively drew Alfred closer to her.

"Good heavens!" Anne said. "You do not think Mrs. Clay was pushed?"

"I have no real proof—only my own instincts and a few utterances made by Mrs. Clay before she died." Plus Bald Betsy's flight across the room at Mangled Maggie's hands, which Elizabeth decided not to mention. She was afraid her suggestion sounded preposterous enough. "But Miss Darcy saw Mr. Elliot on the Cobb that morning, not long before the accident, and for a man in no hurry to marry Mrs. Clay before her death, he moved swiftly in his attempt to obtain custody of Alfred afterward. After all that I have learned about him, I cannot help but speculate about his sudden interest in the child after the accident, and whether that interest took a more malicious form before it."

Mrs. Smith, whose gentle features generally bore either a smile or the appearance of being close to breaking into one, now regarded Elizabeth with the most grave expression Elizabeth had yet seen on her. "I would not be at all surprised to learn that Mr. Elliot tried to harm Alfred before he was born. Nor that he still harbors designs on Sir Walter's title."

Mrs. Wentworth looked a little pale. "These are very serious suspicions."

"I do not voice them lightly," Elizabeth said. "Nor do I mean to alarm you. I only wish to share my concerns with you and Captain Wentworth, Alfred's guardians, and leave you to make your own determination about whether additional vigilance regarding Mr. Elliot is warranted. You, after all, know the gentleman far better than I. Indeed, I hope my conjecture turns out to be entirely groundless."

Twenty-four

They were now able to speak to each other and consult.

—Persuasion

A verdict having been rendered on the monumental issue of how best to steady a wobbly chair, and the offending object having been removed for repair to another part of the house, Captain Wentworth turned, with some hesitancy, to Darcy.

"I suppose we ought to return to the sitting room."

Darcy sincerely hoped the ladies' conversation had not progressed to Alfred's digestive functions. "I suppose we should."

Neither man made the slightest motion toward the door.

"Perhaps after a glass of wine?"

"That is an excellent suggestion."

Captain Wentworth went to a side table upon which rested a decanter. Above it hung a print of the *Victory* leading the British fleet at Trafalgar, its sails full and its course unwavering. On another wall hung two paintings of individual ships—a sleek frigate and an older sloop. Maps and nautical instruments also adorned the walls and shelves. Darcy recognized some items, such as a compass, but could not begin to guess the purpose of others. The entire chamber, with its oak paneling and solid furniture, created the impression of a captain's cabin. Even the windows offered a view of the sea, and Darcy wondered whether Wentworth had chosen this room as his study for that reason.

"Do you miss the sea?" Darcy asked.

"I do." Wentworth removed the stopper from the decanter. "However," he said, with a grin, "I have found marriage a highly agreeable alternative to living on a warship full of men. And should I become too sentimental about nautical life, Alfred now wakes me during the night as regularly as a ship's bell. Perhaps I should assign him the middle watch, so he can earn his keep."

Darcy recalled how disruptive—though joyful—Lily-Anne's arrival had been in their own household, despite their having had, like the Wentworths, the assistance of nurses, and despite, unlike the Wentworths, their having had months in which to prepare for their new condition as parents. "Alfred joined your household rather suddenly."

The wine poured, Captain Wentworth replaced the decanter and picked up the two glasses. "Indeed, I thought Mrs. Wentworth and I would enjoy a little more time to ourselves before having a child to care for. I do not, however, regret our decision to take him." He glanced at the print of Admiral Nelson's flagship before turning and handing one of the glasses to Darcy. "'England expects every man to do his duty,'" he said with a shrug. "Sometimes duty calls with a softer voice, and is performed in less dramatic ways."

"Were you at Trafalgar?"

"No, though like nearly every sailor who served in the year five, I wish I could say I was. The biggest battle I saw was the action off San Domingo a few months later. That day made me a commander." He gestured toward the painting of the sloop, and a nostalgic expression crossed his countenance. "My first ship was that little sloop—the *Asp*—and I was sent straight back to the West Indies in her."

"My cousin served in the West Indies, aboard the *Magna Carta*."

"Indeed? What is his name?"

"Gerard Fitzwilliam. He died in action about three years ago."

"The war claimed the lives of many good men," Captain Wentworth said. "I am sorry that your cousin was among them."

"So am I. He had just been made lieutenant, and looked forward to a glorious career." Darcy paused. "Actually, I wonder if I might ask your assistance in a matter pertaining to him."

"What sort of assistance?"

"I have questions regarding the circumstances of his death. There seem to be . . . irregularities in written and oral accounts that I have been unable to reconcile. However, my own ignorance of naval protocol and routines might lead me to imagine improprieties where none exist."

"That is entirely possible. A ship is its own floating domain, one that no outsider can fully comprehend without having spent time aboard. Tell me your concerns."

Wentworth listened as Darcy recounted what he knew of Gerard's time aboard the *Magna Carta*—the little information his family had been given at the time of his death, Lieutenant St. Clair's personal but belated delivery of his sea chest, Darcy's discovery of the diary and pendant, his recent conversations with St. Clair and Captain Tourner. Wentworth asked occasional questions, his brow becoming increasingly furrowed. When Darcy had done, Wentworth refilled their wineglasses.

"You initiated this discussion by saying that you had questions about your cousin's death, but a substantial portion of what you have told me pertains to the mysterious appearance of the gold figurines, not the battle." The captain returned Darcy's glass to him. "I take this to mean that you suspect the events are related—that your cousin, and perhaps the cook, did not die in legitimate melee with the French, but by the hand of one of their own shipmates?"

"Based on my limited knowledge, I believe it is possible that the battle provided an opportunity for the owner of those artifacts to ensure their existence remained a secret. From what I have told you, do you concur?"

"Unless naval victuals have improved exceedingly since I was in the West Indies, I would certainly describe gold idols in a sugar cask as irregular. One certainly wants to know how they came to be there."

"Is there any reason someone with a rightful purpose for possessing the objects would hide them in a sugar cask rather than in his sea chest or among his other possessions?"

Wentworth thought a moment. "There is not much privacy on a ship. While officers enjoy more than the men, even an admiral's belongings are packed up and his furniture moved to the hold in preparation for a battle. An officer's cabin is dismantled—canvas walls removed, chests and furnishings stowed—to entirely clear the deck for the gun crews. Seamen's hammocks are rolled up and put to other use, and even when not in battle, several messmates might share a sea chest. So no matter what a man's rank, there is a great deal of moving things about, by many hands, and not under the immediate supervision of their owners, who are performing their own duties. Whereas items secured in the hold or on the orlop deck, where an officer's stores would be, stay put until needed or until the voyage ends. So I suppose it is possible that someone might believe treasures such as you describe would be safer in storage." He paused. "But were they mine, I would secure them in a locked chest."

"Then I think we can assume that their owner did not come by them honestly, which means their discovery was a threat."

"Even so, it is a great leap from theft to murder. In the navy, murder is one of the few crimes punishable by death—usually hanging."

"Is that not all the more reason why the mayhem of battle would provide an ideal opportunity for a thief fearing exposure to commit one—or two—with little risk of being caught? And is it not further possible that in the fervor of battle, if a chance to silence someone who knew too much suddenly presented itself, the thief might seize it without pausing to consider the consequences?"

"It is," Wentworth conceded. "But we also cannot dismiss the possibility that however wrongfully the artifacts might have come to be in that cask, the deaths of your cousin and the cook could have been the legitimate result of battle."

"I agree. I am not seeking an individual to blame for my cousin's death if no one is guilty of it. The French collectively provide a sufficient object of resentment. And in truth, I would rather remember Gerard as having died for the preservation of England, than for private greed. However, if this discovery cost him his life . . . I want to know."

"You and Mrs. Darcy saved my godson's life; the least I can do is help you put to rest questions about your cousin's death. I suppose we should begin with who beyond Lieutenant Fitzwilliam and the cook knew about the idols."

"Lieutenant St. Clair, who allegedly was going to raise the issue with the captain after his dinner guests left the ship."

"Have you directly asked Lieutenant St. Clair or Captain Tourner about the artifacts?"

"I thought it best not to betray my knowledge of them."

Wentworth nodded. "That was prudent, until we have a better sense of what—and whom—we are dealing with. I know Tourner by reputation only, and St. Clair not at all. Did the latter mention other captains under whom he has served?"

"Only a Captain Croft, who I understand is an admiral now."

"Yes, he is rear admiral of the white—and my brother-in-law. Did St. Clair serve under him as a lieutenant?"

"A midshipman."

"Croft should be able to give us a better sense of St. Clair's character—at least, St. Clair in his younger years. Naval life can change a man. He might also be familiar with Captain Tourner. As luck would have it, Mrs. Wentworth and I will see the Crofts this week; I can speak to the admiral then. Now, who else might have known about the gold figures?"

Gerard's diary had not indicated that any other individuals learned of them from him or the cook. Darcy pondered broader possibilities. "How would any cask of sugar have gotten aboard the ship? Who would have handled it?"

"The cask would have been loaded with the other provisions within a few days of leaving port—rats are enough of a nuisance once at sea; there is no reason to give them an early start at the food. Since this was a cask purchased for the wardroom mess, it would have been stored below in an area reserved for the lieutenants' provisions, and brought up to the galley when needed."

"If St. Clair acted as caterer for the mess, would he have overseen the loading?"

"It is not inconceivable. However, as first lieutenant he had more important responsibilities, so I expect someone else oversaw the loading."

"Perhaps the midshipman who maintained the wardroom's inventory?"

The suggestion appeared to puzzle Captain Wentworth. "St. Clair assigned a midshipman to monitor the lieutenants' private stores?"

"I do not know whether he did so regularly, but my cousin wrote that the cook encountered a midshipman taking inventory of the wardroom's provisions the week before the idols were discovered."

"That is rather unusual."

"The cook also received a hostile response for having surprised him. Perhaps this midshipman is someone we should learn more about?"

"If we can. Did your cousin happen to mention his name?"

"Musgrove." Darcy had noted at Alfred's christening that Sir Walter's youngest daughter was married to a Musgrove, and wondered whether they might be related to the midshipman. He therefore had held back the name at first, unsure whether Captain Wentworth might be able to maintain objectivity about the man's possible involvement should a connexion indeed exist.

Captain Wentworth's brows rose. "Richard Musgrove?"

"I do not know—Gerard wrote only 'Mr. Musgrove.'"

"Hmm. I had a midshipman on the *Laconia* named Musgrove—a very troublesome fellow—went by the nickname Dick. Ironically, he became a distant relation of mine posthumously upon my marriage. If this is the same man, I would not be at all surprised if he were involved in something he should not have been. I will see if I can learn whether he wound up on the *Magna Carta* after leaving me."

"There was one other person aboard the *Magna Carta* with whom you might be familiar. I believe the Mr. Smith my cousin refers to in his diary is the same Mr. Smith whose estate you are helping to settle for his widow. Your friend told Mrs. Darcy that her husband traveled to the West Indies about that same time, in the company of Mr. William Elliot."

"He did indeed, though I do not know the nature of the business he conducted on that trip. His papers are a hodgepodge of important documents and trivial memorandums—no order to them whatsoever—and I have found nothing about the journey save for a note from Elliot confirming westward passage booked aboard a merchant vessel. From the rest of the papers, I have determined that he inherited a goodly sized sugar plantation from his father, and that when it came into the son's possession, it was a lucrative holding. Its primary business was producing rum and sugar for export to England. The income was not extraordinary, as the British government imposes such high taxes on those imports and requires the sugar to be refined in England, so that our own refiners can monopolize the industry. But the plantation provided enough to maintain a gentleman's style of living. By the time of Mr. Smith's journey, however, the estate had fallen into financial straits. Much of the problem derived from his extravagant spending, but his income had also decreased. I expect he traveled to Jamaica to meet with the plantation's overseer, to personally examine his accounts and methods of management."

"Have you asked Mr. Elliot about the purpose of the trip?"

"You witnessed the amount of cooperation I have received from Mr. Elliot."

"Yes, he advised you repeatedly to drop the matter altogether." Darcy paused. "In fact, despite his ostensible reason for approaching us—to enquire of *me* after Alfred's well-being—he seemed far more interested in talking to you. Or, more to the point, in making a great show of *not* talking to you about Mrs. Smith's estate."

"Perhaps because he made such a failure of it—if not by exerting influence over Smith during his life, then as executor after his death," Wentworth said. "He has told Mrs. Smith that the property is so deep in arrears on its taxes that it has been seized, and that recovery is impossible. However, when it comes to increasing the size of his own fortune, Mr. Elliot is a talented schemer. Had he applied his shrewdness to the Smith estate, I have no doubt it would have become a profitable concern once more."

"Particularly," Darcy said, "since having traveled with Smith to the plantation, he likely saw the entire operation and gained intimate knowledge of its potential."

Darcy was having trouble comprehending Mr. Elliot's actions and motives. One would think that after Mr. Clay's betrayal with Mr. Elliot's wife, Mr. Elliot would have done better by the friend who had remained loyal to him. Apparently, however, Mr. Elliot was loyal only to himself, though his friends might drop dead around him: both of the Clays, his wife—

Mr. Smith.

Mr. Elliot seemed to have lost an extraordinary number of friends in the past three years.

"I understand Mr. Smith died almost immediately upon returning home," Darcy said. "Do you know how?"

"Some sort of illness. It upsets Mrs. Smith to talk about it, so I have never enquired into the particulars, as they have no bearing on the issue of the estate. All that matters is that Smith is dead; the law cares not how he came to be thus, so long as it occurred by natural means."

Or means that appeared natural. A push could look like an accidental fall; poison could disguise itself as illness.

A killer could masquerade as a friend.

Twenty-five

The listener's proverbial fate was not absolutely hers: she had heard no evil of herself.

—Persuasion

*U*pon leaving the Wentworths' home, Elizabeth and Darcy found their steps leading them not to their own cottage, but back to the Cobb. A boundary between the quiet village and the untamed sea, the ancient breakwater was the only place where it felt natural to entertain conjecture on subjects that also lay beyond the limits of civilized behavior. As they walked along the lower wall, passing the gin shop and following the curve toward the quay, Elizabeth recounted the ladies' sitting room conversation.

"You shared with Mrs. Wentworth your suspicions regarding Mrs. Clay's death?" Darcy sounded somewhat surprised.

"I had not planned on doing so overtly," Elizabeth replied, "but when the opportunity arose in the course of conversation, I thought I should—not only to encourage watchfulness on Alfred's behalf, but also to increase the likelihood of her revealing any pertinent family business to someone outside the family, should she think of something useful to our probe. I was a bit apprehensive about how Mrs. Wentworth would respond, but she appreciated my concern for Alfred, and as you saw, she was as cordial as ever when we parted."

Darcy laughed.

"What is so amusing?" she asked.

"While you were engaged in murderous conjecture with the ladies, I was telling her husband my suspicions regarding Gerard's death."

Elizabeth released a laugh of her own. "Can you imagine the conclusions they will draw when they compare conversations? They will think us the most distrustful couple they have ever met."

"We probably are." Darcy took her arm as she trod over an especially uneven series of stones. It was a calm day; not needing to hug the wall for shelter from the wind, they were walking closer to the harbor's edge than on previous promenades along the lower Cobb.

"We have good reason. For a resort where visitors come to improve their health, Lyme seems to attract a great many people with mysterious deaths in their past—and present. We can but hope that nobody notices we are not ourselves exempt."

"Yes, but we solve the murders; we do not commit them."

"Even so," Elizabeth said, "one of these days I would like to journey from Pemberley without encountering a single corpse. The count is climbing rather high on this holiday, if we include all the ones we have learned about secondhand. I added another today—Mrs. Elliot."

"Mr. Elliot's wife died mysteriously?"

"She took a fatal tumble down a set of steps. Apparently, women of his acquaintance suffer an alarming degree of clumsiness on staircases."

"While the men suffer by other means. Captain Wentworth told me today that Mr. Smith died of illness."

"How mundane of Mr. Smith. There is little inspiration for scandal in that. At least when Mr. Clay's heart gave out, he was engaged in something interesting." She paused. "Actually, now that I think on it, Mrs. Smith said only that Mr. Clay died in the act—she never specified how. Mr. Elliot could have walked in on Mr. Clay with Mrs. Elliot and shot him, for all we know. However, even without that additional drama, the members of Mr. Elliot's erstwhile coterie all died rather spectacularly, except for Mr. Smith."

"And Mrs. Smith."

She drew a sharp breath, a disturbing new thought overtaking her. She had not previously considered the fact that of the three couples, Mrs. Smith was the only person still alive besides Mr. Elliot. "Four people dead within three years—everybody Mr. Elliot was close to, save one. Do you think Mrs. Smith might be in danger? She knows so many of his secrets, and her repeated applications to Mr. Elliot regarding Mr. Smith's estate have made her an annoyance he would prefer just disappear. Her compromised health renders her all the more vulnerable to treachery."

"It is probably a good thing that she is living with the Wentworths at present, and that she has turned matters over to Captain Wentworth, who I daresay is equal to any challenge Mr. Elliot could present," Darcy replied. "That being said, she perhaps ought to exercise caution around staircases—or anywhere else Mr. Elliot is present—though I do not foresee her climbing up and down stairs unassisted anytime soon."

They stopped as he said this. They had reached Granny's Teeth.

"She is hopeful on that point," Elizabeth told him. "I do not think she will ever try these steps—good heavens, I would not attempt them myself—but a less hazardous set might be possible for her to negotiate by herself one day. She said the sea has improved her health remarkably."

"It seems Mrs. Smith says a great many things whenever you are together. She is a wellspring of information about herself and everybody she has ever known."

"I myself was a little taken aback by how much she divulged to someone with whom she is only recently acquainted," Elizabeth said, "but I believe her health has so circumscribed her society that she has few people to talk to, and little news of herself to talk about. I think, too, that the kindness your sister and I showed her upon our first meeting accelerated the degree of intimacy she perceives between us."

"Well, she has certainly painted unflattering portraits of both Mr. Elliot and Mrs. Clay."

"Their own actions did that. I confess, I have lost much of the sympathy I had for Mrs. Clay, and at this point might not go out of my way to explore the circumstances of her death any further were it merely a matter of justice for her. We could simply share our suspicions with the coroner and walk away with a clear conscience. But the more I learn about Mr. Elliot, the more I fear for the safety of Alfred and Mrs. Smith, and even of the Wentworths now that they have taken both of them into their home. Too, the fact that Mr. Elliot was frequently aboard the *Magna Carta* at the time your cousin served on it makes him a figure about whom we ought to learn all we can."

"I concur," Darcy said. "In fact, I feel even more strongly about probing his connexion to the *Magna Carta*. The gold pendants were found in a sugar cask—one of those, I would wager, that Gerard wrote came from Mr. Smith's plantation. In the absence of Mr. Smith, we are left with Mr. Elliot as the only person at hand who might lend insight into how the artifacts could have come to be there—if we can pry the intelligence out of him without his realizing it."

"He also would have been present during the battle in which Lieutenant Fitzwilliam died—though he would have observed it from the *Montego,* if he observed it at all and did not take refuge in his cabin throughout the action."

"Unless he was on the *Magna Carta* when it occurred. Gerard wrote that Captain Tourner was entertaining Mr. Smith when Gerard brought the figurines to Lieutenant St. Clair's attention, and St. Clair told me there were passengers aboard during the melee. Perhaps Mr. Smith and his companions could not safely return to the *Montego* before the *Magna Carta* became engaged. The crew would have been too busy preparing for battle to transport them back to the merchant ship."

Darcy's reference to Mr. Smith's "companions" prompted another thought. "Your cousin wrote that the captain regularly entertained three passengers from the *Montego,* but named only Mr. Smith. I believe we can safely assume Mr. Elliot was the second, and the one who made a point of his status as a future baronet—that sounds just like him. I wonder who the third passenger was."

"That is a question I would rather not pose directly to Mr. Elliot if I can help it. Perhaps Mrs. Smith knows."

"If she does not, Lieutenant St. Clair would."

"I hesitate to ask him, as well. I do not want to alert either of them to our suspicions. Both Lieutenant St. Clair and Mr. Elliot seem to have a considerable number of dead people in their past, though in St. Clair's case it is a hazard of his profession."

Elizabeth looked past Darcy's shoulder, toward the section of the Cobb they had just walked. "Perhaps it is not his profession, but the company he keeps."

About five-and-twenty yards away, near the wooden doors of the gin shop, were two men: Lieutenant St. Clair and Mr. Elliot. They stood against the wall, so deep in conversation that they took no notice of Elizabeth and Darcy.

"That is an intriguing tête-à-tête," Elizabeth said. "What do you suppose they are discussing?"

Darcy studied them a moment, then took her hand. "Do not say a word." His voice was so low against the rhythm of the tide that Elizabeth barely made out his instruction. He led her away from the water's edge, angling toward the wall until they were flush against it, closer to Mr. Elliot and Lieutenant St. Clair but still a good sixty feet from where they continued to converse. Darcy leaned against the wall, his back to the gentlemen, and raised a finger to his lips.

". . . appreciate your interest, but you are making this application too late. We are settled on Tourner."

Elizabeth regarded Darcy in disbelief. The conversation was quite audible, yet there was nobody nearby. In fact, the voices sounded like Mr. Elliot and Lieutenant St. Clair, who had not moved from their distant position. *Is that . . . ?* she mouthed.

Darcy nodded.

How? she wanted to ask, but St. Clair was still speaking.

". . . hoped I might persuade you. I have spent nearly my whole career navigating the trade winds and currents of the West Indian routes."

"Tourner has experience as a captain that you cannot match."

"Tourner lacks boldness. He should have retired even before the war ended. Your ship needs a master who can protect its cargo from those who would seize it. I have commanded prize vessels into port, led boarding and landing parties, directed battles when the captain has been incapacitated. Whether a situation demands decisiveness, diplomacy, or discretion, I will answer. You saw for yourself on the *Magna Carta* how expediently I can dispatch a problem."

"I did, and I thank you again for your deft handling of it, though you must admit that Tourner helped. However, your previous service to me does not change the fact that in the matter of engaging a master for the *Black Cormorant,* I have my partner's wishes to consider, and Tourner is his choice. I am sorry." Mr. Elliot began walking, headed toward Elizabeth and Darcy.

St. Clair fell into step beside him. "Perhaps I could meet with your partner? Allow me an opportunity to convince him of my fitness."

"Such a meeting is not possible."

Apprehension took hold of Elizabeth as the pair ambled closer. She and Darcy ought to move, so as not to be caught eavesdropping on them. But then she realized the two men had no idea their conversation could be overheard from such a distance. Amazingly, as the distance closed, she and Darcy were yet able to hear their discussion.

"I do not question that you are a highly capable officer," Mr. Elliot said. "Were we not already decided on Tourner, we would certainly consider you. I also sympathize with your present lack of employment. I suggest you talk to Captain Tourner. Though he takes direction from me, this will be his ship and his crew. He knows your abilities; perhaps he will want you for his mate."

"Then I definitely shall take up the matter with him. In fact, I . . ." The sound of St. Clair's voice died.

Elizabeth met Darcy's gaze. "They are drawing close," she murmured.

Darcy nodded. "It is indeed a fine day," he said in a perfectly ordinary volume as he moved away from the wall and turned as if to go. "So fine, in fact, that I am reluctant to return to the cottage, but I suppose— Oh, hello." He greeted Mr. Elliot and Lieutenant St. Clair as they approached.

"We were just saying that very thing, were we not, Lieutenant?" Mr. Elliot's words came smoothly, but the ease of his manner did not quite reach his eyes. "I hope the weather holds through the week. I hear a new ship is to be launched."

The launch had been a subject of anticipation throughout Lyme for at least a se'nnight. Apparently such events were a spectacle that drew even the most casually interested observers. The Harvilles planned to take their boys, and had encouraged the Darcys to attend.

"It is a merchant ship, I understand," Darcy said.

"Yes, an Indiaman, the largest vessel Lyme's shipyards have ever built," Mr. Elliot said. "Or so I am told." The hint of pride in his voice betrayed his feigned indifference.

"Does it belong to the East India Company?" Elizabeth asked.

"No, I believe she is a West Indiaman, owned by a group of individual investors. I am afraid, Mrs. Darcy, that exhausts the intelligence I have on the subject. Perhaps Lieutenant St. Clair possesses more?"

St. Clair, who to this point had been attending Mr. Elliot with the same deaf ear to that gentleman's pretended lack of interest as were the Darcys, now continued Elliot's performance. "Only that she should have little trouble hiring a crew. There are many able seamen in Lyme eager to sign on with her."

Mr. Elliot appeared satisfied with St. Clair's answer.

Elizabeth was not. She wanted to know why Mr. Elliot and Lieutenant St. Clair were understating their knowledge of the *Black Cormorant*. She wanted to know the meaning of the conversation she and Darcy had just overheard. She wanted to know how in heaven's name she had been able to overhear it in the first place.

"Do you plan to observe the launch?" she asked them.

"I hear she is a handsome ship," Lieutenant St. Clair replied. "I would like to obtain a closer look at her."

"And you, Mr. Elliot?"

"Perhaps. It is something to do in Lyme besides bathing or visiting the Assembly Rooms."

"There is always fossil-hunting."

He smiled. "Only for those who do not mind getting their hands dirty."

Mr. Elliot's smiles increasingly caused Elizabeth's flesh to creep. Despite his perfectly manicured nails, she suspected his hands were as dirty as his secrets.

They were off the Cobb and halfway along the Walk that connected the hamlet to Lyme proper before Elizabeth felt comfortable discussing what had just transpired, without fear of being mysteriously overheard.

"So, Mr. Elliot owns partial interest in a new merchant ship," she said, "but does not want anybody to know."

"He does not want *us* to know," Darcy replied. "Apparently he is not hiding the fact from Captain Tourner or Lieutenant St. Clair."

"Well, no wonder he has continued in Lyme since Mrs. Clay's death. I thought it curious that he did not go home. Now we know what has occupied him—overseeing the completion of the *Black Cormorant.*"

"And hiring someone to command her."

"How was it that we could hear the conversation between Mr. Elliot and Lieutenant St. Clair from such a distance?" she asked. "Moreover, how did you know we would be able to?"

"The day Ben Harville wandered onto the Cobb, I discovered quite by accident that the curve of the wall lends it unusual acoustical properties. I was standing just past the gin shop, while Captain Harville and Captain Wentworth stood where you and I were today, and I heard them speaking. Believe me—I was as astonished as you. I hypothesized that the effect worked in both directions, but I was not certain until now."

"Did you tell the captains?"

"I told neither of them, nor did they seem aware of it. Apparently the phenomenon is not broadly known, or Lieutenant St. Clair and Mr. Elliot would have exercised more caution."

"Or at least not stood there immediately afterward equivocating to us, disassociating themselves from the very ship they had been discussing. How long do you suppose the two of them have been in collusion? Did it begin aboard the *Magna Carta,* or predate that voyage?"

"That depends on what they are colluding about."

"Well, at present Lieutenant St. Clair wants employment from Mr. Elliot, but some sort of anonymous partner is standing in the way, along with Captain Tourner. It sounds as if at one time St. Clair and Tourner were on more cooperative terms—jointly taking care of Mr.

Elliot's 'problem'—but that now St. Clair is willing to step over him to get what he wants."

"They say there is no honor among thieves. I expect that applies to scoundrels of any type."

"Yes, but I thought there was some honor among His Majesty's sea officers." They passed the steps upon which they had first encountered Lieutenant St. Clair, the afternoon they had arrived in Lyme. Elizabeth recalled the impression he had made on her then, and the following day when he had delivered the sea chest. "Lieutenant St. Clair disappoints me. I did not want to believe him capable of treachery, but having discovered him to be on such familiar terms with Mr. Elliot, who we know to be a snake, only causes me to wonder which of them is *more* lacking in honor, and—"

She stopped. She had been about to say "which one is the bigger thief." But from "thief" her mind leaped farther ahead—to the as-yet-unknown thief of two particular objects.

"And?" Darcy prompted.

"And whether Lieutenant St. Clair handled Mr. Elliot's problem and the problem of the gold artifacts in a single shot—because they were the same problem."

"You believe Mr. Elliot was involved with the idols?" Darcy asked.

"I am not sure what I believe, but somehow he was a party to them—directly or indirectly. If he did not handle them himself, he had knowledge of them. Let us consider what we *do* know: The figurines were found in a cask of sugar that, let us assume, came from Mr. Smith's plantation. As his friend and advisor, Mr. Elliot was intimately familiar with Mr. Smith's business—to hear Mrs. Smith tell it, perhaps more familiar than Mr. Smith himself. From your cousin's diary, we know that Elliot and Smith, as well as Lieutenant St. Clair, were frequent dinner guests of Captain Tourner, so they were all well acquainted. And we know that St. Clair, as caterer for his mess, arranged to have the cask brought on board.

"Now," she continued, "what if this particular cask was meant to be stored with St. Clair's personal belongings, but mistakenly ended up with the mess provisions? A cask that was never meant to be used during the voyage gets opened, the artifacts are discovered, and suddenly Mr. Elliot and Lieutenant St. Clair have a problem that St. Clair does not want brought to the captain's attention—at least, not by your cousin."

"Or not while the captain was in Mr. Smith's company."

"Yes, we do not know how far the collusion extended."

"Or why, if Mr. Elliot was the one behind the gold's presence in the sugar cask," Darcy said, "he did not simply transport the artifacts with his own belongings aboard the *Montego*."

"He thought they would be safer on a ship of war?" Elizabeth sighed. "I have not worked out all the details, and my theory probably has more holes than a leaky rowboat. What did Captain Wentworth have to say about all of this?"

"He thought there were enough irregularities in what I described to warrant investigation. Obviously, he does not know about the conversation we just overheard, which I shall inform him of without delay. Mr. Elliot's character he already knows better than we do; in fact, he described him as a 'talented schemer.'"

"See? Mr. Elliot must have a hand in this somehow."

"Wentworth is not personally acquainted with Lieutenant St. Clair or Captain Tourner, though he might know the midshipman who conducted the inventory—Mr. Musgrove."

"I had forgotten about the midshipman. What did the captain say of him?"

"If he is indeed the Mr. Musgrove who served under Captain Wentworth, he was a troublemaker. As for St. Clair and Tourner, Wentworth said he would learn what he could about them and their service histories, including applying to Admiral Croft for information. Croft is Wentworth's brother-in-law, so he anticipates the admiral will readily assist us. He plans to speak with him this week."

"I look forward to the results of that discussion," Elizabeth said. "In the meantime, we must call upon the Wentworths once more, so that you can tell the captain our latest news before he meets with the admiral, and I can consult Mrs. Wentworth on a point of fashion."

"Fashion?" Darcy took her arm as they reached the end of the Walk and began the arduous climb up Broad Street. "After all this discussion of villainy, that is where your thoughts have carried you?"

"I want to know what one wears to a launch. We need to see Mr. Elliot's new ship."

Twenty-six

He had, in fact, though his sisters were now doing all they could for him, by calling him "poor Richard," been nothing better than a thick-headed, unfeeling, unprofitable Dick Musgrove, who had never done any thing to entitle himself to more than the abbreviation of his name, living or dead.

—Persuasion

True to his word, Captain Wentworth performed discreet enquiries into the naval careers of Lieutenant St. Clair, Captain Tourner, and Mr. Musgrove.

The last was simplest. Dick Musgrove was a younger brother of Charles Musgrove, husband of Anne's sister Mary. Captain Wentworth was on genial terms with the entire Musgrove family, including Charles and Dick's parents, and already knew part of Dick's history.

A troublesome youth, Dick Musgrove had been sent off to sea in hopes that naval discipline would make a better man of him. It had not. By the time Captain Wentworth had the misfortune to inherit him, he was as lazy, brutish, and self-serving a midshipman as Wentworth had ever dealt with, and the captain's efforts to instill sense and better self-regulation in the recalcitrant young man had proved as futile as raising sail in a dead calm. Wentworth had literally breathed a sigh of relief when, in consequence of another ship's heavy casualties, Musgrove had transferred to another frigate in desperate need of midshipmen. Any pangs of conscience Wentworth might have felt at passing off a problem officer to Dick's new captain were alleviated by that captain's having passed off a different problem midshipman to Wentworth the year before. It was simply the way of things.

But death and time have a softening effect on memory, resulting in Dick's mother recalling him more fondly in death than he had ever deserved in life. Whenever the senior Mrs. Musgrove indulged in sighing over her "poor Richard," she fancied Wentworth a sympathetic listener. No other captain, she said, had taken such good care of her son during his years in service. (That much was probably true.) And so, when Wentworth wrote to Mrs. Musgrove seeking names of the ships on which Dick had served after leaving the *Laconia,* she had been happy to review her son's old letters (most of them requests for money) and send him by return post a chronological list.

Dick had indeed served under Captain Tourner aboard the *Magna Carta.* It had been the last ship on the list.

Wentworth anticipated similar ease of obtaining intelligence regarding Lieutenant St. Clair. A letter to one of his own former instructors at the Naval College in Portsmouth had yielded a comprehensive summary of St. Clair's history, and he now looked forward to obtaining a more personal account from Admiral Croft. Wentworth's sister and her husband were come for a brief visit to satisfy Mrs. Croft's desire to meet Alfred, and the admiral's desire to tease Wentworth about his sudden and unexpected new commission as a foster father.

"Well, well, Frederick!" The admiral issued a hearty laugh. "Master and commander of the Elliot heir! This was a sea change you did not see coming, I warrant. How are you liking your new course?"

"I find it quite satisfactory," Wentworth replied.

"I suppose a young fellow like you needs something to do now that the peace has set us all ashore, but I expected your new wife to have provided sufficient occupation. Women are quite good at finding little tasks and errands for their husbands to attend to, are you not, Sophy?"

Mrs. Croft cast the admiral a look of affectionate exasperation. "Pay him no mind," she said to Wentworth and Anne. "He has been as eager as I to meet your new charge."

"Charge, ha! I wager the little commodore is already the one issuing orders. Deny it if you can, Frederick. There! I see in your face I have got the truth of it. Well, where is he? Let us determine whether he passes muster."

Alfred indeed passed inspection. When the proper number of compliments had been paid and signs of promise observed, they all gathered in the sitting room, where they were joined by Mrs. Smith. Later, Wentworth and the admiral retreated to the study.

Though he had seen the room before, Croft looked round and nodded appreciatively. "I have been thinking of making over the study at Kellynch Hall in this manner. Do you think Sir Walter would approve?"

Wentworth thought Sir Walter would die of an apoplectic seizure at the very suggestion, and told the admiral so.

Croft laughed. "He probably would. Though I suppose the question would then fall to his heir, and you could persuade Alfred to decide in my favor."

"No persuasion will be required. Alfred will grow up adoring his aunt and uncle Croft."

"Well, even if he does not, I have no doubt he will turn out a fine young man. You always did well by your boys and midshipmen."

"Those among them who were disposed to take direction," Wentworth replied, thinking of Dick Musgrove.

"As I told you when you received your first command, there are always a few maggots in the flour. You just do your best to keep them from contaminating the remainder."

Wentworth recalled the conversation. Admiral Croft, for all his present status and power, was a salty old sailor at heart. In a profession where promotion was often driven by influential connexions, he had advanced largely by his own merit, and for this Croft won Frederick Wentworth's respect even before he won the affections of Frederick's sister, Sophia. He was a forthright, sensible man of sound judgment, and when he gave advice, Wentworth listened.

"One of your own former midshipmen is presently in Lyme," Wentworth said. "Andrew St. Clair."

"Is he? I shall have to look him up. Do you know where he is lodging?"

"At the George, I believe. He lent assistance the day of Mrs. Clay's accident. Alfred is fortunate that he happened along."

"I am not surprised. I remember him as a quick-witted fellow."

"Might I enquire what else you recall about him?"

The admiral shrugged. "I took him on straight out of the Naval College. There are some captains, you know, who do not want College Volunteers—they think the young men are too bookish, and prefer their officers-in-training to have acquired all of their knowledge aboard ship, as they did. But I believe a mixture is good, and St. Clair was the most promising of his class. He quickly moved up the ranks to midshipman and master's mate before being made lieutenant. When he received his commission with the *Temper,* I was sorry to lose him."

"Have you followed his career since?"

"Our paths crossed occasionally while I was in the West Indies, but after the Admiralty sent me to the East—well, it is difficult enough to keep abreast of people and developments in your own fleet and at home, let alone a single officer on the other side of the world. Why do you ask?"

"I have heard his name mentioned in connexion with some incidents aboard the *Magna Carta* during his period as first lieutenant."

"What sort of incidents?" Croft's earlier jocularity had faded; he was now more the flag officer preparing to hear an unwelcome report.

"The discovery of some unusual cargo. And the action with the *Dangereuse.*"

"Where did you hear of this?"

"A friend whose cousin served with him."

The admiral was quiet for a moment. Standing beside a shelf upon which rested several nautical instruments, he picked up Wentworth's sextant. "Assure your friend that if there was anything amiss, the Admiralty would have addressed it."

"The Admiralty was busy fighting a war when these incidents occurred. The lords might not even be aware of them."

"Because they might not exist. Or they might not be what they appear." He slid the sextant's arm along its scale. "You are hearing of this thirdhand, years after the fact. Jettison it from your thoughts."

"That will not be easy."

"Frederick, if something inappropriate did happen aboard that ship, for the sake of your career, you do not want to be involved. Not every enemy should be engaged; sometimes it is best to let one pass." He returned the sextant to the shelf. "I will pay a call to St. Clair if it will relieve your conscience, but I want you to drop the matter."

Wentworth knew not what to say. This was a side of Croft he had seldom seen. In all the years of their acquaintance, he had known Croft primarily as a brother and mentor, not as a commanding officer. They had spent most of the war on different seas. Wentworth had never been on the admiral's flagship during action, had not seen him plot strategy, had not heard him issue orders.

Had not felt the weight of words he left unsaid.

Admiral Croft, sensing Wentworth's discomfort, forced a laugh. "Come, Frederick, do not a new wife and son warrant more of your attention than some long-ago incidents on a ship you were not even responsible for? You are a husband and father—you have new orders now. Take care of your family. And of Mrs. Smith. That good lady was saying again today how your friendship has improved her condition tremendously. By the way, she mentioned something about your helping her reclaim her husband's estate?"

The admiral's being more himself again, Wentworth shook off his own unease. "Yes. Mr. Smith's West Indian property is enmeshed in a legal tangle."

"Then that is another matter you should drop. If there are solicitors involved, they are the only ones sure of seeing any money. Let the pirates sort it out."

When Darcy next met with Wentworth, he sensed disquietude in the captain. They retired to Wentworth's study, where his host poured wine as before and invited Darcy to take a seat. He chose the newly mended chair, commenting that it seemed the repair had proved successful.

"I wish I could say the same for my enquiries," Wentworth replied.

Darcy wished so, too, and had come in expectation of hearing something useful to their investigation. He would not, however, allow disappointment to overtake him until he heard Wentworth out. "Were you able to learn anything?"

"I was. To begin with, the Musgrove your cousin mentioned is in fact the Dick Musgrove I knew. He not only served aboard the *Magna Carta* at the same time as your cousin, he also died on it—though in a different action. I asked his mother to forward me a copy of the letter Captain Tourner sent at the time."

He handed Darcy the letter. It included few particulars, and was very similar to what the Fitzwilliams had received from Captain Tourner upon Gerard's death: *It is with deep regret that I must write to inform you . . . died in action against . . . fought bravely . . . take comfort in knowing . . . an honorable death in service to His Majesty. . . .* So similar, in fact, that it was almost the same letter.

Darcy returned the letter to Wentworth. "What about Lieutenant St. Clair?"

"His history required more probing than I anticipated." Wentworth folded the letter and set it on his otherwise clear desk. "Andrew St. Clair has had a curious career. He comes from a landed but not extraordinarily wealthy family, and entered the Royal Naval College at age thirteen. He completed his Plan of Learning in just two years' time, earning the notice of the Lords of the Admiralty, and after a year at sea he was raised to the rate of midshipman. He distinguished himself both during and outside of battle; under Captain—now Admiral—Croft, he was on several occasions chosen to navigate captured prize ships into port, and eventually served as a master's mate—sort of a senior midshipman, with more responsibility. He sat for the lieutenant's examination as soon as he was eligible, passed on his first attempt, and was promoted at nineteen to second lieutenant of the war sloop *Temper*.

"The *Temper* saw considerable action, and Lieutenant St. Clair performed well enough to earn appointment to a ship of the line, the *Claudius.* Since he moved to the *Magna Carta,* however, his career seems to have stalled. Though from there he went on to ships that have participated in significant battles and taken prizes, he has bounced from appointment to appointment in a series of essentially lateral positions, never receiving promotion above lieutenant."

"Is that unusual?"

"Given the promise he demonstrated early in his career, I would expect him to have made post-captain by now, but he has not even risen to commander. It could simply be that other candidates with superior naval connexions have been given preference, but when I hear of a record such as this—frequent moves between ships, with no true advancement—it often signals a troublesome officer that every captain wishes to quietly pass off to someone else. We all suffer them. The fact that the beginnings of St. Clair's professional stagnancy appear to coincide with his service aboard the *Magna Carta*—scene of the dubious behavior you reported to me—leads me to wonder if that is indeed the case here."

"Did Admiral Croft offer any insight?"

Wentworth hesitated. "No. In fact, he discouraged me from pursuing this further. Most of what I did manage to learn, I obtained from other sources before I spoke with him."

"Were you able to discover anything about the *Magna Carta*'s action with the *Dangereuse,* beyond what St. Clair imparted to me?"

"Very little. From what I did find out, it seems the engagement was a debacle. The *Magna Carta* was escorting two merchant vessels—the *Montego* and the *Port Royal*. They were approached by a French frigate and a war sloop. The *Port Royal* made off with haste—merchant ships often do in such situations, getting out of the way and letting their warship escort do its job—but the *Montego* remained. Tourner initially had the advantage of position; as the French ship advanced, he had an opportunity to wear round and rake her, but he would not engage. Instead, he tried to outrun the *Dangereuse*. The French closed in, started firing broadsides, and crippled the *Magna Carta* to the point where they grappled and boarded. Were it not for the *Montego* firing some lucky shots that dismasted the sloop, Tourner would surely have been boarded by the crews of both French vessels and lost his ship. As it was, the *Magna Carta* was fortunate enough to prevail in melee and force the French boarding party to retreat. Tourner was lucky to avoid a court-martial over the encounter."

"Why would he not engage?"

"That, I could not determine. The only person who knows with certainty is Captain Tourner himself. And perhaps his second-in-command: Lieutenant St. Clair."

Twenty-seven

"Nothing can exceed the accommodations of a man-of-war; I speak, you know, of the higher rates. When you come to a frigate, of course, you are more confined."

—Mrs. Croft, *Persuasion*

*T*he grandest vessel Lyme's shipyards had ever produced, the *Black Cormorant* was a source of pride even to those who had not toiled at her creation. Built to cross oceans and return with exotic goods, she possessed the size and strength of a small warship. Her holds were spacious enough to carry the large cargos required to make transatlantic voyages worthwhile, and her deck would eventually bear cannons enough to protect them.

It was a morning launch, the timing dictated not by any human creature's convenience, but the tide. The ocean lapped onto the shore, as if reaching to draw in its newest pearl. When the water had come in as far as it could, the ship would be released to meet it.

All Lyme, it seemed, had turned out for the event. Visitors and residents, mariners and merchants, gentlemen and ladies, young and old, all crowded the shore to witness her first entry into the sea that would carry her to lands most of those gathered would never look upon, save in their own imaginations. Even the excise men took a break from their work, leaving the Customs House to observe the proceedings—probably calculating in their minds how much revenue would be generated by the merchantman's cargo holds when full.

Elizabeth, Darcy, and Georgiana recognized numerous people; Lily-Anne had come, too, but had a far more restricted circle of acquaintance. Thankfully, while the adults scanned the crowd for individuals they knew, the toddler was content to quietly observe the busy scene from her father's arms. The Harvilles and their sons were some distance away, separated from the Darcys by too many people to allow for any greeting more personal than a wave. Sir Walter and Miss Elliot, their black mourning clothes a somber—though, of course, elegant—contrast to the more festive attire of those around them, surveyed the scene with an air of royalty looking down upon the masses. Elizabeth also spotted Mr. Sawyer, the surgeon who had attended Mrs. Clay. She had yet to sight the Wentworths.

"I do not see Miss Ashford," Georgiana said. "She told me that she planned to come."

"Perhaps she is watching from the other side of the ship," Elizabeth said. She speculated that Georgiana's disappointment more likely derived from the absence of the brother who would accompany Miss Ashford, but she kept the thought to herself as Georgiana continued to survey the spectators.

"Mr. Elliot has secured himself a position close to the proceedings," Darcy observed.

Elizabeth followed his gaze to the ship. Mr. Elliot stood near the bow, the end farthest from the water. Between him and the vessel, a cluster of yard workers made some sort of preparation to the wooden rails alongside the cradle on which the long hull rested, its bow higher than its stern. At the moment, his back was to the ship as he scanned the crowd.

"Though not quite close enough to be mistaken for, say, one of the owners," she replied. "I wonder if he is seeking someone in particular. Captain Tourner, perhaps?"

"No—that is Tourner over there."

Darcy directed her gaze toward a corpulent, weathered man dressed in civilian attire that nevertheless created a naval impression; perhaps it was the gold lace on his cuffs. He stood not far from

Mr. Elliot, who surely would have seen him by now were he the individual he sought. The captain was engaged in conversation with the man who appeared to be directing the proceedings.

Mr. Elliot's gaze traveled until it reached the Darcys. Recognition crossed his countenance, and Elizabeth felt obliged to nod in acknowledgment. "Oh, dear," she said. "I hope he was not seeking us."

As Mr. Elliot made a nod of his own, an "Oh!" from Georgiana drew Elizabeth's attention.

"Here comes Miss Ashford," Georgiana said, "and Sir Laurence."

Elizabeth turned round to see the pair not approaching, but already upon them. The baronet greeted them—including Lily-Anne—with his usual congeniality. Elizabeth expected her daughter to flirt with Sir Laurence again, as she so often did when he came to call at the cottage, but apparently she had decided to leave the baronet to her aunt. She burrowed her face into the crook of Darcy's neck.

Elizabeth apologized to the baronet. "I think she is overwhelmed by all the people."

"Do not give it another moment's thought. *I* am overwhelmed by the number of people here this morning," Sir Laurence assured her. "We were fortunate to identify your party in the crush."

"This is indeed quite a crowd," Georgiana said.

"It is quite a ship," Sir Laurence replied. "Two years in the building. A thirty-two-gun is not a vessel Lyme sees launched every day."

"But where *are* the guns?" Georgiana turned toward the ship. "I do not see any."

"That is because the ship is not fully fitted out yet," he said. "She is like a young lady preparing for her coming-out ball. She may already have put on her gown, but her hair must still be arranged, her headdress secured, her gloves, shoes, and jewels donned. Right now she is but half dressed."

Sir Laurence's manner toward Georgiana had grown warmer upon each meeting—more attentive, more eager to please. In creating his image of a woman getting dressed, the baronet doubtless had a particular young lady in mind.

The comparison brought a slight flush to Georgiana's cheeks. She understood him. But instead of demurely changing the subject, as she might have done during their early acquaintance, she looked him straight in the eye. "If she is but half dressed, then why is she going out in public?"

Sir Laurence laughed. "Because she is a very solidly built young lady, and it will be difficult enough to get her out of her chamber without the added weight of all her accessories. She is already wearing some of them, such as her coppering, but imagine the struggle of moving her with a gundeck full of twelve-pounders."

"She has two gundecks, does she not?" Georgiana turned toward the ship. "Is that not what all those square openings on the sides are? For the cannons to fire through?"

Sir Laurence placed one hand on her shoulder and pointed with the other. "If you look closely, Miss Darcy," he said softly, "you will notice that she is a clever lady who knows how to dress herself to advantage. The lower row of square doors are not true gun ports, but the work of a skilled painter, creating the illusion of a second deck to discourage rogues who might take inappropriate interest in her."

He dropped his hand but remained close to her. The contact had been brief—just long enough to direct Georgiana's attention, ended before Darcy could even intervene—but it had revealed more about the baronet's intentions toward Georgiana than the baronet had revealed about the gun ports.

Elizabeth glanced at her husband—and in his answering look saw resignation. If Georgiana was receptive to Sir Laurence's addresses, he was, too.

Sir Laurence was remarkably well informed on the subject of ships, and took obvious pleasure in sharing his knowledge with Georgiana— who took equally obvious delight in receiving it. In fact, he seemed in elevated spirits today as he pointed out additional features of the *Black Cormorant* to his captivated listener.

Soon, the initiation of the launch drew their collective attention. A few dignitaries said a few words, then the dockworkers moved into position. At the master shipbuilder's command, the props supporting the stern were knocked away, and amid the cheers of the crowd, the *Black Cormorant* slid down the rails and into the water. Lily-Anne clapped her hands at the spectacle—as did everybody else assembled.

"What will happen to the ship now?" Georgiana asked.

"That smaller vessel over there will tow her to the quay, where they will finish fitting her out," Sir Laurence replied. "She is such a large ship, however, that once she has anchors and other necessities, she might moor outside the Cobb at times if the harbor is particularly busy."

As the crowd began to disband, Elizabeth looked for Mr. Elliot, wondering whether he would simply depart along with everybody else. Apparently, he had. She did, however, sight Lieutenant St. Clair, whom she had not previously seen at the launch. He was speaking to Captain Tourner, who was shaking his head.

She stepped closer to Darcy. "I wish we could hear that conversation. It does not appear to be going well."

Tourner shook his head again and started to walk away. St. Clair said something that caused him to turn around. He shrugged, said something back, and walked off. St. Clair did not follow.

Meanwhile, Georgiana and Sir Laurence apparently at last had become aware that there were other people around them, for Miss Ashford was now participating in their conversation.

"Never?" Miss Ashford looked at Georgiana with an incredulous expression.

"Never."

"Well, we must correct that posthaste," Sir Laurence declared. "Mr. Darcy, your sister is telling us that she has never in her life been in a boat of any kind. I at first thought she was jesting. Are you similarly deprived?"

"I have crossed the Channel, and raced friends on occasion during my Cambridge years."

"Very good. And you, Mrs. Darcy?"

"The closest I have ever come to being upon the water are the bathing machines here in Lyme."

"Oh, dear. Then you must allow me to engage a boat to take us all out on a pleasure excursion—not far, just enough for you to see the coast of Lyme Bay from the water. What do you say?"

Elizabeth hesitated. She had never felt a particularly intense longing to experience sailing. But since meeting the Harvilles and the

Wentworths and others whose lives revolved around the sea, since reading Gerard's descriptions of shipboard life in the early parts of his journal, she had developed a curiosity about how it feels to leave the land.

Darcy looked at Elizabeth. "Would you like to go?"

Georgiana positively radiated her desire to accept the invitation. Elizabeth could not deny her.

"Thank you, Sir Laurence," Elizabeth replied. "We happily accept."

"Splendid. I shall make all the arrangements. Business takes me out of Lyme for a few days, but we shall go as soon as I return."

The beach from which the ship had been launched lay adjacent to Cobb Hamlet, into which the Darcys and Ashfords walked together, then parted company. Sir Laurence's house, high on the cliff, was more directly reached by a road that led north from the hamlet, while the Darcys headed east toward the familiar Walk that would lead to Broad Street.

The hamlet, however, was flooded by a sea of dispersing spectators, many of them stopping in the middle of roads to greet neighbors and exclaim over what an exciting event they had all just witnessed. Lily-Anne clung to Darcy as he, Elizabeth, and Georgiana moved through all the people. They met with so much congestion that they found their progress utterly halted a few yards away from the entrance of the Sheet Anchor. The lane was blocked not only by pedestrians like themselves, but two coaches and a curricle whose drivers had for some inexplicable reason decided that this would be a good time to try to navigate the narrow road. Their party moved aside in order to give the vehicles as much space as possible in which to maneuver, and wound up flush against the building's wall.

Lily-Anne, who had behaved very well all morning considering the crush of people, grew impatient in Darcy's hold and expressed her wish to transfer to her mother's. Elizabeth took her, but before long the child was clamoring to stand and stretch her cramped legs. Elizabeth could not fault her, and, after extracting a promise from Lily to remain at her side, lowered her daughter to the ground—whereupon Lily giggled and bolted into the crowd.

Before either Elizabeth or Darcy could react, a passer-by scooped her up. "I think not, young lady." It was Lieutenant St. Clair.

He delivered Lily-Anne back to Elizabeth and greeted them all affably. Elizabeth and Darcy thanked him for intercepting Lily's flight.

"Were I small enough to dodge through everybody's legs and escape this crowd sooner, I would be tempted, too," St. Clair replied.

Given all the conjecture they had engaged in regarding St. Clair, Elizabeth and Darcy were not as easy in their manner toward him as was Georgiana, who, ignorant of their suspicions, was as agreeable as ever. Lily-Anne, however, seemed to take the most delight in St. Clair's joining them. As the adults talked, she repeatedly raised her head from Elizabeth's shoulder to smile at the sea officer.

Apparently, her daughter was a flirt after all. And a fickle one at that.

Darcy's obvious displeasure at Lily-Anne's disobedience was compounded by her playful attention toward Lieutenant St. Clair. "Give her to me," he said to Elizabeth. She transferred their daughter to him, and he excused himself to take her several feet away, where he could admonish their child without being overheard by St. Clair. Darcy was not given to public reprimands, particularly before a person they had cause to mistrust.

"Did you enjoy the launch?" Lieutenant St. Clair asked Georgiana and Elizabeth.

"Very much," Georgiana replied.

"Had I seen you there, I would have joined you to explain what was happening."

"That is most thoughtful of you," Georgiana said, "but Sir Laurence and his sister were with us, and he told us all about the *Black Cormorant* as she was launched. Sir Laurence knows a great deal about ships."

"Does he?" St. Clair's expression was equally curious and bemused.

"Well, not as much as you do, of course. But enough to narrate today's event and describe different parts of the vessel."

"So you now know a jib from a topsail?" he asked sportively. "A yardarm from a boom?"

St. Clair had such a disarming manner that Elizabeth found it much easier to speculate about his involvement in Gerard's death from a distance than in person. She glanced at Darcy, who, though still engaged with Lily-Anne, observed St. Clair. He did not appear overjoyed that the suspicious officer conversed with his sister. Elizabeth remained close to them, to monitor their discussion.

"He did not go into that much detail," Georgiana said. "Though what I did learn about ships made me want to know more. If you are going to tutor me, however, I hope we will start with something simpler than jibs and booms."

"We can start with whatever you wish. Though jibs and booms are not themselves difficult to comprehend—it is how to use them effectively that requires training and experience."

As the coaches and curricle still had pedestrian traffic halted, their party would not be advancing homeward anytime soon. Georgiana said, "All right, then. What is a jib?"

"A triangular sail at the front of the ship."

"And a boom?"

"A long pole run out to extend the foot of a sail." He smiled. "Were we on a ship, I would point them out to you, of course. But see? This is not so hard. What next?"

She glanced beyond his head, at the sign hanging above the tavern door. "What is a sheet anchor?"

His expression became more serious. "A sheet anchor is the largest and heaviest of a ship's anchors—the one every sailor hopes will never be used."

At his sober reply, her manner became more serious, as well. "Why is that?" she asked.

"Because it is the one whose strength is relied upon in the most dire crisis," he said. "The last hope when all else has failed."

To Georgiana's disappointment, Sir Laurence's business took him away from Lyme for a full se'nnight. She consoled herself during this period by enjoying the company of Miss Ashford, who again had been left behind in the care of her chaperone. Already friends, the two young ladies became close as sisters—a state each privately wished would soon be realized. Georgiana was so frequently at the Ashfords' house during Sir Laurence's absence that she knew their rooms almost as intimately as the Darcys' own. Elizabeth was treated daily to descriptions of the baronet's taste in furnishings, art, books, and anything else that reflected well on him.

"He truly is a most attentive brother," Georgiana said to Elizabeth one day after returning from yet another afternoon spent with Miss Ashford, "like my own. Miss Ashford says he is always remembering her with small gifts, and will probably surprise her with something when he returns from his present trip. She showed me several lovely pieces of jewelry he has given her, as well as a few animal figurines—a gold turtle, a porcelain hare, and an ebony cat. She collects them, and whenever he sees an unusual one, he acquires it for her. She said the cat came from Egypt. Is that not a sign of good character in a man? Not the presents themselves, or the money spent—the thoughtfulness. I think how a man treats his sister or mother is a test of how he will treat a wife."

Elizabeth agreed. The manner in which Darcy took care of his sister had influenced Elizabeth's own affections for him. And still did. It was under his guardianship that Georgiana had developed into the remarkable young woman she had become, and Elizabeth trusted that under his influence, Lily-Anne would grow to be as accomplished and amiable as her aunt.

While Georgiana was enjoying the company of Miss Ashford, Elizabeth and Darcy occupied themselves by watching the *Black Cormorant* take form.

The ship appeared closer to completion each time Elizabeth saw her in the harbor. Masts, rigging, and sails gave it a more finished outward appearance to her untrained eye. The status of the lower decks was less apparent. Thus far no guns peeked through the gun ports—real or painted—but it seemed that something or other was being hoisted or lowered on the ship whenever she visited the Cobb. Captain Wentworth, lending his powers of observation, mentioned things like tillers, sweeps, and capstans, but to her this was a foreign language. He further observed that although the vessel looked to have plenty of seamen already hired and expediting the fitting out, only some of them appeared to be living aboard yet.

She believed that Captain Tourner had already moved into his cabin. As Sir Laurence had predicted, the ship spent part of its time moored outside the seawall, where it could better withstand the shifts of wind and tide than could the fishing vessels and other small watercraft that called the harbor home. She and Darcy had seen Tourner being rowed out to the ship one day in a boat whose cargo comprised assorted chests and furnishings, including a handsome desk and a large wardrobe. She found it amazing that many captains and admirals furnished their cabins as they would their homes, but Captain Wentworth had pointed out that, for most of a captain's time, his cabin *was* his home, and that a man was better able to deal with the demands and crises of command if he were comfortable.

At last, to Georgiana's happiness, Sir Laurence returned to Lyme. The Darcys' cottage was his first call.

"Wish for fair weather on the morn, Miss Darcy. I came to you by way of the harbor, where I found a skipper delighted to take us out in his boat. At this time tomorrow afternoon, we shall be upon the water."

"I have been looking forward to it all week," Georgiana said.

"As have I." He regarded her in great earnest. "There is something very particular I plan to ask you when we are away from shore."

Georgiana fairly floated through the rest of the evening. As the sun set that night, she watched the sky for signs of clouds. Not one appeared on the horizon to trouble her.

Twenty-eight

"Being lost in only a sloop, nobody would have thought about me."
—*Captain Wentworth,* Persuasion

On the morning of the boat excursion, a heavy blanket stretched across the sky, creating a seascape so grey that the Portland lighthouse and other familiar landmarks of Lyme Bay disappeared from sight, and patches of fog enveloped parts of the harbor. At noon, the sun, grown impatient with this moodiness, attempted to dispel it by lancing the clouds. The resulting rays of light were rays of hope to Georgiana.

"There is no need to postpone our excursion, is there?" Georgiana asked Darcy. Her expression was more than merely optimistic; it was determined.

Darcy knew how much this afternoon's plans meant to his sister. Elizabeth had been present when Sir Laurence mentioned his "particular" question, and Elizabeth had, in turn, shared his statement with Darcy. He was nearly as pleased by the hint as Georgiana, and he did not want to disappoint her.

"We will keep a watch on the weather," he said. The day indeed appeared to be improving.

By the designated hour of departure, the sky remained grey, but the fog had dissipated, no rain had fallen, and the sun appeared more often than not. The wind was steady, strong enough to fill sails. As Darcy, Elizabeth, Georgiana, Sir Laurence, and Miss Ashford gathered at the harbor, it looked as if this would prove a pleasant day for sailing after all.

"Are you ready for one of the most memorable days of your life?" Sir Laurence asked Georgiana.

She answered him with a smile brighter than any Darcy had seen on her before. "I am."

They boarded the boat, seating the three ladies first, next the two gentlemen. All seemed part of a tacit conspiracy to ensure that Sir Laurence and Georgiana sat beside each other. Darcy and Elizabeth shared a seat with Miss Ashford.

The skipper oared them out of the harbor and made sail. They were off.

Darcy leaned toward Elizabeth and spoke into her ear. "Are you enjoying yourself thus far?"

"Yes." She glanced toward Georgiana. "Though not, I think, as much as a certain other passenger. Perhaps you ought to declare yourself to me again."

"Will you accept my first offer this time?"

"Perhaps."

They passed the *Black Cormorant*, moored just beyond the Cobb. Sir Laurence admired the ship's new rigging and speculated that she might have already taken a trial cruise.

"She is becoming a fine-looking ship," Georgiana said, though she had her eyes so much on Sir Laurence that Darcy could not have said how much of the merchant vessel his sister actually saw. For his part, Sir Laurence heard her praise as if she were complimenting his own appearance.

The wind propelled the boat across the waves. Unused to the movement, Georgiana several times placed a hand on Sir Laurence's arm to steady herself. They skirted the coastline of the bay, its rugged terrain so very different when viewed from the water. It was a highly pleasant beginning.

Until the wind shifted. No longer their ally, it teased their sails and tormented their skipper with its indecision over which way to blow. It wanted to gust strongly, of that it was sure. As strongly as the waves of the incoming tide leaped toward shore in ever-higher swells.

"Are we still safe?" Georgiana asked Sir Laurence.

"Most assuredly," he replied. "We have an experienced skipper. Nevertheless, I shall tell him to turn back."

Georgiana did not appear convinced. Neither did Elizabeth, who now rested an anxious hand on Darcy's arm.

They turned around, the skipper working hard to control his boat while the silent, apprehensive ladies clung to their seats against the force of each wave, and the gentlemen assisted with minor tasks as directed. The skipper had seen worse, he assured them, and so had his boat. There was nothing to dread.

Thus they tossed their way toward Lyme, gratefully watching the Cobb rise in the distance. They neared once more the *Black Cormorant,* the great vessel impervious to the forces that bedeviled the small watercraft. The skipper would have to give the merchant ship a wide berth to avoid being driven into it.

As they skirted round its side, a great breaking wave caught them. It heeled the boat to such extreme that its passengers slid to one side with the force, upsetting the vessel's balance.

The boat overturned, and all were suddenly, shockingly, plunged into the water.

Darcy surfaced first. He had reached for Elizabeth just as the boat capsized—but had lost hold of her hand. Panic seized him until he spotted her nearby, struggling to reach the surface, weighted down by her skirts. He pulled her up. Struggling to keep both himself and her afloat, he looked round wildly for the others. On the opposite side of the capsized boat, Sir Laurence supported Miss Ashford.

The skipper and Georgiana were missing.

From the *Black Cormorant* came a shout for ropes as a man dove from one of its gun ports.

He entered the water some yards away. For an agonizing, endless minute, he, too, disappeared from sight.

At last he surfaced. With Georgiana.

He held her securely as she gasped and choked and coughed up water on him. So violent were her convulsions that she could not at first open her eyes to see her rescuer's face. When at last she could, she was as surprised as the rest of them to recognize him.

Lieutenant St. Clair was relieved to have her expelling seawater on him. It meant she was alive.

But no one, including him, was out of danger.

"Hold on to the capsized boat, if you can," he shouted to the others above the crash of the waves. "Is everyone accounted for?"

"The skipper is missing," Darcy replied.

"No—he is here," called Sir Laurence as he reached the boat with Miss Ashford. "Caught in the rigging. It looks as if he bashed his head when the boat overturned."

The *Black Cormorant*'s crew tossed down ropes, their ends already looped and knotted. St. Clair swam to the one that fell closest to him, never letting go of Georgiana. He slipped the loop over Georgiana's head and under her arms, instructing the gentlemen to do the same for Mrs. Darcy and Miss Ashford. Holding Georgiana from behind, he wrapped her cold, stiff fingers around the rope.

"Can you hold on while they pull you up?"

She tried to speak but still could not; spasms of coughing yet shook her. But she managed to nod.

"It will not be a smooth ascent. Try to use your legs to keep from banging against the side of the ship."

She nodded again. A particularly intense cough seized her, and more water came up. When the spasm had passed, he bent his head to her ear. "Do not be afraid, Georgiana. You can do this. Are you ready?"

"Yes," she gasped.

He signaled to the waiting crewmen. When the rope became taut, he released her. One of her hands flew from the rope to grab his arm. But the panic passed, and she let go.

His gaze did not leave her until he saw her safely pulled onto the deck.

———

In years to come, Elizabeth would wonder whether the dreamlike haze in which she recalled that day was the result of terror or a bump to her head as the boat capsized. For now, she believed the latter, for she had an extraordinary headache.

Her feet no sooner touched the deck than she went to Georgiana, who was prone and still coughing up seawater, though not as violently as she had before. Georgiana waved her away. "Please—" She twice cleared her throat before she could continue. "Tell me what is happening with the others."

"They are just pulling Miss Ashford aboard now. I will go see about the men."

Elizabeth was so flustered, feeling that she ought to check on Miss Ashford but wanting nothing more than to look over the side for Darcy, that she barely noticed a crewman who approached to offer his assistance. "Is there anything we can do for the lady?"

"I do not suppose you have a surgeon on board?"

"No, ma'am, only a skeleton crew."

"Some blankets, then?"

Sir Laurence appeared next. Elizabeth decided to let him check on his sister, freeing herself and her conscience to go see how her husband fared. She watched the seamen hoist him up, not releasing her breath until he was on deck and in her arms.

Lieutenant St. Clair was the final person hauled aboard, after the dead skipper, whom he had disentangled from the rigging and looped a rope around. Though St. Clair had assisted his own ascent by using the rope to climb up the side, he was clearly exhausted. He panted with exertion, his wet shirt adhered to him, his hair had come loose from its knot.

And he was in better shape than the rest of them.

Sir Laurence and Darcy were equally drenched and bedraggled, though their shorter hair prevented them from appearing quite the ruffian St. Clair did. Sir Laurence's coat was a sodden mess, but nonetheless lent him a slightly more dignified appearance than that of St. Clair, who had shed his altogether. The ladies' wet gowns clung to them; fortunately for their modesty, all had worn fabric heavier than muslin. Like St. Clair, their hair hung wet and unbound.

Miss Ashford had swallowed a great deal of seawater, which she was now vomiting into a bucket. Though Sir Laurence attended her, murmuring words of brotherly concern, his divided attention kept straying to Georgiana, who had not yet been able to raise herself from the deck after she had sunk upon it. She had waved away not only Elizabeth but also him and Darcy, insisting that she would be fine in just another minute. She shivered. Elizabeth wondered where the blankets were.

St. Clair went to Georgiana. "Are you all right, Miss Darcy?"

She coughed again and forced herself to stand. "I will be, if everybody would simply—" She raised a hand to her head and started to sway.

St. Clair caught her before she fell. Her knees buckled, and suddenly she was seized by shaking she was powerless to stop. As he brought his arms around her to draw her against him more securely, Elizabeth thought she saw his own hands tremble.

He held her silently while aftershock sobs escaped her with unladylike force. No one dared intervene. But St. Clair's gaze swept the deck, and he was conscious of all the eyes upon them. Darcy's were wary. Sir Laurence's were hostile.

The blankets finally arrived, enough for them all. Darcy draped Elizabeth's over her shoulders. She then took another for Georgiana.

As Elizabeth approached, St. Clair whispered something to Georgiana. Calmer now, she drew a deep breath and slowly exhaled. Another whisper. She nodded and opened her eyes. Then she stepped back, avoiding his gaze as he helped put the blanket around her. When she reached up to take the blanket edges into her own grasp, their fingers touched.

She still did not look at him, but at her feet. "Thank you, Lieutenant." A blush crept across her cheeks. At least one part of her person had begun to recover its warmth.

His hands lingered a moment more before he dropped them. "I am once more your servant, Miss Darcy."

Elizabeth put her own arm around Georgiana and led her to where she had been standing with Darcy. As St. Clair accepted a blanket for himself from the seaman, Sir Laurence strode forward.

"Where is the ship's master?" he asked a crewman.

"I don't know, sir. None of us has seen Captain Tourner for hours. I thought he had gone ashore with—"

"Miss Darcy clearly needs a comfortable place in which to recover. My sister is also ill, and I cannot imagine Mrs. Darcy wants to stand on an open deck shivering. I am sure he would not mind allowing the ladies use of his cabin."

Lieutenant St. Clair's gaze darted to a door beneath the quarterdeck, then to Georgiana.

"Of course, sir," said the crewman.

Elizabeth appreciated the baronet's solicitude, but knew she would derive more comfort from Darcy's presence than from Captain Tourner's furnishings. "I thank you for my share of your concern, Sir Laurence, but I would rather stay with my husband."

"As you wish, Mrs. Darcy," Sir Laurence said.

St. Clair again glanced at the cabin door. "Perhaps Miss Darcy and Miss Ashford would also prefer to remain here on the main deck, close to their brothers."

"As my sister is too ill to answer for herself, I will speak for her recovery being better served by the privacy of the master's quarters," Sir Laurence replied. "Miss Darcy, would you not rather go rest in the cabin with her?"

Georgiana appeared too exhausted to long remain standing under her own power. "I would very much like to sit down."

Miss Ashford and Georgiana went into the cabin. When the door closed, Sir Laurence turned to St. Clair.

"That was all most heroic, Lieutenant." The baronet cast aside the blanket he had been using. His eyes were hard as stone.

"Now, kindly explain how you came to be on this ship."

Twenty-nine

He brought senses and nerves that could be instantly useful . . . he
was obeyed.

—Persuasion

*L*ieutenant St. Clair hesitated. "With respect, Sir Laurence, I
fail to see how that matter concerns you."

"It is not a matter of concern, but curiosity. We are all so fortunate that you happened to be aboard, and happened to observe our
mishap."

"I was aboard to meet with Captain Tourner."

"Indeed? As we have just heard, Captain Tourner is not here. He
must have forgotten your appointment. Did he send a boat for you,
to bring you out to the ship? Perhaps we can all use it to return to
land, since he is not available to steer the vessel into the harbor."

"I doubt the ladies will want to hazard another small boat on
these waters."

"Hmm. I suppose you are correct in that." He glanced toward the
door through which Georgiana and Miss Ashford had passed. "So,
this *meeting* that was to have taken place. Is that why you were in his
cabin? Were you awaiting his return?"

"His cabin?"

"Yes, Lieutenant. His cabin. The cabin we all saw you dive from.

233

Through the gun port." He looked pointedly at St. Clair's shirt. "And in which, I wager, we would find your coat and waistcoat, were we to look. Shall I ask Miss Darcy whether they are in there?"

The baronet's gaze was direct and unyielding; the officer's shifted to the cabin entrance.

"Yes, I was waiting for him, and watching out the window for his return."

"What were you to meet about?"

"Again, sir, I do not see where—"

"Indulge me."

"I had hoped to persuade him to hire me on as his first mate," St. Clair said.

"Indeed? How fortuitous! Then you will not mind taking the wheel now and guiding us into the harbor."

St. Clair regarded the baronet incredulously. "You are suggesting that I take control of a ship without its master's permission?"

"This is an emergency, Lieutenant. We need to get the ladies to shore, and as you noted, they cannot endure transport on another small boat. Do not worry—I know one of the owners of this vessel. If there is a problem, I will make it right. And if you do well, I will put in a word for you. Consider this an audition for the job."

Elizabeth thought Sir Laurence was being incredibly presumptuous, both in the authoritative tone he was taking with the man who had just saved all their lives, and in his commandeering of the ship. He was clearly jealous of St. Clair—jealous that the lieutenant had rescued Georgiana from the sea when the baronet could not, jealous that it had been St. Clair who had happened to be standing close enough to catch her just now, and to whom she had cleaved during her emotional collapse. Elizabeth was, however, so wet and weary, that she did not care what motivated the baronet, or what connexions he flaunted, or how pompous he had to become, if it meant they could get off this ship and onto land one minute sooner.

"Very well," St. Clair said, "but I will need the crew's cooperation."

"I will take care of that, too."

Lieutenant St. Clair assumed command of the wheel, and they raised anchor. Despite the choppy sea, it was a smooth, short, uneventful trip into the harbor. Until they reached the dock.

And a scream came from the captain's cabin.

Thirty

They were sick with horror.

—Persuasion

s it turned out, Captain Tourner was aboard the *Black Cormorant* after all.

In his wardrobe. With a head wound that made the skipper's look like a scratch.

Georgiana, wearing a gentleman's coat over her wet dress, was shaking once more. "We—we were cold and looking for more dry clothes. . . ."

Miss Ashford rushed to a basin and was ill again. Elizabeth looked as stunned as Darcy felt. Sir Laurence, too, surveyed the scene in disbelief before leveling an accusing glare at St. Clair.

"I am guessing, Lieutenant, that Captain Tourner declined your application for employment?"

Though the baronet was quick to judgment, Darcy did note that St. Clair appeared the only person not shocked by the discovery.

"I am not responsible for this."

"Indeed? Even had we not all seen you dive from this cabin, you admitted to being in it earlier. Is that not your waistcoat on the floor? It appears far too small for Tourner. So do the shoes beside it."

Georgiana looked down at the coat she was wearing, then at St. Clair. "Is this yours, too?"

St. Clair's gaze remained on Sir Laurence. "That does not mean I killed him."

"Then who did? Mr. Darcy, what do you think? Does not all the evidence lead to the lieutenant? He sneaked aboard, killed the captain, then remained hidden in his cabin waiting for an opportunity to slip away. No wonder he tried to discourage my sister and yours from coming in here."

When Darcy considered additional evidence of which the baronet was unaware—the conversation between St. Clair and Mr. Elliot that he and Elizabeth had overheard on the Cobb, the argument between St. Clair and Tourner that they had observed at the ship launch, the history between the captain and the lieutenant going back to the *Magna Carta*—he had to admit that St. Clair looked very guilty.

He addressed Lieutenant St. Clair. "Can you provide another explanation for how the captain came to be hidden in his wardrobe?"

"If I am being accused of murdering a fellow naval officer, this is a matter for the Admiralty to adjudicate. Anything further that I have to say on the subject will be said to them."

"Very well," said Sir Laurence. "Then let us go."

"I will help you escort him," Darcy said. If Lieutenant St. Clair were, in fact, guilty, he deserved whatever justice his court-martial determined.

"May I retrieve my shoes?" St. Clair asked.

"By all means," said Sir Laurence. "They are evidence. The waistcoat should come with us, as well."

St. Clair crossed the room. As he put on his shoes and picked up the waistcoat, Georgiana watched, her face a confusion of disappointment.

"Lieutenant?"

He turned toward her, his expression unreadable. "Yes, Miss Darcy?"

She took off his coat and held it out to him. "Take this, too."

The Darcys spent the next day simply recovering from their trial by sea. Early the following morning, a note arrived from Captain Wentworth. He had news, and asked that they all—Darcy, Elizabeth, and Georgiana—come to his home posthaste. He further requested that they bring the artifact and Lieutenant Fitzwilliam's diary.

Anne Wentworth herself opened the door to them. "I am glad you were able to come directly. We are gathered in my husband's study."

Darcy wondered who "we" comprised. He was kept in suspense by a brief stop in the sitting room, where Mrs. Smith sat alone, wearing a light shawl. When they entered, she was struggling to her feet with the aid of her cane, but sat back down upon recognizing them.

"Oh!" She laughed. "When I heard the door, I thought you were the sedan chair, come early. I expect it this half hour."

"Are you quite certain you wish to go alone this morning?" Mrs. Wentworth asked. "As I said before, I cannot accompany you just now, but am happy to do so later."

"No, no—this is my usual time, and I can see you are busy today. I will forgo seabathing this week, with Nurse Rooke visiting her sister in Bath, but I want to sit on the Cobb and take in the air. I will be fine—the chair men will help me to the bench, and come back for me when I specify. Do not give me another thought. You are so good to me, Anne—I wish I could be of more use to you in return, but I can at least be of minimal trouble."

"Very well, then. But the housekeeper has gone to market, so I will wait with you to let in the chair bearers."

"I can manage that, too, though I may be slow."

They compromised on Mrs. Wentworth's assisting Mrs. Smith to a settee in the front hall, where she could wait within easy distance of the door. When Mrs. Smith was moved, the Darcys and Mrs. Wentworth proceeded to the study.

A uniformed Captain Wentworth and another naval officer—an admiral, by the stripes on his cuffs—were already seated at the round table, but the admiral rose upon the ladies' entrance. Another officer stood facing the window, and turned upon the Darcys' arrival.

"Lieutenant St. Clair," Georgiana blurted.

Darcy, too, was surprised. He had not expected St. Clair to be at liberty until after his court-martial—if then.

"Miss Darcy." He studied her, searching for something. "You look well," he said finally. "I hope your health has not suffered as a result of your ordeal?"

"No, I—my health has not suffered."

"I am glad to hear it."

Georgiana's emotional state, however, had certainly been affected. She had not spoken of either Lieutenant St. Clair or Sir Laurence since disembarking the *Black Cormorant,* and when Sir Laurence had called yesterday to enquire after her, she had declined to see him, pleading fatigue. Darcy did not know what thoughts were presently somersaulting through her mind, but from her expression—hopeful but guarded—he expected she was struggling to understand how any human being could take one life and save another in the same hour. Darcy, too, was having trouble reconciling the man who yesterday had rescued them at great personal risk with what he had learned about St. Clair both before and after the event.

"How is it that you are here?" she asked. "I thought you would be in gaol, or wherever it is that the navy keeps men awaiting court-martial."

"It is a long story, one that the admiral will explain, and that I wanted you to hear."

Captain Wentworth introduced the Darcys to the man at his side, Admiral Croft.

"Well, Miss Darcy," Admiral Croft said after the formalities had been exchanged, "I hear you had quite a time of it the other day. I am glad you are still with us."

"Thank you, sir."

"Your brother and his wife are here at my request, for I believe they possess information vital to the navy, but as St. Clair said, you are here solely at his." He motioned them into seats at the table, upon which was spread a map of the West Indies and the Spanish American coast. Mrs. Wentworth took the chair closest to her husband; Elizabeth and Darcy the next two. Georgiana sat to Darcy's right, beside two empty chairs. St. Clair remained standing near the window.

Admiral Croft also remained standing. "Before I begin, you all must swear to keep secret anything you hear in this room today. In return, I give my assurance that you may speak with full latitude—do not fear that anything you reveal will be used against you or reflect poorly on family members connected with the navy. Further—" He looked at Lieutenant St. Clair with an expression of respect. "I vouch for the character of this young fellow. Whatever accusations have been fired at him or whatever suspicions you may harbor, you can speak as freely before him as you would to me or Captain Wentworth."

They all gave their promises.

"Thank you." Admiral Croft again looked at the young officer. "There are many whose lives will depend upon your secrecy."

Georgiana's gaze followed the admiral's. "Including Lieutenant St. Clair?" she asked.

"Actually," the admiral said, "this gentleman is not Lieutenant St. Clair."

Thirty-one

"Well, now, you shall hear something that will surprise you."
—Admiral Croft, Persuasion

H e is *Captain* St. Clair," Admiral Croft continued, "and has been for three years. However, none outside the Admiralty know his true rank because he is working for us on special detail, one best performed by an officer who is—or appears to be—a lieutenant."

All eyes were suddenly upon the newly acknowledged captain. Having spent years of his life deliberately deflecting attention, he now shifted self-consciously under so much of it, all at once.

"Congratulations, Captain," Wentworth said.

"Thank you," St. Clair replied, "but pray, do not congratulate me prematurely—I have not yet successfully completed my assignment."

"You will, my boy," the admiral said. "We are finally traveling under full sail." He turned to Darcy. "Captain Wentworth tells me that you recently received a diary belonging to your late cousin, who served with St. Clair on the *Magna Carta.*"

"I did." Darcy glanced at St. Clair. "It was in his sea chest."

"He says that it holds information about a pair of gold artifacts found aboard, and that you have one of them. Captain St. Clair and I would like to see the artifact—and the diary."

Though Darcy trusted the admiral—primarily based on his connexion to Captain Wentworth—he had not yet heard enough to surrender the pendant and Gerard's journal without reservation. "You have said that those at the highest level of the Royal Navy are behind Captain St. Clair's assignment. Might I ask why two small figurines hidden in a sugar cask on a ship years ago warrant such present attention by the Admiralty?"

"Because we are talking about a hoard of gold," St. Clair said, "hidden in hundreds of casks, aboard multiple ships, over a period of years."

"Captain St. Clair has been investigating a smuggling ring," the admiral said, "one that has been using Royal Navy ships to transport gold from the West Indies to England. The thieves, unfortunately, include numerous naval officers and seamen, along with corrupt revenue men and private individuals."

"And my cousin happened upon this?"

"Yes." St. Clair came forward and stood behind an empty chair, resting his hands on its back. "Though at that time, we were just beginning to learn of it ourselves. I initially became aware of something illicit going on in the region during my first tour of the West Indies, when I was aboard the *Claudius*. On a voyage between Central America and Jamaica, I noticed that our waterline was higher than it should have been for the weight our ship was carrying—the weight written in the manifest, that is. Our cargo was heavier than what had been recorded, enough to make the ship sit lower in the water than it ought."

"You monitor weight that closely?" Elizabeth asked.

"Weight and its distribution are serious matters on a vessel of any size. They affect balance, speed, and maneuvering," St. Clair explained. "Yet when I brought the discrepancy to my captain's attention, he dismissed it as an arithmetic error and said we were almost to port, so I should not concern myself about it. I left the matter alone as far as the captain knew, but I wondered whether what I had observed might be evidence of smuggling. This was not a great leap—the practice is widespread, and we had spent one night moored off an uninhabited part of the Costa Rican coast for reasons the captain never made altogether clear—but I had no idea what the contraband was, or who among the crew was involved. On that same voyage, we had one crewman kill another over a gold figurine that was obviously beyond the means of either of them to have purchased. The killer claimed they had found it, but never revealed where before he was hanged. At the time, I made no connexion between the incident and my smuggling suspicions."

The faint sound of a baby's cry drifted from the nursery. Mrs. Wentworth started and glanced at the closed door, but remained in the study while Mrs. Logan quieted her charge.

Captain St. Clair continued. "Our next port after Jamaica was the Bahamas." He leaned over the table and identified the islands for them on the map. "There, I was able to meet with Admiral Croft, whom I had always respected and trusted when he was my captain. When I shared my suspicions about the weight discrepancy with him, he said he had received reports of other suspicious cargoes, officers, and ships, and asked if I would quietly investigate them. I was appointed to the *Magna Carta,* and have continued the investigation ever since."

"Is not enforcement of excise laws the province of customs officials?" Darcy asked.

"Primarily," said Admiral Croft, "and we have been working in cooperation with them. The Articles of War, however, forbid His Majesty's officers from receiving and transporting goods aboard naval ships for personal gain. The Admiralty, therefore, has a strong interest in identifying and prosecuting any officers or seamen involved in such misconduct."

Darcy looked up at Captain St. Clair. "So when my cousin came to you with the information that the cook had found gold idols in a sugar cask—"

"That is when I first started piecing together what was occurring. Since then, gathering information aboard other ships and from other sources, I have gained what I believe is a comprehensive understanding of the operation, and in the past several weeks most of the remaining questions have been answered. We need to identify just a few more individuals, and then we can move forward with arrests and seizures."

"We want to perform them all at once," Admiral Croft said, "so that the ringleaders do not have an opportunity to rally their forces. And frankly, until now the war has prevented the Admiralty from devoting more resources to the smuggling investigation. Now that Bonaparte is defeated, we can address other matters we had been forced to defer."

"What we did not anticipate," St. Clair resumed, "was that private investigations undertaken by Captain Wentworth and you, Mr. Darcy, would overlap our efforts and in some cases interfere with them, by inadvertently alerting certain suspects to the fact that *someone* is examining their activities more closely than a guilty person wants. They are becoming nervous—which can be beneficial, because nervous people make mistakes. At the same time, they are getting desperate, which makes them unpredictable."

"You are speaking of my queries regarding my cousin's death?"

"Yes, and of Captain Wentworth's enquiries on behalf of Mrs. Smith."

"Mrs. Smith?" Anne Wentworth exclaimed. "She barely has anything to live on. She cannot possibly be involved in smuggling."

"In her case, it is because of the smuggling that she has nothing to live on," the admiral said.

Mrs. Wentworth regarded him with confusion. "I do not understand."

"Here is what we have learned," St. Clair said. "Some years ago, a naval ship needing to replenish its supply of fresh water stopped along the coast of Central America and sent a landing party onto shore. Deep in the jungle, they discovered more than mere water— they came upon a cave full of gold, a forgotten Spanish treasure trove of ancient artifacts once seized from the natives. They kept the discovery secret from the rest of their shipmates, planning to go back and retrieve it. The fortunes of war being what they are, and greed being the corrupting force it is, most members of the original landing party have died for a variety of reasons, but the story survived

and eventually found its way to the ears of someone with the connexions to do something about collecting the gold. Over the years—
impeded by not only our wars with the Americans and French, but
also the revolutions still sweeping Spanish America—the cache has
gradually been moved to Jamaica. That is what the extra weight was
on the *Claudius*—large amounts being transported at once, loaded
under cover of darkness. From there it has begun to be smuggled in
small quantities aboard Royal Navy ships and transported to England."

"In sugar casks packed at Mr. Smith's plantation," Darcy finished.

"Precisely," St. Clair said.

"The admiral, Captain St. Clair, and I discussed part of this before you arrived," Wentworth said to Darcy. "Apparently, Smith's
plantation was being used as a middle stage even before his trip to
Jamaica with Mr. Elliot. The business they conducted while there
refined the procedure and strengthened relations with the people
they relied upon to perform that end of the operation."

"What happened after Mr. Smith's death?"

"Nothing at all," St. Clair said. "The business has continued to run
as profitably as it ever did. The estate has not been sequestered—that
is a lie Mr. Elliot told Mrs. Smith to maintain control over the plantation and see the transport of the entire cache through to completion.
Meanwhile, he has been embezzling its legitimate profits, channeling
most of them into the smuggling operation."

"He has been stealing from a poor widow?" Mrs. Wentworth exclaimed.

"Not any longer," Admiral Croft said. "Captain Wentworth's
sounding has made officials both here and in Spanish Town look
more closely at the estate. It may be seized while an audit is conducted, but Frederick and I will make the revenue men see the injustice of her situation."

"If the smugglers have so much gold, and most of Mrs. Smith's
money, why do they not simply build their own ship to transport it?"
Elizabeth asked.

"Because the British Navy rules the waves." Admiral Croft, whose
slow pacing had taken him round the table several times in the

course of their discussion, reached the empty chair beside Captain Wentworth and sat down.

"A private ship is more likely to be captured by an enemy vessel or privateer," St. Clair said, "and those that do reach England are scrutinized by customs agents. Naval cargoes are subject to naval inspection—and we have identified plenty of dishonest workers paid to overlook violations—but nobody examines the personal possessions of naval officers." He took the last remaining seat, beside Georgiana. "Now that the war is over, however, there are fewer naval ships crossing the ocean, and many of the corrupt personnel—from captains down—are no longer in a position to transport the gold. Also, the seas are safer than they were for merchant ships. So building a private trading vessel is *precisely* what our smugglers are doing at present."

"The *Black Cormorant*," Elizabeth said.

"You, Mrs. Darcy, may come work for me anytime," said the admiral.

"No wonder Mr. Elliot wanted Captain Tourner as his ship's master," Elizabeth added. "Tourner had for years already been smuggling the contraband for him and his mysterious partner."

Both St. Clair and the admiral regarded Elizabeth curiously. "How do you know about Mr. Elliot's anonymous partner?" St. Clair asked.

"Mr. Darcy and I overheard the two of you talking. You were trying to persuade him to hire you, and asked to meet with his partner."

St. Clair stared at her. "I thought he and I finished that conversation long before we met you and Mr. Darcy near the quay."

Elizabeth looked at Darcy in rueful realization. She had just betrayed their discovery of the Cobb's odd acoustical properties.

"You might as well tell them now," Darcy said. "The knowledge could prove useful."

Elizabeth described the whispering effect, which they all found astonishing.

"Well! If that is not the strangest thing I have heard this week, I do not know what is." The admiral laughed and turned to St. Clair. "Instead of investigating the thieves, you could have just sat on the Cobb and waited for them to stroll along incriminating themselves."

"That would certainly be easier than extricating information from Mr. Elliot."

"Have you been able to determine the identity of his partner?" Darcy asked.

"I have long had my suspicions," St. Clair said, "but they were confirmed two days ago on the *Black Cormorant*." He paused, then looked at Georgiana. "It is Sir Laurence."

"Sir Laurence?" she exclaimed, her astonishment echoed by all but the admiral. Darcy could hardly himself believe it, and for a moment thought St. Clair's indictment was reciprocity for the baronet's accusations against St. Clair. But then he recalled how well informed Sir Laurence had been about the merchant vessel on the day of its launch, how he had described it with such pride to Georgiana. Darcy had thought his sister's suitor had wanted to impress her with his knowledge—now he realized the baronet had wanted to impress her with the ship itself.

Georgiana yet regarded St. Clair in disbelief. "That cannot be."

"I am afraid it is, Miss Darcy. I am sorry—I know you consider him and his sister your friends. But I not only heard him discuss his ownership of the *Black Cormorant* with Captain Tourner—" St. Clair paused again, longer this time, his expression holding the regret of one about to give pain. "I saw him kill Tourner."

"No!" She shook her head vehemently. "No—I know Sir Laurence. He could not possibly have committed such a wicked act."

She looked to her brother with eyes that implored him to somehow refute St. Clair's assertion. He would to heaven he could. Were it true, the baronet had sent Georgiana into Tourner's cabin knowing the dead captain's body was in the wardrobe—setting her up to make the discovery that would incriminate St. Clair. It was an act almost as unconscionable as the murder itself.

"How did you come to bear witness?" Darcy asked St. Clair.

"I went aboard earlier in the day, when the ship was still docked in the harbor, to talk to Tourner about coming on as first mate. The thought of serving under him again was abhorrent. I had originally—as you overheard, Mrs. Darcy—hoped to get hired on as the master, because I thought there would be a greater chance of direct contact with those at the highest level of the conspiracy; I had long suspected Sir Laurence was a party to the smuggling, but could never find any real evidence connecting him to it. Nearly everything goes through Mr. Elliot—Elliot is the middleman. But Mr. Elliot's partner was determined to have Tourner, so my choices were serving as second-in-command or watching the ship sail off, taking with it the opportunity to finally complete this investigation."

From the front of the house, the sound of a door opening indicated that Mrs. Smith's chair bearers had arrived. St. Clair, however, ignored the noise and continued.

"I met with Tourner. He was quite full of himself—and not a little rum—and so condescending that I almost decided I would rather give up the investigation altogether than spend months sailing to Jamaica and back as his subordinate. Tourner said he would consider me. When we had done with our conversation, he could not trouble himself to see me off the ship, and I decided to have a covert look about. Tourner left his cabin for a while, and I sneaked back in to see what I could find. Unfortunately, Sir Laurence came aboard—so eager to see how his new ship handled now that she was fitted out enough for a run that he insisted Tourner take him on a test cruise."

"If he goes to such trouble to distance himself from association with the smuggling, was he not concerned about the crew seeing him aboard?" Darcy asked.

"To them he was merely Tourner's aristocratic friend, not the ship's owner. Even so, that core crew is carefully chosen, every one of them a seaman who has worked on another ship the conspirators have used, who can be trusted to follow orders and keep his mouth shut."

As St. Clair spoke, Georgiana rose and walked away from the table. Doubtless, what the captain was about to describe would be painful for her to hear, and Darcy could not blame her for wanting to listen from a place where her countenance could not be observed by everyone in the room. St. Clair's concerned gaze followed her until she reached the window and looked upon the sea, her back to them all.

He returned his attention to those at the table and continued. "During the cruise, Sir Laurence was on deck with Tourner, but as the ship headed back it came to a stop not far from the Cobb. As the anchors lowered, I heard Sir Laurence and Tourner coming into Tourner's cabin, so I hid in his cot, drew closed the bed curtains, and lay still. I dared not shift enough to peer through the curtains; as you saw, the cot is suspended, and I feared any movement would draw notice.

"They shared a drink in celebration of the ship's performance. The bottle poured more after that—I know not how many times for each of them, but I expect the balance listed to one side—and Tourner's speech became less guarded. 'We will be able to move the gold in greater quantities now,' he said. 'That should please you. I could see in your face when you first laid eyes upon it that you wanted to get it to England in all haste.' Sir Laurence made no reply. Tourner continued, saying that Mr. Elliot had told him everything was arranged with their friends among the preventive men. Sir Laurence confirmed that Tourner should encounter no trouble from the revenue authorities upon his return, and enquired how soon the *Black Cormorant* could set sail.

"Tourner said that the ship was nearly fitted out. The guns were to be installed the following day; all she needed was the rest of her crew. He then put my name forward for his mate. Sir Laurence rejected me irrefutably. Tourner declared that, as master, the *Black Cormorant* was his ship and he should be able to choose whomever he wanted. Sir Laurence said no, the *Black Cormorant* was *his* ship, and the argument escalated from there."

Though it was warm in the study, Georgiana crossed her arms in front of her and rubbed her hands against them as if cold. She continued to stand facing the window, but stole surreptitious glances at St. Clair.

"Tourner was a man emboldened by liquor," St. Clair said. "In my days as his second, half my job while preparing for battle was privately monitoring his consumption so I knew what to anticipate during the action. He took offense at Sir Laurence's manner—he was a senior captain in His Majesty's navy, by God, deserving of respect. Then he reminded Sir Laurence how long he had been part of their 'private business'—and of how much he knew.

"They were not loud; in fact, Sir Laurence's anger was icy. They were engaged so intensely with each other, however, that I slowly shifted enough to peek through a crevice in the bed curtains. Sir Laurence's back was to me. He picked up the empty bottle from the table and pretended to examine it. 'If you indeed know so much about my business,' he said, 'then you know that I cannot afford a ship's master unable to hold his liquor—or his tongue.' Then he took the bottle and struck Tourner in the head."

"Tourner fell. Sir Laurence stepped around the body and went to the window—I suppose to see whether he might be able to simply drop Tourner overboard without being observed. I took advantage of this opportunity to lie back down so as to ensure my own presence remained unknown. I heard Sir Laurence utter an oath, then sounds of him opening the wardrobe and moving the body."

The horror Darcy experienced as he listened to St. Clair's narrative derived not from Tourner's death—the corrupt captain bore some responsibility for his own fate—but from the knowledge that the person who had so dispassionately taken Tourner's life was the very man to whom he had been willing to entrust Georgiana's. He had failed in his duty to protect his sister, and her stricken expression as she now stared at St. Clair pricked him with guilt. Thankfully, though St. Clair noticed that Darcy's gaze was upon Georgiana, he did not turn round to observe the effect of his revelations upon her. Instead, he continued his tale at a point that no longer focused on the baronet.

"At last, Sir Laurence left," he said, "and I heard one of the boats being lowered. I looked out the window to see how busy the quay was—and that is when I realized we were not in the harbor, but anchored outside of it. I was trapped on a ship I was not supposed to be on, in a room with the corpse of the only person aboard, to my knowledge, with the authority and skills to navigate the vessel back into the harbor so I could disembark.

"I decided that my best chance of escape lay in waiting for low tide at night, lowering myself down the side of the ship, and swimming for shore. As time passed, however, the water became choppier. I was looking out the window, reconsidering my plan, when your boat neared, heading toward port. A breaker was coming toward you, and I thought at first the wave was going to drive you into the side of the ship, but then the boat capsized altogether. I saw you all get tossed into the water, Miss Darcy farther away than the others. You know the rest from there. I stripped off my coat and shoes, and dove."

"Realizing that to do so would expose to Sir Laurence your presence on the ship—in the very cabin where he had left Tourner's body?" Darcy asked.

"You would never have been able to find Miss Darcy—not in time, not with two other ladies also needing assistance."

Georgiana regarded him in quiet contemplation. "You compromised your investigation—more than three years' work—to save me?"

St. Clair turned then, to face her. Darcy could no longer see the young captain's expression.

"How could I not?"

The admiral regarded his protégé with esteem, but also resignation. "It was an honorable act, and when Captain St. Clair informed me of it, I said I would have expected no less of him. From a tactical standpoint, however, our line has been cut. Whether Sir Laurence believes St. Clair acted independently in boarding the ship—a mere out-of-work sea officer seeking employment—or realizes he had official motives, we have lost any chance he had of gaining the baronet's trust. We now must take a different tack."

St. Clair turned to Darcy. "We need to apprehend as many of the conspirators as possible so that all the work done to this point is not lost. Therefore, I would like to see Lieutenant Fitzwilliam's diary, in hopes that it will provide evidence."

Darcy handed the journal to St. Clair. "There are but two passages pertaining specifically to the artifacts."

"I am interested in everything your cousin observed from the time he joined the *Magna Carta*."

As Captain St. Clair opened the volume, Georgiana returned to her seat and leaned toward Darcy. "May I see the gold figurine?" she whispered.

He withdrew the pendant from his pocket and gave it to her. She frowned upon first receiving it. Indeed, it was not the sort of objet d'art that he expected would appeal to a young lady whose taste ran toward more classical images. She traced its lines with a fingertip, her expression troubled.

St. Clair, meanwhile, commenced reading. He skimmed quickly, pausing to offer an occasional explanation or remark. "Lieutenant Wilton—it was he who oversaw the loading of the contraband sugar casks onto the ship. They were all supposed to go to the captain's private stores, but one of them accidentally wound up among our mess's provisions. . . ." He nodded. "Yes, Tourner never initiated engagements when he had contraband aboard—I think he feared discovery if he lost and the ship was seized. . . ." A few pages later: "I would much rather have dined with my own mess than accept Tourner's invitations. But Mr. Smith's rum had the favorable effect of loosening Tourner's lips, and when we were alone he would boast of the fortune upon which he would retire. Occasionally he would mutter hints that the fortune did not consist entirely of prize money, and I would ply him for particulars."

When he neared the end of the diary, he said Musgrove's name aloud. "I had your cousin to thank for that lead, Mr. Darcy, as I never ordered an inventory. Musgrove was an accessory to the conspiracy, though his was a minor role. He was simply not clever enough to be entrusted with much responsibility or information."

"How did he die?" Anne Wentworth asked.

"He was impaled by a large splinter of the hull when a cannonball struck the ship. It was probably the most glorious moment of an otherwise unambitious career."

St. Clair returned his attention to the diary, his eyes moving more slowly over the final entry. "He told me of only one idol," he said. "He must not have trusted me—not completely—and withheld the other to offer as evidence to someone else if I failed to act." He released a heavy breath and looked at Darcy. "Indeed, his caution was warranted, for he was surrounded by conspirators, and I could just as well have been one of them. At the time of my last conversation with him, even I could not guess the extent of the larger plot he and Hart had happened upon."

Darcy at last voiced the question he had been wanting to ask since this discussion began—indeed, since he had first read the page to which the journal in St. Clair's hands was now turned. "Did Gerard die as a result of it?"

"As a result of the scheme, or of my ignorance?" St. Clair closed the diary but did not hand it back to Darcy. His face held regret. "Both, I believe. When he came to me with news of the discovery, I needed time to ponder what it meant, and to determine how to proceed. I knew enough of Tourner's character to distrust the captain, so I discouraged Lieutenant Fitzwilliam from reporting the incident to him. However, as we now know, there were others aboard who were also part of the conspiracy, and I did not consider that the conversation between your cousin and Hart might have been overheard."

"By whom?" Darcy asked.

"Lieutenant Wilton's cabin adjoined Lieutenant Fitzwilliam's, and canvas walls are hardly soundproof."

A weight settled on Darcy's chest. "Did Lieutenant Wilton shoot my cousin during the battle?"

"No. But I believe he reported the conversation between Hart and Lieutenant Fitzwilliam to the captain, for I saw him go into Tourner's cabin just before your cousin came to me about the figurine. I thought nothing of it at the time, because there were any number of official matters about which he might have needed to inform the captain, even though Tourner was entertaining Mr. Elliot and the others. But after the battle with the *Dangereuse,* as I began to amass more information and realized Wilton was in collusion with the conspirators, I suspected he had told Tourner that Lieutenant Fitzwilliam had become aware of their illegal commerce. And that Tourner's guests also learned that Fitzwilliam had knowledge of it."

"What led you to that conclusion?" Darcy asked.

"When the *Dangereuse* retreated, she was forced to leave behind some of her boarding party, who became our prisoners. One of them, an officer, told me just before we turned them over to the British authorities that he had seen Lieutenant Fitzwilliam shot by a civilian gentleman aboard."

"Which gentleman?"

"His words were veiled, but he said he had been shocked to witness a future baronet shoot one of His Majesty's officers."

Though Darcy had sought the truth about Gerard's death, when it came, he was unprepared for the cold sickness that spread through him. "Can this Frenchman's word be trusted?"

"Had he told me immediately, or during the time he was in our custody, I might have thought he was lying in an attempt to use the information in exchange for better treatment. But based upon his timing—when he had nothing to gain for telling me—and upon the honorable conduct I observed in him during his captivity, I believed him. I have since learned that he is a secret Royalist, with connexions to both the French and English aristocracy."

"Was he acquainted with Mr. Elliot?" Elizabeth asked. "Is that how the prisoner knew he was a future baronet?"

"If he was, he never let on to that fact during his captivity. Even so, Captain Tourner continued to entertain Mr. Elliot and his companions in the weeks after the prisoners were taken, so I imagine the French officer overheard some of our men talking about the gentlemen and learned more about them that way." St. Clair paused. "Mr. Elliot, however, was not the only future baronet aboard the *Magna Carta* on the day your cousin died."

"Who was the other?" Darcy asked.

Georgiana's hand closed round the pendant she yet held. "Sir Laurence."

Thirty-two

*It now became necessary for the party to consider what was best
to be done.*

—Persuasion

*G*eorgiana looked ill as she searched St. Clair's face for confirmation. "Sir Laurence came into his baronetcy two and a half years
ago—after the events aboard the *Magna Carta* that you have been
describing. It is he of whom you speak, is it not?"

"Yes," St. Clair said. "Of course, he was simply 'Mr. Ashford' then."

"But already a gentleman who enjoyed the life of an aristocrat,"
Georgiana said.

Elizabeth heard the revelation with only mild surprise; as their
discussion had progressed, she had begun to harbor her own suspicions about the identity of Captain Tourner's third guest. "Was he
traveling with Mr. Smith and Mr. Elliot?" she asked.

"He had traveled to visit his godfather, the Duke of Manchester—
Governor of Jamaica," St. Clair said. "Once, while I dined with the
three gentlemen at the captain's table, Sir Laurence mentioned that
he had shared a slight acquaintance with Mr. Elliot and Mr. Smith in
London, and by happenstance had booked passage on the same ship
to the West Indies. English society on the island is so limited that
they could not help but meet each other periodically during their

time there, which advanced their acquaintance. Sir Laurence, however, was definitely a detached third party to the well-established friendship of the other two, and seemed perfectly content to remain so."

"When do you think he became part of the conspiracy?" Darcy asked. "He told us at the launch that the *Black Cormorant* had been two years in its construction."

"If he was involved in Lieutenant Fitzwilliam's death, then he was involved in the conspiracy by the time the *Montego* and *Magna Carta* set sail for England—possibly before they ever departed London; after all, we have only their word for it that their London acquaintance was slight. In fact, that is the supposition I have been exploring most recently. I think Mr. Elliot and Mr. Smith approached Sir Laurence as a potential investor back in London, and that he traveled to the Caribbean to see the cache of gold for himself before deciding to finance the building of a merchant ship."

"I notice that you continually refer to Mr. Elliot and Mr. Smith in tandem," Mrs. Wentworth said. "Are you certain that Mr. Smith knew about the smuggling? At the risk of appearing naïve, I have always received the impression from Mrs. Smith that Mr. Elliot led his friend so thoroughly that it is possible all of this transpired around Mr. Smith without his even realizing it. Has anybody spoken to Mrs. Smith about it?" She turned to her husband. "Has any evidence been found among his papers that implicates him—or that could illuminate the role of Sir Laurence?"

"I have read all the documents and memorandums Mrs. Smith turned over to me," Captain Wentworth said. "I saw nothing obvious—but at the time, I was not looking for allusions to smuggling or association with Sir Laurence Ashford. I will look through them all again as soon as this discussion concludes."

"I would like to read them with you," said St. Clair.

"Of course. Are there other individuals or details we should look for?"

"I have not yet been able to determine the end recipient of the artifacts once they reach England. Mr. Elliot arranges for the casks to be retrieved once unloaded from the ships; I believe they are moved temporarily to a hiding spot on property he owns near Sidmouth. But once the artifacts are removed from the casks, they seem to disappear. I suspect they are being melted down for their gold value alone."

"No," Elizabeth said. "If Sir Laurence is investing in this enterprise, he would not be a party to the destruction of artifacts." She glanced at Georgiana, giving her an opportunity to express her opinion—after all, Georgiana knew Sir Laurence better than did anybody else in the room—but Georgiana was looking at the pendant again. Elizabeth turned to St. Clair and Admiral Croft to explain. "The baronet and his sister came to dinner one night, and the conversation drifted onto the subject of the marbles Lord Elgin removed from the Parthenon. Sir Laurence emphatically asserted his support for Elgin. He considers the earl a hero for having rescued the sculptures from the neglect and deterioration they suffered since the country came under Ottoman control."

"In fact," Darcy added, "he said that Lord Elgin's actions were justified whether executed legally or not, and that he would have done the same."

"He *has* done the same," Elizabeth said. "Like Elgin, he has arranged transport of ancient treasures from a part of the world whose conquerors did not appreciate their value, who indeed melted down much of the other gold they found."

"And Spanish America remains in such a state of political upheaval that had the artifacts been found and seized by local government before they were removed to Jamaica, their fate would have been uncertain." St. Clair nodded. "I can see Sir Laurence excusing his activities on those grounds. But if the gold is not being melted, where is it going?"

"I think I may know," Georgiana said quietly. All regarded her expectantly, but she did not immediately speak again. Instead, she held the bird pendant out to St. Clair. "Do all of the artifacts resemble this one?"

St. Clair placed his hand under hers and raised it to examine the idol. "An informant who claimed to have viewed the entire cache described all manner of items—pendants such as this one, figurines depicting various animals, jewelry, ritual objects, and more. Of the pieces I have seen myself, yes, this is representative of their style."

"Might turtles be among the animal figures?" she asked.

"They could indeed. The idol Lieutenant Fitzwilliam turned over to me was a tree frog." He looked at her earnestly, her hand still resting in his. "Miss Darcy, if you possess any intelligence on the subject, pray disclose it to me—even if it is only conjecture."

"Sir Laurence has kept at least some of the artifacts for himself. I have seen only one—a turtle figurine he gave to his sister. But he told me he has an extensive collection of art from around the world, and after all I have heard this morning, I am supposing it includes numerous relics from Central America. However, he is not given to excess—at least, not from what I have seen. He could not possibly intend to keep the entire hoard for himself once it is transported to England, could he? It sounds as if there is too much of it for any one person to enjoy simply for its aesthetic or historic value."

"Yet he cannot give it away to the British Museum as Lord Elgin has done," Elizabeth said, "or attempt to sell it to the government, without exposing the illegal means by which he acquired it."

"No, but he could quietly sell pieces to individuals who share his appreciation and discretion," Darcy said.

"Private collectors." St. Clair took the pendant from Georgiana and released her hand. "Of course. Sir Laurence doubtless has friends with the same interests he does, and has had time to develop an underground market of collectors eager to acquire the artifacts." One could see the rapidity with which his mind was working through this newest possibility. "In fact, now that construction of the *Black Cormorant* is finished and the war is over, the ship can transport the objects to buyers not only in England but also in countries and ports previously inaccessible. He will easily earn back his investment and profit quite handsomely, even after Mr. Elliot and all the other participants are paid off."

"Not if we have anything to say about it," Admiral Croft declared.

St. Clair turned to Georgiana. "Thank you, Miss Darcy. I had been unable to physically connect Sir Laurence with the artifacts, and one cannot level accusations against a baronet—the Governor of Jamaica's godson, no less—without evidence that cannot be dismissed or minimized. But if you have seen one of the artifacts among his possessions—"

"Among his sister's possessions," she corrected. "At their house here in Lyme. The majority of his collection, however, is at Thornberry, his country house in Somerset."

"Admiral, is this enough for a search warrant to be issued?" St. Clair asked.

"When combined with your testimony about Captain Tourner's murder, I should certainly hope so. We shall want his Somerset estate searched, as well. Even then, the artifacts might be hidden."

"Is this the final bit of evidence you needed to proceed with all of the arrests?" Darcy asked.

"There is one other main conspirator whom we have been unable to identify: the man who initiates contact with the high-level naval officers whose ships they have been using," St. Clair said. "We know of individual corrupt officers, such as Tourner, who are part of the ring, but not the liaison."

"It is not Mr. Elliot?" Darcy asked.

"Mr. Elliot does not have naval connections of his own, so I am unsure how he and Mr. Smith recruited new captains and other officers to their conspiracy—at least, not initially; once some were on board, those individuals might have made their own recommendations. Nor am I sure how Mr. Elliot or Mr. Smith came to learn of the cache of gold in the first place."

"Perhaps we should ask Mrs. Smith about other associates Mr. Elliot might have," Mrs. Wentworth suggested. "She is not here now; she is on the Cobb—I heard the chair arrive for her—but she knows more about Mr. Elliot's past than does anybody else, and when she learns he has been stealing from her all these years, I expect she will be more than happy to assist this investigation in whatever way she can."

Thinking back upon the information Mrs. Smith had already shared, it seemed to Elizabeth that one of Mr. Elliot's most significant past associates had been missing entirely from this discussion.

"Could the liaison have been Mr. Clay?" she asked. "The Smiths, the Elliots, and the Clays were very close friends. If two of the gentlemen were conspiring in a fortune-making scheme, would not all three? Mr. Smith owned the plantation, Mr. Elliot attended to the details . . . did Mr. Clay possess naval connexions?"

"Not to my knowledge." Mrs. Wentworth thought a moment, then added, "But I recall Mrs. Clay once saying that *she* had known a great deal of the profession."

She did, Elizabeth thought. Biblically. And then another thought struck her.

"Perhaps, Captain St. Clair, you have been unable to identify the man who acted as the conspirators' naval liaison because that individual is not a man."

His brows rose. "I confess, that notion never occurred to me."

"According to Mrs. Smith, Mrs. Clay had affairs with numerous naval officers, before and after Mr. Clay's death," Elizabeth said. "What if one of them told Mrs. Clay of the treasure hoard? And what if she, in turn, told Mr. Elliot?"

"Why Mr. Elliot?"

"Of her closest friends, he was the one who possessed both the cleverness and the means to do something with the information."

"She also might have recognized in him a kindred scheming nature," Mrs. Wentworth added.

St. Clair nodded. "All right. Would she have confided her source to Mr. Elliot?"

"Apparently, the only person among their set who did not know about her extramarital affairs was Mr. Clay, and even he might have been turning a blind eye," Elizabeth said. "So, yes, for the purposes of our present discussion, let us assume she told Mr. Elliot. He definitely became aware of her naval paramours at some point, for he mentioned them in a quarrel that I overheard the night before Mrs. Clay died, and which I am certain was between the two of them. She was accusing him of unfaithfulness, and he—"

Elizabeth stopped as parts of the argument suddenly returned to her mind. *I saw you leave the Sheet Anchor with one of them, and later walking on the Cobb with the other . . . I thought the business had ended,*

but you have been carrying on behind my back. . . . *never would have begun had I not been so foolish as to introduce you.* . . . *Where is my share of
what they have received all these years?*

"The business" . . . Mrs. Clay's "share" . . . a meeting at the Sheet
Anchor—a pub frequented by sailors and Captain Tourner in particular. And Mr. Elliot's response: *You are hardly guiltless yourself. Unless
you are an utter fool, you will keep your mouth shut.*

She gasped. All this while, she had assumed that Mrs. Clay and
Mr. Elliot had argued about sexual infidelity.

"I thought that Mr. Elliot's assignations had been with other
women." She looked at Darcy. "But now, after learning of his smuggling enterprise—"

She saw in Darcy's eyes that he followed her reasoning. "I believe
you are right. She was in fact referring to meetings with other members of the conspiracy."

Elizabeth turned to St. Clair and Admiral Croft. "Mrs. Clay was
furious that 'business' she thought was over had continued without
her knowledge. She said that she had made the introductions, and
she wanted her share of the money they had received. I wonder if,
when Mr. Smith died, Mr. Elliot told Mrs. Clay a similar lie to the
one he told Mrs. Smith—that legal issues surrounding the West Indian plantation had forced them to stop or suspend the smuggling."

"What did Mr. Elliot have to say in his defense?" St. Clair asked.

"That his recent meetings were none of her concern. But then she
threatened to tell what she knew. Mr. Elliot warned her to keep silent,
lest she incriminate herself along with him."

From somewhere in the house, a clock chimed. The hour was later
than Elizabeth realized. Admiral Croft rose. "Time and tide waiteth
for no man, and neither will the smugglers." He began to slowly pace
around the table again. "The course of our discussion has led us here:
Mrs. Clay learned of the treasure from one of her naval acquaintances, and told Mr. Elliot about it. Mr. Elliot rigged up a plan to use
Mr. Smith's plantation to hide the treasure in sugar casks headed for
England, and with Mrs. Clay's help, he recruited officers to transport
the treasure aboard their ships. Once the gold reaches England, it

goes to Sir Laurence, who keeps some of it for himself and sells the rest to other collectors. The baronet has also financed the construction of the *Black Cormorant,* which is ready to set sail."

"Except it now has no master," St. Clair said. "And somehow I do not think he is going to hire me for the post."

"Aye, there will be no more sailing under false colors for you," the admiral said. "But I also hope there is no need." His pacing had brought him to a shelf upon which Wentworth's compass rested. He picked it up, contemplating it a moment before turning to face them.

"We are navigating by guess and by God," he said. "I wish we had more evidence before engaging the enemy—it is St. Clair's word against the baronet's as to what occurred in Captain Tourner's cabin, and Sir Laurence has powerful friends. But we are out of time. I believe that we have enough to arrest Sir Laurence and Mr. Elliot, and to detain them long enough to execute search warrants on their houses. We had just better pray that we find what we expect."

The admiral set the compass back on the shelf. "If we are mistaken, the investigation is sunk."

Thirty-three

Pity for him was all over. But this was the only point of relief. In every other respect, in looking around her, or penetrating forward, she saw more to distrust and to apprehend.

—Persuasion

*A*dmiral Croft departed to coordinate with the customs collector and other local authorities the simultaneous arrest of Sir Laurence, Mr. Elliot, and lesser conspirators who could be found in Lyme. Once the ringleaders were apprehended, a telegraphic dispatch would be sent to the Admiralty from the signal house at Lambert's Castle to initiate the arrests of corrupt officers and conspirators in other ports.

Though Captain St. Clair wanted to accompany him, upon the admiral's order, he remained at the Wentworths' home. "We cannot risk your being seen by Sir Laurence or his accomplices," the admiral told him as they stood in the study doorway. "Your liberty in the wake of Captain Tourner's murder is as good as a signal flag. Once all is in place, I will come collect you before the warrants are executed. I assure you, Captain—I would not deny you the satisfaction of being present when at last we deliver our broadside."

Georgiana, meanwhile, rose and went back to the window on the opposite side of the room. Elizabeth followed. She attempted to read her sister-in-law's expression as she gazed upon the sea, but Georgiana's face was inscrutable.

"Georgiana?"

Georgiana attempted to draw a deep breath, but it came in the short tugs of one trying to maintain composure. She released it—an equally shaky effort—but managed to hold herself together. "I am the most extraordinary fool."

"Do not berate yourself so. Sir Laurence deceived everyone, myself and your brother included."

"But I spent more time with him and Miss Ashford than did anybody else. Of us all, I should have suspected that something about him was not as it seemed."

"You are not by nature a suspicious person."

"Perhaps I should be." She turned from the window, her expression rueful. "At least, when I am near the sea—that is where Mr. Wickham duped me, too."

"I do not think the sea is to blame. In fact, it seems rather to reveal character—it did in the case of Captain St. Clair."

Georgiana had not looked at St. Clair since their discussion broke up, but now hazarded a glance in his direction. The admiral having departed, he was talking to Darcy, but both men had half an eye on Georgiana. Upon being caught observing her, St. Clair immediately averted his gaze; Darcy questioned Elizabeth with his. He wanted to know his sister's state, which Elizabeth silently assured him was sound. Or would be. Captain St. Clair's expression had also shown concern, though of a less brotherly sort.

"I underestimated Captain St. Clair, as well," Georgiana said. "All in all, I have not proved myself a very good judge of men."

"Neither have we. Darcy and I were fairly convinced that St. Clair was involved with Lieutenant Fitzwilliam's death."

"But see—you knew there was more beneath the surface. He *was* involved with Gerard's death; he has spent years trying to bring the conspirators to justice—while I was daydreaming about a marriage offer from Gerard's killer." She shuddered. "Had my wish been granted, I dare not contemplate what my life would have been as Lady Ashford. Captain St. Clair delivered me from more than the sea."

That gentleman and Darcy were at that moment also discussing the subject of Lieutenant Fitzwilliam's death.

"As you said earlier, there was more than one future baronet aboard the *Magna Carta* at the time my cousin died," Darcy said, "but you never definitively stated which one shot him. Was it Sir Laurence?"

"I wish I could tell you with certainty," St. Clair replied. "My instincts say it was Sir Laurence, but it could have been either of them. In preparation for battle, the pistol cases were opened, and every man was armed. And as I explained to you before, in the chaos of a boarding action, it is challenge enough to remain aware of all that is happening in one's immediate surrounds. We are fortunate Lieutenant Fitzwilliam's death was witnessed by anyone at all."

Anne Wentworth quit the study, her mission threefold: to ascertain whether Mrs. Smith had yet returned from the Cobb, to order refreshments for her guests, and to check on Alfred. Captain Wentworth asked her to send Mrs. Smith to them if she were indeed home. He then crossed to a tall bookcase and lifted down from a shelf an inlaid box.

"This contains all of Mr. Smith's papers that his widow turned over to me."

He brought the box to the table. Captain St. Clair, Darcy, and Elizabeth came over. As Darcy rolled up the map and put it aside, Wentworth opened the box and withdrew the papers. They each took a handful and commenced reading. Georgiana remained by the window, her thoughts too full to read anything closely, and unlikely to become more settled by closer proximity to Captain St. Clair.

Elizabeth read through several letters, including a few from Mr. Elliot. The pile held correspondence from other individuals, as well. One sloppily folded letter—apparently from Mr. Smith's mother— had at some time come into unfortunate contact with a sticky substance of indeterminate origin. After skimming three full pages of trivial family news—no wonder the Smiths had suffered financial woes, if his mother's letters were always so voluminous—Elizabeth found stuck to the back of the fourth page a torn fragment from a note in a different hand.

Such proof is regrettable, but there is nothing to be done about it. Fortunately, her spouse is determined not to notice, and yours too naïve to suspect. If it comes to it, she can claim her grandfather or some other long-dead relation had red hair.

Elizabeth reread the lines, then shuffled through the remaining papers in her pile. Darcy interrupted his own reading to question her with a glance.

"I am looking for the other pieces of a torn note," she explained. "Have you any fragments in your stack?"

Darcy set down the letter he had been perusing and started to riffle through the other papers in front of him. He had not gotten far, however, when Anne Wentworth returned to the study.

"Frederick." Anne's face was pale, her voice unsteady. "Alfred is missing."

Thirty-four

*"We must be decided, and without the loss of another minute.
Every minute is valuable."*

—*Captain Wentworth,* Persuasion

*M*rs. Logan was in tears.

"I fed him and put him down to sleep. Then I went out—I needed to go to the market, and I thought to perform the errand while he napped. You were all in the study—it seemed like such an important meeting; I did not want to disturb you—I told Mrs. Smith I was going. I expected to return before her chair arrived, but I was delayed—so many people about on market day. When I got back, I went upstairs immediately to check on Alfred—he was not in his cradle—"

The servants were summoned, but unable to provide any further intelligence. The housekeeper had returned from the market just after Mrs. Logan, and the others, going about their own duties elsewhere in the house, with no reason to enter the nursery, had not observed anything unusual.

Alfred was too small to have wandered off on his own, and a baby was not something one was likely to misplace. Yet they searched the house and garden anyway. He was nowhere on the premises.

They reconvened in the sitting room. Captain Wentworth, his

own worry evident, reassured his wife that they would find Alfred. "Do not panic yet. Sir Walter has not seen his son since the christening—perhaps he or your sister retrieved the boy for a visit. It would be very like them not to think to inform us." Wentworth himself did not sound convinced of this possibility.

"My father would have sent a servant to collect him. And even if he had come himself, he would not have entered our house, gone upstairs to the nursery, taken Alfred from his cradle, and departed without a word to anybody."

No, Darcy thought, but another Elliot might. He met Captain Wentworth's eyes. "Do you think perhaps Mr. Elliot—"

"I can name no one else more probable," he replied.

Mrs. Wentworth glanced toward the entry hall. "He must have come after Mrs. Smith departed for the Cobb, or surely she would have alerted us."

"Unless he used the rear door and stairs," Captain Wentworth said. "Someone planning to steal a child would hardly want to make an obvious entrance."

"I am reluctant to voice this thought," St. Clair said, "but if Mr. Elliot did encounter Mrs. Smith, she would not have presented a very imposing obstacle. He could easily overpower a crippled woman, particularly if he had someone else with him. Lyme is full of his fellow conspirators—the crew of the *Black Cormorant* alone must number at least two hundred. Any one of them could have accompanied him."

"Mrs. Smith is the only one of his past associates still alive to incriminate him," Elizabeth added, "and he knows she bears him ill will."

"Good heavens, Frederick—he might have taken Mrs. Smith, too." Mrs. Wentworth sank into a chair. "If only Nurse Rooke had been here with her and not in Bath."

Captain Wentworth took her hand. "Let us not allow our conjecture to run wild," he said. "Mrs. Smith could very well be sitting on her bench at the harbor, perfectly safe and utterly oblivious to our alarm. In fact, someone ought to see whether she is indeed there, for if so, she may be able to tell us something that could lead us to Alfred. I would do so myself, but I am going to the Lion this moment to determine whether Mr. Elliot is there with the child."

"I will accompany you," Darcy said. "If Mr. Elliot does have Alfred, there is no predicting what he might do." *Or what he might have already done.*

Darcy left that last thought unspoken—Mrs. Wentworth was worried enough—but he could see in her husband's countenance that Captain Wentworth realized the truth. If Mr. Elliot, or someone acting on his behalf, had taken Alfred with the intention of harming him, the deed had likely already been accomplished—or was taking place now—and in a place more remote than his rooms at the Lion.

Wentworth nodded. "Let us go at once."

"I will come, as well." St. Clair's manner indicated that he, too, recognized the reality of Alfred's plight.

"You cannot, Captain," Wentworth said. "You are under the admiral's orders to stay here."

"If Mr. Elliot is guilty of the child's disappearance, I can aid you. I have been watching the gentleman closely—"

"So have I." Captain Wentworth looked at his wife. "For some time. I know what he is." He paused, then looked back at St. Clair. "Besides, what possible pretext could you give for showing up at Mr. Elliot's door? He has surely been in communication with Sir Laurence and knows about your arrest. He thinks you are in a brig. What explanation could you offer that would not raise his guard about all three of us?"

The gentlemen moved out of the room and into the hall.

"You are right," St. Clair conceded. "My appearance would sabotage not only the smuggling investigation, but also the very rescue I was trying to assist." He released a frustrated sigh. "And yet I feel I must do something."

Darcy looked past him, through the doorway, to where the ladies yet clustered in the sitting room. Elizabeth had moved closer to Mrs. Wentworth and was offering words of comfort. Georgiana stood a little apart, appearing, to Darcy's eye, more vulnerable than she had an hour ago. Alfred's kidnapping made him all the more apprehensive about Mr. Elliot's fellow conspirator. He did not think Sir Laurence would try to harm Georgiana, but he did not want her former suitor to even attempt to speak to her again. Until Sir Laurence was arrested, Darcy could not be easy about letting Georgiana out of his sight.

He turned to the man who mere days ago he had been determined to keep at a distance from his sister. "Captain St. Clair, only the urgency of Alfred's disappearance impels me to leave Miss Darcy anywhere but under my direct watch while Sir Laurence remains at liberty, lest he try to contact her. If you would undertake her protection in my absence, I would consider it a great service."

"Of course." In those two simple words, an understanding passed between them. Darcy knew he need not have even voiced the request, and St. Clair recognized the trust it represented.

St. Clair walked them to the front entry, offering whatever random points of information he could quickly call to mind about Mr. Elliot and his habits. As they reached the door, where they were entirely safe from the ladies' hearing, he detained them a moment longer.

"If Mr. Elliot is not at the Lion with Alfred and Mrs. Smith, he may have gone to his property near Sidmouth. There are old quarry caves on the grounds, perfect for hiding smuggled goods." He paused. "Or . . ."

The two captains' eyes met.

"I understand," Wentworth said.

Captain St. Clair returned to the sitting room to find Georgiana alone. She stood near the window, watching Mr. Darcy and Captain Wentworth recede down the street. The housekeeper had set out tea. No one had touched it.

"Where have Mrs. Darcy and Mrs. Wentworth gone?" he asked.

"Up to the nursery. Mrs. Wentworth is terribly distressed, as one might expect, and wanted to wait in there until Captain Wentworth comes back. She wishes she could have gone with him."

"So do I. It is harder to wait than to act. Why did you not go upstairs with them?"

She took a seat, but perched on the edge of the chair. Except for the briefest of glances, she had not looked at him—not directly—

since he reentered the room. "I do not know Mrs. Wentworth as well as Mrs. Darcy does. I felt my presence would be an intrusion at a time when Mrs. Wentworth needs whatever peace she can find." .

She studied her hands, dropped them back in her lap, smoothed a wrinkle from her skirt. At last she rose from the chair but yet maintained her distance, going to the table and bringing a teacup to the pot. She poured, but stopped when the cup was but half full. She set down the pot and simply stared at it.

He took a few steps toward her, but halted when the sound of his approach appeared to distress her. "Are you all right, Miss Darcy?"

"Everybody keeps asking me that."

"It must be difficult to have had Sir Laurence's true character revealed to you so suddenly—perhaps the more so for having heard it from me."

She looked at him then. Her eyes were troubled, but it was not resentment that filled them. "You have been rescuing me since the moment we met. By now you must regret ever catching me on the Walk."

His answering gaze was earnest and unwavering. "Quite the opposite. You did, after all, save my investigation today."

"If I have not cost you it."

"Miss Darcy—" He took another step toward her.

"Lieuten— *Captain*." She swallowed. "I have not properly thanked you for—I have been trying to find the words—" She turned her head away, struggling to control a countenance that threatened to reveal more than she wanted it to. "The other day, in the water—I owe you such a debt, I cannot express—"

He closed the distance between them. "Miss Darcy." He reached toward her, but withdrew his hand before touching her. "You owe me nothing," he said gently. "Pray, do not let a sense of obligation to me cause you more distress."

"I owe you my life." She looked up at him. "When the boat capsized, and I was under the water—" Her voice broke, and she swallowed again. "I was never so frightened in all my days."

"Nor was I."

She studied his face, her own disbelieving. "That cannot be true," she said. "You have been aboard embattled ships, with cannonballs flying and wounded comrades falling all around you."

His expression was all seriousness; his voice, little more than a whisper.

"Yes, I have."

She was the first to break their gaze, turning to busy herself with the tea things once more.

"I—my conduct toward you when we found Captain Tourner—" She picked up the half-full teacup but did not drink, in need not of refreshment, but something to do with her hands. "Forgive me. I did not know what to think."

"There is nothing to forgive. You were in shock. And even were you not, the evidence was condemning, and I could not at that moment freely speak in my own defense."

She added sugar to the tea, but the tea had gone cold, and the wet, brown lump sat undissolved in the cup. "I did not want to believe you capable of murder, but Sir Laurence was so persuasive." She finally looked at him again. "And when my own brother helped take you away—"

"In point of fact, I was grateful for Mr. Darcy's escort. I knew that once I was in the navy's custody and had an opportunity to send word to the Admiralty, I would be safe, but Sir Laurence easily could have ensured I never reached the base."

The teacup clattered in its saucer. "You thought he might make an attempt on your life?"

"You saw what he is capable of." St. Clair took the teacup from her before she spilled it. "But Sir Laurence could not act with Mr. Darcy present. Here—" He poured her a fresh cup of tea. "Come sit down, and let us talk about something else."

"It is kind of you to try to distract me, but I cannot imagine a subject exists that could divert my thoughts from Sir Laurence and the present crisis."

"We shall do our best to find one," he said, leading her to the sofa. "And should we fail, I believe I still owe you definitions of topsails and yardarms."

———

Despite Mrs. Wentworth's apparent calmness, Elizabeth could feel the anxiety radiating from her, and understood it as only another parent can. Lily-Anne had disappeared once—wandered out of sight one afternoon while they were picnicking beside the stream at Pemberley—and the minutes until she and Darcy found her were the most sickening of Elizabeth's life. She had held herself together while they searched—then burst into sobs upon her daughter's discovery.

Mrs. Wentworth ran her hand along the headboard of the empty cradle. "Frederick will find him," she said in a voice that sounded more an attempt to convince herself than Elizabeth. "If Alfred can be found."

"He has Mr. Darcy to help him," Elizabeth said. "Darcy has found missing people before—my youngest sister, for one." Lydia's disappearance had been a voluntary elopement, but Elizabeth told herself that if Darcy could locate her wayward sister in all of London, he could find Alfred in Lyme.

"Alfred has become more than a brother to me. Though he has been with us but a short while, I have come to love him as a son. And Mrs. Smith—I fear for her, too. If only we knew whether she is on the Cobb or missing, as well." She stepped away from the cradle and looked out the window toward the sea. "It is always women's lot to wait."

"Apparently we are all confined to quarters—and we are not the ones who have done anything wrong."

"I am not under any orders from the admiral. And it feels unnatural—it feels wrong—to sit idle when one's child is in danger. If Lily-Anne were missing, what would you do?"

Elizabeth knew exactly what she would do. All the Sir Laurences and Mr. Elliots in the world could not prevent her from taking some kind of action to find her daughter. Yet she did not want to lead Mrs. Wentworth astray. "I would go to the Cobb and ascertain whether Mrs. Smith is there. Captain Wentworth said somebody ought, and I agree. However, when he said that, I do not think you were the 'somebody' he had in mind, and I do not want to advise you to act against your husband's wishes."

"I was contemplating it before you said it aloud. Do you think I would be endangering myself? I do not want to add to Captain Wentworth's trouble."

"With Mr. Elliot's whereabouts unknown, you should not go alone, but if we go together I believe we will be safe. If there is any sign of trouble, the Harvilles' cottage is nearby, and there will be plenty of other people about."

"What will Mr. Darcy say? I doubt he would want you to go, with Sir Laurence's ship in the harbor."

Mrs. Wentworth was correct about the likelihood of Darcy's endorsing this plan. But Elizabeth hoped the intelligence their mission yielded would abate any displeasure at how it had been obtained. "As he is not here to voice an objection, I think Captain St. Clair will prove a greater obstacle."

"Not if we use the back stairs."

Thirty-five

"Let me plead for my—present friend I cannot call him, but for my former friend. Where can you look for a more suitable match? Where could you expect a more gentlemanlike, agreeable man? Let me recommend Mr. Elliot."
— *Mrs. Smith to Anne Elliot,* Persuasion

*E*lizabeth and Mrs. Wentworth completed the walk to Cobb Hamlet in as much haste as possible without drawing undue attention to themselves. It seemed every elderly, infirm, fat, idle, or just plain slow person in Lyme had turned out on market day for a leisurely stroll, determined to put themselves in the two ladies' path and wander oblivious to the fact that anybody might want to pass them. In truth, however, this was only their perception, distorted by the urgency of their errand. Nor was the number of boats that obscured their view across the harbor once they reached the shore any greater than what it ought to have been.

The fog, however, was a different matter. The sun had declined to show itself this morning, instead allowing the mist to linger in patches that shrouded sections of the seawall, including the one most of interest to them. They could see figures near the bench—a woman seated, a man standing.

Despite the gloomy atmosphere, Elizabeth observed the woman hopefully. "Is that Mrs. Smith? I cannot tell."

"Nor can I," said Mrs. Wentworth. "We shall have to move closer."

They walked along the lower wall, forcing themselves to proceed slowly so as not to catch the figures' notice. The angle from which they viewed the couple altered as they progressed along the curve. The gentleman, his back to them, now blocked their view of the woman. When Elizabeth and Mrs. Wentworth were nearly as far as the gin shop, however, he glanced toward the beach, momentarily offering them his profile. Then he put one hand on the wall and leaned against it, shifting just enough to open up their line of sight to the bench.

The woman was indeed Mrs. Smith.

Anne gasped and grabbed Elizabeth's arm. In her lap was Alfred.

And the gentleman to whom she was speaking, ever so collectedly, was Mr. Elliot.

"What do we do to help her?" Mrs. Wentworth whispered.

Elizabeth took in the pair—Mrs. Smith's cool manner of address, Mr. Elliot's casual stance. As he tossed back his head and issued a laugh that carried to Elizabeth's ears, an unsettling thought overtook her.

Perhaps Mrs. Smith did not want their help.

She and Mr. Elliot were, after all, old acquaintances whose years of friendship outnumbered their years of estrangement. Mrs. Smith had shared a great many of Mr. Elliot's secrets—how many of hers did he know? And was the greatest one of all, that they were even now in league with each other?

Was that the reason Mrs. Smith was the only one of Mr. Elliot's former set still alive?

So many questions entered Elizabeth's thoughts at once that she could not contemplate them all. Was Mrs. Smith as poor as she claimed? Did she know about the smuggling? Did she know more about Mrs. Clay's death than she had let on? And Alfred—what in heaven's name was she doing sitting so nonchalantly on the Cobb with the Wentworths' missing child on her lap? Had she helped Mr. Elliot steal the baby? Had she let him in the house?

Or was an endangered Mrs. Smith calmly trying to negotiate for her and Alfred's lives with a devil so cold-blooded that he could laugh as he bargained? If only she could hear what they were saying.

Then she recalled that she could.

She turned to Mrs. Wentworth, whom she had kept in suspense while these thoughts had been flying through her mind. "I know that you trust Mrs. Smith, but at this moment, I am not sure I do. Let us listen to them a while—and pray they remain so absorbed in their conversation that they do not notice us through the fog."

Mrs. Wentworth regarded her with doubt, but nodded.

Elizabeth took Mrs. Wentworth's arm and led her forward. "After we pass the gin shop, we should be able to hear them. Stand as Mr. Elliot does—close to the wall, with your back to them, blocking me from view. Be sure to remain silent yourself."

They passed the wooden doors, walked several yards farther, and drew near the wall.

". . . and all of this has led you to the conclusion that, your own husband's fortune having been exhausted, you somehow possess a claim upon mine." Mr. Elliot laughed again, an eerie, hollow sound in the mist. "My dear Mrs. Smith, what elixirs has your doctor been prescribing that induce such imagination? Smuggling, and gold, and—are there pirates, too, perchance? You could support yourself as a novelist—this is better than *Robinson Crusoe*."

"Do not mock me. I know what I heard."

"And just whom did you hear this from?"

"Mrs. Clay. In this very spot. The morning she died."

"Impossible. She never would have confided in you. She did not even know you were in Lyme—you are so much altered that I myself did not recognize you until I saw you at Alfred's christening with Anne Wentworth."

Elizabeth had seen Mrs. Smith in that "very spot"—on her bench—on that unforgettable morning. It was her customary place, where she sat each day, almost invisible in her familiarity, watching other people.

And, Elizabeth now realized, listening to them.

In all her hours on that bench, week upon week, Mrs. Smith must have discovered the Cobb's acoustical phenomenon. She was perfectly positioned to overhear all sorts of conversations—including one of Mrs. Clay's.

"I heard it from both Mrs. Clay and from you," Mrs. Smith continued. "She took great pleasure in telling you that she had returned to Sir Walter. She did not reveal that she had just married him, only that when she left you the night before, she had put into action a plan that she had initiated after learning of his being in Lyme and of your betrayal. You had been lying to her, but she was again under Sir Walter's protection, and she wanted her share of the gold now that she was no longer under yours."

That, Elizabeth at last understood, was why Mrs. Clay had been on the Cobb the morning after her wedding. She had met with Mr. Elliot to continue the discussion Elizabeth had overheard the night before. *So long as you live under my protection, my assignations are my business.* Her marriage to Sir Walter had freed her of dependence on Mr. Elliot, empowering her to force him into relinquishing the profits she believed rightfully hers.

Or so she had thought. Then she took a tumble off the Cobb—doubtless helped over its edge by Mr. Elliot.

"You have also been lying to *me*," Mrs. Smith said, "and I want *my* share of the money my husband's property has helped you acquire."

"Indeed? And do you want Mrs. Clay's share, too, now that she can no longer claim it for herself? Is that why you caused her accident?"

Silence followed. Elizabeth tried to look past Mrs. Wentworth to see Mrs. Smith's reaction, but Mr. Elliot yet blocked her view.

"Ha! It *was* you," Mr. Elliot continued. "I was guessing, but I can see from your expression that I am right. In the excitement of the ship's explosion, you thought nobody saw you push her, did you not? But as I was leaving the Cobb, the sound of the blast caused me to turn around. I saw two women on the high wall—one of them falling, and the other with an arm extended toward her. I was too far away to see you clearly, so I did not know it was you until this moment. I still do not know how you reached the upper wall or got away in your pathetic, crippled state. But if you stopped me here this morning to threaten me with secrets, I suggest you consider the magnitude of this one before proceeding further."

Mrs. Wentworth's eyes were wide. Indeed, Elizabeth, for all her

speculation on the subject of Mrs. Clay's death, had never anticipated this.

In a moment, however, she realized that Mrs. Wentworth's apprehensive expression was due only in part to Mr. Elliot's revelation.
The rest was caused by something behind Elizabeth.

She turned round to see Darcy and Captain Wentworth striding
toward them. Unfortunately, she and Anne were not the only persons to notice their approach. Mr. Elliot also turned—spying both
the gentlemen and their wives.

"Well. Look who is come."

"I trust you will explain to me later how you came to be here." Darcy's heart had nearly stopped when he saw Elizabeth on the seawall
in such proximity to Mr. Elliot. When he and Wentworth had failed
to find Mr. Elliot at the Lion, they had decided to seek Mrs. Smith on
the Cobb before making the fifteen-mile journey to Sidmouth. They
had not expected to find their wives there.

Knowing Elizabeth, however, Darcy probably should have. "I
cannot believe Captain St. Clair approved this scheme," he added.

"Captain St. Clair does not know," Elizabeth replied. They and the
Wentworths had edged away from the face of the wall, to a distance
where they could speak without danger of being overheard by Mrs.
Smith and Mr. Elliot. "But we will have to share the details later, for
at present I must tell you what we have just learned. Mrs. Smith
pushed Mrs. Clay off the wall—at least, that is what Mr. Elliot has
accused her of, and she did not deny it."

"Mrs. Smith?" Darcy said. "How is that possible?"

"I do not know," Elizabeth said. "We might have found out had
you and Captain Wentworth not arrived when you did. They have
noticed us now." Both Mr. Elliot and Mrs. Smith were looking at their
party.

"Her legs have been getting stronger," Mrs. Wentworth said. "I
have observed her moving into and out of chairs more easily, and
walking short distances—a few steps—within the house, but I
thought her still quite dependent upon her cane. How she managed

the steps here on the Cobb—even I would not venture up Granny's Teeth—"

"She might have used the other stairs just round the bend, behind the quay—the ones we came down after the ship exploded," Elizabeth said. "They are not far, especially if her legs are stronger than she has led you to believe. If she took care, she could manage them the same way she managed the stairs this morning at your house. I wager it was she who went up to the nursery and took Alfred."

"And it is I who will take him back." Captain Wentworth began walking toward the pair. The others fell into step.

"When we reach them, there is no use pretending we did not hear their discussion—with Mrs. Smith, at any rate," Elizabeth said. "Look where her bench is, Darcy—she is ideally situated to overhear conversations, and in fact heard one between Mrs. Clay and Mr. Elliot shortly before Mrs. Clay died. I do not know whether Mr. Elliot is aware of the phenomenon; I think perhaps not, for his speech to her was unguarded." She paused. "For that matter, so was hers—I wonder whether she realizes the whispering effect works in both directions."

"I cannot believe Mrs. Smith would act so falsely by us," Mrs. Wentworth said, "or harm Mrs. Clay. She is my friend. We must give her an opportunity to explain."

As they neared the bench, they were able to obtain a closer look at Alfred. The child was wrapped in a blanket and appeared to be sleeping. Mrs. Smith smiled at the Wentworths. "Why, good morning, Anne." Mr. Elliot also offered a greeting, but without the smile. Caution pervaded his normally smooth manner.

"Good morning," Anne stammered.

Captain Wentworth went straight to Mrs. Smith and took Alfred. "You have given us quite a fright, Mrs. Smith. We have been looking for Alfred."

"Yes," Anne added. "How did the two of you come to bring him here?"

"I had nothing to do with the child," Mr. Elliot declared. "He was with Mrs. Smith when I happened upon them." He glanced at the quay, where the *Black Cormorant* was docked. The merchantman had acquired her guns since Darcy had last seen her. Darcy wondered whether it was Mrs. Smith or the ship that had brought Mr. Elliot to the Cobb.

"I did not mean to alarm you," Mrs. Smith said. "Did you not find my note?"

Captain Wentworth passed the sleeping baby to his wife, who held him tightly. As Alfred nestled against her—a welcome sign that he was sound—the anxiety in her face diminished but did not disappear. "No," Mrs. Wentworth said. "There was no note."

"I left it in—well, now, where did I leave it? All was such a bustle when we quit the house. The chair bearers were impatient. I had wanted to linger a few minutes more for Mrs. Logan to return, but they said they had other customers waiting. So I decided to bring Alfred with me."

"Why did you not simply leave him sleeping in the nursery?" Captain Wentworth asked.

"I thought he might enjoy the outing, and the sea air has been so therapeutic for me that I believed he could benefit from it as well. Besides, he was not in the nursery when the chair arrived—he was already with me. I had heard him crying earlier, after Mrs. Logan went out. You were in the study with your guests—I did not think you wished to be disturbed. So I went to the nursery myself to quiet him. He would not settle down without being held, and the sedan chair was due to arrive, so I brought him downstairs with me so that I might watch for it."

"How did you negotiate the stairs?" Mrs. Wentworth asked.

Mrs. Smith smiled brightly. "On my own legs, I am proud to say. I have been improving beyond your knowledge, Anne! The sea has done wonders for my health. You and Captain Wentworth have been so good to me that I wanted to surprise you some future morning by leaving behind my cane and walking with you all the way down to the Cobb on my own. I am not quite that strong yet—it is a long, steep walk, but I have been practicing by climbing and descending the stairs when you are not at home."

Mrs. Wentworth regarded her in astonishment. It was not, however, the delighted amazement that Mrs. Smith had hoped to arouse in her friend. It was a sober, wary shock. Her gaze drifted from Mrs. Smith to the wall behind her, and up to the edge of the parapet from which Mrs. Clay had fallen. "And is that," she said, her voice small, as if muting it would negate the possibility of what she was about to ask, "how you came to be standing on the upper Cobb the morning Mrs. Clay died?"

Mrs. Smith's cheerful glow transformed into a panicked flush.

"I can explain."

Admiral Croft returned to the Wentworths' home in a great flurry. He entered the sitting room so intent upon his mission that he did not realize he interrupted two people who had been engaged for some time in private conversation.

"I have the warrants," he announced. "The customs officers and our own forces stand ready. Here—I brought your sword. Where is Wentworth?"

"With Mr. Darcy." Captain St. Clair rose from the sofa to accept the sword; Georgiana also stood. "They are tracking down Mr. Elliot." He summarized Alfred's disappearance.

Admiral Croft frowned. "This is most alarming. How is Mrs. Wentworth taking it?"

"Not well. She is upstairs in the nursery. Mrs. Darcy is with her."

The admiral nodded. "We will not disturb them." He looked at Georgiana. "Miss Darcy, please assure Mrs. Wentworth that Captain St. Clair and I have gone to apprehend Mr. Elliot. Sir Laurence, as well."

"I will, sir. I am sure the news will relieve her."

Admiral Croft bowed. "Let us make haste, Captain." He quit the room.

Captain St. Clair put on his hat and girded his sword. From bicorne to boots, he looked every inch an officer prepared for battle.

"You do not expect to fight Sir Laurence, do you?" Georgiana asked.

"If the baronet is as intelligent as he thinks he is, he will surrender without resistance. But if not, I am prepared." Her anxious expression gave him pause. "We intend to take him alive, if that is the source of your concern."

"No, it is not."

Hand on his sword hilt, he took a step toward her. "I had been wanting to warn you of him for some time, but feared you would interpret my words as—well, it does not matter now. When next you see me, Sir Laurence will no longer be a threat to anybody."

He took leave of her, then went to meet the admiral in the hall. He had nearly quit the room when Georgiana's voice stopped him.

"Captain—"

He turned round. "Yes, Miss Darcy?"

She advanced until she stood just before him. "Do take care."

He regarded her a long moment, his eyes full of hopeful determination. "I shall."

"Show a leg, Captain St. Clair," called the admiral from the entry hall. "Sir Laurence and Mr. Elliot will not be kept waiting."

Thirty-six

"We were a thoughtless, gay set, without any strict rules of conduct. We lived for enjoyment. I think differently now: time and sickness and sorrow have given me other notions."
— Mrs. Smith to Anne Elliot, Persuasion

*I*t was an accident."

Mr. Elliot chuckled at Mrs. Smith's declaration. "Undoubtedly."

Mrs. Smith stared at him a moment, appearing to weigh something in her mind, then turned to the others and gave Anne Wentworth her full address.

"I was here that morning, as usual. The weather started to turn, and Mrs. Rooke left to summon the sedan chair early to take me home. She had barely started away when I became aware of a conversation going on above me on the upper wall. I recognized the voices—they belonged to Mrs. Clay and Mr. Elliot.

"I had seen them together on the Cobb numerous times before, but though they sometimes walked right past my bench, they never saw me—nobody notices a cripple; indeed, passers-by avert their gazes to avoid my eyes—and I am so changed that the two of them never realized how close they strolled to a discarded remnant of their past. I saw them in their fine clothes, saw her belly great with evidence of yet another illicit dalliance, and never did anything to

284

draw their attention as they walked past. Betrayed by them both, I wanted nothing to do with them.

"That morning, they argued, and I learned that their treachery had gone further than I had previously known. Moreover, I learned that Mrs. Clay had left Mr. Elliot and taken up residence with your father. The news angered Mr. Elliot, but it incensed me." Mrs. Smith's face contorted in disgust. "She made me ill"—her voice shook—"with her loose ways and string of lovers. There I was, impoverished and alone, my husband dead, no fortune to ease my physical comfort, no children to console me. Privation and poor health were my sole legacy from the careless days of our youth, while she had attained everything she ever wanted."

She fingered her locket, with its miniature of the late Mr. Smith, and turned to Mr. Elliot. "And you—you sickened me in other ways. Not only have you been living in luxury off a fortune my husband's property made possible, but *you*—my 'friend'—kept another secret from me for so many years."

"You were happier not knowing," Mr. Elliot said.

"I suspected. When I asked you directly, you denied any knowledge—I had to learn years later from your wife. However, when I sorted through my husband's papers after he died, I found a note from you proving that you knew from the start. I tore it to pieces, not wanting any reminder of how thoroughly deceived I had been by everyone around me. Now I wish I had kept it, as further evidence of what a heartless creature you are."

Mr. Elliot shrugged. "It was not my secret to tell."

"No, it was my husband's—and hers."

Elizabeth realized she had read a fragment of that note, and understood the betrayal Mrs. Smith referred to. The portrait of Mr. Smith in the locket his widow now gripped in her fist depicted a man with red hair—as red as that of Mrs. Clay's second son.

Mrs. Smith turned back to Anne Wentworth. "If you have not already inferred, Mrs. Clay's liaisons did not begin and end with naval officers."

"Oh, Frances . . ." Anne's expression softened, and she went to sit beside Mrs. Smith.

While Captain Wentworth attended Mrs. Smith's speech, he seemed distracted. His gaze strayed repeatedly to the *Black Cormorant*. Its deck was astir today, though its crew went about their work quietly.

"With my husband no longer able to confess," Mrs. Smith continued, "I decided to confront Mrs. Clay. I wanted to see remorse in one of them. I wanted to hear the truth from *somebody*.

"I left my bench and walked to the steps around that bend." She pointed toward the southern end of the Cobb, where stood the far stairs behind the quay. "By the time I climbed to the top and reached Mrs. Clay, Mr. Elliot had gone."

Mr. Elliot, too, seemed attentive to the activity aboard the *Black Cormorant*. His gaze had drifted to the ship, but at the mention of his name it returned to Mrs. Smith.

Captain Wentworth leaned toward Darcy. "She is preparing to make sail." Only Elizabeth stood close enough to overhear him; Mrs. Smith continued as if he had not spoken.

"Mrs. Clay was looking upon the harbor when I spoke her name. She turned round, and for a moment she did not know me. But then she recognized traces of my former self in my present face. There was no greeting, no warmth of encountering an old friend after a span of years. She only asked what I was doing in Lyme. I replied that I had come for my health. She made no enquiry into how I fared," she said bitterly, "not even the most minimal civility.

"I, on the other hand, asked after her, and she gleefully announced her new status as Lady Elliot. When I enquired after her boys, she could barely give any account of them—it was clear that they seldom entered her thoughts. The injustice of it overpowered me. Indulged by men of wealth, she had now married one, and would know a life of comfort that surpassed even what she enjoyed during our former years together, neglecting the child that should have been mine even while carrying another."

Mrs. Smith's voice cracked, and one of the hands that had been strong enough to carry Alfred now shook as Anne Wentworth took it into her own.

"I asked about her younger son, and whether he had grown to bear the image of his father. She replied that he little resembled Mr.

Clay. 'That is not what I asked,' I said. She at last had the decency to look ashamed. She took a step back, and said she did not understand my meaning. She was close to the wall's edge, but not right upon it. 'That surprises me,' I said, 'for I understand *you* perfectly.' I moved another step toward her. 'But if you truly do not comprehend, I will state my query more plainly. Is he my husband's child?'

"She stared at me for what must have been half a minute at least, the wind whipping her hair and cloak, the gloom deepening. I could see in her calculating visage an internal deliberation over whether any purpose would be served by attempting to maintain the lie any longer. At last she answered. 'Yes, he is.'

"At that moment, a thunderbolt pierced the sky. Arriving as it did, so swiftly upon her confession, it seemed a divine condemnation of her sin. She started, and took another step backward, coming precariously close to the edge of the seawall. I realized her peril and moved toward her to pull her back to safety. But Mrs. Clay interpreted my advance as threatening, and put up her hands to ward me away."

Mrs. Smith's voice had become thick. She swallowed, blinking watery eyes. "I called out to warn her that she was close to the edge, but people were shouting about a ship on fire and my voice was drowned by their cries and the wind. Then the ship exploded. The blast so startled her that she lost her balance. I reached for her, but she was already too far into her fall for my fingers to more than brush her sleeve."

Mrs. Smith looked beseechingly at Anne.

"It was an accident. An unfortunate, regrettable accident."

"Yet you did not summon anybody to help her," Darcy said.

"My own thinking was not clear immediately following," Mrs. Smith replied. "I was shocked by the explosion and from the horror of witnessing such a dreadful fall. I assumed Mrs. Clay was dead, having tumbled so far, especially in her condition. Also, I was frightened that someone might have seen the accident and misconstrued what occurred—as Mr. Elliot did. I started walking along the upper wall toward shore, faster than I had realized myself capable of, spurred by fear and the pandemonium around me. I had covered half the distance before my mind settled enough for me to consider that perhaps she had not died. I looked back, and by then you were attending her. So I continued to the main steps, where I met the sedan chair when it and my nurse arrived a few minutes later. She was surprised to find me waiting there, but I told her that after the explosion someone had helped me that far."

She turned back to Anne Wentworth. "My dear friend, *you* believe me, do you not? You, who have known me even longer than did Mrs. Clay. As much as I resented her, I did not push her. I could never do such a thing."

Anne pressed Mrs. Smith's hand. "Of course you could not."

Darcy was less certain.

However, it was Mr. Elliot who, though not meaning to, now commanded Darcy's attention. The gaze that had periodically shifted toward the *Black Cormorant* throughout Mrs. Smith's confession now looked past Darcy, toward shore. The casual stance in which he had so confidently goaded Mrs. Smith now adopted a more defensive air.

Darcy turned. A detachment of Royal Marines had arrived on the Cobb. They marched in formation along the lower wall, their red coats a striking display of color in the gloom. Admiral Croft and Captain St. Clair accompanied them.

"Well, this has been a fascinating explanation," Mr. Elliot said. "However, further reminiscing will have to wait, for you have delayed my errand too long as it is." He moved past the ladies on the bench and headed toward the quay. Captain Wentworth, however, interposed himself.

"I am afraid, Mr. Elliot, that I must detain you a little longer," he said. "I believe Admiral Croft has business with you."

"What business could the admiral possibly have with me?"

Admiral Croft reached their party and came to a stop. "A warrant for your arrest." Captain St. Clair and two marines remained with him while the rest continued to the quay. "And another authorizing the search of your property in Sidmouth."

"Whatever for?"

"Smuggled artifacts."

"This is outrageous." He glared at Captain St. Clair. "You will find no evidence there."

"Regardless of what is discovered," Captain Wentworth said, "we already have enough to free Mr. Smith's plantation from your control and try you for stealing from his widow."

"Truly, Captain Wentworth?" Mrs. Smith exclaimed. "I will at last have income from my husband's estate to support myself?"

"Truly."

"Oh, Anne! Is this not the most wonderful news?" Mrs. Smith smiled triumphantly at Mr. Elliot as the pair of marines led him away.

Captain St. Clair noted the baby in Anne Wentworth's arms. "It was Mr. Elliot, then, who stole the child? Is Alfred well?"

"Actually, my friend Mrs. Smith had him," Mrs. Wentworth replied. "He is fine."

"I am relieved to hear it."

"Have you already arrested Sir Laurence?" Darcy asked.

"He was not at home," St. Clair replied. "We believe he is on his ship. If so, he will not be aboard much longer."

A revenue cutter had entered the port, effectively blocking the merchantman's ability to exit it. Meanwhile, the marines had been joined by a group of customs officials who had emerged from the harbormaster's office. Together, they swarmed the *Black Cormorant*.

Just as the admiral, St. Clair, Wentworth, and Darcy walked up the gang-board from the quay to the deck, the marine sergeant emerged from the master's cabin with Sir Laurence. Another man was with the baronet. Darcy did not recognize him, but Captain St. Clair did.

"Lieutenant Wilton," St. Clair muttered. "Apparently, Sir Laurence wasted no time in finding another ship's master. We shall relieve him of command, as well."

Admiral Croft turned to St. Clair. "You may do the honors, Captain. You have earned the pleasure."

St. Clair stepped forward. "This ship is hereby seized by the crown," he announced. "And you, Sir Laurence—along with all her crew—are under arrest for the illegal import and sale of foreign goods, and for conspiring to defraud His Majesty King George of revenues rightfully his."

"These charges are made on whose word, Lieutenant?" Sir Laurence regarded St. Clair disdainfully. "That of a killer?"

"That of Captain St. Clair," said the admiral, "senior officer in His Majesty's navy, who has been investigating you and your fellow conspirators under the orders and authority of the Lords Commissioners of the Admiralty."

The admiral's reply gave Sir Laurence pause, but only for a moment. "You must be very confident to arrest me," he said. "I have influential friends."

"We shall see if they remain your friends when they learn you are a thief," St. Clair replied. "Not to mention a murderer." He looked to the sergeant. "Take him."

As the arrests were made, Darcy and Captain Wentworth rejoined their wives back on the Cobb. They watched Sir Laurence being led away.

"What a relief to finally see Sir Laurence exposed as a murderer," Mrs. Smith muttered.

Captain Wentworth regarded her in puzzlement. "How did you come to know about Captain Tourner?"

"Captain Tourner? I have no idea who you refer to. I was thinking of another man entirely—one whom my husband told me about before he died. On his voyage home from the West Indies, Mr. Smith and his companions were involved in a very frightening battle in which they had to defend themselves. My husband took down a French sailor with his pistol, but he said Sir Laurence's shot struck a young British lieutenant."

"Intentionally?" Darcy asked.

"My husband said it appeared so, but he could not comprehend why Sir Laurence would do such a thing. The incident troubled him greatly. He raved about it repeatedly in the delirium of his final days."

"Did he name the officer?" Darcy asked.

"Fitz-something. Fitzgerald? No—that is not it. I am sorry—I have long forgotten. At the time, my attention was absorbed by utterances he made of a more personal nature."

Darcy looked once more at Sir Laurence. The gentleman Darcy would have welcomed into his family had dispassionately stolen the life of one of its members. Even now, the baronet left the Cobb with an outward air of dignity that belied the dark soul within.

Elizabeth slipped her hand into Darcy's. "At last, you have your answer—we know for certain it was Sir Laurence who killed your cousin. Why do you look so troubled?"

"I am contemplating how much of Sir Laurence's beguiling was his doing, and how much was mine. I believe I allowed his title and fortune to blind me to his true character."

"He is well practiced at deceit."

"I thought I was well practiced at unmasking it."

Thirty-seven

"While we were together, you know, there was nothing to be feared."
—Mrs. *Croft*, Persuasion

*A*fter their time beside the sea, London felt cramped and noisy to Darcy. Its streets seemed too level, its buildings too numerous, its air too close. Though their town house was, as ever, an oasis of peace amidst the urban din, he was glad their time in the city would be of short duration. Soon they could return home to Pemberley, stopping en route to deliver Gerard's sea chest to Riveton Hall—the final destination of its long journey.

First, however, Darcy was obliged to testify against Mr. Elliot and Sir Laurence in the Court of Admiralty. Artifacts had been found on both their properties—in the quarry caves at Sidmouth and in Sir Laurence's art collection at Thornberry. When the evidence was combined with the testimony of Captain St. Clair, Admiral Croft, Darcy, and others, it was expected that the trials would be resolved fairly quickly. The numerous courts-martial for the corrupt naval officers would continue much longer.

Captain St. Clair called upon them nearly every evening. The Darcys had him to dinner more than once; in turn, they had dined at the home of St. Clair's London sister, with whom he was staying.

In his company and under his tutelage, Georgiana's interest in things nautical had blossomed. She proved an apt and eager pupil, soon conversant in the jargon of man-o'-wars and seventy-fours, and she took particular pleasure in hearing him describe life aboard ship and the lands across the Atlantic where he had spent so much of his career. He, in turn, seemed as taken with her intellect, her conversation, and her gentle manner as he had been with her appearance on the evening he had first seen her. After years of hearing little in the way of music beyond fiddle tunes and sea ballads sung by men's voices, he took particular pleasure in listening to her perform on the harp and piano, and he was delighted to be able to speak with her in languages he had acquired in his travels.

Now that the naval officer was free to represent himself honestly, Darcy found that he liked the young captain quite well—well enough that when he discovered his sister reading the *Navy List* in the drawing room one afternoon, he sat down on the sofa and looked at it with her.

They talked—about Mr. Wickham and Sir Laurence, about trust broken and judgment deceived. They forgave each other—and most important, forgave themselves—for their perceived failure to recognize such determined scoundrels until nearly too late. They shuddered at what might have been, and looked forward to what might be.

"Sir Laurence is a criminal, and I am grateful to have escaped the future I thought I wanted," Georgiana said, "but I did learn something from him. The more I reflect upon my conversations with him, the more I realize how much they were about him—his interests, his tastes, his opinions—and how little about me. I think he had decided to acquire a wife, and I answered his criteria. Had we wed, I would have become simply another object in his collection. Next time, I shall hold out for a man who expresses at least passing curiosity about what I think, and feel, and want."

"What is it that you want, Georgiana?"

"Purpose, foremost—something more meaningful than endless balls and dinners and theatre parties. Variety—of places and people and activity. And a home of my own." She paused. "I believe it is time I left Pemberley to you and Elizabeth and your children."

They were in no hurry for her to go. "Pemberley is your home as long as you want it."

"I know it is. But I would like to be mistress of my own. It does not have to be a grand home, just mine—and my husband's, of course."

Darcy smiled. "I am glad to hear you intend to let him share it, whoever the poor fellow may be."

"You should indeed feel sorry for him, as my previous failures have increased my requirements. I want a man of integrity and principle, whom I can respect and admire, who respects and appreciates me in turn, and who makes me feel safe, happy, and loved." She paused. "In short, I want what Elizabeth has."

He smiled again at her praise, but said very seriously, "That is what I want for you, too."

She picked up the *Navy List*, still in her lap, and set it aside. "And if he looks handsome in blue, so much the better."

He laughed and put his arm around her. She rested her head against him, as she had when she was small. She was more than ten years his junior, and they had lost their mother on the day she was born. He had been protecting Georgiana her entire life; it would take just such a man to persuade him to relinquish that role.

"He is in a dangerous profession," Darcy said. Though they had not spoken directly of St. Clair throughout their discussion, there was no need to identify the "he" by name. "I would not want to see your heart broken like Miss Wright's."

"I have given this much consideration," she replied. "Nobody lives in perfect safety, and we are at peace now, which makes his profession less dangerous than it was. But even should war come again—it is a risk I am willing to take."

They had been in town a fortnight when a captain in full dress uniform came to call. He entered their drawing room a striking figure. Gold lace edged the collar, lapels, pockets, and tails of his dark blue coat; an additional two rows of gold distinction lace striped his cuffs. The insignia of his two epaulettes—a crown over a silver anchor with a rope twined round it—marked him as a captain of seniority;

the symbol also adorned the gilt buttons of his coat and breeches. Another anchor—sans crown—graced the gold and ivory hilt of his sword. His tall bicorne hat easily added another foot to his height— and to the aura of authority he projected.

This was a commander whose presence instilled courage, an officer whose conduct exemplified honor, a leader whose integrity inspired trust.

A man who, judging from the glow in her eyes, Georgiana would follow anywhere.

"Captain St. Clair." Her lips pursed as she tried to greet him with an appearance of dignity that matched his, and to restrain the smile that wanted to spread across her countenance. But the image he presented proved too great a force for her to disguise its effect on her, and her eyes betrayed the pride and happiness she took in seeing him at last able to publicly assume the rank to which merit had raised him years ago.

"Good evening, Miss Darcy." He removed his hat and tucked it under his arm.

"The tailor has finally finished your new uniform, I see."

"Do you approve it?"

The smile would not be checked any longer. "It will do."

"I have come direct from the Admiralty," he said. "The board has appointed me captain of the *Black Cormorant,* now a Royal Navy frigate renamed the *Perseverance.*"

"There is no one more deserving of that ship." Her smile spread farther. "Your own command at last! Where will you be stationed?"

"I am under orders to the West Indies, to retrieve the remaining cache of gold."

"Oh!—so far away." Her smile faded, but she quickly recovered it. "But a part of the world you know well. And an important commission."

"It is, indeed—and a profitable one. I will receive a captain's share of whatever treasure we bring from there. Meanwhile, the Lords Commissioners have approved and released to me a reward of fifteen thousand pounds from contraband already seized, for my service in bringing the smugglers to justice."

Though St. Clair addressed Georgiana, his gaze shifted to meet Darcy's. As their eyes met, Darcy could see that this information was directed equally to him. And he knew why.

Fifteen thousand pounds, combined with Georgiana's marriage settlement—not to mention whatever prize resulted from St. Clair's retrieval of the remaining treasure—would provide a more than ample income upon which to wed.

"This is all very good news, Captain," Darcy said. "In fact, I am sure Mrs. Darcy will want to hear it directly. If you will excuse me, I shall go find her."

"Of course."

"I believe she is in the nursery," he added deliberately. "It may take me a while to disengage her from Lily-Anne."

Andrew St. Clair, like any clever captain, knew how to employ an opportunity to advantage. There was one commission that he coveted even more than the post to which the Admiralty had just appointed him, and he now made his application with all the determination and hope for success of an officer initiating the most important engagement of his life.

In little more than a minute, Georgiana's hand was in his.

In the next, it was his forever.

By the third, she was in his arms, and this time, with no other eyes upon them, he could hold her as tightly and for as long as they both wished. He did, then kissed her.

And laughed.

She pulled away just enough to look up at his face. "What amuses you?"

"The last time I had the privilege of holding you close, you were coughing up seawater on me. This is far preferable."

He kissed her again and reluctantly released her, but she did not go far. She smoothed the lapels of his coat, her fingertips lingering on the gold lace.

"When do you leave for the West Indies?"

"As soon as I can raise a crew, which should not take much time.

I have served on enough ships that I know many dependable men now seeking work, and officers I can rely upon. We shall have a fine complement."

"How long will you be away?"

"Only as long as I must. Even so, it will be a journey of at least three or four months. Perhaps longer."

Though a faint shadow passed across her face, she allowed it to stay only a moment before forcing away the evidence of her disappointment. "I suppose that is not too long to wait to become Mrs. St. Clair."

"I had rather hoped Mrs. St. Clair would accompany me." He again took her hands in his. "Though you will have every comfort in my power to provide, a captain's cabin is a long way from Pemberley, and life aboard ship is not easy. But if you come with me, you will see such wonders as I hope will make the inconveniences worthwhile. And I dare hope my companionship will offer some attraction."

He drew her closer. "What say you, Georgiana? Do you want to see the New World with me?"

"I do." Her expression reflected such happiness that it could be matched only by his own.

Nevertheless, he searched her face for signs of doubt. "Are you certain that you want to board a ship again—this ship in particular—after the accident at Lyme?"

"I am certain," she said without hesitation. Then she smiled. "How else will I ever have an opportunity to see a bo'sun standing on the fo'c'sle?"

He laughed. "Pronounced like a true sailor—you have learned well. Next I shall teach you to swim."

"I shall master that, too."

"I have no doubt."

"Nor do I—about any part of your proposal." Her countenance became solemn. "Though I am not as traveled as you, I have seen enough of the world to know that life is not all clear sailing. Whether we are on a ship or on the shore, there will be storms to weather. But whatever comes—" She pressed his hands, still holding hers, and regarded him with perfect surety.

"So long as you are with me, Captain, I know I have a sheet anchor."

Epilogue

Who can be in doubt of what followed? When any two young people take it into their heads to marry, they are pretty sure by perseverance to carry their point.

—Persuasion

While Captain St. Clair oversaw the hiring of his crew and the refitting of his ship, Georgiana attended to the inviting of their wedding guests and the fitting of her trousseau. High on the list of invitees—after all their relations—were Admiral and Mrs. Croft, with whom Georgiana formed a fast and firm friendship, and St. Clair's strengthened. In preparing for life aboard a frigate, Georgiana benefited tremendously from the experience of Mrs. Croft, who, inseparable from the admiral, had spent most of her marriage on warships. Her advice was practical and comprehensive, and her nostalgia for the sea and foreign ports made Georgiana all the more eager to embark on her new life.

Pemberley being too distant from any royal dockyard where Captain St. Clair could supervise the nautical preparations, the couple were married in London, in a ceremony attended by the bride's family, friends of both parties, and the full complement of St. Clair siblings and other relations. Georgiana found her new family to be everything she could have hoped, and was so warmly embraced by them as to make her look forward to more fully knowing them in time.

Following the celebration, the Darcys removed to the home of Elizabeth's aunt and uncle Gardiner so that the newlyweds could enjoy a few days' solitude in the vacated town house before setting off on their Jamaican honeymoon cruise in the company of two hundred fifty sailors.

Georgiana and her captain were not the only individuals navigating a new course: Mrs. Smith soon left the hospitality of the Wentworths. Though they accepted Mrs. Clay's death as an accident and Anne Wentworth did in fact find a note from Mrs. Smith when they returned home from the Cobb following Alfred's disappearance—a note that apparently drifted onto the floor under the front hall settee in the bustle of the sedan chair's arrival—both Captain and Mrs. Wentworth were left with an unsettled feeling about their houseguest that they were unable to entirely overcome. Mrs. Smith's mobility and income restored, she and her hosts mutually decided that her removal to a dwelling of her own, with faithful Nurse Rooke as her companion, was a desirable domestic arrangement. The separation marked a return to independence for her and a return to privacy for the newlyweds-turned-new parents. She moved back to Bath, where with winter approaching, she could continue her recovery by availing herself of the greater number of hot baths and legitimate medical practitioners in the city.

Sir Walter and Miss Elliot also quit Lyme for Bath, but for entirely different motives than Mrs. Smith's. Though the baronet, too, had come to Lyme for health reasons, he and his daughter found the society of the small village too restricted, its diversions too limited, its shops inadequate, and the sea the very enemy to one's complexion and youthful appearance that Sir Walter had always believed it to be. They retreated to the elegance of Bath, where they lived in supercilious bliss, oblivious to the fact that the greater consequence of their neighbors reduced their own, and that the superior charms of other, younger ladies cast in sharp relief the inferiority of Miss Elliot's.

Walter Alfred Henry Arthur Elliot was much in his father's speech, if not in his presence. Until Alfred reached a more interesting age—defined by Sir Walter as being old enough to read the entire *Baronetage* unassisted—the baronet was content to see his heir only occasionally. Under the Wentworths' loving guidance, and in the companionship and affection of foster siblings who came along over the years, Alfred grew into a sensible and likable young man despite Sir Walter's best efforts. When the time came for him to assume the baronetcy, he did so with seriousness and respect for the generations-old tradition he was entering, and proved himself a more worthy heir to his title than the man from whom he inherited it.

Elizabeth and Darcy, after seeing Captain and Mrs. Andrew St. Clair off on their new life, returned home to Pemberley with Lily-Anne. There, they enjoyed a welcome holiday from the "holiday" they had spent beside the sea. The accidents at Lyme, however, had brought them the friendship of the Wentworths and the addition of Captain St. Clair to their family, and so they would always look upon their experience there as more pleasurable than not.

Before too much time passed, they were once more taken with the idea of travel. As they readied for sleep one night, Darcy again mentioned the possibility of a foreign destination.

"I am all in favor of journeying abroad," Elizabeth said, closing her book and setting it on the night table. "Georgiana is not the only Darcy with an interest in seeing more of the world. When do you want to go?"

On the other side of the bed, Darcy extinguished his candle, lifted the coverlet, and climbed beneath. "I had originally contemplated this coming summer, though now that Georgiana is no longer a Darcy but a St. Clair, we will be booking passage for only three instead of four."

"We might need to delay that departure. This summer will be a little busy."

"Why?"

Elizabeth offered him only an enigmatic smile before blowing out her own candle and curling up beside him.

"When we do go, however," she said as the firelight teased the darkness, "we shall indeed have to book passage for four."

Author's Note

Dear Readers,

When I have the good fortune to hear from you, whether in person or via e-mail, I am often asked about the amount and type of research I do for my novels. The simple answer is that it varies with the needs of each book. I always endeavor to be as thorough as I can, using primary sources (when available), reference books and other secondary sources, Internet resources (carefully evaluated), museums, hands-on experience, expert interviews, and anything else useful that I happen upon. When possible, I also visit a book's settings to see them for myself and get a true sense of place. I never know what little detail—seemingly insignificant at the time—will prick my memory months later and become a critical component of the story.

Research for this novel took me from the cliffs of England's Jurassic Coast to the decks of the HMS *Victory* (Admiral Nelson's flagship from the Battle of Trafalgar) to subterranean smuggling caves. Because the book's action occurs almost entirely in Lyme and on the Cobb—real places—I spent a considerable amount of time there, exploring the village and seawall, taking hundreds of pictures, asking questions of everyone I met. There is little room for fudging details in a mystery set somewhere readers can themselves visit.

Fortunately, one of the plot's most unusual details—the Cobb's "whispering gallery"—actually exists. It is not very well publicized—I learned about it from a small reference in "The Book of the Cobb," a short monograph on the Cobb's history for sale locally in Lyme. When I tested out the acoustical effect, I knew I had to use it somehow in the book. The Cobb suffered serious damage from a storm in 1824 and much of it had to be rebuilt, so there is no way of knowing whether the effect existed in Austen's time—but that also means no one can say for certain that it did not. (Fiction writers love that kind of ambiguity!)

Except for Mrs. Smith's bench, the other features of the Cobb that I mention (the gin shop, Granny's Teeth, quay warehouses, steps on the southern arm, etc.) are also real and can still be seen. The shipyards are gone but the hamlet, Walk, and beach are still there—modernized, of course. The building thought to have been Austen's inspiration for Captain Harville's cottage is now a café. The Lion (now the Royal Lion) can still be found on Broad Street, but the Assembly Rooms have long since been torn down. Due to a fire, only the cellar of the Three Cups inn of Austen's day still exists (now the basement of a bookstore). Another Three Cups was built up the street; though now closed, the building remains.

On another historical note, readers particularly well informed about Austen family history might recognize *Perseverance* as the name of the frigate on which Jane's brother Frank (Francis William Austen) first sailed after completing his studies at the Royal Naval College. It is not the same ship Captain St. Clair commands at the end of this novel—St. Clair's ship, like St. Clair himself, is fictional. But I could not think of a more appropriate name for the ship St. Clair and Georgiana sail off in following the events of the story, and the tie to Frank—one of Jane's two naval brothers who inspired *Persuasion*—made it all the more perfect.

I hope you enjoyed *The Deception at Lyme*. To learn more about the

Mr. & Mrs. Darcy Mystery series and forthcoming books, or to sign up for my e-newsletter, visit my website at www.carriebebris.com. While you are there, drop me a note—I love to hear from readers!

With warmest regards,
Carrie Bebris